# THE KUNDALINI EQUATION

## STEVEN BARNES

A TOM DOHERTY ASSOCIATES BOOK

THE KUNDALINI EQUATION

The lines from ''Zomby Woof'' by Frank Zappa that appear on page 281 are used by permission, copyright © 1973 Munchkin Music, ASCAP.

First printing: May 1986

A TOR Book

Published by Tom Doherty Associates
49 West 24 Street
New York, N.Y. 10010

Cover art by Les Edwards

ISBN: 0-812-53150-7
CAN. ED.: 0-812-53151-5

Printed in the United States

0  9  8  7  6  5  4  3  2  1

# Chapter One

## The Legend

*This whole world was enveloped by death—by Hunger. For what is Death but Hunger? And Death bethought himself: would that I had a self!*
—Book One, Verse Two, The Upanishads

## 1500 B.C., Indus Valley, India

In silence, concealed within an angled web of temple rafters, Jiarri notched an arrow to his bowstring and sighted along its shaft at the priest beneath him. The old man was pinned to the bloodstained frescoed wall by spikes through his wrists; his toes barely reached the ground.

*End his pain.* Jiarri lowered his arrow's silver tip. He could do nothing but watch.

The squat, muscular spearmen on either side of the priest snapped to attention as a new figure entered the temple of Kalirangpur.

The newcomer was thick-chested, with the shoulders of an ape. His scarred face mirrored the hideous carnage just beyond the temple's shattered, metal-bound doors. His armor and carriage proclaimed him an officer. Something

1

round and flat beneath one massive arm caught the smoldering torch's glare, throwing it back to the wall in flashes of white.

Behind the officer waddled a small, grotesquely obese figure whose feet slapped a clumsy rhythm on the tile. His rags, matted with filth, fluttered about him like a shroud. A scrap of cloth swathed his face diagonally from scalp to chin, covering his left eye: one of the beggars who sought alms in the marketplace, now licking up behind his true master. Jiarri growled, and aligned the tip of his arrow with the back of the spy's neck.

The officer thumbed back the priest's eyelid, and spat directly into the iris. The old man convulsed, the spikes tugging cruelly at his wrists. The officer said something in a guttural tongue and threw down a silver plate veined with tiny rivulets of gold. It rolled on edge to the priest's feet and clattered to the ground.

The ragged spy snatched it up. "The General wants to know where this came from." His voice was a barely comprehensible mishmash of barbaric consonants. "The etching, the molding, are much finer than anything else in Kalirangpur." His bandaged finger lightly traced the elegantly carved image of a sacred bull. "The General has seen such plates, but they were old, tarnished. This is new, the metal freshly cast."

There was no reply. Like a hawk seizing a rabbit the General's hand flashed out, fingers sinking deeply into the priest's wizened throat. He twisted the old man's head around until their eyes locked.

"You don't have to die," the spy said.

The priest coughed painfully, then spoke for the first time. "All men die."

The spy peeled the bandage away from his face, blinking against the light. "But why die here, today, in agony?" He called sharply, again in the barbarian tongue, and two guards prodded a trio of children into the temple at spearpoint. The priest's knees sagged. He groaned as fresh blood oozed from his wrists.

Two of the children were girls, both nearing womanhood. The youngest was a boy, his initiate's robe ripped and muddied. Although his legs trembled, he stood tall and met the General's gaze squarely.

Silently, Jiarri chanted his admiration.

The General clapped his hands, and both girls were hurled to the ground. He twined his fingers into the hair of the eldest, and jerked her head up, laughing as he made a vulgar hand gesture.

"Just tell us," the spy said. "Tell us about the plates, and we will let your miserable village rot in peace."

The priest's lips trembled silently, a single tear rolling from beneath his sunken eyelids.

"Death holds few terrors for you," the spy whispered. "But these are just children. Children who need you to think clearly. Sanely." His voice was almost brotherly.

The eldest girl screamed piteously, fingernails ripping at the tiles beneath her. One of the soldiers knocked the boy to the floor. With a vicious laugh the spy raised the back of the stained robe.

The air hissed as a sliver of shadow flashed from above. Before the chunky figure could complete his action he was falling, gagging on his own blood, clawing at the feathered shaft which jutted from his throat.

Another hiss: a second arrow was through the priest's chest before anyone could turn. The General whipped his sword from its scabbard in a blur of iron, shattering one of the two torches. Shadows devoured the temple.

Jiarri cursed his own impetuousness, then let the third arrow fly in the direction of the General. He wiggled up through the rafters to the slit in the roof, and pushed out into the night.

The sunbaked brick walls of Kalirangpur were shattered, her woven reed buildings sputtering with flame. Sparks and bits of ash filled the air, spiraling like burning snowflakes. Her people littered the streets, sad dark bundles drifting in the embrace of the river Ganges. Drunken soldiers reeled through the streets, backs and arms sagging with loot.

Jiarri clambered down the roof, sliding along one of the

support poles until he reached the edge. He tightened his leg muscles, closed his eyes to blot out the light, and whispered, "Sun Eagle, your wings," before leaping seventeen feet to the next roof.

His feet struck the crude tile with a crunch. He skittered along the edge until he was once again in darkness. Soldiers streamed out of the temple, surrounding it, screaming up at the empty roof. Of course he had to be there. The leap to the next roof was impossible.

Jiarri smiled grimly. The night was his friend, his lover, and soon he was lost in its arms.

In the mountains north of Kalirangpur, hidden among the peaks like a gilded bird's nest, stood a city. Beyond its gold-veined walls were mirrored domes and jeweled spires that grazed the clouds, temples with arched roofs, houses of cut stone, granaries of kiln-cured brick. On the sheer granite wall behind the city, titanic bulls and tigers contorted in mortal dance.

On a platform atop the highest tower stood two men. The taller of them was also the elder. His face was graven with age, and seemed somehow an infinity of visages joined into one. All of the joy known to man was etched in that face; all of the sorrow, and all of the hope. Every fractional tilt of his head brought to life another combination of light and shadow and texture, another personality, such that his appearance changed subtly from moment to moment.

His name was Ahmara Khan. His forked beard was a pale fluttering wisp. The robe that rippled in the chill wind was undyed, extravagant only in the fineness of its weave.

His eyes were fixed on the southern ridge of mountains: a stubble, a ring of dead, broken teeth. Smoke curled over them poisonously, muddying the sky.

"Soon," Khan said quietly. As he spoke his face seemed that of the wisest and saddest of the gods. "Soon Pah-Dishah joins her sisters. Save yourself. We were fools." He drew his cloak more tightly across his shoulders. "These mountains will hide nothing but our bones."

The younger man touched his grandfather's arm. It was thin and frail, but even here, at the top of the highest wind-whipped tower, it radiated soothing heat, as if he were burning with fever. It was, as always, strangely calming to Jiarri. "I am a Hunter. So long as the city lives, my duty is here."

Khan studied his grandson: the strong, proud jaw and dark eyes, the broad shoulders and wiry arms beneath a thin white tunic. He nodded, resignation and pride mingling in his smile, and turned to enter the temple. Together they wound their way down the staircase.

The air within was hazed with incense and fevered prayers, the floor beaded with kneeling worshipers. Somberly robed figures glided across the tiles, each ritual motion triggering an anguished cry from the faithful. The priests blended their voices in wordless song, their bodies in sacred dance. The tones were always precisely the same, and Jiarri supposed that the identical rhythmic call had echoed in domed temples since the beginning of time.

Theme interwove with theme, pitch and volume climbing until the ceiling hummed. Their feet blurred, robes swirling like storm-tossed leaves. The fluxing patterns of the dance, the cadence of the hymn, and the tang of the incense made his temples pound.

Ahmara Khan appeared on the spiral stairway. The chanting stopped, the final notes vibrating in the ceiling and floor like the last stroke of the gong. Jiarri stayed back, watching his grandfather descend step by slow step.

The worshipers watched him, blind to the frailty and indecision in his step. They saw only Ahmara Khan, their one remaining hope, the high priest who had grown ancient in service to Pah-Dishah. The holiest of men, whose labyrinthine mind might yield one final miracle.

He was joined at the foot of the steps by his eldest priest, who bowed low. The Elder's eyes were deeply ringed. He trembled from weariness and lack of sleep. Perhaps it was the perspiration that steamed from his skin and clothes, or the pools of oil that burned atop their braziers, but the Elder's skin glowed, shone golden. His

eyes were vast and dark, his breath sour and strangely
sweet at the same time. He pressed his lips against Ahmara
Khan's feet, his tears moistening the ground.

Ahmara Khan stared unblinkingly into the haze, as if
blinded by the weight of his knowledge. "There is smoke
over the mountains, carrion birds above Kalirangpur. She
is dead."

An acolyte peeled away Khan's outer garments, slipping
on a darkly purple ceremonial robe. Jiarri shuddered as he
watched the youngster dress his grandfather, and thought
of the boy in the temple of Kalirangpur. Surely dead, or
worse, by now.

Shakily, the elder priest rose to his feet. "Perhaps the
Northerners will be satisfied. Will see that they have raped
our land until it bleeds. Perhaps they will search elsewhere. Perhaps they will not learn of us."

"You dream," Ahmara looked out over the congrega-
tion. They knelt on the marble floor, praying. As he stood
there, gathering their image in his mind, he squared his
shoulders. In the manner that Jiarri did not understand, but
had seen so often, the lines in Ahmara's face caught the
light differently now. He was no longer the coldly mega-
lithic figure: towering, solitary even in the midst of his
brothers. He was the man they had known and trusted all
of their lives, their breathing link to a time when Pah-
Dishah was not alone, was not the only city with walls of
marble rather than mud; which traded in art and science,
rather than fish and grain.

Slowly, reverently, as a man who can smell and taste
the nearness of death, Ahmara Khan lifted his voice in
prayer.

Jiarri held his breath and knocked at his grandfather's
door. Before the high priest could answer he entered, and
with him the two Elders in whom he had confided.

It was mere hours before the dawn, and the flames
guttered in the butter lamps. Coiled parchments, jars of
powdered incense, busts and carvings and hanging murals
mazed the room. Khan was angled over his desk, poring

over scrolls that had been ancient and crumbling before Pah-Dishah's walls parted the mountain wind.

Jiarri bowed humbly, and spoke. "Grandfather, forgive me, please. I am unable to sleep. I must ask you again: Is there no way that Pah-Dishah might be saved?"

One of the Elders stepped forward. As if the ravages of time carved identical runes on those of the priesthood, their faces were remarkably alike. In the shadows of night it was not the skin that shaped the appearance, but rather something in the character. There was fire in the Elder's eyes. His face seemed more than ever a wooden mask, but behind it was a visage graven on a live coal.

"We must speak," the Elder said softly.

The high priest folded his fingers carefully on the desk in front of him. "So it seems."

"We are a wealthy people, but because we furnish medicines and crafts to our neighbors, we have never needed to arm ourselves."

The other priest murmured in assent, his face vanishing into the shadow of his cowl.

Ahmara sighed. "We could never hold our walls against the Northerners. We are a city, not a nation." He paused, and although his gaze rested on the Elder, Jiarri knew whose image was fixed in his grandfather's mind. *Jiarri. Have you betrayed me? Betrayed us all for the sake of a longer life? Jiarri. Tell me the boy I loved and trusted would not . . .*

"I think," Ahmara said neutrally, "that you already understand this. What is it that brings you here? It might be better for you to spend this time in prayer. Or . . ."

"Or?"

"Or to gather your belongings and flee through the gate, to stay ahead of the invaders as long as you can."

"No," the Elder said. "We believe there is another way. Jiarri told us a story, one that you told him years ago, before he became a Hunter."

"A story . . . ?" Ahmara's voice was bland, but his gaze flickered to Jiarri, and there was nothing casual in it at all. His face tautened, the wrinkles flattening until his skin looked like leather stretched on a rack. His eyes were dark, then caught the light in such a way that the pupils blazed brighter than the heart of the sun. Jiarri froze, the light peeling aside his skin, his skull, probing into his brain for a paralyzing moment in which all of his thoughts, all of his intentions were laid out as naked and glistening as tiny skinned animals. Then Ahmara mercifully broke the contact. Jiarri reeled back, shaken.

The Elder continued on obliviously. "Yes. You told Jiarri that once, long ago, the Sun Eagle came to earth fleshed in the bodies of our Hunters, making them warriors such as the world has never seen. Forces of death and destruction who froze the hearts of the strongest men. Regardless of weapons. Regardless of number."

"A story . . ." Khan waved his hand in a gesture of dismissal. The lamp flame softened the lines in his face as he looked away. "A tale to frighten small boys into obedience. A story, nothing more."

The Elder leaned closer. "But a story important enough to be carefully passed from Master to initiate for hundreds of years. More than just a tale, Ahmara Khan. A legacy. A legacy for just such a moment as this, when we have lost all other hope."

Khan shook his head. His hands knotted into fists, and he placed them beneath his desk. "I'm afraid I can place no credence in such—"

"Lies."

Jiarri spun, facing the Elder who had spoken. "You have no right to speak so to Ahmara Khan. You—" The Elder turned a blisteringly cold gaze on him. Jiarri's courage drained away until he felt himself a child, drowning in adult mysteries.

Ahmara lifted a finger, and the Elder closed his eyes.

Jiarri collapsed to his knees. "Must we give up hope because we are discovered and outnumbered?" he said. "Can we not fight, so long as we have strength? I think that you fear for me, and for my brother Hunters." The thousand lines that ridged his grandfather's face seemed mirrors reflecting mirrors, faces within faces.

"Ahmara Khan. If it could only gain us a month. One month. How many people, how much knowledge might be saved? I would be honored to die for my city."

Ahmara Khan rose and turned to the window, looked out over the city. Below, its braziers flickered like fallen stars. "You don't understand," he said finally, staring out into the morning darkness, withered fingers linked tightly at the small of his back. "Such a thing does . . . did exist. But it is not what you think it is. The Hunter ceremony is sanctified to the Earth Heart, which birthed the mother wisdom. The ceremony offers heightened senses, swifter and stronger limbs.

"But it is only a shadow of what once was. Once, in a time before time, such knowledge was common. When boats of metal floated in the air, and men spoke in the God Voice that traveled beyond the horizon. The priests of that time came to see themselves as more than human. Perhaps they were correct. . . ." His voice dropped almost to a whisper, and they had to strain to hear his words.

"They grew jealous, and kept the knowledge for themselves. Then they grew covetous, and warred amongst one another. They tore the moon from the ocean and flung it to the sky. Divided heat from cold and created seasons, rent the ground into valley and mountain, and finally disturbed the beat of the Earth Heart itself, which, in its wrath, brought down their cities, their armies, felled the ships from the sky, and silenced the God Voices that once traveled over the mountains. Men were animals once again, and darkness fell for a time beyond counting. Pah-Dishah and her sisters were the first to crawl from that darkness. It was too soon: men were not yet ready. The time will come—but not if we are selfish." He exhaled fiercely. "You do not speak of Pah-Dishah's salvation. You speak of the end of the world."

The priest who had remained silent spoke now, and his voice echoed as if they were in the temple itself and not in the confines of Ahmara Khan's sanctum sanctorum. "Stories. We are not children, or ignorant farmers to be impressed by such myths. We are men of wisdom! And we know that you hold secrets that can save our people.''

"More than life is at stake here! All of the people of this city may leave it and, by fleeing, save their lives if not their possessions. We stay because Pah-Dishah's walls hold the spirit of our people.'' He pointed to the scrolls, the charts, the carvings and glyphs that crowded the room. "This is our soul. The knowledge of healing, of craft, of harmony.''

"Words,'' the Elder said derisively. "Words will not save our women, or rebuild our walls.''

Khan frowned. His sight wavered, and in that instant the city was a dream carved in ice crystals: born in starlight, dying with the dawn.

"In a single month,'' Jiarri whispered, suddenly close behind him, "vital scrolls could be duplicated, carried to safety. Some trace of Pah-Dishah might survive.''

"The Hunters . . .'' Ahmara Khan's eyes lost focus, drifting.

"You do not understand,'' Jiarri said. "It is right to sacrifice the flower to save the root.''

"Death, Jiarri, is only the portal.'' He sighed hollowly. "Very well. Select only those who have been completely faithful to their diet and meditations. Begin the Cleansing ceremony. Feed them honey and yogurt, and after noon tomorrow, water only. They must not sleep, must not speak, except in answer to your questions. Have these things done, and in five days I will give you further instructions.''

The priests bowed to him, signing their gratitude, and left the room. Jiarri remained behind.

Khan riffled through musty piles of scrolls, hissing when he found the correct stack. He withdrew one slender roll of parchment, and carried it to his desk. He unfurled it as if afraid it would crumble to dust beneath his fingers.

"This one was completed by five successive high priests over a period of a hundred years. I must tell you something, something I have never shared before. Come.'' Jiarri stood beside him, touching shoulders. As they touched, that strange and gentle warmth flowed through him, washing away the tension.

"I do not know anymore. I don't know what the gods give us, and what our minds discover for themselves. What is magic and what is"—he shrugged, trying to find a word—"what is merely knowledge. Technique."

"Does it matter? The gods made us, made our world. We can do nothing without them."

Khan smiled fondly, with pride only marginally soured by fear. "Those of my brotherhood often speak in parables. Symbols. To you, my own flesh, I will speak as one thinking man to another. What I said before, about the gods and their war, is the truth. Whether they created the moon, and the seasons, I do not know. I do know that the knowledge should never have been written down. And once passed to me, I should have had the courage to destroy it. But I was loath to destroy any link to those times, the bright times before the Darkness. The Warrior ceremony is only a fragment of the old knowledge, one easily obtained because the pull of blood is strong. I can place your feet upon the path, Jiarri, but cannot guide you home again."

He rolled the parchment into a tube again. "We will use it, one final time. But then I will burn it and crush the ashes, and all that will exist will be the component threads of knowledge." He pulled his grandson close, kissed his lips with tender strength, then drew back. "Do you understand?"

Jiarri's warm hand clasped Ahmara Khan's. "We are both the city's blood," he said. Although his words were strong, he felt something reach out from his grandfather, something that could not be chained in words, something from within that infinity of faces created by light and shadow and time. Jiarri knew that he was a dead man.

He drew his shoulders back. "We are the only hope. I will gather thirty of the strongest Hunters, and we will begin at once."

As he passed through the doorway his strength drained

from him, and he gripped at the wall. Without turning, he
asked, "How long will it take?"

"For those of you who are purest in mind and body . . .
perhaps twelve days."

*Twelve days.* Jiarri shut the door without another word,
only then collapsing against the wall, cold waves of
apprehension crawling his skin like swarming ants. *Jiarri,*
he swore at himself, *you know the face of death. You have
faced the Bear, and the Snake. You have hunted the lord
Tiger in his lair, and have felt the Sun Eagle work through
you to accomplish these things. What, then, is there to fear
in the Warrior ceremony?*

### Pain

From the strong muscles that held his spine erect, now a
cramping nightmare. From his stomach, empty save for a
paste that tasted of blood and honey. From his lungs,
screaming for oxygen, empty now for an impossibly long
count of ten.

Thirty naked Hunters, seated in concentric rings surrounding Ahmara Khan, chanted in unison. Jiarri's buttocks, flush against the rough tile of a temple antechamber,
had long since become numb. There was no feeling anywhere but in his back, in his spine.

Shoulders revolving slowly, liltingly, thirty nut-brown,
corded bodies swayed in the cramped confines of the
antechamber.

The gong struck, and thirty tortured chests seized a
breath of air. Another breath would not come for a count
of forty. Fight the pain. Retreat within. Slow the body.
Breathe slow, deep. Taste the air, so thick with incense
that every intake of breath was torture. Feel every separate
particle of ash striking the moist membranes of your nose
and throat.

The gong. Exhale for a count of ten, emptying the
organism, hissing air out cautiously, knowing that this was
the most important part. . . .

The emptiness. For ten counts his body screamed, his

closed eyes flashed red, and his stomach burned with fire.
He could not endure. He must breathe. . . .

To his left, one of the Hunters fainted, toppling forward.
Only the strong . . .

He would endure it. Endure fatigue, pain, and

### Fear

Six days now, with but three hours rest a night. During
the last rest break, lying curled on a clean linen, there had
been no sleep. His eyelids might have been translucent,
except that the light shining through them was in his mind,
not in the temple. Now was the time that his mind dredged
up memories, fantasies, fought to break discipline. And
time after time, the constant drone of the chanting chan-
neled his thoughts and feelings like a canal channels water.

The chanting created images of blood and fire, awakened hungers that Jiarri was shocked and ashamed to find
within him.

At first. Then as the hunger grew, hour by long hour, he
stopped resisting, and fell headlong into the darkness.

And there, he felt the death of time itself.

And in that space, where there was nothing, no change,
no matter, no sense of who or what he had been, he heard
the voices. And they cried to him, screamed to him, and
he came to them. They came to him.

Himself.

Not-himself.

The voice/voices shrieking their fear, and confusion,
and Ahmara Khan's voice rising above all: "Be afraid, my
children, my beloved child, but not ashamed. What you
have been, you shall never be again. What you become,
no matter how terrible, is but a further step. Resign yourself to death, and to that thing that craves death. Do not
resist. Open yourself. Open yourself. . . ."

And Jiarri did. And the darkness burst with flame, a
torrent of lava exploding from within him, carrying before
it every dark and dangerous thing within his spirit. Despite
the cleansing, the meditation. So much filth! The greed,

the lust, the anger, the terrible fear, the red wrath and, by the Sun Eagle, the fathomless depths of his

## Hunger

It flowed through and washed over him. With closed eyes he saw its flame racing along his spine, branching out through his muscles, gnawing the flesh from his bones.

A night-gilt, solid shadow that had once been Jiarri melted into the grass surrounding the camp of the Northerners, watching with eyes that were full, glowing moons. Behind him were nine others, once Hunters, now something quite different. Warriors. None came close to another without evoking a warning snarl.

A day of running without rest, without food, pausing only to drink, had brought him to the edge of the camp. Long before he could hear or see them he could scent them, smell the acid of their sweat, the singed meat smoking in the cook pots.

Now he could see them. The starlight was searingly bright, the night sounds both loud and filtered down by a focus of attention so intense that nothing existed save the men in front of him.

They were so terribly weak, and unaware. A moan of frustration broke from his throat. Why did he have to wait? Why?

From another world, a voice so faint it was almost nonexistent whispered to him. *Wait*, it said. *Wait for the first breath of dawn to kiss the horizon. Wait.*

Just words. But words that had a soothing effect when he didn't want to be soothed, that spoke of caution when he craved, more than anything he had ever known, to leap from the shadows, to bring down these slow and stupid creatures. To bury his fingers in their entrails.

The guards who patrolled the perimeters of the camp were competent and alert, but to Jiarri they were like blind, deaf men. He could *feel* their attention waver. Knew that even when they looked directly at him their minds couldn't focus strongly enough to pick him out of the shadows. Knew that the oneness he formed with them was that of predator and prey. A bond stronger than flesh, older than time, realer than the illusion of choice.

They were *his*, and his mouth watered with the need to taste their pulse.

The other Warriors crept away from him, disappearing into the shadows.

There was no betraying noise, but one of the guards was growing nervous. No break in the silence, but something made them, made these . . . *men* . . . unnaturally alert.

The muscles in Jiarri's legs shook, and his fingers dug into the grass in front of him. The growling, purring sound in his throat rumbled through his entire body, but he couldn't feel it, or feel the cold, or feel anything except the presence of the men before him.

Behind them, lit with torches that danced in the early morning wind, were the tents of the hundreds (Thousands? The significance of the numbers seemed to drift away from him. There were Many, and they were Enemy) who dared to enter the mountains, to seek the City.

City. A flood of strange emotion washed through him at the thought of City. An image flashed. City. Yes. Must protect City. Must kill . . . and return to City. Must . . .

He wrenched his attention back to the tents, to the glowing coals that warmed their food. To the shrill, exhausted laughter of the women who warmed their bedrolls. His eyes searched the tents and, easily, found the one he sought. Larger than the others, of richer fabric.

A man appeared in its doorway for a moment. A hard, thick-bodied man who was naked but for a bandaged shoulder.

*General.*

Jiarri sensed something that pulsed *crimson* in the General's head; a fallen star, a precious jewel. He coveted it. The man shouted orders in a voice Jiarri had heard before, long ago, in another life.

The perimeter guards peered out into the darkness, at the mountain, and he knew that they were looking for

(CITY),

knew that come the

(DAWN)
they would be on the move, would
(KILL), would
**(KILL)** . . .
Jiarri made a final, weak effort to pull his mind from
that track, but once found he seemed to roll along it
inexorably, the images of (CITY) and (DAWN) and of
ripping, tearing rage melting together and mingling so that
the first flush of light along the ridge of eastern mountains
snapped the mental links restraining him.

The guard reacted as torpidly as snow melting in the
sun, and even the terror that turned the man's face into a
caricature of humanity spread in slow ripples, the eyes
widening, the mouth contorting. Now the grunting sound
of terror, of pain as Jiarri was on him, ripping with teeth,
tearing with painted fingers.

Just a bare moment to revel in the warmth and moist-
ness, then Jiarri was moving, and the second guard had
barely opened his mouth to scream, raised his spear to cast.

*So easy* . . .

The spear floated through the air, and Jiarri, suddenly
playful, caught it as it snaked lazily by, pivoting without
even a fractional loss of momentum. It arced back as it had
come, a dancing circle that ended with an agonized exhalation and crooked fingers that gripped the stalk of a deadly
night blossom.

*So pretty* . . .

He vaulted the collapsing body, racing now, and saw
the others of his pack converging on the main tent.

This time, the guards had time to react, to draw steel
before Jiarri and his brothers struck. Jiarri went under the
stroke of a sword, fingers outstretched, nails glinting in the
torchlight. It was over in an instant, and as he bestrode the
body, watching the blood gush blackly from the torn throat,
his temples *pulsed*, as if something within were feeding on
the death. He reeled, drunk with pleasure.

He sensed the air pressure a moment too late and spun
on his heel as a spear entered his side.

Jiarri grunted and wrenched the haft from the guard's

hands with a sudden, irresistible surge of strength, grinning at the pain, at the man's shocked expression. At the feel of his own blood flowing from the wound. In the next instant his vision blurred. The man before him was not a man but a bag of organs and brittle bones sheathed in gossamer, the starlight outlining each rounded shape, painting the whole in a violet glow. Jiarri reached softly into the guard's body, slipping his hand under the ribs until he held the warm pulsating object he sought. Then, with the delicate sound of a soap bubble bursting on a flower, the thing came free, showering sweet black droplets.

Soldiers whirled like feathers in the wind, spiraling to the ground. Each replaced by another. And another. And another . . .

To his right, one of the Warriors fell, head sundered from the flowing stump of its neck. Its hands clutched blindly at the dirt, arms twitching as the body crawled aimlessly. Dimming eyes in the severed head blinked hate into the cold morning air.

Jiarri glimpsed his own face in the burnished oval of a shield. Perhaps it was just the curve of the metal, the darkness, the flickering light of the torches, but his face seemed . . . alien.

He wore no hunting snarl or killing grimace. It was something different, as if there were another life, another mind within him. One gnawing its way to the surface with needle teeth. "Feed me death," it whispered seductively, "and I will give you power."

The Dawn churned in chaos as Jiarri plunged on, hungry for the wondrous blood-red jewel within the skull of the man they called General.

All that day he ran, in a place past all exhaustion. His body felt no pain, only a fierce whistling flame that drove him forward, lifting him on a wind of will. Though empty, a mere shell of a human being, still his body stumbled on. Though closer to death than life, still it moved.

The pursuers followed him no farther than the edge of

the camp, as if the dim morning light lent insufficient iron to their shattered courage.

None of the other Warriors ran alongside. Their torn bodies littered the rocks and scrub grass behind him.

But he didn't think of them, or their sacrifice. He thought of nothing, nothing but the

(CITY),

nothing but Pah-Dishah, and the urge to reach her, to see her walls before . . .

Before . . .

There it was, locked up in some corner of his mind so darkly distant that his body had been unable to find it when the wounds and the lack of blood had grown severe. There was

(DEATH),

and it opened loving arms to him.

His steps faltered, his heart stuttered in his chest.

He collapsed, rose for a total of five halting steps, and fell for the last time.

Jiarri crawled now, only the warring interaction of two images,

(CITY)

and

(DEATH),

driving him on.

And on. No thought now, and nothing that resembled life so much as the twitching of an iron filing drawn by the lodestone, or a rock tumbling down a mountainside. But still he moved, until his hands, outstretched, grasped a sandaled foot. He stopped, breath hissing weakly in his throat.

Strong hands lifted him from the dirt, and in the moment of that contact all hurt vanished, replaced by an awesome sense of peace and fulfillment. Pain and

(DEATH)

and the other thing, the growing, hungry thing, were locked up again, unable to reach him.

His grandfather's face was withered with remorse, tears silvering the sunken cheeks.

There were others with his grandfather, but the darkness that streamed in to cloud the periphery of vision made them ghosts, wraiths in thin rags that fluttered from translucent shoulders. A voice might have whispered, "Gods . . . his *face*," but he could not be sure. The darkness was numbing, clouding reason and will.

Ahmara Khan cradled Jiarri's head in his arms, smearing blood on the hem of his robe. He searched his grandson's filming eyes. "Jiarri," he said at last. "Forgive me. I cannot forgive myself."

Death, making its inexorable approach, had burnt away the trance of the previous night, leaving only its sealed memory. At his grandfather's urging he opened the box for just an instant. In that moment all things became appallingly clear, both the pain and the

(HUNGER)

He opened his mouth to speak. All that emerged was a strained, gurgling sound that a dying animal might have made. He tried desperately to place the thoughts, the feelings, the images into words, and failed utterly. His vocal cords would no longer respond. *It was your duty. It was mine,* he thought, trying to speak with his eyes.

*It feeds on death.*

"The scroll is dust," Ahmara Khan whispered. "The people are dispersing, the secrets with them. No one will ever assemble it again. We have won—the path was opened, but with your death it closes again, for all time."

But with the last fragile wisp of reason left to him, Jiarri regretted that his grandfather had made that promise. Knowing, from the chill, calm place that preceded the great darkness, one final Truth: that the desire to comfort can make the noblest soul proclaim that which the heart holds false.

And that the gods love nothing better than to prove a man a liar.

# Chapter Two
## Halfway House

*Darest thou now O soul*
*Walk out with me toward the unknown region*
*Where neither ground is for the feet nor*
*any path to follow?*
　　　　　—Walt Whitman,
　　　　　　　"Darest Thou Now O Soul"

*My father and I were estranged when he died. He wanted it to be so, and at last, so did I. My feelings were mixed. This man had driven me from his house, and for this I hated him. In dying, he gained that Ultimate knowledge, the seeking of which had brought about my dishonor. For this I envied him. But most urgently, I lost forever the chance to show him how wrong he was: about me, about the scrolls, about the Hunger. For this, I mourned.*
　　　　　—Savagi, *The Myth of Love*

# Thursday, December 3.

Adam Ludlum hated hospitals, had since his childhood. The image of a pudgy eight-year-old's splintered, swollen

knee had never faded. Nor had the memory of a night
spent in Children's Hospital, a night filled with terrifyingly
long and agonizingly dull needles that drained fluid and
numbed and brought dreamless sleep. The feelings, the
sights and sounds and smells were still garishly intense.

More than twenty years later new nightmares melded
with the old, like shattered bones knitting in the dark.
Standing at the nurse's station at Saint Martin's convalescent home, he knew it had something to do with the odor.
All of the disinfectant in the world couldn't erase it. Adam
sometimes wondered if it wasn't so much a smell as an
*impact*, the cumulative impact of all the little reminders of
death and decay.

The wet, cool, bubbly sounds. The whispering inter-
com, the blinking red and green lights. The steady *blip
blip* beneath the black and white video screens scanning
the halls and rooms, framing fragile, white-haired figures,
age and disease transmuting their bones to spun sugar,
clutching quad-legged tube-metal walkers, spidering painfully along the polished hallways.

The racks of olive-drab oxygen bottles. The scurrying
doctors consulting thick, metal-backed notebooks filled
with indecipherable glyphs. The polite, disinterested quarter smiles beneath the white caps that said people don't get
well here. This isn't really a hospital. It's sort of a halfway
house for Forest Lawn.

There was a commotion up the hall, and a stocky blond
nurse appeared, pushing a wheelchair. The man seated in
it was cadaverously thin, and his skin hung loosely. Of
medium height, he was a scarecrow of brittle bone and
parchment. He wore a frilly shirt that had been carefully
laced up around his neck. His teeth were stained yellow.
Only his watery gray eyes were truly alive. And soon . . .

Too soon. Only two days ago Adam had sat across the
desk from Dr. Wiley, examining the X rays and reports
fanned across the polished wood-grain surface. They seemed
to pertain to something else, someone else, anything or
anyone but the man shriveling away in a convalescent
home.

Dr. Wiley, a very pale man with short, curly red hair and an irritatingly elusive Southern accent (Texas? Louisiana?), cleared his throat politely, squinting as if a contact lens were scratching his eye. *"The lungs, Mr. Ludlum. The tumors have metastasized, and we now have an invasion of the bone marrow, and a possible emergence in the brain tissue. I'm afraid that the staff at Saint Martin's simply assumed it was senility."*

*"Terminal?"*

*"Lung cancer is very difficult to treat, Mr. Ludlum—we can try chemotherapy, and radiation therapy, but your father is already very weak. It might be months, or he might hang on for a year. We'll do what we can. You are his closest surviving relative, and there are forms to be signed. I'm sure that you understand. . . ."*

The nurse's voice interrupted Adam's thoughts. "Here you are, Gunther," she chirped. "Your son is always on time." The elder Ludlum's face was waxen, disinterested.

The nurse was a large pale woman with bulbous, disapproving eyes and a round head that was just a fraction too large for her slender neck. She lowered her voice and drew Adam to the side. "Your father is very weak. We have to ask you not to excite him this time."

"I didn't do anything," Adam said glumly. "He just got upset."

"Whatever. Please try."

His father looked up at him blankly. Adam smiled, but got no response. He reached down and took his father's hand.

The contrast between hands was startling, and Adam burned with shame. His fingers were bloated sausages in comparison with the brittle sticks of Gunther's fingers. *Fat. God, I'm still so heavy, and I promised . . .*

Gunther's breathing was a thin wheeze. "Adam, I want to go outside."

"Yes, sir."

They wheeled down the hall toward the sun deck, past a huge construction-paper mural depicting improbably small mountains frothed in pink snow, and trees with fluffy blue cotton leaves. Dogs as large as houses frolicked in the grass. The words "Alta Loma Elementary School" were crayoned along the bottom. Just above it were the signatures of the artists, six or seven pleasant scrawls and painstakingly blocked names, most of them unneurotically large and scripted in bright crayon. It was all happiness and health, and as Gunther Ludlum's tired eyes scanned it he sighed.

The observation deck was a concrete terrace that split off from the dining area. There were two other people there, both of them men, both alone, both asleep in the sun, their faces sunken like apricot flesh dried against the pit.

Adam parked his father under a gauzy umbrella, and pulled a chair over next to him. Gunther gestured weakly. "I hope you brought them."

"Sure. I wouldn't forget." Adam opened a new package of Camels, lit one and handed it to his father. Gunther took it with one hard, dry hand and brought it to his lips, inhaling with a wheeze. Smoke trickled from his nose.

There was silence for a long time, then Adam broke it. "I wish you'd stop, sir."

Gunther let out a sharp bark of laughter. "Worried about my health? Little late for that, isn't it? I'll stop smoking when you do."

*Touché*.

Adam sighed and lit a second cigarette, drawing on it deeply. The nicotine soothed away his flash of guilt. "I'm sorry that I didn't call, sir. I've been kind of busy."

His father's hand crept out like an arthritic crab. "S'all right. It's all right, Adam. Are things good at the radio station?"

"Fine, Dad. They're giving me a raise soon." The lie almost caught in his throat. His engineering position hadn't brought a pay raise in thirteen months.

"And Michelle. I want you two to get married, hear me? I'd like to see it before . . ." Gunther's voice weakened, and he coughed, puffing little clots of smoke into the air. They hung there, then faded like discorporating ghosts.

Adam gazed out over the Los Angeles basin. The smog wasn't too bad, and come evening, the streets and boulevards would be gem-encrusted, and beautiful in a cold, inorganic way.

Gunther squeezed his hand softly. "There's just no time, Adam. It passes so quickly. You don't realize that yet. I wish you'd had your mother longer. Would have made a difference. Harriet was a wonderful woman. Knew what being a woman was about." His brow furrowed as he tried to sort back through the memories, then smoothed out as he gave up the effort. "Maybe I should have remarried. . . ."

"Are you still having a problem with the medicine?"

"Yes. Change. The doctor wants to . . ." He inhaled, face screwed up painfully tight. "The medicine. The . . . ah . . . Adam, you know what I'm saying?" His voice was sharp, but there was chagrin mingled with the question.

"The doctor wants to change the dosage."

Gunther's head sank back into the leatherette wheelchair support. "Sometimes I sit . . . can't sleep . . . Do you know how easy it is to fool the nurses, pretend to take the pills?" He cackled softly to himself, smoke puffing in bursts from his nose and mouth.

"Sir—"

"Quiet. I don't want to sleep so much anymore, Adam. Pills . . . help me sleep, but make it hard to think. All I want to do is remember."

"Remember what?"

"One day. Just one day." His voice was a hoarse whisper. "If I could just remember one day, all of the little details. What I ate. Who I talked to. What I wore. What the sun felt like. There were so many good days, Adam. If I could just find and remember one, I think I could die . . . could be happy." He gripped Adam's hand with sudden hook-fingered strength. "I want to see you grow up, boy. When are you going to marry that girl, and show me my grandchild? Adam? When?"

Gunther's head sank back on his chest, and Adam thought

that he had fallen asleep. His breathing was a frighteningly hollow rasp. The cigarette slumped in a suddenly lax hand.

They were quiet like that for a time, and Adam became aware of the barriers he had erected. Barriers that prevented him from looking too deeply. If he looked too deeply, he might really *feel* his father's weakness, might finally understand what it meant. He might not be able to cope.

So old. His father had always been old. Had never been friend, always and only Father, someone strong and unutterably wise and unreachably far above him.

*I wish that I could have seen this man as he was when young. Just once.*

His father's face was a gutted, weathered ruin. *But I do not see my father. I see only a mental reconstruction.* And that was fodder for the game. A wild talent, fascinating and utterly useless, Adam's since childhood.

Well, then . . .

First, the hair. It was thinning and white. Sparse, with the mottled scalp beneath what had once been thick, healthy black growth.

Adam closed his eyes. He imagined his father's hair, each separate white follicle, and felt the mental muscles thickening, quickening, as he changed the follicles to black.

He opened his eyes, and for an instant the illusion was sustained. He closed his eyes again, and applied a mental paintbrush, darkened the hair strongly, absurdly, tarbrush black. He opened his eyes. There it was—overlaying reality like a transparency laid on an animation stand.

His father groaned, and the illusion dissolved. "Sir," Adam said softly, "I reconciled with Micki. Honest. We're going to get married. I just have to show her I can keep my word." He could feel his eyes misting, hear his throat tighten up. "I've broken so many promises to her. You, too. Two years ago I promised I'd lose fifty pounds. You bet me, remember? You offered me three thousand dollars."

Gunther's hand loosened on his. Adam lifted it to his cheek. The skin was dry and cracked, like sunbaked leather.

His father stiffened at the contact. "I couldn't do it for someone else. You can't do anything for someone else. It has to be for me. I'm ready now. Algy's going to introduce me to a man named Culpepper, Dr. Giles Culpepper, and he wrote the book on sports medicine. He's got a conditioning clinic at UCLA."

Gunther closed his eyes. "Another game, Adam? Are you still chasing after miracles? There aren't any miracles in life. Just hard work." Gunther opened his eyes. They were cloudy and unfocused, and lost in the awakening lights of Los Angeles. "There's a bulletin board in the hallway," he whispered. "The children drew it, Adam. They come in sometimes, and they bring us flowers, and sing to us. . . ." His eyelids slid partially closed, his pupils dark crescents hanging at the lower edge. The cigarette fell from his hand.

Silent now, Adam stayed with his father, gazing out over the lights, until the shadows lengthened, the air cooled, and the nurse came and wheeled his father away. Then he left the convalescent home, walked out past the sterile nurse's station, past the mural with the fluffy blue trees and the gargantuan dogs and the guilelessly artful signatures, and never realized that he was crying until he felt the moisture drying on his cheeks.

# Chapter Three

# Trycycle

*Your body's balance of nutrients is similar to the balance required of a circus tightrope walker. . . . It is possible to chemically analyze your food, blood, tissues, hair, and all your waste products . . . however, the procedure is very costly and is usually done only for research purposes.*
—Naola Van Orden, Ph.D., and S. Paul Steed, Ph.D.,
        *The Bio Plan for Lifelong Weight Control*

*The body is wilderness, lover, companion, and ultimately betrayer. Its whims are as a child's, and children must learn to obey. Learning to succor the body is less important than bending it to the will.*
                —Savagi, *Conquest of the Flesh*

## Saturday, December 5.

Adam knew that he was about to die. Like the inexorable, mindless advance of the *marabunta* army ant, pain crept up from the soles of his feet to his calves, investigating each tendon and muscle fiber separately. Finding them

27

wanting, it then proceeded to his knees, and from there to the thighs and hips. Somewhere along the way it had leapfrogged into his lungs, and now, as he pedaled the wheels of a computer-controlled stationary bicycle, he cursed Algernon Swain, he cursed UCLA and Dr. Culpepper, and, most vehemently, he cursed the life preserver of bouncing flesh around his middle.

Due to the rubber mask clamped over his mouth and nose, however, said speculations of Algernon's genealogy and sexual habits were conducted silently. Deprived of the humanizing influence of extreme vulgarity, he glared at his friend and continued to pump, his bare chest swelling and falling like a doomed soufflé in a Julia Child film loop. To illustrate a fifteen-percent grade, the rectangular CRT in front of him utilized a tiny cartoon cyclist scooting up a hill.

Well, trudging, perhaps.

Algernon Swain was a short, thin man with skin that seemed impossibly black for an American. He wore tortoiseshell glasses even thicker than Adam's sweat-steamed wire rims, thick enough to be legendary even back in fourth grade, where he had gained the nickname "Parakeet." Algernon's prematurely salted thatch of short wiry hair had always reminded Adam of twilight over the cactus patch. He and Adam had been friends since kindergarten, growing tighter and tighter until high school graduation sent them to separate colleges. Then, increasingly infrequent lunches and movies had kept alive what there was of those earlier days to cherish. If their friendship was no longer close, it was still comforting and, occasionally, as now, invaluable.

"Just one more little mountain, Adam." Algy stepped to the front, checked the straps on the remote cardiac sensor strapped to Adam's chest, and wiped a sterile gauze swab across his friend's forehead. "The evil doctor needs another perspiration sample. We've got most of the other data." Adam shook his head sharply and a halo of sweat droplets spattered against Algy's glasses. Behind the mouthpiece, Adam managed a grin. *There's your damn sample.*

The sports med testing room was divided into two sections. On one side stood a Universal weight machine, a silvered water tank for measuring lean-muscle mass, a reflexometer, and the stationary bicycle. On the other side of the room was the diagnostic/control apparatus measuring Adam's performance. It monitored his blood pressure, temperature, oxygen consumption rate, and current proximity to cardiac arrest.

The display in front of Adam grew level again, and he could have sworn that the tiny cartoon figure heaved a sigh of relief. Algernon thumped him on the back, plucked the facepiece away, and said, "Aw done, mistah Wudwum."

Adam slumped over the handlebars, counting red and black stars until the herd of elephants tap dancing on his chest thundered off over the horizon.

The door on the far side of the room clicked open. An extremely erect and alert man in his mid-fifties virtually floated in, bouncing on the balls of his feet. A manila file folder was tucked under one muscular, lab-smocked arm.

Adam opened one eye wearily and examined the newcomer. "Dr. Culpepper, if I haven't passed your test, be merciful and shoot me now. I couldn't go through *this* again."

"*If* you are admitted into the program, you and these tests are going to be dear old friends." Culpepper's immediate impact was leonine: his hair was an iron-gray, thick, wavy mass that swept back from his brow in a fall that almost touched his broad shoulders. His face was a network of tiny, pleasant wrinkles that owed more to sun curing than to the ravages of time.

"All right, all right." Adam heaved. His lungs felt like they'd been scoured out with crystal Drano. The taste of old tobacco tar was heavy in his throat, and for a moment he thought he was going to vomit. "Just let me catch my breath first."

"Oh, come now. No more than once a month for the complete physical, once a week for the weighing." Culpepper visually measured the adipose tissue bulging from Adam's side as he hunched over the bike. "Come,

Mr. Ludlum. Join me at the table. You look rather uncomfortable there."

"Thanks. I feel like Jell-O draped over a coathanger." The chest contact pad came free with a sucking *pop*. He dismounted, lost his balance, fell into Algernon's supporting arms. The moment of dizziness passed, and he wobbled over to a small metal table set up at a corner of the lab.

"Adam, are you sure you're all right?" Algy's licorice face was serious, creased with concern. "I never let your heartbeat go above 180, but—"

"S'cool." The room was still spinning. "Will you let me die here for a minute? I'll be fine."

Algy nodded and hurried back to the monitoring station. The older man crossed his legs with elegant fluidity, watching Swain's dark fingers fly over the control boards. "Frankly," Culpepper said quietly, "this program was devised to take fit athletes in prime condition and take them to world-class performance levels. You may be aware that the Soviets are far ahead of us in the *coordination* of the individual factors that contribute to performance. We're part of an effort to compensate for that, a central control for all of the data that come through the sports department. Diets, performances, injury, strategy, psychological motivation, just about everything that influences an athlete. Algernon has coordinated a battery of tests: skin scrapings, hair and nail tissue, urine and feces, perspiration, etcetera."

"I thought the Russians just used a lot of anabolic steroids and that sort of thing."

"Steroids contribute to muscle mass and athletic performance, there can be no doubt of that." Algy stiffened noticeably, attention jerked from the keyboard. He bit back a comment and continued typing. Culpepper laughed. "A bone of contention there. I believe that athletes should have any tool to elicit the maximum performance. That is, after all, what the game is."

"No comment," Algy said. "It's your show, Dr. C."

"Algernon is a good man," the doctor said, more quietly now, "but in some ways, he doesn't understand the athletic personality as well as he might. Did you know that when they asked several hundred athletes if they would use a drug that guaranteed championship performance, but would kill them within a year, over half of them said yes?" He laughed. "The proper job of the winner is *winning*." He turned his silver-gray eyes on Adam, who suddenly felt as if he were staring into two dry wells. "Mr. Ludlum, are you a winner?"

Adam nodded, still locked into those gunmetal eyes.

"I wonder. In effect, Adam, you're asking a Rolls-Royce mechanic to overhaul a Honda. The truth is that I haven't the time or the temperament to deal with your bad habits."

He spread the sheet out in front of Adam. "Look at this," he said bluntly, "and tell me why I should take you on."

| Adam Ludlum | % | Fat/Lean | lb/Fat | lb/Tot weight |
|---|---|---|---|---|
| Age: 33 | 36.1 | 132.9 | 75.1 | 208.0 |
| Sex: M | 35.8 | 132.9 | 74.1 | 207.0 |
| Activ Level: 0 | 34.9 | 132.9 | 71.1 | 204.0 |
| Height: 70.5 | 34.2 | 132.9 | 69.1 | 202.0 |
| Weight: 208 | 33.9 | 132.9 | 68.1 | 201.0 |
| Vit Capac: 2.1 | 33.2 | 132.9 | 66.1 | 199.0 |
| Spiro Temp: 32 | 32.6 | 132.9 | 64.1 | 197.0 |
| Tare Wt: 1.61 | 31.9 | 132.9 | 62.1 | 195.0 |
| $H_2O$ Weight: 2.9 | 31.5 | 132.9 | 61.1 | 194.0 |
| Lung Capac: 2.22 liters | | | | |

Vital Lung Capacity = 53.55% Normal

*Recommended % Fat = 17.00*
*Recommended Weight = 160.1 lb*

Adam stared at the sheet for almost two minutes before pushing it away, leaving four damp fingerprints. "What does it mean?"

"Your 'vital capacity' is the amount of air your lungs

hold, measured in liters. 'Spiro Temp' is the temperature of the measuring apparatus, used as a reference. 'Tare wt' is the weight of the scale. Read the second line. What it means is that at a weight of two hundred and eight pounds, you are carrying seventy-five pounds of fat. That's thirty-six point one percent, more than twice what it should be." He pointed at the four columns of numbers. "The last vertical row represents your weight as you begin to shape up. The others show the varying proportions of fat and muscle you would have at the different weights."

"So this is me?"

"Part of you, yes," Algy called over his shoulder. "There are psychological factors that Dr. C hasn't dropped into his equation."

"You mean Mr. Ludlum's proclivity for fad diets? Have you tried the Beer and Nutmeg diet? It's been on all the talk shows."

Adam's ears burned, but he forced himself to stay calm.

Culpepper cleared his throat, smiling sardonically. "Notice, Mr. Ludlum, that the computer program as designed doesn't cover the degree of weight loss that you need. We would need extra work in your case. Extra supervision. We are overcrowded and understaffed, Mr. Ludlum. I would like you to tell me why we should invest our time in you."

Algernon's voice betrayed his annoyance. "Doctor, you've read his assessment sheets. You've been complaining for months that you can't find someone who can visualize clearly enough for your mental rehearsal sessions. Adam is almost a freak at visualization. Not Tesla level, but damned close."

Behind him, a dot matrix printer was zipping across sheets of fanfold paper, and Algernon's chair creaked. "Aw done." He plopped down at the conference table's fourth chair.

Culpepper sighed. "Mr. Ludlum—you were saying?"

"Because you *have* to," Adam said under his breath.

"Excuse me?"

His face felt hot, flushed, but the thoughts, once begun,

emerged in a gush. "I'll work like nobody you've ever had in here. I can correlate my own data. I'll do research for you. I'll do *anything*, because I really believe that you're the best chance I have."

"Why?"

"I've tried everything, dammit. I've tried to lose weight, and my smoking goes up. I try to cut down my smoking, and my drinking goes up. I get nothing but grief working at the radio station, and it's sedentary to boot. I feel as if all my stress outlets are hooked together—"

"Which they are," Culpepper said soberly. He pulled one of the personal information sheets from the folder and examined it. "Stress. Hmmm . . . have you ever tried sex as a substitute for food?"

"Dr. Culpepper, if I ate as infrequently as I've gotten laid these past three months, we'd be holding this conversation through a Ouija board. If you'll pardon the non sequitur, celibacy sucks."

"Evocatively phrased. Why don't you explain what has held you back in the past?"

"I don't really understand. And I always thought I had to understand before I could do anything about it. But maybe that's wrong. Maybe what I have to give up is having to understand."

Culpepper sat back in his seat, face darkened in confusion. "Well, you have a rather direct attitude about all of this. The deciding factor might be that Algernon is willing to spend some extra time to make up for that expended upon you. I expect you to be worth it, Adam. I assume you're already worth it to Algernon. Now you have to show me."

*I'm in!* Adam suppressed his excitement as he pulled on his shirt. He squinted at a series of branching graphs, labeled with geometrical symbols and words like "Behavmod" and "KC input-out." "It looks like you've got things divided up into intellectual, physical, and emotional components. Why intellectual?"

"If you're going to be a part of this program, you should finish reading my book, young man. Now then,

Algernon told me that the only form of exercise you ever stuck with was some form of karate.''

"Kenpo, under Mitchell Shackley."

"Ah. I seem to remember that name. Were you proficient?"

"Not really."

"Did you enjoy it?"

"Is that important?"

Algernon nodded vigorously. "It's vital, Adam. You're much more likely to stick to an exercise program if you enjoy it."

"And you're much more capable of dealing with a problem if you understand it." Culpepper leaned back in his chair. "What we're talking about here is a technique used by hurdlers, called framing and sighting. By creating a precise image of your goal, it then becomes possible to determine the most expedient route to it. That's the first step. The next is to break that route up into bite-sized pieces that won't gag you, pardon the mangled metaphor—"

"He never metaphor he didn't like," Algernon said innocently.

Adam glared. "You've always had a simile bent."

Dr. Culpepper winced and continued. "As I was saying, break it up into manageable pieces and take them one baby step at a time."

"That makes sense."

"Let's put it another way," he said. "What do you know about behavior modification?"

"Electrocuting rats and making puppies drool?"

"That's just the tabloid headlines. We're talking here about how individuals can coordinate their efforts to create a desired effect. Self-modification comes in five steps. First, you identify the habitual program you want to change. Second, you identify the program that you want to change it to. Third, and this is usually the step that people forget or ignore—you raise your energy level to its highest state."

"Why?"

"Because when your energy level is down, it's always easier to stay in a familiar groove, even if it's a destructive pattern. Hence, the young are always more adventurous, and the expression 'You can't teach an old dog new tricks.' "

He ticked off on his fingers. "A program to change, something to change it to, raise your energy level . . . right? Fourth, practice the new program. Fifth, either reward yourself for success, or fail successfully—"

"Fail successfully?"

"Certainly. A successful failure is one in which you learn something about yourself, and about the process of positive growth. Last, and most important, you must start the whole process over again. You have to keep trying."

"It's a cycle, then."

"That's it exactly," Culpepper interjected. "A trycycle."

Adam and Algernon rolled their eyes, and Culpepper chuckled with satisfaction, then sat back in his chair and looked at Adam carefully. "Mr. Ludlum," he said at last, "we are going to try an experiment and allow a nonathlete into the program. Perhaps some good will come of it. At any rate, I am going to ask you for a concrete action on your part: lose at least ten pounds. When you have done that, come back. If you can't, I must assume insufficient motivation. Agreed?"

Algy nudged him under the table.

"Uh—yeah! Sure. That's fine. Thank you. Both of you. You won't regret this."

"We'll see. Well—you'll excuse me?"

He nodded to both of them and stood.

Adam rose from his chair, head spinning. *I'm in! I'm*— "Once again, thanks for letting me into the program."

Culpepper gathered his papers. He patted his pockets until he produced a muffled jangle of keys. "As I said before, thank your friend. And let's not sing hosannas quite so quickly, shall we? After all, we're still not certain we'll get any results at all."

The door banged shut behind him.

Adam and Algernon stared at each other for a long moment, then whooped. Adam yanked Algernon from his seat and spun him around. "Goddamn! You beautiful bastard. You did it. *Christ* that man is a hard-ass.'"

"Hey, you're thanking me now. Let's just see if you still feel that way in a few weeks. You've got weight to lose."

"In six weeks I'm going to be twenty pounds lighter, and on my way to the slim, trim buns of my jaded youth."

"I've always hoped you were a closet case, Ludlum. You just watch those buns around Culpepper. He's a little nutty."

"How so?"

"He gets results. He breaks heads, but gets results." For a moment Algernon looked as if he was about to say something more, but held it back. "He doesn't give a damn about you, you know."

"I kind of got that feeling, yes."

"But if you can get in, you'll get the best there is." Algernon laced his fingers, suddenly terribly interested in their interplay. "Adam," he said reluctantly, "I've seen you do this to yourself over and over. You've tried every gimmick diet and fad exercise program that's come along. I'm not going to jolly you, man. You don't have much chance of making it this time, either."

A burst of protest was the first thing that came to mind, then as the truth of Algernon's words came home, Adam calmed, and thought, and finally sighed. "I can understand how you feel. I'm not sure I believe in myself anymore, either."

"Then why do you keep doing this to yourself?"

Adam's eyes burned. He clenched his teeth hard, driving the emotions back to neutral. "My father is dying, Algy, and I'm scared. I look around, I look at myself, and suddenly I see, maybe for the first time, really, that I'm not a kid anymore. The future doesn't look infinite anymore. Every year there seem to be fewer months between Christmases. God, I used to think that was bullshit, something adults said to scare you, but it's the truth. Time *flies* by, and everything changes but Ludlum.

"My relationship with Micki has nose-dived, and nothing's happening at work. I feel like a rat in one of those endurance experiments, dumped into a pool of water and paddling and swimming around without a hope in hell of reaching the shore. Just feeling myself run out of energy, and getting more water up my nose all the time. I'm a thirty-three-year-old man who can't trust himself to keep his word." Adam was staring at his hands. Pudgy, pale hands with fingernails chewed ragged to the quick. "We were Boy Scouts once, Algy. Remember how they told us to be 'good campers'? Do you remember what a 'good camper' is?"

Algy's eyes narrowed as he scanned his memories, then he grinned. "Right. 'Only leave footprints, only take pictures.' "

"That's my life. I want more than that. I want to leave something more than footprints. I can't handle it anymore. If I can't win this time, it feels like I'll never win. Can you understand that?"

Algy nodded soberly. "I'm here. I care. Use me, Adam. Don't be afraid to ask."

"I won't." The years suddenly fell away, and both of them were just kids again, just "Chunky" Ludlum and "Parakeet" Swain. First to raise their hands in science or algebra, last to be chosen for any game but murderball. Yet and still, in their own private universe, they were kings. Dropping ammonium triiodide and tapioca pudding "torpedoes" from the fire escape, rigging "Thumper" Watson's locker with a potassium permanganate and aluminum powder booby trap. A friendship forged as a bulwark against the devastating, casual humiliations of prepubescent monsters terrified of the changes exploding in their own bodies. A friendship, born strong, tempered through travail. Not even their fierce competition for Micki had diminished it. As with so many truly powerful bonds, it waned now only through neglect.

Adam gripped Algy's hand, hard. "Listen, I've got to meet Micki."

Algy smiled softly, only the tiniest touch of regret in his eyes. "Say hi to her for me."

"I will." Adam paused at the door, looking back at the small, thin man with the spray of wiry hair and the Coke bottle glasses. His friend. Maybe his only real friend. "Algy, thanks. Really."

"Asshole," he sniffed. "Don't thank me. Just—this time—do it for real, will you?"

# Chapter Four
## The Good Life

*When we find we are without friends, the thing to do is at once to send our thought out to the whole world; send it full of love and affection.*
—Ernest Holmes, *The Science of Mind*

*When we wish to attract others, this . . . thing is simplicity itself. All crave human companionship. The company of equals, the worship of followers, the discipline of a strong leader. Show your intended where they fit in the order of things. Control by leading, subvert by following, force those marching shoulder to shoulder to conform to your rhythm.*
—Savagi, *The Myth of Love*

Adam pulled his metallic blue-green Cortina compact to the curb, peering through rain-streaked windows at the two-bedroom, partially renovated green house a half block south of Wilshire Boulevard in Santa Monica. The house was in better repair than most of its neighbors, although its orange tiled roof had psoriasis, and the exterior paint was faded and flaked. Block lettering on the wet, blotchy sign announced, ''GOOD LIFE bookstore. Health and metaphysical literature. Herbal remedies, incense, I Ching, Kabbalah, Astrology. Special classes in vegetarianism and natural birth. Used books around the corner.''

A scrawny, hungry-looking girl in a rough cotton tunic stood at one side of the store's walkway, a sticklike figure hunched beneath the branches of the fir tree that towered rather improbably in Good Life's front yard. She was attempting to hand damp slips of paper to Good Life customers as they left the store.

As he walked up the path their eyes met. Her face was hollow, her teeth chipped and stained brownish yellow. Her eyes were hard, bright, darkly ringed points: set in that moist, waxy face they were oddly unsettling, but held his for an uncomfortably long moment before he broke contact and kept walking. She clutched at his arm with fingers that dug in like calipers. It *hurt*. He stopped, shocked by the strength of that grip.

''Please,'' she whined. He winced, trying to twist his arm away, to no avail. ''Read the truth. The Messiah was here. He will return soon.''

''Nobody'll be happier than me.'' Adam tugged at his arm. She relaxed her grip, but it was still impossible to pull free. ''Are you some kind of weight lifter, or what?''

She pulled him closer. Her breath was very sharp, and sour. She smelled as if a rat had crawled into her tunic and died. ''Health? Peace? Savagi can give. And more. Savagi was here. He will return. Please. Read.'' She thrust two of the pamphlets into his hand. He was about to refuse when he realized she was trembling.

*You've been lucky today. Why not share a little of it?* He dug into his pocket, and found his wallet, pulling out three dollar bills. ''All right, you win. Will this handle it?''

Gratitude lit her thin, pockmarked face until it was almost beautiful. ''There's much more. Come to the Temple of the Earth Heart. Free dinner. Meet his children. Please.''

Free dinner? That idea scored happily until a warning bell rang in the back of his mind. *This woman looks like*

*Miss Bangladesh. Why is she inviting me to a free feed?*
He had a sudden image of a cult of binge/purge masochists
who watch, with vast, hungry-puppy eyes, while their
guests wolf heaping bowls of brown rice and bean sprouts.

*And concluded the banquet by . . .*

Where had that last thought come from? It seemed
familiar, and vaguely disquieting. A bit of children's
doggerel.

Adam's eagerness to get out of the rain deadened its
reverberations. He smiled noncommittally. Her expression
changed again, sharpening so suddenly that it gave him the
absolute willies. "Anything you want, Savagi can give.
Anything. Read Savagi. Trust Savagi."

Adam folded the leaflets and shoved them into his coat
pocket, hurrying into the bookstore. The door slammed
shut, putting a barrier of wood and stenciled glass between
his ears and the whining voice.

Bookracks and hanging rugs, the sweet, musky smell of
incense, the tinkling, faintly metallic music of crystal wind
chimes, and the press of a crowd all hit him in the same
instant. He was overwhelmed, dizzy, and took a moment
to regain his equilibrium.

The cash register sang merrily, and he sidled in the
other direction, hiding behind a shelf. He peered between
the halftoned book covers and spotted her instantly.

Micki was almost a foot shorter than the other girl
behind the counter. Only her head and shoulders projected
above the counter as she logged packages. The teenaged
boy buying a stack of posters said something funny, and
Micki's heart-shaped face caught the light, glowing as she
laughed. When she shook her head, her brown hair shim-
mied in ringlets, the highlights sparkling.

Her cheeks bore the slightest trace of blush, her mouth
just a hint of lipstick—the carefully created illusion of the
Natural Look. Aside from a tiny pair of copper earrings,
she wore no jewelry.

Micki owned the bookstore, had for six years now. She
lived in the back, often worked twelve hours a day, and by

force of will had taken it from bankruptcy to a thriving business.

He tore his eyes away. There were pamphlets and over-sized paperbacks everywhere, and he picked up a stack of the cheapest of them, treatises on *"Atlantis—Mythtery of the Ages, Sexual Secrets of the UFOs,* and *Colonic Irrigation.* There was even one by the man called Savagi, entitled *Conquest of the Flesh.*

Curious, he flipped the book over and examined the hand-colored photograph on the back. Savagi seemed to be an exotic wrinkle collector, his face holding enough tiny folds of flesh for an entire VFW parade. He was a small, nut-brown man, his hair wrapped Sikh-like in a turban, withered arms folded placidly in front of him. Adam had the impression that his chest was large, perhaps dispropor-tionate to the rest of his body. Despite the poor reproduc-tion, the old man radiated immense vitality and intelligence.

Especially the eyes. They didn't seem printed on the paper so much as punched through it, as though they contained something beyond the halftone's ink and paper. The eyes were like windows into the deepest, coldest night that had ever darkened the sky.

When he finally wrenched his gaze from the photo, the crowd had thinned, and he snuck a glimpse of Micki. She was still at the cash register, although her head was turned to speak to the other, taller, girl behind the counter. Adam carried his load of books to the front and plopped them down. Micki's head was still turned, and she didn't see him.

"Excuse me, Miss Cappelotti." He adjusted his glasses, clearing his throat with a rolling, theatrical resonance. "This book, ah, *Conquest of the Flesh*, guarantees salvation. Considering that the legitimacy of the offer will be impossible to determine until *after* the customer's demise, how are the refunds handled?"

"In your case, they'll be printed on asbestos." Her expression was playful, but the voice was guarded. Her tanned, slender fingers slipped the books from his hand. "I—don't really have time to talk right now."

"I thought that maybe we could catch some lunch."

She closed her eyes, sighing. "I thought we'd decided—"

"No. *You* decided."

"Adam, it's just not going to work. I care about you. Very much. But you can't build a life on broken promises." Her voice almost caught when she said that, then she stopped, and softened it. "I've got a store to run, Adam. If you want these books—"

He took her hands gently. "What I want is just a few minutes of your time. Just lunch, Micki."

Her eyes. Those hypnotically mismatched eyes that he had adored since seventh grade. The left one green, the right blue. And both so bright and reflective it often seemed she wore silvered contact lenses.

She pushed his hands away. "No."

There was both sweetness and finality in the words, but something inside him bared its teeth.

"Micki . . . we owe ourselves more than that."

"Adam"—there was a vast weariness in the single syllable—"we went over everything that has to be said three months ago. Nothing's changed."

There was a customer behind him in line now, an older man with a road map of veins etching his cheek. The man shuffled his feet impatiently.

"*I've* changed. If this was three months ago I'd just walk away from here and bury myself in a chocolate sundae at Swenson's."

The other girl behind the counter, a tall, stocky Latina with braids and braces, leaned forward. "I'll raise you a banana split."

"I fold. Your face or mine?"

"I like him, Boss. Give him a chance." With deceptive sweetness, she added, "Don't you have lunch break in about five minutes, Micki? I could take the register. . . ."

Micki was shaking, but it was difficult to tell whether it was rage or suppressed laughter. In a stage whisper she said, "Well thanks a bunch, Donna."

"Any time."

She turned to Adam, peering at him as if for the first

time. "Damn you. Sometimes I could just . . . I assume you can wait for me to grab my coat?"

"Just barely."

Micki glared at Donna and left the counter, smiling weakly at the customers. She spun around as she passed the cash register. "And Donna Maria—about that raise you wanted—"

A flash of metal-lined teeth. "Forget it, Boss. I work for love."


"You're still smoking."

It wasn't a question, and Adam silently cursed his Ultra Brite. He sat across the table from Micki in a tiny Oriental restaurant a few blocks south of the Good Life. Plates smeared with red and golden brown sauces, specks of brown rice, and tiny cubes of pork littered the table between them.

A plump, smiling Chinese lady floated from table to table with never less than a dozen dishes crowding her arms. She nodded to them as if to say "just a minute." They had received the identical nod five times in the past seven minutes.

He looked at himself in the mirror behind their booth. It was far too easy to picture the diet and exercise books filling his apartment, the weight-loss slogans plastered over his refrigerator and bathroom mirror. The bloated, bathing-suited "before" picture still waiting a triumphant "after." In the past three weeks, he had gained two pounds. It was crazy.

"It's true. I don't smoke around you. And I still eat too much. But I'm trying something new—and it's going to work this time."

"Oh, Adam, you've said that so damned often. . . ." Her voice died away. Micki covered her face, sighing hard. "Adam, I don't want to hurt you. I never did. When we started seeing each other, your weight didn't bother me. It bothered *you*. But in the past two years I've seen you lie to yourself so many times. You were going to start karate again—"

"After Shackley, everybody else looked *sick*."

"Then you could have gotten into another sport. Listen, Adam, it's too damned easy to come up with reasons to fail." She raised a hand to cut off his protest. "The whole thing is out of control. You love showing me off. If I'm not wearing the shortest, or the tightest, or the sheerest, you feel cheated. Well, all right—I love myself, and I love keeping myself healthy. But what is the statement you're making about yourself when you demand that of me, and then let yourself—"

"Micki, I was wrong. I've been trying. . . ."

"No. No trying. You either do it or you don't, but it's for you now, and just for you. Leave me out of it."

She turned sideways, facing away from him. Adam fought to find a correlation between this woman who seemed infinitely distant and the woman who, only three months before, had lain beside him in his apartment, both of them covered with the light, sweet dew of lovemaking, and told him that it was the last time. She had been so open and caring, trying so hard not to hurt him. Knowing that it was impossible.

*"You're not going to change. All right. I don't have a right to expect you to. But I do have a right to want for myself what you want for yourself. And I want someone who respects himself more. On every level. I'm going to have that in my life. I'm sorry it couldn't have been with you."*

"I can't let you do this to yourself. It's not your fault that the chemistry isn't there. You'll be a hell of a catch for some lady." She paused and wiped her mouth nervously. "I think it's time you started looking for her."

Adam's stomach was starting to cramp, to sour and knot up as if the fried noodles had been rancid. "I'm—" He choked back the word "try." He was getting damned sick of that word. "I'm doing something about it. Forget everything I've ever said before. This time it's for real."

"I—don't think I want anybody trying that hard for me."

"I'm not just trying. And it's not for you. It's for me."

"I just can't handle it anymore. I shouldn't have come."
She pushed her chair back.

"Won't you even let me drive you to the store?"

"It's not far."

She put a five-dollar bill on the table. "I'm not sorry
about any of it, Adam. I'm glad we tried. And . . . I think
I'm glad it's over."

Adam watched her leave, numb and pissed for not even
being angry with her.

Then something broke inside him, and he pushed himself out to the aisle, humiliatingly conscious of the excess
flesh that wedged him tightly between table and seat.

The blood pounded in his ears as he ran to the street
corner. Heaving for breath, he spun to a stop as he saw
her.

Her eyes were red, and she seemed somehow smaller
than her sixty-four inches.

He didn't touch her, although his yearning to hold her
was blindingly strong. "Micki—"

"Adam, leave it, will you? Don't make me regret any
of it. Can't you just . . ." The tears were beginning to
spill, and she was fighting a losing battle for control.

"Micki, I'll make you a deal. A month. Give me a
month. Maybe six weeks. I won't call you, I won't come
to see you. You just see me at the end of that time. If I
haven't made changes that you can see and feel, I'll just
walk away."

She gazed at the blinking green and orange neon shop
signs that lined the wet streets. There was something
pathetic about neon in the daytime. Bleached of light and
color, they just looked fragile, vulnerable, their pale illu-
mination competing unsuccessfully with the noise and
rush that pulled the customers north to Westwood, south to
the Marina.

Adam studied her carefully, afraid that her answer might
be no, and that this could really be it, after all of their
time together, all of the time circling and darting in the
mating dance. That the end might come before there
was any chance to finish sharing the feelings, alibing

the failures, reaching the emotional parity so often craved, so seldom achieved.

When it came down to it, one side always wanted things to work more than the other. One always had to resist the urge to crawl, to beg, to try to make it right. *One person kisses the cheek, the other presents it to be kissed.*

But there was no regret in him. Her hair, dark with coppery highlights, stirred softly in the breeze, reminding him of massed wind or water, something natural and un-controllable, and for a moment it seemed impossible that he had ever nestled his face in that hair, breathed its perfume, made those lips cry out in pleasure.

"Six weeks, Micki. You won't hear a word from me."

"Oh, Adam." She was crying as she turned away from the window. "I thought that it was all done."

*Yes, I'll try once more. Just once.* She didn't have to say it. There was little hope, only an acknowledgment of possibility, and a willingness to go one final mile.

No words of thanks would come, but when he touched her hand, it seemed as if a tiny jolt of static electricity leaped between them.

Suddenly she pulled his head down and touched her lips to his in a very brief, almost sisterly kiss. Almost. "For luck."

Then she turned, and walked quickly away, back toward her store.

# Chapter Five
## Heart and Soul

*As the mind of Man has grown, so have grown his faculties. His arms reach farther, his eyes see more clearly. He has created machines which make him the swiftest and strongest of creatures. And yet his basic aims have never changed. In lieu of attaining Ecstasy, or even peace, we play games with each other, with our lives, with our very souls. The rules grow daily more complex. The stakes have never changed.*
*—Savagi, Death of the Soul*

The room's single window was masked with Reynolds Wrap, the foil taped to the shade, the shade thumbtacked to the bottom of the frame. Still, golden threads of sunlight streamed in through cracks where the foil had been folded once too often.

The threads brought a pale dawn to Adam's bachelor apartment, painting dim valleys of light and shadow among the skeletal branches of his bookracks, the clumps of unsorted underwear gracing the chairs, and the forlornly bent rabbit ears of the television set. Sprawled magazines and manuals cluttered the room's single table.

Adam flicked the light switch, surveying his kingdom

until the light browned out. He jiggled the bulb, tightened it, and it flared warmly to life.

In the kitchenette, a black fur ball with a splotchy orange tail raised its head from the sink and mewed plaintively. It shook itself, bounded out, and raced across the room, burying its claws affectionately in his leg.

"Hi, BeDoss. How're you keeping, guy?" The cat mewed hungrily as he picked it up and edged toward the kitchen. "And what little present did you leave me, eh?"

The whiff of cat stink hit him like a slap across the nose, and Adam shrieked "You little bastard!" and switched the faucet on, washing the brown nuggets down the drain. In a few moments the garbage disposal was gurgling happily. BeDoss sat on the floor licking his paws with a pink tongue, gazing up at Adam unrepentantly.

Adam knew that expression well. *Well if you'd clean my catbox more often . . .*

Adam unbuttoned his shirt and kicked his shoes off, then nudged a heap of underwear aside until he found the familiar comfort of his J. C. Waterwalkers. The cheap leather uppers had worn out twice in the last four years, but the tire-tread soles threatened to hang in there until the Second Coming.

BeDoss followed him back into the tiny kitchenette, rubbing frantically at his feet as Adam started up the coffeepot, then peeled the metal strip from the rim of BeDoss's can of Kitty Krunch.

*Well, you've done it this time. Six weeks. You dumb shit. What can you do in six weeks that you couldn't do in six years?*

He ground his heel on that thought, crushing it before it could crawl away and breed. While the coffee warmed, Adam poured the Kitty Krunch into the red rubber feeding dish. BeDoss mewed his undying fidelity and abandoned Adam's ankle.

Adam pulled a couple of beers from the refrigerator, then cleared the apartment's single desk by the simple expedient of dumping the books and magazines on his unmade bed. The desk light fizzled for a moment before flicking to life.

"Soul." The object on his desk was the approximate size and shape of an office typewriter, and gleamed like the first toy out of the box on Christmas morning.

His Sol-20 computer weighed fifty-two pounds, had cost him three months' salary and about a hundred hours of spare time. When Adam carried it home from the shop, it was just a carton—a series of cartons, actually, with its wires and various small connections still undone, its parts still wrapped and boxed and cannistered, waiting for the Computer Fairy to come and breathe life into them.

Its top and front were metallic, burnished black and stainless. But its sides were wood-grain, textured to the touch and altogether lovely, some meld of technology and earth magic, and over the years his upgrading of its capacities from 8000 to 512,000 bytes of memory had merely deepened their relationship. He had tinkered with so much, changed so much, and adjusted so much that a cynic might have even suggested that it was no longer the same machine.

Whatever it was, it was his, and operational from its 512K of memory to its five-inch CRT and the whirring fan in its guts. He ran his fingers gingerly along the siding, as if the wood and metal were as fragile as butterfly wings. "Well, stinker, at least *you* still love me."

From a plastic file box he pulled the 5¼-inch DataLine modem software, and booted it up. It immediately gave him a list of the information service's specifications. A hundred-dollar membership fee plus ten dollars an hour bought him access to one of the best services in the country, with over 500 separate categories of information available. From technical paper abstracts to news reports, stock reports, games (he had sworn to himself that he wouldn't be caught dead playing Adventure on DataLine; the game, a series of interlocking verbal puzzles involving rooms, tunnels, caves, treasures, and trolls was monstrously addictive, and a wonderful way to chew up sixty or eighty dollars' worth of time before you knew it), word processing and word-processing aids, research services, bulletin boards, and enough more to make him dizzy.

Almost as dizzy as holding Micki.

Michelle Annelle Cappelotti.

He could never even *pretend* not to love her. She was still as beautiful to him as she had been the first time he saw her, almost twenty years before.

When was that? Seventh grade? Seventh grade, and the teacher was Mrs. Benjamin, the algebra instructor who always looked like she had just stepped out of the "before" panel of a hemorrhoid ad. Mrs. Benjamin, who looked at the girl sitting in the fourth seat of the row next to the construction-paper patchwork bulletin board and said, "*Michelle Cappelotti.*"

"Michelle." Now that the thoughts had started they had a tempo, a momentum of their own, and there was no way to stop them. He was blinded by the memory of the first day, of the dark lustrous hair and the straight little nose, the eyes that were hypnotically mismatched.

Micki.

The closet door stood open, and on the back of it hung a white cotton karate uniform he hadn't worn in over five years. The brown belt was still folded over the hook. It dangled there like an innocent man on the gallows, silently accusing, asking him when he would put it on again, go back to Mitchell Shackley's Kenpo Karate School, and pick up where he'd left off.

Too late now. Shackley was gone, studying or teaching in Nepal somewhere. At least, that was the rumor.

Adam's face sank down into his arms, enfolding him in darkness. He shook, exhuming corpses that had laid rotting in their graves for half a decade.

He could still remember Shackley's parting words, one muscular, callused hand resting on Adam's shoulder as he pronounced sentence.

"*You've been here for six years, Adam. But there's a difference between six years of training and one year six times. You earned your brown belt four years ago, and you're just not going to go any further until you tame the*

*demons. I'm getting tired of watching you tread water.
You don't come to class often enough. You've learned the
katas, but you won't compete, and you won't fight.''*
Shackley pursed his lips in frustration, smoothing a knot
out of his graying Fu Manchu mustache with the tip of a
finger. Adam had seen those fingers shatter Coke bottles
and pine boards suspended from tissue paper, and respected Shackley as he did few living men.

*''There's something blocking you, Adam, and you won't
let me help you. I can't just take your money and run. I
want you to make up your mind about this, decide if it's
what you really want, decide if you want to be honest with
me about what's bothering you. Take a rest from this for a
while. Think about it. Then when you're ready, come on
back and talk to me.''*

A rest. Sixty months of rest.

He popped the top on a can of Brew 102 and propped
his feet up on the windowledge. When his feet hit the
shade, it rattled up abruptly, exposing a cold, wet street
framed by the yellow neon ''Villa Reymondo'' sign with
the broken ''y'' that buzzed at night.

Adam took another sip, grimacing. The suds were terrible, but by God he was going to drain the last bitter drop.
There was logic in there somewhere, but he wouldn't have
wanted a shrink probing around for it.

He emptied the can and gazed out at the clock on the
billboard across the street, above the burnt wreckage of the
Hollywood Ranch Market. He could remember when its
huge clock raced at dizzying speed, tracing a day's passage in a handful of seconds.

If he concentrated, he could build the market again, and
it amused him to do it. There . . . there were the timbers
going up, and a magical brush stole the darkness from the
charred boards. Workmen were scuttling about like tiny
ants, and in a matter of moments, the market was alive
again, the yellow-white fluorescent lights flooding over the
counters chockfull of green melons and golden ears of
corn, and the twenty-four-hour snack bar visible from his
window, and . . .

He blinked, and it was all gone. It seemed so real, right down to the sounds and smells. He'd never met anyone who claimed a more vivid imagination. Or a more useless talent.

There was nothing across the street but one hell of a view. This was supposed to be a turning point, the Great Moment in his life. The least reality owed him was a rainbow.

Soul's READY TO LOAD message stared at him. Adam popped open the other can of beer and licked away the foam, running his thumb along the thick fold of flesh at his midsection.

Adam switched on his modem connection, and hit Control 1. The word DATADIET appeared on the screen, as the batch file listing all necessary commands, passwords, and identification ran through the modem.

The phone number was busy the first time, so his modem paused and then tried again.

Adam flexed his hands. They were greasy with sweat. He pulled a box of Ding-Dongs from the cupboard and munched into the chocolate and cream, watching the clock.

At one and a half Dongs, he got through. The batch file took him straight through the menus and the Health submenu to where "Diet" was sandwiched (and for Adam, that was a visual image. A literal sandwich, with sprigs of lettuce, and a little mustard around the edge . . .) between "Calories" and "Exercise." DataLine examined his private, rented data niche in their magnetic bowels, evaluated it, and rendered its electronic opinion.

And there was everything that Culpepper had known about him at a glance. The weeks and weeks of insufficient calories burned, exercise taken, information given . . . The goddamn machine virtually called him a liar. According to its record of the past nine months of his life, the best he could hope for in forty-two days was a loss of about six pounds, and for that to reappear as soon as he relaxed for a moment.

The figures and polite suggestions stared at him unwaveringly, yellow-white letters glowing on the screen.

*Six weeks.*

How do you remake yourself in six weeks? How do you even begin?

*And how much do you care, Adam?*

The "y" outside his window fizzled at him. The traffic below was a moan of white noise, isolating him with his thoughts.

*How much do you care?*

It wasn't just Micki. It wasn't just his father.

How many ways can you lose and still feel like a human being? How many times can you pretend that you don't really want something, without beginning to feel that there's just nothing of value in your life?

*How much do you care?*

There was a sharp edge jutting into his back, and he reached behind him and pulled it out. It was Savagi's *Conquest of the Flesh*, and he cocked his arm to throw it across the room. But the light from the overhead bulb caught the slick paper just right, and the appalling magnetism of the man's eyes captured him, and he began to thumb through it.

Just sixty-four pages long, it was divided into eight sections: "Beginnings," "Diet," "Breathing," "Body Disciplines," "Body Magick," "Fasting," "Endings," and "Toward a New Purpose." Almost idly, he turned to "Fasting."

What was it that Culpepper's book had called fasting? "The last refuge of the uninformed?"

*How much do you care?*

He thought of Micki: hair lustrous in the darkness, eyes brilliant in the light.

He thought of his father: *"When, Adam, when?"*

Of Mitchell Shackley: *"When you make up your mind . . ."*

Of the University of Southern California.

*Now why was it that you dropped out of school at a BA? And what is it that you feel every time you hear someone call Algy* Doctor *Swain? And how often would you even* see *your best friend if he didn't reach out to you, and how much longer will he keep doing that?*

*How much do you care?*

*What will you try?*

There was a message stamped in dark blue on the inside cover of the book. "Come to the feast!" it read. "All ills cured. All questions answered. Come to the celebration! Savagi loves you! 7 P.M. every Saturday and Sunday."

Seven o'clock. Adam glanced at his wristwatch and laughed to himself. A joke, that's all. Stick with Culpepper and the UCLA program.

Again, he examined the picture of Savagi. There was something direct and awesomely no-bullshit in that expression.

*What have I got to lose? Might as well try just everything at once, you know? And I'll just do a little synthesizing of my own.*

*Might as well check out these ding-a-lings. And the Nutrisystem. And the Carnation diet plan, and Herbal Life . . .*

But those were afterthoughts. What he really wanted to do was to get another look at the woman whose fingers had damned near ripped his forearm off. *Something* had happened then.

Good. It was settled then. He leaned back and disconnected DataLine, disconcerted that he had daydreamed away precious minutes. The CRT light dwindled to a dot and disappeared.

There was time to shower, and then head into West Hollywood to the Temple of the Earth Heart.

For a meeting with Savagi, or whoever the hell he was.

*And concluded the banquet by . . .*

He shook his head clear. Now, where *had* that bit of poem come from?

# Chapter Six
# Children of the Earth Heart

*. . . if you relieve one symptom in a chronically anxious patient, something else will crop up, some other autonomic dysfunction will occur. When dealing with any imbalanced state, it is important to recognize the potential for developing alternate symptoms and ultimately other disease processes . . . [therefore] you should work to put your whole body, mind, emotions and spirit in tune.*
—C. Norman Shealy, M.D., *90 Days to Self-Health*

*There is only one path to realignment with the powers of the universe. That path is the body. The body is the doorway. The animal drives: breath, sleep, food, drink and sex. It is through misuse of these that Mankind lost Divinity. It is through discipline that GodHead will be reattained.*
—Savagi, *Conquest of the Flesh*

His lungs ached for a cigarette. Now was the time that Adam wanted to roll back against his chair and draw deeply on a Benson & Hedges Menthol, teasing the smoke down into his lungs, feeling the rush of blood in his head, the yammering of tiny nicotine receptors in his brain as they got their fix.

But this wasn't the time for that. He had scraped the last bit of brown rice and fish mush from his bowl with the wooden spoon provided by the Temple of the Earth Heart.

"Feast," he said to himself, instantly realizing that the grumble was unjustified. The meal had been free, and joyfully given, served by acolytes in rose-petal linen robes, who hummed sweetly as they wove through the rough, low, round wooden tables that dotted the floor of the dining hall.

The temple looked as if it had once been a restaurant, with a bookstore branching off to the side. The ceiling was low and intimate, and smoked by the wicks of countless candles. The smell of old incense was in the wood, and he rather liked it. He felt comfortable, even if the Children of the Earth Heart made his back teeth grit.

His food was served by the thin brunette who had accosted him in front of the Good Life. She was transformed from that afternoon: her clothing freshly washed, her teeth brushed, her frail body almost attractive beneath the thin robe.

Almost? That was a lie. She was damned attractive as she bent over his table, smiling shyly, and it was somehow disturbing. By no stretch of the imagination could she be considered pretty, but when she looked at him, which she did *often*, there was something in those dark, short-lashed eyes, that was pure invitation, and it was impossible not to wonder if there weren't back rooms in the temple, dark, padded alcoves where prospective New Faithful could sample a little earth magic.

Hookers for Christ. Hadn't that been what those girls, the little Hollywood street preachers of the sixties, had been called? *They'll do anything, anything you want, upside down and swinging from the ceiling, if you read Second Timothy with them after. . . .*

Then she was gone on to another table with her pot of mushy rice and fish, and maybe the flirtation started all over again. Except that she peered back over her shoulder at him, and smiled shyly, briefly, through chipped teeth.

The visitors to the temple were an interesting lot. A couple were tourists, there merely and clearly to check out the local wacko action, grins barely suppressed. Three looked just plain hungry, a girl in ill-fitting shorts and two young men in clothes that looked like they'd been hooked out of a Goodwill box. And a half dozen, Adam included, who seemed politely interested.

As the meal came to an end Adam expected the Sermon, but instead, there was an influx of Children, smiling, their hair conspicuously clean and braided or shaven, gathering around the tables, one or two of them to every guest, spiriting them off to private corners to talk about the wonders of Savagi. Adam expected the thin girl to come to him, but she didn't.

Instead, a tall man in his late forties strode to Adam. In some ways he reminded Adam of Culpepper. But this man's hair was golden and cherubically curled. His eyes were hazel, cat's-eye marble clear and fever-bright. His face was so gaunt that Adam would have considered him unhealthy save for his infectious energy.

"Greetings, Brother. My name is Kevin Dearborne."

"Adam Ludlum." He shook Dearborne's hand. The offered hand was warm and dry, and Adam felt very little pressure. It pumped up and down in an even, practiced stroke. It shouldn't have been alarming at all, but it was. *He could crush my hand to a paste.* The thought was there, instantly, without any provocation.

"You came to talk," Dearborne said. "You spoke to Sylvia earlier today."

"Sylvia—oh, yes, at the Good Life." Adam laughed self-consciously. "Guess I sort of expected you people to have names like Jowatha and Fizier or something."

There was no offense taken in those improbably large eyes. "Oh, no. Savagi taught us that it is possible to control and to guide ego, but not to destroy it. One never eradicates the root completely, so why try?"

"Makes sense to me."

Kevin's large, thin hand cradled Adam's arm. "Come. Let's talk." Adam felt himself plucked from the cushion by a strength that was wholly intimidating.

Together, they walked to a side alcove. Behind the hanging white curtains was a selection of books and pamphlets, herbs and tiny jars of salve. Monochrome and color pictures of Savagi lined the walls. From every corner and every wall, those dead, flaming eyes stared. Adam suddenly found it difficult to breathe, and would have left the room had it not been for Kevin Dearborne's large, insistent hand on his shoulder.

Dearborne set Adam down on a bench, sitting opposite him in a wicker chair. As the curtain dropped, the rest of the world seemed to vanish. Suddenly he was very alone with Dearborne, who sat, largely in shadow, inspecting Adam unblinkingly.

"Who are you?" Dearborne asked. "I feel as if we have met before."

The air crawled with chill currents. Adam suddenly wished that he'd brought another jacket. "No—I don't think so. But maybe at the Good Life?"

"No." Dearborne shook his head, and watched Adam quietly. "I was mistaken. We have never met before. But you are different, as Sylvia said you were."

*Oh, come on. How many people do . . . you . . .* Adam's objections died unspoken as he sat in the alcove. Dearborne's breathing, his words and phrasing, were slow and measured. As if he was a professional hypnotist.

"I'm not sure why I came here." Adam said, still fighting to regain equilibrium.

"You were supposed to. You felt something different, didn't you? We recognize our own. Sometime, in another life, you touched the Light. You plumbed the Earth Heart. You were meant to return."

"What is this? All of this?"

"Savagi," Dearborne said. "He was . . . the greatest of men." Dearborne's voice still had that low, measured, somnambulant quality, and Adam found it difficult to keep his attention focused. Surrounded by pictures of Savagi, Adam was slipping into someplace dark and still. The metallic tingle of the music spiraled away and away until the two men were totally, utterly alone.

"You will read of him. Much of him, I think. He rediscovered the ancient ways, and was driven from his grandfather's house in India. He came to the United States, where he could teach. Small men, jealous men, who could not follow his teaching, defamed him. And one such man . . ." For a moment Dearborne's eyes flamed, something so bright and hard and feral behind the polite facade that Adam was taken totally aback. But then, like a grate swinging shut on the blinding fury of a blast furnace, Dearborne's face became neutral, and then pleasant again.

"Could not follow . . . ?" Adam found that the breath came more difficultly, that he was struggling for each sip of air. Dearborne seemed to expand, filling the space like a genie exploding from its crystal dungeon. The voice. His voice. *Don't get sucked in* . . .

But Dearborne's voice, and his eyes, his bright hazel eyes, bright as Savagi's were dark, held him absolutely.

"A master leads where few can follow. Intelligence. Sensitivity. Dedication. Purity of intent. There are forces in the universe, Adam. One must know which side one is on. One must be dedicated to the Earth Heart to tap it."

"W-what are you talking about? Earth Heart?"

Dearborne reached out and took Adam's hand. His whole body tingled. "The core of our world. A molten sea of nickel-iron, generating a vast field of energy. I think you are ready for Power."

How often had Dearborne given this speech to prospective converts? "What is it that you think I want?"

"Your weight. You smoke. You drink. You have sexual problems." That last struck Adam right where it was meant to, and his thighs pressed together tightly.

"We can help you. You can help us."

More than anything in the world, what Adam wanted

was to rise and leave the alcove, leave the temple. There was only one thing that stopped him, one question that he had finally screwed up his courage to ask. "You . . . and Sylvia . . . seem so strong. I don't understand."

"Human beings are afraid of their . . . our strength. When we treat ourselves as healthy animals, our animal powers increase. They say that most people use only a fraction of their minds. This is even more true of our bodies. Human strength is barely tapped. We tap the mind, the body. We ride the currents of the Earth Heart. The path is only for the chosen. Not for those out there who came to gawk or beg. You. You are the right one."

"How do you know?" He couldn't help himself from asking, despite the whispering voice that said, "What's born every minute, Adam? Fill in the blanks, Adam: A———and his———soon are———.

"We know our own." When Dearborne stood, his muscles and joints meshed together like the gears of a great machine. He had never felt such physical power from a human being—not even Shackley. What Shackley had was focus, coordination of his human energies. Dearborne was a blast furnace; Shackley, a laser beam.

Dearborne selected pamphlets from the surrounding tables. Looked at Adam carefully, selected two more and put one back. A plastic case containing a set of three cassettes. A box of tea. "These are the things that you need. Trust me for a week. Then either throw them away, or continue."

"How much?" To his intense shame, Adam found that he was already fumbling for his checkbook.

"One hundred and ten dollars. It is not inexpensive. But it is what you need."

Adam's hands shook as he wrote the check out. *I can't believe I'm doing this. Jesus. This guy could be making a fortune selling refrigerators.*

He ripped off the check and handed it over. He was too conscious of his breathing, the sound of his heartbeat thudding in his chest. "I don't know why I'm doing this," he said finally.

"Yes you do," Dearborne said mildly. "It is your choice. Your yearning. Nothing I could say would sway you if it were not true. You must welcome the change, or there is no change at all."

"I think . . . I'm ready to change," Adam said. "I have to tell you honestly—I splurge. I try weird things, and go great guns for a couple of weeks, and then—"

"All we ask is a couple of weeks. From the right person."

He nodded, and exchanged the check for the box. "Thanks for the time, and the meal." He was already starting to feel foolish. *Fifty cents' worth of rice and fish, and here I go carting out a hundred and ten bucks worth of paper and tape. Wonder who got the best of that deal?*

With a last nod to Kevin Dearborne, Adam tucked the box under one arm and left the alcove, heading through the tables. Many of the other guests had already gone, being either more resistant to the pitch, or perhaps, as Dearborne had implied, been subjected to less intense efforts.

A hundred and ten dollars! How had he *done* something as stupid as that. He needed to go back and return . . .

But then there was the memory of Sylvia's grip, and of Dearborne's hand, the large, warm fingers that could have crushed his like a hydraulic press. Maybe there *was* something. And they were all so thin. . . .

Adam grinned to himself, and left the building feeling more optimistic than he had in weeks. In such a good mood, in fact, that he didn't really notice the two men— one black, one white—both in business suits, who entered the Temple of the Earth Heart as he left.

But they noticed him.

Winston Gates moved aside for the young man with the box of pamphlets and the half yard of grin to pass. He had to move quickly, for not only was the young man bliss- fully oblivious, but also quite wide enough to crowd the doorway.

He nudged his partner, Doug Patterson. "Swear to God

I'm going to nail Dearborne. Just wish there was a law against inflicting sappy smiles."

"There isn't, so get off it." Doug was three inches taller than Gates, fifteen years younger and several shades lighter. He walked with a limp gained in pursuing a suspect who, unable to climb a chain link fence, had turned and pumped three shots into Doug's legs and side.

Doug had graduated from patrolman to investigator, and no longer chased suspects on foot. He did, however, spend three hours a week, every week, on the pistol range.

Gates had been to the Temple of the Earth Heart twice before, and on neither occasion had the business been pleasant.

A young man in a clean saffron robe met them at the first hallway. "Yes?" the momentary question, and automatic smile vanished as the boy recognized Gates. "Inspector Gates. Again. When will you stop harassing us?"

"Friend, you don't know what harassment *is* yet. I think that you had better get Brother Dearborne out here. Now."

The boy glared defiantly. "You'll see. The Messiah is returning soon."

Doug laughed harshly. "I don't think he went out for pizza, kid."

The boy opened his mouth, shut it, and then took off for the back of the temple.

The waiting room was decorated with pictures of another, grander building that the Temple of the Earth Heart had owned, but these were harder times. There were a few pictures of elder temple members, but the one overwhelmingly prevalent image was of a bearded, wrinkled man with deep-set eyes and a mouth that seemed to never have borne a smile. The gold foil label beneath it read, "Savagi. ?–1977. Our eternal love, the Children of the Earth Heart."

"Hey, Win. Isn't 'baby of the earth' another name for a potato bug?"

"Jerusalem cricket, if you don't mind."

Doug thumped the plaque with his forefinger. "Think

the rest of them are in on it? Might just be the one wacko."

"You rarely see one maggot traveling by itself," Gates said cheerlessly. The sound of soft-soled shoes on wood whispered down the hall toward them. Gates steeled himself and turned to face Dearborne.

The man coming down the hall was so full of life and at the same time so utterly calm that Gates ran a list of statistics through his mind to shield himself from the almost overwhelming charisma.

Kevin Dearborne. Sixty-one years old, six feet even, approximately one hundred and fifty-five pounds. Three arrests, no convictions.

That was almost all that was known of the man. At least, all that the files of the LAPD could say with certainty.

"Inspectors Gates, Patterson." Dearborne's smile was perfunctory at best. "How may I help you today?" Dearborne and Patterson examined each other. There was genuine tension in the air: Patterson was an inch taller than Dearborne, and thirty years younger, but there was something about the older man that was altogether physically foreboding.

Gates took a photograph out of his jacket pocket. It pictured a young man, perhaps Doug's age, with a rather round face, limp blond hair, and unhealthily pale skin. Gates handed it to Dearborne.

"I'm sorry," the thin man said after a few seconds, handing it back. "I don't believe I know this person."

"How about this one?" Gates handed over a second picture. This was a young girl, perhaps seventeen years old. She was Hispanic, quite pretty, with a full, smiling mouth and teeth that shone brilliantly in a happy smile.

There was a moment's pause, and the slightest of flinches. "No, I don't believe I know her, either. But then, so many people come in and out of these doors."

"Yeah, well, I doubt if either of them will be darkening your door in the future." He handed Dearborne a third picture, this one black and white, once again of the girl.

She was lying on the floor of her jail cell. She was very dead, her skull like a hard-boiled egg that had flipped to the kitchen tile. The lack of color was a blessing: blood oozed darkly from her nose and mouth and ears.

Dearborne was very still. "Savagi protect us," he said quietly. "What happened?"

"Sanchez. Carla Sanchez," Patterson said. "Arrested yesterday for the murder of one Hector Cawthorn. It took three officers to subdue her, Dearborne. She put one of our men in the emergency ward."

"Was it . . . drugs?"

"PCP? Angel dust? Not according to the blood tests, and as you can see, we had plenty of blood to test. Sometime last night, she grabbed the bars of her cell and lobotomized herself. Do you have any idea how much strength that takes? Knock yourself out, sure. Fracture your skull, maybe. But crush it like a cracker? Naturally, I thought of you."

"Why me?" Dearborne said, but there was a slight breech in his self-confidence now, one that he tried to hide with an imperious flip of the photograph as he handed it back.

"The MO on the murder and the suicide. Doesn't it remind you of anything? Judd, last year. He *was* one of your Children. He was linked to two murders that were just like Cawthorn's."

"The heads?"

"Yeah. Cawthorn's head was crushed. Torn open. No sign of metal at the scene. Brain tissue mutilated. The trail went back to Sanchez. And just like Judd, she killed herself. And just like Judd, she had some of your pamphlets in her apartment."

"I don't know this woman," Dearborne said, his armor back in place. "If she had any of our literature—well, they are available in resale outlets. As for poor Judd, I always maintained that he was innocent. Perhaps this Sanchez woman was the culprit. I hope she was."

"Yeah, you and about fourteen grieving families across the United States. Fourteen cases of brain mutilation—

some say brain-eating—in the past twelve years. There have only been two real suspects, and both times the trail led back to you, here in LA. I think it stinks, and I'm going to find out what the connection is. Believe it.''

"Inspector," Dearborne said quietly, "I'm sure you will. But you won't be happy with what you find. There *is* no connection, except that the temple has often opened its doors to homeless people. Even under *this* administration, I doubt if that is against the law. One of those people was Judd. Another was probably one of this Sanchez woman's victims." He breathed deeply. "But do you know something, Inspectors? I'm not sure that you have a legal right to show me disgusting photographs of that nature. I suspect that that borders on harassment. I'm going to ask you not to come back here again. We are engaged in holy work. These are the Last Times, gentlemen. And each of us must understand which side of the battle we serve. It is your only salvation. Are you saved, Inspector Gates?"

Gates chewed at his mustache, and sighed. "All right, Dearborne. We're going. But we'll be back, believe it.''

They turned to leave, conscious of Dearborne's eyes on them the entire time. Just before they got to the door, Patterson turned. "Dearborne," he said sharply, "you got any idea how a hundred-thirty-pound woman could get strong enough to tear a man's skull apart with her bare hands?"

Dearborne smiled benevolently. "If it weren't such a barbarous occurrence, I would say that it sounded like a miracle, wouldn't you?"

Then the door closed behind him.

Gates and Patterson walked slowly back to their car. "Well, that might be it," Patterson said at last. "Not exactly a neat package, but it might tie up."

"Unless the killings start up again," Gates said. He pulled a stick of beef jerky from his pocket and bit into it. "Barbecue sauce," he said. "Jeeze. Thought I'd grabbed a teriyaki. Gotta pay more attention." Gates walked around to the driver's side of their unmarked beige Plymouth Duster.

"Hey, Win," Patterson called, "if it wasn't angel dust, what do *you* think it was?"

"Karate," he mumbled, taking another bite. "Vitamins. How the hell do I know? I just hope it doesn't start up again."

"Vitamins." Patterson snorted. "Jesus, you're weird."

# Chapter Seven

## The Fast

*[Fasts] are not to be used indiscriminately. Like major surgery or the use of potent drugs, they are to be employed with a high degree of selection and never without close and qualified supervision.*
—Dr. Garfield G. Duncan, Pennsylvania Hospital, Philadelphia

> *Everythin' in life is food*
> *Never seemed so real*
> *Hungry for you, starvin', girl*
> *You're my favorite meal.*
> —Stukka Mann and Jo Mama, "Pink Lunch"

*Deprived of flesh or grain, the body must quiet and center itself. It will tremble, and weaken. The bowels will churn foully, and none but the strong persist for more than a handful of days. But ah, the purity of mind that rewards he who is master of his animal spirit . . . !*

—Savagi, *Conquest of the Flesh*

# Wednesday, December 9.

Adam fished around in his pocket until he found a roll of sugarless antacid mints, peeled one pinkish tablet free, and popped it between his teeth. As he chewed, the burning sensation in his stomach dimmed until he was able to focus on the bank of meters and lights on the sound-control panel in front of him, and the ranting of KCOC's champion DJ.

"—must be postmarked by midnight of the fifteenth. Remember, all entries in the Eddie Down Your Chimney contest must be printed legibly on the back of a self-addressed, stamped nude photograph. In the case of a tie, the winner will be decided by an oral exam. All entries become the property of the boys in the mail room."

Eddie Roach was the short, ferret-faced man on the far side of the glass wall separating the engineering side from the studio. His thin black hair receded above his ears, creating a widow's peak effect that was positively demonic when he went full tilt into his comedy routines. His chronically bloodshot eyes were concealed behind wrap-around sunglasses.

His shoulders hunched as he locked himself into his spiel. "And hey, I know everybody out there's heard of Roach Motels? Well that's just not hip enough for *my* fans. Keep an eye out for Big Eddie's Roach Brothels. Roaches check in, catch horrible diseases, and give 'em to their kids and old ladies. Heyyyy . . ." He flashed his eyebrows at Adam, who grinned weakly in reply. Eddie's forehead wrinkled, but he continued.

Now lowering his voice to a passable impression of a soap opera announcer: "Now let's tune in to Jo Mama's mysterioso lead singer Stukka Mann, who complains that his love life has been a little too hot lately." He popped his fingers and pointed at Adam, who fumbled as he clicked the tape cart into its slot. There was a second and a half of dead air, and then Mann's screeching rendition of

"Don't Let the Sun Go Down on Me" blasted from the loudspeaker.

Eddie peered at Adam through the soundproof glass. He took off his shades, small dark eyes curious. "Hey, 'engineer.' You OD'd or what?"

Adam tore his attention away from his innards. "I'm sorry, Eddie, that won't happen again."

"You've screwed up all morning, Lardlum. Why don't you grease your ears so you can get your head out of your ass?"

The walls receded, then suddenly fluxed until they seemed just an arm's breadth apart. Adam closed his eyes, searching for something in the fog. "Uh . . . I'm sorry, Eddie. What did you say?"

Eddie's mouth opened and then snapped shut like a fish gasping for water. "Something is wrong with you, and I ain't sure I like it. If you've got a bug, stay home. I don't need you passing your diseases to me. We ain't that tight."

"I'm, ah . . . I'm just on a diet, that's all. Maybe I'm not getting enough sleep." He pulled up his glasses and rubbed at his eyes. His lids itched.

There was a knock on the door, and an enormous mane of pale red hair entered. Slender fingers brushed the hair aside, and the face of Morgan Iadiapaolo, KCOC's relief engineer, emerged. "Knock knock. Twelve o'clock. Drop your socks and grab your lunch." She looked around the room with wide, guileless eyes. "Time for a break, Adam. Where's your munchies?"

Adam patted his thermos. "Right here."

"Oh." Morgan's eyes flickered from the thermos to his face and back again. "One of those liquid protein diets?"

"Well, not exactly. . . ."

"Good. I've heard they can be pretty dangerous. Your body can't hack that. Especially *your* body."

"I'll try to remember." He stumbled out of the control room. The lavatory was only a few short steps down the hall, but he barely managed to make it before the taste in his stomach leaped up to his mouth and splashed against his teeth.

There was nothing but fluid in his stomach, had been nothing for days, but it actually hurt to vomit. His stomach flamed and spasmed until there was nothing left. He steadied himself, waiting for the fit to pass. The others had, this one would as well.

Adam fought to remember what he knew about starvation. *The body calls up its glycogen reserves in the liver and converts them to glucose as needed by the brain. Blood pressure falls as a result of massive water loss.* . . . But those were just the facts of it. The results were lightheadedness, rank breath, and a stomach that foamed with acid.

And HUNGER. Never in his life had he felt anything like it, anything so palpably present, as if there were something within him that would devour the lining of his stomach if he didn't feed it.

Hunger had always been a chronic problem. Now it was horribly acute.

But now Adam had an ally.

He closed his eyes and visualized his mouth, peeled the skin back from his cheeks until he was staring into the pinkish flesh beneath. (The image actually overlaid reality in the mirror, like a plastic transparency. "This will be the most difficult thing to achieve," Savagi had warned. A joke: for Adam, it was the easiest thing in the world.)

First he had to slow the action of the three salivary glands around his jaws. Once he had them visualized clearly, he darkened the image, minimizing blood and fluid flow to the area. When the basic effect was attained, he painted a mental picture of the entire digestive apparatus, especially the pancreas and gall bladder. Traveled as far as his visualization would take him through the thirty-three-foot-long coiled tube that links mouth to anus, calming everything along the way. Relaxing according to the very specific guidelines laid down in *Conquest of the Flesh*. It felt as if he were playing black light through his innards, but the burning, cramping demand of hunger slowly cooled.

He breathed deeply, and brought his mind up to the

throat. To the thyroid gland, its twin lobes curving around the larynx and trachea. Gently, gently, he bathed it in white light. It was harder to hold this image, but grew a little easier every day. If this worked, it would increase his metabolic rate, and produce weight loss.

Adam continued the process, visualizing each portion of the "Hunger Circuit" in order, following Savagi's instructions precisely.

And in a few moments, the hunger was gone. Completely.

A mouthful of cold tea from the thermos gargled the awful taste out of his mouth. The herb tea purchased from the Temple of the Earth Heart (he had looked up the ingredients: just a simple cleansing mixture of peppermint and chamomile, nothing fancy). The perspiration on his skin felt sticky: a handful of cold water briskly rubbed into his face brought him back to life. He left the lavatory and ran directly into Mrs. Tanaka, KCOC's station manager.

She peered up at him. "Adam . . . will you come with me, please?"

He trudged along behind her, passing the jingling typewriters and busily purring phones in the sales pit. He overheard snatches of conversation as he passed the desks:

"Look, I know that we missed your spot yesterday: we had that news break, the plane crash? I'll make it up today. . . ."

". . . deal you can get. People don't buy what they see or read when they want sound equipment. It's what they *hear*. . . ."

"Hello, darling. I want to know why George and I weren't invited to your party, and Ed Lasky and Mitzi were. That was tacky. . . ."

Adam sighed.

KCOC's offices were lodged in a converted restaurant, with high, wood-beamed ceilings with exposed piping and wiring. The original builders had cut enormous skylights, and KCOC's architects had added three rows of fluorescent lamps. There were plants everywhere: a fern shadowing every desk, a rubber plant in every hall, an avocado tree in every office. The air smelled *green*. It was supposed to create a cheery atmosphere, and most of the time it succeeded. At this moment, though, he felt like a straggler on the Bataan Death March.

Tanaka's office was large, and seemed even more so because of her size. It was packed with wooden objects, not a single frond in sight. Tiny sculptures, matchstick constructs, Chinese puzzle balls, and other gewgaws filled every nook. She motioned to one of the nearest chairs, and sat behind her desk, watching him carefully. He felt too hot, then absurdly cold, then hot, the sensations spinning around and around like dragonflies chasing each other in the sun. He was dizzy, he was centered; he was starving, he never wanted to see food again.

When he finally focused his eyes on Tanaka, he realized that she was staring at him. "Adam . . ."

"Is there something wrong with my work?"

"Eddie's been complaining again. We do what we can to humor him: he *does* get the ratings. Usually we'd just brush it off. But you *have* been making mistakes. And you—" She drummed her fingers on the desk. "I don't know how to put this delicately. Your *smell* has changed, Adam. And it isn't pleasant."

His face flamed with embarrassment, and he wanted to sink right into the carpet. "I'm so sorry. I'm on a fast, and my system is cleaning itself out. I've eaten a lot of crap over the years, and some of it is coming out in my perspiration. I'm very sorry." He felt like hell, and an automatic voice rose in the back of his mind. *These people are decent to you, and here you are taking your problems out on them. Why not just break the fast?*

"I see. And how long are you planning to continue this?"

"Maybe just till the end of the week. If everything is still all right, perhaps longer. If it doesn't interfere with my work," he added hastily.

"Adam, how long has it been since you've eaten?"

The word "eaten" triggered a chain of thoughts, thoughts of sandwiches, of chocolate Mallomars and maraschino cherries. Of steak and shrimp platters at the Sizzler. Of blood-red lobsters marching arm in arm with corn dogs slathered in mustard. . . .

"Three days, ma'am. Four since I've had any solid food."

"Adam"—she stifled a laugh—"I have to admit that I never pictured you as the kind of person who could handle a fast. However, I cannot complain about any effort to improve your health. I am aware of the problems you've had."

She paused, looking down at a 5 × 7 card in her hand. "Well, I notice that you have two weeks of vacation and the same amount of sick leave stored up." She put the card down and met his eyes cleanly. "I suggest that you take that time, and get this situation sorted out." Her voice seemed to echo, to become many voices.

His head was pounding now, not unpleasantly, just an increased perception of the flow of blood, of the ceaseless pounding of his heart. "I think that that would be a terrific idea."

Tanaka's voices seemed pitched louder than they had to be, and were bouncing across the room at him, ricocheting at increasing speed.

"*Good*," they said. "I'm going to call my secretary, and have her make out a check in the amount of your vacation pay. You take it . . ." The voices were fighting with one another now, tearing one another apart, an interference pattern of ripples that was growing wider and wilder, the radar soundings of a thousand bats whirling, squealing in their eternal night. It was all he could do to keep upright in the chair. At some point they said, "*Adam*," and he managed to nod his head as if he had been listening. Finding her hand felt like threading a needle with swollen fingers, but he managed to shake it, and as he did, the fit ended as quickly as it had begun. His vision steadied itself. The sounds around him became intelligible. He managed to leave the office without wobbling too much.

# Thursday, December 10.

"How long will you be gone?" Algy asked. Their phone connection was poor, and Algy's voice crackled.

"A month. Maybe a little more. I'm going to visit my aunt in Tampa. Dad asked me to go for him."

"Your aunt. Right." Algy hesitated. "Is there anything wrong, Adam? We *always* get together on our birthday. I've got the tapes from last year all ready to go."

Adam ground his teeth, overwhelmed with guilt. "I know, Man—I was looking forward to getting drunk, listening to last year's ruckus, and laying down a new one. . . . I'm sorry, really."

Algy sighed. "If there's something wrong, you can tell me. They still have you on file in sports med. They should have taken you off, you know. You didn't check in. They'll hop on that little screw-up pretty soon."

"I'll be back, Algy, and . . . you'll be proud of me." Adam closed his eyes, listening to the seesaw rumbling in his stomach. He felt good, but fatigued.

"All right, tough guy. If you need anything, you know where to come. Don't let me down, Mr. Ludlum. I'm counting on you."

The line disconnected.

*Not even "Have a nice trip."*

*He doesn't believe me for a second.*

Adam dropped the phone back on the receiver, and braced his elbows on his knees, looking down at the thick, heavy shelf of flesh lying there.

The sight was too depressing. He needed to get to work.

Adam booted up Soul and entered his data disk, scanned the information already entered, and turned to the stack of magazines, clipped articles, and books at his desk.

The first magazine was the July 1962 issue of *Muscle and Health*. A red and black boundary surrounded a picture of a bearded little man lifting a pair of long-handled hammers by their ends. The caption read, "The Little Atlas."

There was another, clearer picture of Savagi inside. He was standing on a stage identified as Madison Square Garden. Dim rows of blurred faces faded into darkness beyond the center platform. Savagi was bare-chested, the flesh hanging from his rib cage as if he had slipped into the wrong man's skin that morning.

The heads of the sledgehammers were almost two yards away from his shoulders. Muscles stood out from the old man's arms in cords and knots. The caption read, "Fifty-Six Pounds on 32-Inch Handles: A Total of Over 1,800 Inch-Pounds on the Mighty Savagi's Wrists!"

Adam looked from the page to his computer screen. How to make sense of it? On the surface, it seemed no more than a typical strongman stunt. But it was too easy to see Dearborne's smiling face, or remember the girl's grip on his arm.

How to pan out the gold?

He fumbled for his copy of *Conquest of the Flesh*, thumbing through it quickly. "The body is like a horse or a dog," it read, "which despises a weakling but recognizes and gladly obeys a true master. In a fast, once mastery is achieved, the body will release its poisons and also a special essence from the glands . . . which will invigorate and stimulate in a manner not seen since childhood."

The combination of simplistic philosophy and accurate observation was maddening. Adam pulled a stack of print-outs from a wooden box next to Soul. He thumbed through the pages until he found what he was looking for, a reference from BIOSIS, the *Biological Abstracts* data base available from his umbrella service, DataLine.

"The body *does* release fat-soluble toxins during a fast," Adam typed. "But that comment about the 'essence.' Could Savagi have been talking about forcing the pituitary to release GH, human growth hormones? A lot of things release growth hormones: high-intensity exercise, hypogly-cemia, trauma, sleep, dopaminergic stimulants, such amino acids as L-arginine and L-ornithine. And several prescription drugs highly sought after by professional athletes. GH triggers additional muscle growth and burns fat. Any college biology student might know that, but Savagi gave no evidence of any Western scientific training, and so that concept must have come from the same epistemological matrix as the rest of his system of behavioral and structural modification.''

Adam rubbed his temples. There was a headache brewing back there somewhere, but it felt good to get his ideas down on paper.

"Maybe Savagi was a little nuts. In *Conquest of the Flesh* he talks about the 'Air Fire' circling in the blood. It's ridiculous to listen to until you substitute adenosine triphosphate and the Krebs cycle for his mystical bullshit.

"The visualizations that I'm doing obviously have something to do with shutting down that yammering appetite alarm in my head. If it's so damned effective, though, why don't more people use it? Lack of visualization ability?

"One thing that Savagi and Culpepper agree on: you have to focus yourself in a direction. There has to be an ultimate goal, the very conception of which takes you past any immediate blockages. All right. I've got every karate movement I ever learned from Mitchell Shackley locked in my memory. In my notebooks. I'm going to study them, hone them like I never did before. But I have to give it everything, just everything, or it won't work.''

# Friday, December 11.

*Inhale . . . feel the breath sinking deeply into your body, pulled so deeply that it warms your toes. Then, stay there for a time, feeling. Absorb the sensation, bathe in it, let it flow through you. . . .*

*Relax deeply. Your body is limp, and heavy, and warm. . . .*

Adam had a chart of the human brain in front of him,

one of the few color plates in any of Savagi's texts. Some areas were laid out in black, others in white, some in red.

It was his task to visualize the map as clearly as possible. There were anterior and posterior charts, and a cross section. The breathing exercises made it easy to sink deeply into the vision. In fact, in a way that he couldn't phrase precisely in words, it seemed that he had waited a terribly long time for the discipline of the breathing, and his body hungered for it.

The vision.

He floated above himself, saw himself sitting, cross-legged, on the floor. Attempting the knee-cracking contortion of the full lotus was beyond him.

Down. From that vantage point, he saw a pitifully overweight man, the flesh hanging sad inches over his beltline, more than just pudgy, shadowing into obesity, promising heart disease and kidney weakness, and all of the other flesh failures that obesity brought into existence.

But then he was down through the dark brown hair, concentrating, concentrating, seeking the light within. Now he was there, within the grayish folds, the curvilinear, convoluted dark places within the human brain, thirty billion cells divided into two hemispheres.

The charts made it all easy to visualize: the outer, grayish layer of the cortex surrounding a thicker layer of white material. He could almost make out the individual nerve fibers, but not quite. His concentration was not yet so acute. But he could identify the four main lobes of each hemisphere: the frontal, temporal, parietal, and occipital. And he clearly followed the curving bridge of the corpus callosum that connected the hemispheres.

For now, he sank down through the hypothalamus to the twin lobes of the pituitary, painted it with white light, felt, in his state of deep relaxation, the answering tingle of the thyroid.

He pulled himself up out of the depths of his trance, feeling the light recede to a pinpoint in his mind, and exhaled harshly, feeling energized.

Adam was shaking, and the floor beneath him was

spattered with dark droplets of sweat, but it was easy to ride that rush of energy, and put on his jogging shoes before it vanished. Before he could change his mind he left the apartment.

Puffing and blowing, he made it down four flights of stairs. Dusk was just painting its shadows along the sidewalk. Adam walked north until he reached Fountain, then turned away from the main flow of traffic and began to jog.

Every step was torture, and he hadn't gone ten paces before he had to stop, his vision blurring and his stomach screaming at him. He ground his teeth and started again, counting every hard strike of his heel against the pavement.

*Just to the next corner.* He pushed harder than he ever had in his life. His legs felt like they were stuffed with gravel, and there was nothing in his world but pain. He made it three blocks before his body quit, and he leaned against the street sign, gasping, sweat flowing off of him in a sheet.

# Monday, December 14.

He sat at Soul's console, surrounded by books, a steaming mug of tea next to his hand.

Thinking about breathing. Breathing helped to kill the hunger. Or maybe it was the meditation?

Whatever it was, it was a blessing. He remembered the voice of Mitch Shackley, as the karate instructor exhorted his students to produce "meditation waves" with their breathing. *"Exhale longer than you inhale,"* he would say. *"This increases the amount of oxygen debt, and starts a chain reaction, as your body struggles to get the oxygen that it needs. Your breathing deepens, your system slows down, and more meditation waves are created."*

Shackley had given them a perfectly simplified explanation of the physiological effects of breathing on meditation, *sans* words like "carbon dioxide," "arterial blood," or "alpha rhythm." Like Savagi, Mitchell Shackley never let facts stand in the way of truth.

But the breathing patterns taught in martial arts classes were nursery rhymes compared to the symphonies of breath and will orchestrated in Savagi's *Conquest of the Flesh.*

"Breath of Life," it said. "Transform yourself. Master your body."

It was a strange world that the pamphlet introduced him to. A world of inhalation/retention/exhalation cycles. Of constricted anal and throat muscles, of "energy pathways" (a physicist would choke on the loose usage of the term "energy" in metaphysics texts, but once again, truth was not always contained in facts) of color visualizations, of sight and sound and smell.

It was difficult for him to even attempt the drills at first, but concentrating on his breathing made his hunger less urgent. The sensation of oxygen starvation was stronger than any other bodily need.

So when he woke up in the morning, the first thing he did was boot up Soul, and slip in the disk labeled "Health" and see where he was on his weight chart. The graph line was finally starting to dip. He had lost three pounds.

He lay down on the floor and stretched the simple Yoga postures in Savagi's books: the Twist; the Stomach Lift, or *Uddiyana*; the Plow; and the dreaded Cobra. When the kinks began to leave his muscles, it was time to find out just how much karate he could remember.

He started with the prearranged solo fighting exercise called Wo Ying Chuan, Invisible Fist, that he had once learned under Shackley's watchful eye.

Wo Ying Chuan, performed by a master, was a staccato thunderstorm of eye jabs and elbow strikes, punches and kicks, sweeps, stomps, and snakelike evasions. Adam remembered watching Shackley perform the *kata* at the Long Beach International Karate Championships, remembered an audience of 10,000 holding their breath as they thrilled to the sight of a man in total command of his craft. Now fast, now slow . . . now soft and curving, now hard and awesomely linear. For Adam, it had always been the ultimate expression of Shackley's art.

But expressed through Adam's mind and body, the movements were a pitiful jumble. He stumbled, he forgot or scrambled entire sections of the 108 techniques. His hands and feet moved so slowly that drunken tree sloths could have bobbed and weaved and jabbed him half to death. It was frustrating beyond tolerance. He let the frustration stay in his mind, let it create a bare thread of connection between the floor and the outgoing fist. Just enough to let a trickle of feeling run back and forth, reinforcing itself. Then, before he could fumble into another failure, he stopped.

Adam uncurled from his bed, sputtering as he moved BeDoss's rear end out of his face. The cat purred deliciously, rubbing against Adam with affectionate disregard for his master's feelings. Adam picked the animal up and stared into BeDoss's lazily slanted amber eyes. "Why do cats think that the highest form of compliment is sticking their butts in your mouth? Huh? Can you answer me?"

BeDoss gave him an *I could, but I won't* yawn and Adam dropped him gently to the floor.

Adam sat up in the bed and pinched his nostrils between his fingers, freeing the left one for a four-second inhalation. He held the breath for twelve seconds, and then exhaled for four through the right nostril, starting the cycle over again on the right side.

After ten rounds of breathing, he was fully awake. An eleventh round, and energy jolted through him in a blast, like gasoline sprayed on a spark plug.

Head buzzing, he stood tall, slapped his sides, and dropped his right foot back as he went into a Cat Stance. Palm block. Eye jab. (Balance *shift!*) Arm break. Claw to face. Elbow-knee stroke. Sweep . . .

Then to Soul to record the results in carefully constructed data fields. He broke the inhalation/retention/exhalation/pause cycles into their separate categories, experimented with lengthening or shortening each, and adapted his spread-sheet/graphics program to visualize it. Never meant to run on a computer as ancient as Soul, it was not color, not mouse-driven, and he still hadn't licked the dropout problem when he saved files. But he could still make pie and bar graphs, and manipulate them by changing the numbers or, conversely, alter the numerical equations by shifting the visuals.

Computer. Exercise. Tea. Sleep. The parameters of his world tightened in on him, sealed him into a womb of discipline without a door or a window. Slowly, one tiny piece at a time, Adam Ludlum began to master his body.

# Wednesday, December 23.

Adam lay motionless, uncertain whether he was awake or asleep. His heart trip-hammered in his chest, danced crazily, turned cartwheels of rhythm, an ethereal Buddy Rich pounding "Beat me daddy eight to the bar" on his rib cage. Then, as he visualized his heart, relaxed the muscles in his chest, followed the instructions in Savagi's texts and made his body warm and heavy, it slowed and steadied.

He sniffed his armpits. No matter how much time he spent in the shower his body odor remained terrible, so he was glad that he didn't have to interact with friends or business associates. His urine was dark and fetid, and he increased the amount of water he drank threefold. His face was beginning to clear. . . .

The telephone rang. He started, and reached for the telephone. Overreached, actually, knocking the receiver from the cradle. But he caught it before it could complete its fall. Staring at his own hand, he propped the earpiece between shoulder and cheek.

"Adam? Adam? I can't hear you very well."

*Oh, God,* he thought to himself. *Father.* "I'm sorry, sir."

There was a long pause. "Something is wrong, Adam. I

know that there's something wrong. What's happening, Adam—''

"Nothing, sir. I've—" He stopped, trying to find the right words. "There's just something that I have to work out, and I have to do it in my own time. That's all. Please."

Gunther was silent, but in that silence Adam could see the rippling of the corded throat, the slow movement of withered, translucent eyelids, could hear the wheezing ancient lungs. "You're all I have left," he said at last. "Can't you come and see me? It's Christmas. Please, Adam."

*There just isn't any reason not to see your father at Christmas. You wanted to have good news, to show him and tell him that his only child had finally done it. But if you have to bathe in Hexol, you'll be there.*

"Sir . . . of course I'll be there. How could you even doubt it?"

There was silence on the other end of the line, and then the click of the receiver being dropped on the cradle.

Sir. Adam. Christmastime, perhaps the very last Christmas for Adam to share with his father, and there was more ritual than warmth between them. There shouldn't have been, needn't have been.

But there was.

Adam folded his legs into a half lotus and sank back into the meditation again.

He breathed. As he breathed he saw the colors flowing through his lungs, out into his bloodstream, up into his brain. And this time, it was easy to hold the image of the macrobrain structure. What was happening, what was exciting him, was that now he could hold, and visualize, the individual nerve conduits within the cerebral cortex. He painted them varying colors, so that he could make them out, but they grew daily clearer: green, hoselike afferent cells, purple globular neurogliaform cells, red squidlike pyramidal cells. All of them regulating life, conducting their vital business. Now as small as knots of thread. But soon. Growing larger soon . . .

No. Not soon. *Now.* The thought, calm and purposeful, sounded like a muffled shot in his darkness. He had waited, and waited, and the waiting was over.

Rationally, he knew that he could only visualize what he had studied. And yet there was clearly a feedback loop that took the information stored in his brain and turned it in upon itself, accelerated the process of studying itself, so that the deeper he sank into Savagi's texts, into his own texts of macro and micro neuroanatomy, the faster he progressed.

A nerve fiber. With great effort, he brought back a single nerve fiber in its myelin sheath, its nucleus, the dendrites exploding away from the cell like a forest of cacti. And here he could see the spark of thought, the actual flow of nerve messages from the tip to tip of the dendritic spines, leaping across the synapses!

Dazzling, staggering, the image was so clear. But even in watching the sizzle of his thoughts he knew: Not enough! Not enough! He was more than this, and he bathed the vision in white light, watching the accelerated growth of new dendritic spines, watching the sparks grow fatter and faster, color and now sound, the infinitely varied electrical sizzle of the most complex computer switchboard in the universe retooling itself for . . . what?

There was no time for that thought now. He played leapfrog with a single spark, a single nerve signal, soaring over it, around it . . . sinking into it and suddenly lost in memory.

Darkness. Then light.

Adam followed a thread of light that led down the spinal cord, a shaft of golden luminescence that called to him, sucked at him. In an avalanche, fragments of memories and sensations flew at him, buffeted him, flying and twisting as he fell through the light toward something that was immeasurably bright at the base.

The memories were like chips of a video screen. There was a touch from a friend, there the screech of a car as it collided with his bike (remember that, Adam, remember the visit to Children's Hospital that followed?) and there your first kiss from Micki, in the prop room behind the auditorium at LA High. All of the excitement and the taste of the soda-pop-flavored lipstick, and the tingling, swelling pressure in your pants as she opened her mouth . . .

And *there* a slap from a drunken telephone repairman, and *there* having the living shit pounded out of you in the middle of gym class by Thumper Watson, and *there* . . . and *there* . . .

He was falling now, out of control, directly into the center of the fire, and there was nothing but the incredibly pure and white light.

And in the middle of the light, a pool of lava, its surface erupting with thick, oily bubbles. Fire spurted like morning glory blossoms, the overwhelming stench of earth salts so thick it was a physical presence. Somehow sweet. Beckoning. Magnetic . . .

# Chapter Eight
## Christmas Day

*My knees are weak through fasting, and my flesh failest of fatness.*

—Psalms 109:24

## Friday, December 25.

Strips of red and green crepe paper hung from the ceiling of Saint Martin's reception room. Dangling with them were a few strands of tinsel, and a couple of silvery bulbs, suspended by wires from the ceiling as if waiting for a tree to sprout under them. Burl Ives's "Have Yourself a Merry Little Christmas" was crooning from hidden speakers.

Adam blew on his palms, trying to get some circulation into them. He *knew* how absurd it was to complain about a California Christmas. It was forty-two degrees outside, and most of the rest of the country was digging out from under a blizzard. In a few days New York's City Fathers would be piously mourning the first grannysicles of the season, found frozen to their cats in unheated Bronx apartments.

But still, his fingers were numb, and he worked them to get the blood going.

"Merry Christmas, Mr. Ludlum," the girl at the desk said cheerfully. Adam waved his greeting. "Have a Christmas cookie?"

His vision swam. With unintentional sadism, she held out a tray of red and green tree-shaped confections. He took one and stared at it as if it had dropped from the moon, measuring its unfamiliar weight in the palm of his hand.

"You'll have to visit your father in his room today. He's not feeling very well."

"That's fine. Thank you." He followed a green line painted on the floor back to a branching corridor, searching for Room 117. The cookie was burning a hole in his hand, and before he could go any farther he took a nibble, and then a bite, tasting the sugar melt in his mouth, the hint of cinnamon, the delicate texture of ground hazelnuts. His knees sagged as he wolfed it down. His stomach cramped fiercely, the sugar rush hitting so fast that the hall whirled.

Staggering now, he found his father's room and virtually collapsed across the threshold.

The shape on the bed was motionless when Adam sat next to it. For a long time Adam just gazed down on his father.

Gunther seemed relaxed, if more fragile than when Adam had seen him last. His skin was more waxen, his eyelids thinner, more starkly veined. A thin plastic oxygen tube hissed air into his nose.

Something beyond sadness stirred within Adam. *There's a difference between caring and warmth. It shouldn't be true, but it is. And here is the man you've honored all your life. He's dying now, and that has to be the loneliest thing in the world, and he's cubbyholed in this hospice.*

*What about warmth, Adam? When was the last time that you just felt warm and . . .*

*Protective?*

Gunther's eyelids fluttered open, and for a moment

there was no recognition in the gray orbs beneath. Adam
reached out and took his father's hand.

"It's just me, sir. Merry Christmas."

"Adam . . . ?"

"Yes, sir." Adam took the box from under his arm, and
laid it on the bed gently. "Just a little something."

His father gazed at it, and the corners of his mouth
twitched. "Help me . . . ?"

Adam helped his father up to a sitting position, could
feel the diseased flutter of Gunther's heart against his
hand. When his father was upright and balanced, Adam
peeled away the simple wrappings, pushed back the tissue
paper. Beneath was a blue satin robe, gold threads woven
around the edge of the collar.

"I think it will look nice on you, sir. I hope you like
it."

Gunther nodded, squeezed his son's hand. "You . . .
look tired, Adam."

"Yes, sir. But glad to see you."

"I'm glad to see you, too, Adam." Adam brushed a
strand of his father's stiff white hair back, wiped a crumb
of dried mucus from the corner of his eye. Beneath his thin
hospital shirt, Gunther's bony chest moved shallowly with
each labored breath. "I wish . . . I wish that I had a
present for you."

"There is something, sir," Adam said nervously, "something I wanted to ask you."

"Whatever you want, Adam." The hiss of the oxygen
tube was almost inaudible.

"Listen to me, sir. Please, don't cut me off this time. I
remember Mother dying when I was seven." Adam suddenly stiffened, so intense were the images that fought
their way into his mind. *I don't want the images, just the
words, just . . .* But it was too late, and he suddenly knew
why the single cinnamon and hazelnut cookie had staggered him.

*Kitchen. Strong, sweet, warm smells, and someone warm
gazing down, unutterably beautiful. A steaming tray lifted
from the oven, hot air shimmering like water in a frog*

*pond. And his mother would bend down, shoveling a brown crescent up with a spatula, and slide a steaming, soft, crumbling cookie onto a napkin and give it to him, the bit of flour and brown sugar and cinnamon and hazelnuts burning against his palm, and then kiss his forehead as he downed it greedily, heating his tongue and the back of his throat until the tears gushed from his eyes, and ohgod, ohgod it tasted so good, and he was so happy, so very happy that he could just die.*

Gunther's hand on his wrist, suddenly strong. "Adam, Get hold of yourself."

Back in the present with jarring suddenness, Adam fought for equlibrium, and found it at the cost of his composure. His eyes spilled wetness now, and he made no effort to hide it.

"I remember," he said huskily, "when Mom died. The way everyone looked at me: 'poor little darling.' I remember how the other kids stopped playing with me, like they were afraid that they'd catch something nasty, and their mommies would go away, too.

"I remember a lot of things, and one of them is that you were never quite the same toward me. I never . . . we never talked about it, but I know it's true, sir. I guess I just need to know: Did you blame me somehow? You never said it, but I always wondered."

Gunther turned his face away, toward a window that looked out on an empty courtyard. A few leaves were blowing around out there, chasing each other in little dust devils.

"For God's sake, be a man, Adam, can't you? I can't stand to see you sniveling."

His voice stamped a seal on the last words, but Adam broke it. "Sir, please. I don't . . . I don't know how much longer I'm going to have you. How many more chances I'll have to ask." Adam shook his head miserably, wiping his cheek with the back of his hand. "Would you really want me to live not ever knowing for sure?"

For a long time there was silence in the room, then Gunther said; "No, Adam, I don't blame you. All right? Is that enough?'' Gunther's voice was brittle, the strength and command only a shell of what it had been . . . of what it had always been, and Adam stared back into the watery gray eyes until Gunther lowered his head, released a long, sour exhalation. ''I've left so many things undone, and there's no more time, just none. Adam, I had so much hope for you. So many dreams. . . .''

Under the thin blankets, Gunther's limbs twitched uncomfortably. His body shook as if someone were piling weights on his brittle ribs.

''I couldn't give you a lot of the things you needed, Adam, and I'm sorry for that. But even when I hated myself, I loved you. You have to believe that. And Adam''—he drew into himself, and his voice, already weak, sounded like the last wheeze of a ruptured balloon— ''Adam . . . I'm proud to call you my son.''

''Thank you, sir,'' Adam whispered. ''I can't even tell you how much I needed that.''

Gunther smiled wearily. ''It's not much of a Christmas present, Adam.''

Adam held his father's hand tightly, then bent and kissed his forehead. ''It's the best damn present anybody ever gave me.''

# Chapter Nine

## Endurance Vile

*I sometimes lose all track of time. Not just minutes, but sometimes I seem to lose track of years. If I'm on an especially long run, I'll sometimes lose track of where I am. I'll imagine I'm in a timeless state, where I'm one with all runners, with all of history.*
—Kathi Page, quoted in *The Running Mind* by Jim Lilliefors

*There are limitations to what the human mind and body can accomplish. That is, to what "ordinary mind" and "ordinary body" can accomplish. But time itself is a creation of the mind, and within our history is the heritage of our bestial ancestors, an indomitable force which, once tapped, reveals the true animal power within us. A force which is easier to unleash than to control.*
—Savagi, *Death of the Soul*

# Thursday, December 31.

11:37 P.M.

Beyond the chain link fence surrounding Hollywood
High School, car horns were squealing and children were
testing the M-80s and cannon crackers that would shortly
usher in the new year.

Adam hunched down, bracing his knuckles against the
gravel of the quarter-mile oval behind the school, stretching his calf muscles, and thinking.

Thinking that although he had lost eighteen of the fifty
pounds he needed to lose, a new wall now loomed before
him: an emotional cul-de-sac that limited further growth.
The barrier remained as intractable as death.

Death? Why did that image bob up, as it did with
increasing frequency? He had lost eighteen pounds in a
little under four weeks. There couldn't be anything wrong
with that, could there?

Could there?

It was chilly as Adam started to run. Once again, he felt
himself to have no energy save that which he drew from
the breathing.

He started at a pace not much greater than walking, a
smooth, effortless glide. It couldn't take effort. After all
(he reminded himself), he had no strength. None at all.
None save that of the air that carried him, the air that
circulated in his lungs, cleansed the fatigue toxins from his
bloodstream. For a fleeting instant, gustatorial hallucina-
tions flitted in his mind: the memory of a long-ago submarine sandwich, the provolone and onions especially intense.
He banished the mouth-watering phantom back into limbo.

The icy caress of the breeze was invigorating. His limbs
pumped in measured strides, coordinated with his breathing. Coordination. He inhaled for four strides, held it for
sixteen strides, exhaled for eight strides, and then began
the cycle over again. His lungs, his legs burned. The

pulses of light coalesced and swirled until he had them under control, pulsing in balance with the breathing.

Adam concentrated on the piece of track ahead of him, focusing on a space always just a few paces away. The sensation of floating became stronger, and as it did, a spot of light appeared in his vision. Suddenly the image of the volcano was alive again.

It roiled with leaping tongues of flame. Glowing liquid rock jetted in fountains before his eyes. Most disconcertingly, it was sitting right there in the middle of his vision, not like a hallucination at all, but like an actual geyser of lava somehow sliding away and away before him, always just out of reach. And as he watched, the shower of magma parted, and in its midst was a beautiful golden runner with clean strong limbs and flowing hair, so beautiful it was almost androgynous. It looked back over its shoulder at him, and he was shocked to see his own face. With the slightest nod, it beckoned him on.

Its skin flowed with molten metal. Golden threads trailed out behind the runner, fastening to Adam's shoulders, his hips, his feet, pulling him forward.

Now the speed increased. Every step carried unnatural impetus, whipped him around the track at greater and greater velocity. The walls blurred as the sound of his breathing became a piercing whistle, transubstantiating pain and leaden limbs into wind, tingeing that wind with fire.

As Adam watched, the runner's skin sprouted hair, wiry golden fuzz, beautiful, wonderful, and Adam ran faster, trying to catch up. It seemed he was running behind some ultimate ancestor, something that had run in days before steel, or concrete, when blood and bone and primal fury were stronger than conscious thought.

Faster and faster. Perspiration flowed profusely. Even at midnight, the heat was fierce. It was impossible to form an image of himself anymore. It was too difficult to evaluate the sensations and the twinges, the feeling of each successive foot strike as it reverberated, rolling up the trembling calves, up through the unsteady knees. (Even as he thought about them, he could feel his body realigning itself, so that each step was smoother than the one before, so that the grinding sensation in his knee steadily diminished. His hips were loosening up, and the change came from there, from deep within his body. He felt his spine straightening as he thought about it, as his consciousness traveled up. His shoulders relaxed, his head suspended as if by a string from above.)

It was beautiful, fearfully beautiful. There was no strength, and it didn't seem to matter because he was weightless, floating around the track at exhilarating speed.

And then the beauty became anxiety, and he told himself, *Slow down.* Time to stop, to go back home, to end the experiment.

*Stop.*

And he couldn't. The thought wouldn't penetrate to any level where the muscles and sinews and nerves and blood vessels interconnected. They continued to move on their own, propelled by breath and will, and the part that cried *halt* was less than the part that drove him on. The golden man in front of him turned and grinned. The face was beautifully inhuman, its fur dissolved to scales and reptilian skin that shone blue-hot in the dim light. Something hideously triumphant, something from beyond nightmare or imagination. It was Adam and something from within him, subhuman, transhuman.

Adam lost count of the laps, the circuits of the track, knowing only a steadily escalating fear as his body emptied itself, lifted on a wind of will.

The night was filled with sound, and through sweat-blurred eyes he glimpsed the moonlit clouds painted with the bursting fire of skyrockets, man-made lightnings, the echo of small thunders filling the darkness. The sound of people screaming and laughing, strings of firecrackers banging like percussive popcorn.

Numb to the joy and the hope, Adam staggered around the track, knees burning and ankles twisting beneath him. Still his body wouldn't stop. He couldn't move a finger, except to keep his arms pumping steadily. His breathing was locked into the same strange rhythm. With what little strength remained to him, Adam made a mental scan of his body. He could alter his stride by a mere half-inch, affect the swing of his arms even less. It was hopeless.

He finally came to his eyelids, and with a total concentration of will, he closed them. He kept running, on automatic, in total darkness, his feet burning, blistered, torn. He hit a concrete guide strip at the rim of the track and stumbled, body trying to regain balance.

*Let go.*

He was floating, drifting in darkness, and hit the ground without easing his fall. He felt his upper lip split, teeth driven through it, felt the concussion as his forehead smashed down onto gravel, tearing skin. His legs still twitched in the air.

Twitched, and kicked, and finally stilled.

His breathing steadied.

His heartbeat rate dropped.

A single droplet of perspiration slid down his cheek, dripping into the grass. He felt its track cooling on his cheek.

He opened his eyes. A snail, silver-black in the moonlight, glided across the darkness, laying a glistening trail. Its body was translucent, and its antennae writhed torpidly as it flowed up to his face. It looked at him, no more than a thumb's thickness from his eye, then turned and slid silently away.

Adam lay in the wet grass, bruised and bleeding, feet raw, lungs aching, legs burning, beyond exhaustion or thought. Waves of heat and light rolled through his body in a crackling aurora.

*Feeling.*

# Friday, January 8.

Light. Even with his eyes closed, there was light, a place that he slid into without effort, where his body, filled with air now, healed itself.

The bruises and wounds of New Year's had mended
themselves, as quickly as scraped knees had healed when
he was eight years old. There was no ache anymore, and
only the faintest of discolorations to tell that it had happened at all.

The light. Was it beneath him? Within? Perhaps both
within the earth and within his mind. Insane, perhaps, but
sanity didn't seem terribly important at the moment. It was
so powerful, pleasantly irresistible. It was all things, and it
called him closer. Beckoned him soothingly. And he drifted
closer to the heart of it. . . .

Something called him out of it. A sound, a shrill sound.
The telephone. It had rung on and off for the past three
days.

He ignored it, staying in the dark place, watching the
lights.

# Wednesday, January 13.

Micki hit the bell at the front desk a fourth time, glancing impatiently at the clock. Three o'clock. *The manager
should be working the desk. Somebody should be.*

She tucked her purse up more tightly beneath her arm,
nervously aware of the growing dampness there. Aware
that the air was cool, almost cold, and that only her own
sense of unease caused the damp stickiness.

The lobby of Adam's apartment was familiar enough to
her—she had spent dozens of nights in his cramped, gener-
ally untidy living space. The building had to have been
elegant once, designed in a vaguely Mediterranean motif.
Its open courtyard was tiled with dark red brick, interrupted by a series of avocado trees fenced with low benches.
In the summer the courtyard was pleasant; now it was just
dank, and chill, and depressing. The new wrought-iron
security doors wouldn't open unless Adam buzzed her up,
and so far he hadn't answered her rings. The office was to
the left of the courtyard, its front desk usually staffed.

She rang the bell again, then gave up as an elderly woman lugged a fully laden wicker-wire shopping cart into the courtyard. She was struggling with the lock when inspiration flashed and Micki ran across the courtyard.

"Can I help?"

She was rewarded with a broad smile full of square, white, store-bought teeth.

"Thank you. You know, so many young people won't even think of helping a lady. It's nice to see one who will. You live on the fourth floor, don't you?" The woman was wearing layers of orange and white sweaters, very clean and much patched. The dry, sweet smell of baby powder followed her in a cloud. The woman continued to rattle on as Micki helped her in, pushing the cart to the elevator.

"I don't live here," Micki said defiantly. "I'm visiting a friend."

"Oh." The woman smiled conspiratorially. "A young man? Now, don't let him take advantage of you. Nope. You've got to hold your face cards back, pretty thing like you."

The old lady was just beginning to really warm up to her subject when the elevator reached the fifth floor. Micki left quickly.

The carpet strip in the middle of the hall was well-worn and smudged with muddy heelmarks. The fluorescent halos overhead were a little too bright for her taste, and cast hard-edged shadows.

Adam's door, Number 514.

She knocked, hard. "Adam? Adam, I know you're there."

There was no answer from inside. She leaned her ear against the door. She knew he was there. He had to be.

"Adam, I called your work, and they said you were at home. Your landlady told me she thought you were sick."

There was still no answer, and she opened her purse, fishing out her key ring.

She held his key up to the dim light. Why had she kept it when they broke up? Whatever the motivations, she hoped that the locksmith who had installed the security doors hadn't changed Adam's lock.

He hadn't, and the door clicked open.

The glowing circles overhead cast a column of light into the darkness. The first thing that she noticed was how *clean* the room was. Adam was many things, but none of them was neat.

For an embarrassing moment, she wondered if she had entered the wrong apartment. Then she stepped in, and shut the door behind her.

"Adam?"

With a pitiful whine, BeDoss jumped across the room, throwing himself at Micki's feet, rubbing frantically. She bent to pick him up, saying, "Poor baby—"

Then froze.

Adam sat cross-legged in a corner of the room, staring at her, through her as if she wasn't there at all. Even across the room she could hear the low, steady whistle of his breathing.

"Adam?" She took a step forward, aware that her throat was tightening uncomfortably. She fumbled for the light switch, and stifled a scream when the darkness flashed into light.

Adam wore a two-week beard, and beneath it his face looked lined, haggard. The flesh sagged on his cheeks. His eyes were darkly ringed, his hair wild and unkempt.

"Adam?"

She took another step forward, and then another, and then ran to him, all caution and reservation vanishing. She threw her arms around him, and pressed her cheek against his stubbled face. "Adam . . . I can't believe you. I called you at work last week. They said that they hadn't heard from you for over a month. You didn't come to the Christmas party. Your landlady said that she had seen you, and that you looked half dead." Her fingers twined in his hair, and she forced him to look at her. "Are you all right? Adam?"

"All . . . right."

She buried her head against his chest. "You haven't

eaten, have you? I can't take responsibility for this. If you're hurting yourself to prove something to me, it's childish and just *stupid*." She was trying to be harsh, but the right words just wouldn't come.

He tried to lift his hand to stroke her cheek, but his hand would only move a few inches. "Not for you. For . . . me. Had to . . ."

"Adam. Call this off. I'll get a doctor. I'll . . ."

Again he shook his head, more shallowly this time. "Not doctor," he whispered. "All right. All right. Maybe for first time. Need . . ."

Her hands traced the new hollows of his face. "You've lost so much weight. Oh, Adam, this was *stupid*. Brave, but stupid."

"Need you to stay. Just a while. Get me . . . get me some juice. Health-food store. Green drink." He swallowed, hard. "Parsley and spinach juice. And bouillon."

She nodded. "I will, Adam. I never thought . . ."

Her emotions were such a ball of snakes that she couldn't sort head from tail. What surfaced most strongly was fear, and a sort of ghastly, grudging respect.

"Don't worry," he whispered, his voice just a rasp. "I was coming back up anyway." He paused, and the slightest of smiles played on that wasted face. "At least, for a little while."

# Chapter Ten

## The Dragon

### Thursday, January 21.

Kevin Dearborne stood by the window, curls of incense smoke coiling around him like misty serpents.

"I expected to see you before now," he said. "Why didn't you come to me?"

Adam smiled uncertainly. Sylvia sat just behind him and to the right, and another member of the temple was seated to his left, bracketing him. From the corner of his eye he could see the intensity of the expression on Sylvia's thin face. It was the kind of desperate politeness he had seen on the faces of dogs begging for table scraps. Jesus, it gave him the willies.

"I . . . wanted to do it myself," he began. His voice died as he heard the lie in his words. Dearborne turned, and in the dim, haze-filtered light his silhouette seemed momentarily changed, less that of a man than of . . . what?

It didn't make sense, and Adam swallowed hard, and continued.

"I have questions."

"Of course you do." Kevin sat on a bench in front of

him. The impression of strength was as powerful as before, only . . .

Only . . .

Kevin reached out and touched Adam's hand, and Adam's hackles raised at the contact. "We are *one*," Dearborne said. The overhead light filtered through the halo of golden hair, making it seem to glow. "You belong here, as one of us. You have much to learn from us . . . and we from you."

Kevin's hand tightened on Adam's, and tightened until Adam felt the beginning of pain.

Adam felt himself wavering, falling into Dearborne's spell. An alarm rang in the back of his mind. What was happening?

Dearborne's breathing. Adam's attention flashed to it, realized without comprehending that Dearborne was matching his own breathing pattern. Mirroring him, pacing him. Trying to lead him, but lead him where?

Adam twisted his hand free.

Sylvia moved up more closely, and her smell was almost overpowering. But now, disturbingly, it was not offensive, was somehow stimulating, and he fought for balance. Her hungry-puppy expression was more pointed now. He was her meal of choice.

"After the fast I tried to break my diet. I went to McDonald's for a Big Mac." Sylvia was too close to him, and he turned and looked at her. Her thin face was only inches away, and held the kind of sexual openness that made him feel that he was standing on the brink of a pit.

"Please," he whispered.

"Sylvia," Dearborne said briskly, nodding toward the door.

She stood, eyes still on Adam. Her lips formed the words *I want you* soundlessly, then she turned and left.

For a few moments the room was silent, then Kevin Dearborne chuckled. "She feels you. You are different, Adam. You belong here with us."

Adam wiped his mouth nervously. "I tried to eat this

Big Mac, and it just tasted like filth. I spit it out. I
couldn't eat anything there.''

"You are becoming pure," Dearborne said. "Your essence is burning through the impurities. Your mind and
body are becoming more efficient." Dearborne reached
out and touched Adam, stroked him along his left side,
and Adam's skin tingled at the contact.

*Jesus Christ, what is this place? What am I doing here?*

"Your skin here, and on the back of your arms, is
loose. You have lost weight. Much weight."

"About thirty pounds," he answered. Dearborne's hand
touched him as if he were assessing the body of a prosti-
tute, or a prize show animal. Adam wanted to scream, and
run from the room.

"The skin will tighten if you continue the meditations.
The breathing. Concentrate your efforts there. All else will
flow from the breathing."

"I only used the tapes a few . . . times." Adam closed
his eyes, and the after-mage of Dearborne was not that of a
man at all. It was the reptilian thing, the beautifully inhuman thing, and its claws crooked beckoningly at him.
Adam opened his eyes quickly.

Outside of the room, the members had begun to sing.
He recognized Sylvia's reedy, high voice. The chant was
hypnotically comforting, calmed away his fears.

Fear was ridiculous. He was safe here, and they loved
and cared for him, and he . . .

Kevin smiled, suddenly very close, his breath as warm
and pungent as mulled wine.

"You must come with me. There is a place I want you
to see. You are special, unique. You belong here with us,
and at Pah-Dishah."

"Pah . . . Dishah?"

It was so hard, so hard to think. He wanted to just relax,
let everything go.

Trust them. Trust Dearborne. They care about you.
Love you. Understand you . . .

But every time Adam closed his eyes, tried to relax, he

saw not Dearborne, but the reptilian form. Smiling and hissing and beckoning.

"No . . ."

"Adam. We are your family. Your only family." Dearborne grabbed Adam's hand. Adam felt the man's power, his brute, primal power, the tendons and ligaments working in perfect coordination with each other, crushing into Adam's flesh.

Adam recoiled, shaking, the pain penetrating him like a wave of frost, freezing him to the chair . . .

Until it touched an inviolate place at the base of his spine. The frost dissolved in flame that gushed from the core of him, the core that the fast had touched, and Dearborne jerked his hand back. A shocked expression flashed across his face for a moment. A visage swiftly masked, replaced by the unctuous smile.

Adam stood. "I'm going. I'm not coming back. I . . . I'll do it myself."

"You'll be back," Kevin said confidently. "Soon, you will have no where else to go."

"You're off your nut."

"Until tomorrow, Adam Ludlum."

Adam backed away, almost unsure that they would let him go. He crossed out through the outer chamber, where eight Children of the Earth Heart sang, more softly now, the notes still plucking at his mind. Carefully, as if walking through a nest of snakes, he worked his way to the door.

The air outside smelled unnaturally fresh and clear. He breathed as if a crushing weight had been lifted from his chest.

He looked back at the door. He wasn't sure what he felt from the Children, from this place. From Dearborne. The emotions were mixed, but foremost among them was a terrifyingly strong compulsion to open himself, to trust them with all of his innermost dreams and visions.

Somehow, he knew that to do that was to die. And be reborn as . . .

What?

The wind bit at him through his thin windbreaker, and he hurried to his Cortina, taking only one final look back at the window, where the pale faces of Dearborne and Sylvia watched him, faces smiling with satisfaction.

*You'll be back . . .*

"The hell I will," he whispered to himself, knowing that it was more a prayer than a promise.

# Chapter Eleven
## Wo Ying Chuan

*We are all dancers. We use movement to express ourselves—our hungers, pains, angers, joys, confusions, fears—long before we use words, and we understand the meanings of movements long before we understand those of words.*
—Franklin Stevens, *Dance as Life*

## Tuesday, February 23.

"Name?"

"Micki," she said. "Micki Cappelotti." She leaned over the front desk of the sports medicine building's reception and pointed to her name.

"Sure, hon." The guard hunched over his appointment book, flesh bulging uncomfortably above his belt. His face grew ruddy and made the bald patch surrounded by a thin line of receding hair seem blotchy and sun-freckled. At the sight of Micki, his dark little eyes came alive.

She flickered a smile at him and followed his pointing finger. She pulled her coat more tightly across her shoulders as she walked: the air in the sports med building leeched the heat from her body.

*You should be happy. Adam is doing well.*

But what she felt was unease, and so far there had been nothing she could do to talk herself out of it.

Surprise, surprise. Adam had had one last trick in his magic bag, something that he hadn't pulled out in all of the years that they had known each other. Something had just *changed* in him, as surely as a caterpillar metamorphoses into a butterfly, and in spite of herself she was fascinated.

The halls were cool white tubes stretching off into the distance, splitting and then splitting again, cooled by refrigeration, cooled by the neutral expressions on the firm tanned bodies jogging placidly by on their way to the cafeteria, the lab, the classroom, the track.

Everything was so sterile, so clean. She felt a momentary flicker of guilt that she wasn't happy to be here. But, as with her first visit, there was something that seemed vaguely wrong with the place, slightly skewed, as if there was a subtle difference between fitness and health that was still beyond the reach of Culpepper's computers.

The kinesthetics lab was on the third floor, a long low room with a red bulb and a "Do Not Disturb When Light Is Flashing" sign above the front door.

The light glowed to life as she touched the handle. She cheated, slipping quickly into the room.

Adam was on the other side of a glass partition, standing on a clean white mat, wearing a sparkling blue track suit with white gloves, white shoes, and white bands around wrist, elbow, knee, shoulder, and hip.

He looked like a slightly out of shape business executive, and the transformation was startling. Adam had lost forty-two pounds of fat, and gained ten pounds of muscle. Loose skin had tightened almost magically. There were still bulges at his butt, and traces of sagging flesh around his jowls, but his chest was beginning to firm, and when he . . . when they . . .

She tingled at the next, unavoidable thought.

Making love was just *different* now, as if the change was deeper than the weight loss, the control of his appetite.

Suddenly it had the kind of searing intensity that is usually only found in first encounters, or clandestine, forbidden trysts. He held her so tightly that it should have stifled . . .

But didn't.

She watched him run slowly through Wo Ying Chuan, Invisible Fist.

It was anything but invisible now, as he slowed the movements to a crawl and exaggerated each of them into ellipses and flattened arcs.

Dr. Culpepper was sitting on a high table behind the two videotape cameras recording Adam's every movement. Micki shut the door behind her carefully, softly, and just watched.

Culpepper was tapping his foot against the ground in rough rhythm with Adam's movement. He glanced from Adam to a third screen, where a rare film of Mitchell Shackley performing Wo Ying Chuan was running. Shackley looked to be in his late thirties, prematurely gray, with a thin, rather roguish mustache. He was handsome in an angular way, a man who seemed to be either steel or rubber as the moment or movement demanded. And even to her untrained eye, his motions were absolutely perfect. Of course, she had heard Adam speak of his teacher before, often. And she had seen still pictures. But it just wasn't the same.

Before this moment, Fred Astaire had come closest to her image of perfection in human movement. His effortless grace could make a hat rack or a cane into a living thing.

But Shackley was an eerie level beyond that, as if he moved through a dimension not of mass and velocity but of time and energy. Here, the kicks and punches were just the visible foam atop an invisible tsunami, and the incredible power in his movement was heart-stopping.

She forced herself to watch Adam.

Where not long before his movements were clumsy and forced, there was now an indefinable flow working its way through his arms and legs, a connecting rhythm that coordinated his kicks and strikes into rippling arcs, as economically beautiful as the lash of a whip.

The air in the room didn't seem to be moving. Every eye was focused on the screen, and the man beyond it mimicking the motions.

"My God," Culpepper whispered. "This is phenomenal."

When Adam stopped to rest for a moment, one of the assistants rushed in to swab a sample of perspiration.

"One more time, Adam," Culpepper said, clicking the microphone to life. "Once slow, and then top speed."

Adam gulped air, and nodded. Culpepper saw Micki out of the corner of his eye, and smiled broadly, squeezing her hand. "Michelle. Good of you to come."

She sat next to him. "How is he doing? And where in the world did you find that tape of Shackley. That is him, isn't it?"

"Adam found it through a local television station. Shackley did a guest spot on one of these syndicated health shows about fifteen years ago, and damned if it wasn't still in the production company's vault." He moved a stack of papers to make a little more room for her. "Adam's probably watched it two hundred times. I've never seen anything like him. Improvement so rapid you can see it day by day. It's like he once knew it all—knew everything, and is just sloughing off the rust." His gray eyes were puzzled.

"I think that I know what you're talking about."

He laughed, no less puzzled. "What do you want to discuss? Weight loss? Well, you've seen that." He picked a sheaf of computer printouts from the table between them and handed it to her. They reminded her of the simple spread-sheet graphics Adam ran on his computer, but these were far sharper, shaded into three dimensions, and in full color. Each pie wedge or bar graph represented another of Adam's physical characteristics. For an instant, a chill went through her as she realized that what she was holding was Adam, inside and out, all of his body functions and isnesses boiled down to a short stack of fanfold paper.

Culpepper went on without looking at her. "Strength? Look at the bar graph on the third page." She did, and it looked like a digitalized Everest, so swiftly did the curve climb. "It takes four to eight weeks to increase physiological strength, but *functional* strength can be increased in minutes—by improving technique or increasing confidence. Whatever he's doing with these damned breathing exercises or visualizations is increasing strength faster than I've ever seen.

"How about maximal oxygen consumption? That's the body's capacity to process oxygen. It's measured in milliliters of oxygen consumed per kilogram of body weight per minute of exercise. Training increases it. So does losing body fat. It's roughly equivalent to horsepower—and I'm telling you, Dear, that Adam has about twice the horses under his hood that he had three months ago, and they're breeding fast."

He watched Adam going through his paces again, and there was something in Culpepper's eyes that Micki had never seen one man express toward another: hunger.

Culpepper turned back to Micki and clutched her shoulder anxiously. "Michelle, tell me honestly. Is he putting one over on me somehow? I've read the books he gave me, the Savagi stuff. I've tried it. Members of my track team have tried it. Sure, there's been a little increase in relaxation ability, but nothing like Adam. I've analyzed urine, blood, saliva, and tissue samples, and I can't find any trace of drugs, illegal or otherwise. Even steroids or artificial GH wouldn't explain the explosion in coordination."

"Nothing illegal. He raided my bookstore for some of the fringe health tracts. I've seen him experiment with some strange blender drink concoctions: raw beef blood and brewer's yeast, for instance."

Culpepper scribbled.

Micki watched Adam's shoulder, elbow, and wrist roll

in a continuous wave as an extended outward block flowed through them.

"All sports movement is a matter of sequential joint rotation," Culpepper continued. His voice was a background drone to her now: it was impossible to take her eyes from Adam. "You can approach the linear, but never achieve it. The champion athlete lines up his joints in sequence and executes the arc of movement so quickly and smoothly that it is sometimes perceived as a straight line."

"And the same's true of karate? Adam always tells me that it's not a sport."

Culpepper laughed. "Well, that's a philosophical point of view. From a sport physiologist's point of view, it's just another complex, high-speed contact sport, with the same strategic elements as boxing, multiplied for limbs and targets. All we're trying to do here is smooth out those rotations right now. Building a model of his movement so that we can study it." He sighed and smoothed down a ruffle of dark gray hair. "But Adam is staying ahead of us. We isolate a problem, begin working on it, and by the time we have a solution and call him back in, he's already corrected the problem."

"Isn't that good?"

"What it is is bizarre."

Adam finished the series of movements, and Culpepper leaned forward. "You'll see what I mean now." He flicked on a control at the neck of a microphone. "All right, Adam. Top speed."

A comma of dark hair fell down into Adam's eyes for a moment. For the first time he seemed to see Micki, and grinned at her. "Give me a minute to catch my breath, Doc."

The smile. It was the same that he had always had, and that connected her with the old Adam, made her feel more secure. Thank God that *that* hadn't changed. Yet.

Adam nodded and bowed from the waist, gave a complex hand salute, and began. His punches were a blur, kicks whipping and cracking. His body torqued smoothly, arms and legs meshing like the gears of a deadly machine. The video of Shackley had been rewound, and she watched them—Adam's crisp, quick movement, and the slow-motion demonstration of the older man. Of course, Shackley was cleaner, more direct and sure in his movement. But the resemblance was astonishing.

Adam finished the first sequence, paused a moment, and began again. There was a little frown on his face, and this time he moved more slowly, but smoothly.

"Most human movement comes from the four F's," Culpepper went on. "Feeding, Fleeing, Fighting . . . and making babies. The deeper you can get into the emergency emotional states, the faster you progress, and the more intensely you perform. Assuming your form is good—that the structure of your movement is good—the more energy, the better."

"And if it's not?"

"You can tear your body apart," he said bluntly. "Newspapers love to print stories about women lifting cars off of their children. They rarely print the aftermath, the next day or week when the poor lady finds that she's turned her spine into a pretzel."

Adam finished the smoother sequence, and began again, this time faster, much faster, but a tiny wobble in his posture had worked itself out. There was a gleam in his eye, a kind of satisfaction that she hadn't seen before, and it made her uneasy.

With a jerk so abrupt that it hurt to watch, Adam came to a halt.

"How was that?" He came through the door toweling himself off, then took her in his arms and kissed her wetly.

"Uh, Adam"—Culpepper turned his eyes away momentarily—"why don't you get showered and meet us in the conference room?"

"Right, Chief."

Culpepper watched Adam leave before touching Micki's arm. "That young man has gained a lot of confidence in the past few months. You deserve a lot of credit."

Micki smiled weakly. "No. Whatever he's doing is coming from him. Believe it."

Culpepper watched the video as it played over and over again, and finally told the assistant to turn it off. "You know, there's still a problem with Adam."

"What's that?"

"Spatial relationships. His form is wonderful, but any boxer can look great while he's shadowboxing. He doesn't want to go to a school, or even spar. I think that he's jealous of what he's found, doesn't want to share it. His ego is more than I can control. He needs to get hammered down a little."

*Than I can* control*??*

She changed the subject. "There's only one reason I can think of that Adam might be better at this. Why he's growing so fast. Visualization. He's always been really good at what he calls rotation of higher dimensional constructs. Best part of his IQ tests. You know, imagining what a shape looks like from another direction and all that?"

Culpepper jotted something down on a scrap of paper. "Could be. Nikola Tesla was said to be able to visualize three-dimensional shapes as if they were actually sitting in front of him. Solid. Touchable. If Adam can do *that* . . ."

They went down the hall to the conference room, and as they walked Micki thumbed through the manila folder holding the printouts.

There were several sections inside, labeled "Sleep Disruption," "Dreams," "Digestion," "Meditation," and the thickest section, "Breathing Patterns: Zen, Yogic, Christian."

"He's talked to me," she said, shutting the folder. "But there's really nothing more I can tell you."

"Then as far as you know he's not playing with anything dangerous?"

"If I thought he was, I'd do everything I could to stop him."

"Well, good." Culpepper relaxed suddenly, and his

smile was wide and conspiratorial. "You watch out for that, because I think I've got something special here. Maybe together we can take Adam just as far as he can go. What do you think?" Culpepper held the door for her.

*I think that maybe I just lied to you, Doc.*

"I think that we'll just have to see."

# Chapter Twelve
## Food for Thought

## Wednesday, April 28.

Winston Gates plopped down at his desk at Wilshire Division. Through his window, he could see down to the 7-Eleven store next to the bail bondsman at the corner of Wilshire and Highland. The morning's rain was drying on the parking-lot pavement: the air was warming for the first time that year. Actually, he was happy just to be able to *see* the lot. When his "In" tray was full, it blocked the view. A mountain of paperwork was not what he needed at the moment.

Arlene Cheviot pulled up a chair, cheering him with a smile. The omnipresent office buzz enveloped them, lending a kind of privacy. On the job, Arlene was a rather square-shouldered woman with dark red hair and an unmade face that seemed a little too long. Off-hours, she radiated something totally different. There had been others for both of them, even a short, disastrous marriage for Winston, but they always seemed to gravitate toward each other like magnetized ball bearings.

"Winston, you haven't called for two weeks."

He ran a hand through thinning hair and smiled at her

bleakly. "Damned case is driving me batty. I'm sorry. Things look like they're slacking a bit. Maybe tomorrow night?"

"Busy. My mother. What are you doing tonight?"

He took her hand. It felt so damned smooth and warm that his fatigue melted. "Nibbling your ears I hope."

"You may have to settle for a Tommyburger," Doug Patterson said, coming up behind him. "We've got a live one. Well, he was live before the Skullcracker got hold of him. Come on, Win."

Winston squeezed Arlene's fingers. "I—"

"Listen," she said, pushing herself away from the desk, "call me if you're finished by ten. Beauty sleep."

"Beauty sleep." Winston watched her leave the room with special attention to the subdued syncopation of her walk. "And that, Doug, is a dead waste of time."

"Solid. Let's move, shall we?"

Winston sighed. "Duty, always duty."

"As the nights define the days, so do our duties define our freedoms."

"Who said that?"

"I did, just now. Like it?"

"It sucks."

The victim looked like a child who had toppled over in prayer. His skull was crushed, flattened, and blood pooled out from the enormous fissure like holiday ribbons spreading out from a cake.

Doug grimaced in disgust, and Gates lifted the dimpled sheet of newsprint someone had draped over the head.

"Black. Male. About nineteen. Jesus. Looks like someone took an ice cream scoop to his brain."

"Over here, Winston. Knife. Switchblade."

Winston dropped the sheet again, and looked at the blood-smeared blade lying on the cement behind the bakery.

"Well, he had time to get his knife out," Doug said. "Looks like he used it, too."

"Didn't do him much good. This poor monkey never had a chance."

He turned and peered out at the crowd, held back now by one of the uniformed officers. "Do we have any witnesses?" There wasn't even a ripple of reply, and Gates spat on the ground. "Does anyone know this man?" He flipped through the wallet.

"Carter Pelz. That name mean anything?"

A woman moved up out of the crowd, and she was tight-faced, near tears. "I know him. He was good boy. Not hurt anyone. Why someone, anyone kill him like this? I no understand."

"Neither do I. But I'm going to. Please—talk to the officer right over there. Thank you. Anything you can remember that might help."

He turned just in time to catch the eye of a small, narrow-faced man who immediately turned away.

"Doug," Winston said quickly, "take care of things here. I want to talk with that man."

Gates pushed through the crowd, saw the little man hurrying ahead of him. Before the man could break free of the crowd, Gates had him by the shoulder.

The man was Latino, and his face looked sun-dried and tired. Only his eyes were truly alive, and they were bright with fear. "Say, Friend, don't you want to talk to me?"

The man looked sideways at him. "I see," he said with a broken Spanish accent. "I see, but I no talk."

"Why not?" Gates said gently, edging closer.

"*Diablo*," the little man said. "It was not a human being. It was a demon."

The crowd's attention was caught now, and a swift, frightened mutter swept through it.

The little man's eyes were utterly terrified, and Gates repressed his automatic mockery. He took as much of the officiousness from his voice as he could. "All right. Just tell me what you saw."

His witness exhaled harshly, and Winston caught a whiff of old beer and worse. His teeth carried a week's worth of yellowish brown tartar, but there was still an ember of intelligence glowing in the muddy eyes. The little man held himself and rocked back and forth disconsolately, and made the sign of the cross. "It was terrible, señor. First man walk down the street. I watch. I see other man follow. I want to call out, but I scared. Second man start to run, fast. First pulls knife. They go into alley together. I hear noise. Scream, and then screaming stop. More sounds, then second man come running from alley. *Madre Dios*, señor. He *glows*."

Gates stopped, sucking in air. *Oh, God. Just when I thought I had something . . .*

"Glows."

"*Si*, señor. Glows. He runs, faster than anyone I ever see. And he glows."

"Glows." Gates tried to smile, tried to hide his disappointment, and could barely summon anything except disgust. "Well, thank you. I'll remember that. Glows."

The faces in the crowd around him were a spectrum of responses—everything from amusement to superstitious awe. *Jesus Christ*, he groaned to himself. *I can just see the papers tomorrow.*

He walked back to Doug. The crowd was thinning out. The police photographers had finished shooting their Polaroids, and the meat wagon was shoveling what was left of Pelz from the sidewalk.

If anything, Doug looked even more disgusted than Gates felt. His hands were poked deeply into his raincoat pockets as they watched the plastic zipper bag carry away Pelz.

"Don't go barhopping around here," Doug said flatly.

"Hell of a mugging, yeah."

"Well, no. That's not what I meant. I mean that I figure that there's mercury in the suds. You know what two of the locals told me?"

Gates laughed. "They said that they saw a glowing man running from—"

Patterson closed his eyes numbly. "Don't tell me you heard that shit, too." Doug didn't say anything else, just watched the back of the ambulance close. "I think we need to talk with an expert."

"You've got one in mind?"

"Yeah. We might even be able to catch her if we hurry."

"We'd better catch something. This is getting depressing."

Mrs. Ramos was a short, thin woman with shockingly green eyes and a mane of lustrous black hair that cascaded to her shoulders. She taught history and cultural anthropology with what Doug described as "a mean streak"—a special pleasure in discussing the Inquisition, the children's crusade, fringe religions and cults throughout history. Although it was more than three years ago that Doug had taken a class from her, "Ramos" was the first name to his mind when the subject of cults came up.

"Glowing? No, I can't think of anyone who would add that kind of filigree to a murder. Cranial mutilation is another thing. Doughnut?"

"Sure. Why not?"

"Plain or jelly?" She flipped open the top of a Winchell's box. "The cherry is good." She was smiling at him.

"Fine."

"What you have is evidently some kind of religious fanatic. He uses prayer, and perhaps drugs, to rev his body up to supernormal adrenaline levels. The Moros did it during the Spanish American War. Superhuman strength and speed. The standard issue .38 wouldn't stop them. So many Marines died as a result of midnight throat slittings that they started wearing leather collars. Hence the name 'leatherneck.' "

"And somebody might cover their clothes with phosphorescent paint in connection with such a thing?"

"It's possible. Anything's possible."

Doug leaned forward. "What about the cranial mutilations?"

Mrs. Ramos looked through the pictures as she munched a doughnut. Raspberry jam squished out of the edge and drooled down her chin before she could catch it. "Well, the only thing I can think of is pretty bizarre. The alternative is worse."

"Give me the bizarre one first."

"From what you tell me, the man in the alley fits the pattern of the other fourteen killings? Was there any trace of urine or fecal material in the brainpan in this or the other cases?"

"Yes and, Good Lord, no."

"Human saliva?"

"A little difficult to say. It was a mess. What if there was?"

"Urination or defecation in the brainpan of an enemy is a sign of high contempt." Gates wanted to get out of the room, and away from this homely little woman who talked about these things as if discussing rose pruning.

"Or, he might have taken the brain away to burn it. An offering to his gods." Ramos was thinking carefully. "The last possibility is pretty unpleasant. Brain-eating might have been involved."

"The tabloids made a mint saying that."

She flicked her hands in resignation. "Not a pretty thought, but a far more common practice than many people think. In any culture that has isolated the brain as the center of thought, brain-eating has cropped up as a means of paying respect to a formidable foe, literally 'I take your mind into my body.' Some believed that by eating selected sections of the brain, special abilities that the foe possessed would become yours. I wrote a paper on it in college, theorizing that this was the actual reason that kings and generals so often demanded to be brought the heads of their enemies."

"That's disgusting."

"That was what the instructor thought, too. However, the case was made strongly enough to earn my master's degree. You might consider it. Food for thought, as it were."

"Would you expect any particular pattern for such a person. Is there anything you could tell us that would help?"

"Well, it's probably not over yet."

Winston changed approach. "Have you ever heard of the Temple of the Earth Heart?"

"Vaguely. Used to be big back-to-the-land group in the sixties, weren't they? Don't they have something to do with the legend of Pah-Dishah?"

"What's that?"

"Myth pattern. City in pre-Aryan India. Supposed to have been the final repository of the old knowledge from India's mythical supercivilization. The Earth Heart and so on. Figures in several Hindu tales. Why?"

"It's cropped up in connection. What's the Earth Heart?"

She shrugged. "The legends are vague. Some kind of ground spirit. Read a paper by a man once equating it with the earth's electromagnetic field. Or the earth's core. Something. Typical pseudoscience."

"Does the name Dearborne ring a bell?"

Ramos shook her head.

Winston tried a long shot. "How about Savagi?"

She opened her mouth quickly, closed it, and then reconsidered. "I think he wrote that paper. He was the leader of the temple, wasn't he? Died under mysterious circumstances? Hint of a power struggle, and so on?"

"That's it. Well, it's probably nothing." He swallowed his last bite of doughnut, wiped a sprinkling of sugar from his chin. "Thanks anyway." His forefinger thumped a desktop pencil sharpener disguised as a scaled-down guillotine. "Sounds like you teach a helluva class, though. History was never like this when I was in school."

She chuckled darkly. "We're here every semester, Inspector. Come back any time."

# Chapter Thirteen
## Independence Day

*There are no hidden meanings. All that mystical stuff is just "what's so." A Master is just someone who found out.*

—Werner Erhard

*You ask what the structure of miracles may be. I tell you that it is simple, so simple that most will never grasp it, and fewer master it. There are three elements: First, change your perceptions of yourself. Second, change your perceptions of the world. Third, create a new interaction, with yourself as the power axis.*

—Savagi, *Conversations with the Master*, Metromedia recording. 1959

## Sunday, July 4.

KCOC's office building sat just off Highland Avenue in Hollywood, a two-story stucco monument to bad taste that had somehow escaped every Hollywood beautification project to date.

Micki had always considered it dreadful and wondered how a building could look so incredibly different on the inside.

She pulled Adam's Cortina into the parking lot and braked it with a squeak, glancing at her watch. It was five minutes to eight, and that was a relief. A long week, a long day, but tonight would be time to party with the staff of KCOC. She didn't know them very well, but this would be a perfect opportunity.

A figure was signing out in KCOC's lobby, and she recognized it instantly. A short, tight-faced, hyperenergetic little man burst through the doors, and veered toward her instantly. She got out of the car, not wanting Eddie Roach to have the advantage of height.

"Micki," he said, meeting her halfway across the parking lot. He looked her up and down with an expression that attempted to elevate the leer to an art form. "Good to see so much of you. Guess you'll be showing up at the party tonight?"

She was half a head taller than Eddie, but somehow he made her feel small and vulnerable. She was suddenly sorry that she had worn a clinging thigh-length knit skirt: a potato sack suddenly seemed more appropriate. "I'm here to get Adam."

"Yeah, well, there's no accounting for taste. He's back in the editing booth, flogging a couple of the tape machines." He laughed, and grinned at her challengingly. "Tell the truth: Didn't you like him better when he was a Twinkaholic?"

"What are you talking about?"

"*Nobody* can convince me that he's made all of those changes without some kind of drugs. You know"—he put his thumb to the side of his nose and sniffed—"a little white lunch? Snow for breakfast. He's not the self-controlled type."

"What is your problem, Eddie? What did Adam do to deserve you?"

"Nobody deserves me. I'm a gift to the world."

"Christmas comes but once a year, Eddie. Why don't you go get wrapped?"

He bounced away, gave his familiar hiccuping radio laugh. It sounded no more genuine in person. Just before he got to his car, he turned. "Be sure Mr. Kung Fu shows up tonight. We don't want to miss the fireworks."

"What?"

But Eddie just disappeared into his black Datsun 300 2X with another raucous laugh.

The lock buzzed like a bee in a bottle, and the door popped open.

The offices were deserted, the only light leaking from the back of the building, where the automated broadcasting booth was in operation. A couple of the sales pits had light under their doors, where workaholics were wringing a final desperate dollar from their territories.

And the only sound in the building other than the murmur of the radio was odd music from the back of the studio.

At first the sound was one of a deep, stentorian Yule hymn performed *a cappella* by the Mormon Tabernacle Choir. It grew crisper and clearer as she walked carefully back through the shadows, then suddenly stopped, and repeated the same bars:

> *Yet with the woes of sin and strife*
> *The world has suffered long*
> *Beneath the heav'nly strain have rolled*
> *Two thousand years of wrong . . .*

Repeated again, and then abruptly changed for another hymn, this one accompanied by an organ. A bellow of bass with a frosting of treble that fluttered about the upper register like a flight of angels.

Then it was something else, a song in some language that she couldn't understand at all, and then as she opened the door to the editing room, one of the Mahavishnu Orchestra's symphonic adaptations of a Hindu prayer.

Adam sat at the computer, watching the LCD's bands on the console's twenty-band graphic equalizer, scribbling in his notepad as he played with the bank of cassette tapes.

He still hadn't seen her behind him, so totally absorbed was he. For a moment she just watched him at play. His profile was distinctive now, even his glasses making him seem less a bookworm than a studious collegiate athlete. As he turned side to side, the line of his shoulders was deliciously masculine.

His long, dark hair framed a face that was all intensity and sensitivity, and she was overcome by a wave of affection for him.

There was really no remaining trace of his overweight, at least when he wore clothes. When nude, the love handles remained. She had a sudden strong urge to tug at them right then. He popped another cassette into the third computer and started it up. This was a rhythmic chant number in a Chinese dialect, one of those rounds that sound disharmonic until the listener's ear becomes educated.

"*Hannya Haramita Shingyo,*" she said softly. "That's one of the chant tapes you got from Good Life."

Adam swiveled around in his chair and bounced to his feet. His eyes were extraordinarily alive, and his energy level so infectious it was alarming. "Right you are!" He swept her into his arms and kissed her soundly, and she closed her eyes, rejoicing.

*I can't believe it. Everything is so damned good.*

She felt tears start from the corners of her eyes as she pressed against him in the editing booth, feeling the hard, flat muscles of his abdomen pressing against her, heard the breath growing hot and rapid in her throat. Wanting nothing more than to take him home and rip his clothes off.

He glanced at his watch. "Ye Gods. Late again. Sorry, Micki. I just got lost."

"How's the theory proving out?" She pointed at the little battery of tapes, each humming along merrily.

"I told you that hymns are like mind-altering drugs. Religions use word sounds and pitch to alter consciousness, everyone knows that. What *I'm* saying is that like the *shingyo*, they're also used to teach breathing patterns.'' He picked up and waved a well-scrawled notepad at her. ''Look. I've classified the patterns, and there are linkages. Doesn't matter what religion, or part of the world, or what. They're *all* getting high on carbon dioxide.''

She rubbed his nose. ''Carbon dioxide. And arched roofs, and wine and wafer and dancing and induced fatigue. You've told me all about it before. *We* have a party to go to, and I want to go. I want to eat. Food. Anyone who can down a pint of beef blood three times a week without barfing wouldn't understand—''

''It's good enough for Jack La Lanne,'' he protested weakly.

''Well, I haven't slept with Jackie lately. And your convertible sofa will witness a solo tonight if you don't take me dancing.''

''You can't do this to me.'' He rubbed his temples, scowling. ''I've been working too hard. I've got this terrible stress headache coming on, and I'm scared of Tylenol.''

She pushed him away. ''Ha. Take two aspirins and ball me in the morning. You promised me a chance to boogie. Now, are you coming with me, or does Eddie Roach fill up my dance card?''

Adam opened his mouth and closed it a couple of times, then turned and shut down the console. ''As foul a threat as I've ever heard. Science is one thing. Eddie is something else altogether. Let's go.'' He popped the cassettes out of the players and held four of them in his right hand, still unable to conceal his excitement. ''Do you realize what this means, though? I've run comparisons on over three hundred hymns and chants from every continent on earth, and it turns out that it doesn't matter what they're saying at all. They've all been about the same thing— *breathing*. Honey, I am onto something.''

She grabbed him and snatched the tapes out of his hand. ''Listen, mister,'' she said through clenched teeth. ''You had better get on the stick. All right. You're a genius.

I'm in love with a genius. Do we need any more reassurance tonight?''

Suddenly sheepish: "No, ma'am."

"Good." She kissed him, hard. "And I'm proud of you, you idiot."

She hit the lights as they passed through the door.

Micki leaned back into her cushion, feeling the last of the *rijstafel* settling to its well-deserved reward.

Oei's Table was an extremely exclusive Indonesian restaurant nestled high in the Hollywood hills, not far from the spot where a famous motion-picture director was rumored to have lain upside down on the hood of his car, smoking a particularly strong mixture of illegal herbs. Upon viewing the lights of the San Fernando Valley as if for the first time, said director received a vision of a "mother ship" that spawned a box-office smash, and then a smaller, more intimate and even more hugely profitable pseudosequel.

Those same lights spread out beneath them as they sat in an enormous bay overlooking a steaming swimming pool and sauna filled with 112 of KCOC's employees and guests.

Oei himself was a curious cross between a young and old Peter Lorre: the mischievous, lively face and intelligent eyes of the *Mr. Moto* Lorre, and the plodding, sadly overweight Lorre of *Silk Stockings* or *The Raven*. He scampered here and there among the feasters, balancing a tray of sauces and spices: inspecting, tasting, joking, making sure that his guests were cared for.

His restaurant was a tantalizing mixture of modern and traditionally exotic. Polished, slanted teak ceilings cast angled shadows on handwoven Indonesian rugs. The rugs, inlaid with traditional images of worship, family, and feasting, stretched from wall to wall, their edges nestled under hand-carved tables of Indonesian hardwood.

It was here, buffet style, that Oei and his diminutive servants served Adam and Micki the dozen courses of the *rijstafel* or rice table.

She loved the *gado-gado*, an Indonesian salad of stewed and fresh vegetables topped with a tangy peanut sauce, and the entrees—tangy *sate sapi,* and most especially the ginger-tinged sweet and sour delight of the *pangsit goreng.* Only the *kare ayam*, chicken steeped in coconut milk and curry, was not to her liking. It seemed like an afterthought compared to the succulence of the earlier courses. The dessert of *kue talam*, an insanely rich custard of coconut milk, mung-bean flour, and Javanese brown sugar, eradicated any slight dissatisfaction. Micki leaned back into the pillows lining the recessed, marbled dining area, and groaned in delight.

Oei excused himself, reappearing from behind a veiled recess with twin wands dipped in oil, and treated the assembled guests to a display of whirling, flaming baton acrobatics. Adam, seated next to her, clapped his hands like a six-year-old at his first circus.

Gone was any trace of clumsiness from the Indonesian. His bare feet skated across the floor as if coated with Teflon. He tossed the flaming sticks into the air, caught them with his teeth, with his feet, and finally, panting, kept four blazing brands in the air simultaneously, until the entire restaurant rocked with applause, Adam's louder than any.

When the demonstration was over, Oei bowed deeply and left the floor, and a four-man combo appeared from the shielded alcove and set up their instruments.

The room was filled with such incredible good feelings that something inside her melted as she leaned against Adam's shoulder. All she felt was warmth and security.

*If this is love, I'll take a dozen.*

The guests were moving out onto the floor now, and Adam, square-shouldered and handsome in a denim-patterned sports jacket, was drawing appreciative glances from all corners of the room.

The music was slow, and she caught their reflection in a gold-veined wall mirror. He was six inches taller than she, and she had to admit that the two of them were perfectly matched. Holding him seemed awesomely right.

Adam floated her across the floor, and she was swept up with him in a dream only marginally soured by the sight of Eddie Roach quietly conferring with Oei, pointing a skinny finger at them. Oei, a feather of irritation tickling his composure, headed in their direction.

When the song ended, Oei tapped Adam's shoulder and smiled quizzically. "Mr. . . . Ludlum? Did you enjoy my demonstration?"

"Hell, yes. Terrific, that's all I have to say." There was a dangerous quiet at the center of Oei's question. "Is there some problem?"

"Your friend, Mr. Roach, mentioned that you feel that *Kali* and the Indonesian weapon arts are forms of the Chinese *Wu Shu* and not indigenous art forms, is this correct?"

Adam looked around the room for Eddie. Roach was leaning against a wall, his smug expression only partially hidden by a glass of wine.

"Well, I was really talking about an article in a martial arts magazine. Of course I'd heard of you, and of your demonstrations. I was delighted, really. I meant no offense."

"Nor was any taken." Oei's smile was counterbalanced by the creases wrinkling his forehead. Some of the other guests had stopped dancing, or were only pretending to dance, listening to the conversation with growing interest. "Mr. Roach also told me that you are proficient in the arts."

Adam's smile grew crooked, and she recognized the look in his eye. The staff of KCOC was definitely gathered by now, a semicircle of interested faces.

*Oh, Adam. How much have you been talking about your studies? How many of them are curious?*

As if in answer to Micki's unspoken question, Morgan Iadiapaolo tapped Adam's arm. "Hey, come on, Adam. You've been talking about this stuff all year. How about a little demo?"

Before Adam could open his mouth to protest, there was a smattering of applause, led, Micki noticed, by the redoubtable Mr. Roach.

"I have traveled widely in the East." Oei's voice was low, controlled. "And it has been my pleasure to study with many experts. I was fortunate enough to find a master of the Indian art of *varrman*. *Varrman* is not the most potent of Indian arts—that ultimate ancestor is forgotten now, lost when the Aryans swept into northern India. That was a mystical art, which released the animal fighting instinct through directed dreams." He was looking at Adam curiously, without hostility or challenge, as if the two of them were the only ones in the room.

"Would it be possible to put the original secrets back together?"

Oei shook his round head. "Perhaps. Who knows? There is great reluctance to teach. Perhaps there is reason for the reluctance. At any rate, if you would care to learn, I will show you a bit of the hybrid art I learned."

Adam glanced at Micki, and then at the circle of co-workers around him, in their suits and dresses, their ties and ribbons, and felt the tension. "I'd like that very much."

Oei bowed, and waved his hands to silence the musicians. Walking to the center of the dance floor, now suddenly filled with confused and milling couples, he clapped his hands again. "Ladies and gentlemen, we have an additional bit of entertainment tonight. As sometimes happens, one of your number is not unfamiliar with the martial rigors and would like to learn a bit of the art of my fathers. Would you please give a polite encouragement to Mr. Ludlum."

Adam smiled uneasily as he doffed his jacket. One of the servants, a beautiful olive-skinned girl who couldn't have been more than sixteen, brought Oei a pair of wooden sticks, then handed Adam a second set. They were each twenty-four inches long, of polished rattan.

Mr. Oei placed his sticks beneath his arm, and watched Adam casually. "Now, Mr. Ludlum. How would you use these?"

Adam held them out in front of himself clumsily. He tried to adjust them this way and that, one stick projecting from the top of his right fist, the other from the bottom of his left. Finally he ended up with both of them upright. He made a few feeble thrusts that looked like a combination of fencing and racquetball.

There was a bit of chuckling from the others as they returned to their seats. Adam bit his lip.

"Very good," Oei said jovially. He flipped the sticks from under his arms, and suddenly he was frightening. No Rose Parade majorette ever moved a baton more fluidly or with greater precision. The sticks moved like magic, flipping over and under and around, flowing like living things. He twirled them above his head, he dropped one and passed it from hand to hand, behind his back and in front of his body.

He stopped abruptly, and the room thundered with applause.

Beads of sweat appeared on Oei's forehead, and his silk brocade jacket was damp beneath the armpits.

"That was *kali*, the mother art of the Philippines."

"*Kali*. As in the Indian goddess of creation and destruction?" Adam asked softly.

"Very astute, but not necessarily correct. There are those who say that the name of the art derives from a progenitive village in the Philippines. Like yourself, however, I find it difficult to believe that there is not some kind of connection. At any rate, in terms of technique, *kali* is superior to what remains of *varrman*. *Kali* has its spiritual side, too, especially the *antung-antung*, a magical charm used by filipino stick and knife fighters. *Varrman*, however, has the weight of Yogic tradition behind it, and what I have done is to combine the philosophical approach of *varrman* with the physical technique of *kali*. I believe it possible that this hybrid art is the finest in the world. Would you still like to learn?"

Adam watched those sticks revolving lazily around and around in Oei's hands, and to Micki his expression looked a little sick. As if for the first time, he realized that he had been trapped, and that he couldn't back out. "What the hell. You're not going to hurt me, are you?"

Oei laughed. "Here." He positioned Adam's arms so that they crisscrossed his body, right hand up and left down.

"We'll start with an exercise called the six-count. It's a basic coordination drill." Adam nodded, the fear still on his face as Oei moved his right stick forward. "Hit mine with your right," Oei said. Clumsily, Adam did. "Now your left."

Left, right, up, down, the sticks clattered in a six-count pattern. Right up, left down, right backhand, left up, right down, left backhand, and then the pattern repeated. Over and over. Slowly, because Adam kept missing the strokes.

Time and again, it seemed that he was almost catching on to the basic rhythm, and every time he did, Oei, smiling, sped up just a hair, or began to circle to the left, until Adam lost his balance. Once he actually fell, tripping over his own feet in the effort to keep up with Oei.

"Great going, Ludlum," Eddie called.

Nobody else laughed, and Mrs. Tanaka said quietly, "That was quite nice, Adam. Why don't you try again?"

He smiled and nodded. His knuckles were skinned, but he got up gamely, dusted himself off, and got set to continue.

Micki's heart went out to him. Eddie Roach, chortling into his napkin on the far side of the room, had lost and everyone knew it. Adam would look like a novice, but not like a fool.

This time, Micki noticed, Adam made a conscious effort to shorten his stance from the traditional karate posture to the shorter, crouching *kali* position.

Oei began again.

Adam was controlling his breathing now, and as Oei moved, circling, rat-a-tatting on the rattan, a small furrow of concentration appeared, quickly replaced with a smile. He increased the speed until both of them were moving at a decent clip, then stopped. "Good. A week or so of practice would give you the basics of that one. Why don't we try something a little more complicated? It's called *abaniko*."

This time, Oei's sticks blurred overhead like helicopter rotors. Adam frantically twirled his to match, meeting Oei's stick squarely with a clack. Oei's arcs were smooth and fluid, Adam's wobbling and ugly, but he just barely managed to get them around in time. He stumbled as he stepped around, and as Oei pushed him faster, she heard the breath catch raggedly in his throat, almost a sob. Oei bore in. Adam stumbled, but still managed to catch the flashing sticks once, twice, three times even as he collapsed and fell.

This time he got up and smiled uncomfortably, wiping his hands on his pants. "I'm sorry. Let's try that again."

"Let's mix the two exercises up," Oei said genially. "You're doing so well. Six-count and *abaniko*, alternating."

Without a word, Adam nodded and stepped back in toward Oei.

Once again, Oei dominated Adam so totally that it was almost painful to watch. But twice, when Adam caught the rhythm, he *leaned* in toward Oei and caught him slightly off guard, and Micki saw the restaurateur take a half step backward before regaining his balance and moving forward again. Oei's smile didn't return quite so automatically, and a spot of perspiration glistened on his forehead, rolling down to the tip of a brown nose.

Adam took a fraction of a second to watch Oei's feet as they moved, and this time Micki *saw* Adam's feet shift position, right in the middle of a movement. No one else in the room seemed to realize exactly what had happened, but suddenly he wasn't as clumsy anymore.

Oei's eyes narrowed, and he increased the speed.

Adam fought to control his breathing, and did. Micki realized with a start that her own breathing was starting to speed up.

An uncomfortable expression was growing on Oei's face, and with a start Micki realized that the man *was getting tired*, and Adam was getting stronger. She saw the arc of Oei's movement grow shorter, flatter, and heard the grunt of pain as one of Oei's sticks rapped the corner of Adam's eyeglasses. They flew from his face, slid across the floor, and made a dull cracking sound when they fetched up against the wall.

A discontented mutter wound its way through the room.

"I'm sorry," Oei said. "You didn't adjust quite fast enough. You . . . really are quite good. Are you *sure* that you've never done this before?"

Adam picked the glasses up, examining the cracked lens. He handed them to Micki.

"Never."

"I'm sorry about your glasses. If you wish—"

"Never mind. I need a new prescription anyway. They've gotten too strong." He watched Oei, watched the man's breathing patterns, and Micki knew that Adam sensed what she had: Oei had hit Adam to give himself a chance to rest.

"Well," Oei said, wiping his face with the back of an unsteady hand, "I think you might be interested in a little of the real thing now. Those were just drills, and probably not of tremendous interest to you."

Micki could feel what had happened. It wasn't just Adam who was trapped. Oei was trapped, too. She looked across the room, at Eddie. He bounced up and down on his floor cushion, so excited by what he had placed in motion that he was probably about to wet his seat.

"No, I think they're very interesting," Adam said.

"At any rate, I'd like you to feel a little of my hybrid art. Would you like to switch to plastic or bamboo sticks? I'm afraid that I might touch you a few times."

"Go ahead," Adam said flatly. "I'll see whatever you'd like to show me."

Oei nodded and came in again. Slowly this time, but totally out of sequence. The right and left hands acted together or independently, jabbed or thrust or cut over from odd angles, and Adam, once confident, was thrown into confusion again. The movement was slow, but even as Micki watched it began to move faster and faster, Oei coldly confident, Adam stumbling, trying hopelessly to coordinate mind and body. He turned toward her for a moment, and his face was pained, humiliated, carried a "what am I doing here" quality that was heart-wrenching. Oei smacked Adam's knuckle, nicked his head, spun the stick down to graze his knee.

Always a light, kissing touch, just a touch. Adam was drenched in sweat now, great dark flowers blooming across his shirt. The sticks were slipping in his fingers, and he was exhausted.

Again, their eyes met for a moment, and she could almost hear him scream "help," and she started to stand up, to call a halt to it, when something very disturbing happened.

Oei threw a low kick, a cross-stepping movement that was blended smoothly with the *clacketty-clacketty* of the twenty-four-inch rattan batons. Adam's attention was totally on keeping his head on his shoulders, and there was no way that he could see that kick.

But he countered it anyway. He counter-kicked, stop-kicked, met Oei's shins with the bottom of his foot, and the smaller man's rhythm was thrown off for a bare instant, in which Micki *saw* Adam shift his weight again, and in the next instant again, until his posture—crouched, balanced—was almost a mirror image of Oei's.

Oei came in again, very fast now, and he was hitting Adam repeatedly. Every time Adam shifted position defensively he was hit. Oei, smiling, teeth showing, but no longer coldly confident, was putting a little more into the touches.

A murmur was growing in the room. Something was happening. They could feel it even if they couldn't understand it. Only Micki, her eyes educated through months of observation, could have told them exactly what they were seeing: if Adam's attention was high, *Oei could only hit him high*, and if Adam, panicked, paid too much attention to his feet and legs, then *Oei could only hit him in the legs*. Everywhere Adam's attention was *not*, he couldn't be hit, and Oei, aware of it even if Adam wasn't, was growing more frustrated.

There was a blur, a whirlwind of rattan, and Adam groaned. The stick jerked spastically in his left hand even before the sound of a meaty *smack* registered on her hearing.

And that was when the third thing happened.

The room went dead silent. You could absolutely *feel* Adam's attention narrow to exclude the other guests, the servants, even his own body. Suddenly there was nothing in his universe but Oei. And with that shift in attention, Oei's dominance suddenly dissolved. A confused, uncomprehending look replaced the former confidence, and he stumbled as he began to give ground.

Adam's movements were as smooth as Oei's in terms of the large circles, and they dipped and interwove, peaked and valleyed, swooped up and down and sideways, were concentric rings and figure eights, growing smoother and more controlled even as Micki watched. As she watched, the radius of those circles grew shorter and shorter, and the circles grew tighter and faster.

Oei sobbed in frustration and threw himself forward, and Micki knew that in that instant, embarrassed, humiliated in his own restaurant, in front of his guests, his employees, for that bare moment Oei forgot where he was and what he was doing, and was trying to kill Adam. She could no longer see the movements, couldn't distinguish thrust from parry, counter from explosive drive. All she could see was that Adam's face was growing more feral, more lit from within by a light not familiar and wholly frightening, and Oei's fear grew like a tangible thing. Adam's confidence and poise ballooned as if it were glutting itself on Oei's terror.

Adam's stick reached through, almost slowly, and Oei's head jerked back. Adam's foot reached out casually and hit Oei's knee, freezing Oei's movement for an instant. Adam's sticks danced up the man's body, twirled and hopped, hit the man along his side at least twelve times in a staccato jig. Just touches. Totally controlled, the last one ending in a savage jab to the windpipe that penetrated a quarter inch.

Oei gagged and dropped his sticks, staggering back to clutch his throat.

The tableau was frozen for a moment. The sticks twitched in Adam's hands as if they were alive.

"Who . . . are you?" Oei croaked at last.

Adam paused in confusion, as if he didn't have an answer to the question. The muscles along his jawline spasmed as if they were being fed regular pulses of electric shock.

The silence in the room was painful. Oei scuttled backward, watching Adam's swiveling sticks. "No one . . . can do what you just did."

Adam looked down at his hands, and slowly, the sticks ceased to move, lost their life, dropped from his hands. He took a nervous step backward, looked at the figures of his friends and co-workers as if they were strangers. Subtly, almost without moving, they were pulling back toward the wall, frightened.

"I . . ."

"Leave," Oei croaked. "I don't know what just happened, and I do not want to know. I do not know what path it is you follow, but if I were you, I would stop."

"Stop?"

"You are young. You have time. You are attempting to cheat time, and time will destroy you. I know you now," he said, and his eyes were more afraid. "I saw you in the jungles in Burma, and once a missionary in India spoke of you." Oei was heaving for breath. "Yogis have written of you."

"And Savagi?"

The silence now was thick enough to strangle, and Micki felt as if she were watching through a curtain of muddy water. "That one. So. I was right. If you follow him, then I have said too much." He drew himself up with ruined dignity, sliding the fear back behind his pride as if it were dirty linen to be hidden from company. He bowed to his customers. "If you will excuse me, please." He swallowed, hard, and left the floor.

Adam nodded, and tears had started from the corners of his eyes. "Mr. Oei," he said, "I'm sorry. I really am."

Oei stopped, but did not turn around. "I will say a prayer for you," he said softly. "It may not be enough."

The musical combo attempted to play again, but there was no spirit there, and no one went back to the dance floor. The party began to break up.

Adam's hands were on the wheel of his Cortina, but he didn't seem to be able to move. The car was still parked on the immense, oval drive in front of Oei's Table. Above them, the lights on the upper floor were flicking off one by one, leaving the restaurant in deep shadow. One by one the cars of the other employees and guests were circling the drive and drifting away into the night. A few of them said goodnight to Adam. None of them touched him. Not a pat on the shoulder, not a shake of the hand.

"What did he mean by all of that?" Micki asked.

"I guess he was just . . . upset. Wanted to spook me. He was embarrassed, that was all."

"You . . . kind of went into overdrive there, didn't you?"

Adam laughed, and held up his hands. They were shaking, and the skin on the palms was torn and wrinkled, oozing blood. "I guess that's what you call it. I don't really remember that much."

He laid one of his hands on her knee. She could feel the trembling, the sweat and blood, and she took his hand and held it, felt the heat coursing through it.

He gripped her hand tightly, and when he turned to look at her, the same hangdog expression was etched across his face. "I don't know what's happening, but it's big, and it's good."

"Is it?"

"It has to be. I mean, it's everything that I ever wanted. When you get everything that you want, that's what they call good, isn't it. Isn't it?"

His hand was burning hot, and she put it to her cheek. His eyes were bottomless, and for the first time she discerned the faint cry of anguish buried in the bravado. A faint voice in her mind was crying, *Walk away. Get out of the car now and just walk away while there is still time.*

But he *needed* her. Too obviously he was a lost little boy, playing with toys that were somehow growing bigger than he was. Toy soldiers who were suddenly fixing bayonets, panda bears who were developing a taste for meat, Zoid Giant Zrks who craned their creaking mechanobrontosoid necks to bare sharp, gleaming teeth.

The heat in his hand was penetrating her, warming her cheek, relaxing her, and draining down into her crotch, where a sweet, liquid feeling began to flame. Suddenly, she was hot and tingly all over, and kissed the palm of his hand. Her lips felt swollen, and she was almost too filled with emotion to speak, but she managed to say, "I don't know, Adam. I don't know what it is. All I know is that I want you to take me home. Now." She took his hand and pressed it against the place that felt so warm, so very hot.

He caressed her for a minute, then raised his hand and flicked the tip of his tongue across the moisture glistening on the pads of his fingers. She felt as if she were going to faint.

Adam turned the key in the ignition, and pulled the car around the silent oval and out of the gate.

In the building behind them, a single, silent man in a darkened upper window watched, triggered a control that started an automatic gate closing behind them. He closed the curtains, and though he retired immediately, and took a sedative, he was unable to sleep that evening.

# Chapter Fourteen
## The California Bash

*My chemistry had been changed in some way: certain preferred foods became unpalatable, certain colors and music were now jarringly offensive.*
— Lawrence Blair, *Rhythms of Vision*

## Saturday, August 14.

For a six-week period between the beginning of May and the middle of June, the Paramount Ranch in Agoura Hills, Southern California, is famous for an Elizabethan eccentricity known as the Renaissance Pleasure Faire. From weekend to weekend the past lives again, enlivened by fresh hot breads and spiced meats, unamplified bawdy songs, street vendors, exhibitions of horsemanship, and the lusty goings-on of Chipping-under-Oakwood village. Tens of thousands of people turn out every weekend to broil in the sun like so many barbecued cutlets.

But the Pleasure Faire had been gone for two months, the gilded robes and frilled dresses neatly folded and packed, the horses corralled and their copious, fragrant droppings swept away. The California Bash was ready to roll.

139

For the past four years KCOC and Metrocom promotions had co-sponsored the Bash, which drew as many people in two days as the Pleasure Faire did in six weekends.

The stage was a vast, prefabricated shell erected on a gentle hillside on the northeastern corner of the ranch, with speakers suspended thirty feet above the ground, anchored to the stages, wired to the trees, and suspended on tubular-frame stands amid the swarming audience itself.

The crowd itself swallowed any semblance of individuality among the participants: it was a thick, flowing liquid rolling from the refreshment stands to the overburdened, pungent urinals. From the wooden water barrels at the outermost edges of the crowd to the lip of the stage itself, the fenced area was patrolled by patient, alert security guards.

The KCOC remote trailers were parked up behind the shell, in an area often used to park show horses. The ground was flattened more by hooves than tire treads. The air was unusually humid, thick with the dank aroma of horse manure.

Adam Ludlum sat in the third trailer back, listening to the sounds from the stage, to the closing bars of a song called "Chain Dance" wailed by Stukka Mann, the lead singer of Eddie Roach's favorite group, Jo Mama.

His eyesight blurred. Reflexively, he brushed at glasses that weren't there anymore. He hadn't worn them very often since the night at Oei's.

His hands controlled the lines and levels from the recording truck to the microwave relays that beamed the signal back to KCOC and to the satellite that relayed the audio and video to cable and FM stations all over the country. Those unfortunates without stereo televisions would rely on their local FM stations for sound.

There was a buzzing sound in his head, and it grew more irritating as the song pulsed to a close. On his monitor, the three-man/two-woman group was doing its usual turns and gyrations, a sort of coitus ex machina with one another's bodies and guitars, whipping the audience into a frenzy. He could feel the cheering through the floor of the trailer, felt it vibrating in his bones. It was giving him a headache.

*So burn another number*
*Or pop another beer*
*If you can't take it with you,*
*Lemme use it while you're here.*
*Baby lemme lemme use it while you're here.*

The noise coming through the headphones hurt him, and he peeled them off and groaned in gratitude when Morgan Iadiapaolo swung in through the door, carrying a matched set of Michelobs.

"Adam, it's Madam. Sweetheart, you've been here since five this morning. Hain't you take a break yet?"

Adam looked up with the palest of smiles. "Break? What is break?"

"You speak beer?" Morgan sat in the empty seat next to him, waving a can temptingly under Adam's nose.

Adam sniffed regretfully. "Nothing but club soda for me, thanks. Trying to get cleaned out. I tell you what you could do, though. Watch the board for a couple of minutes? I gotta choke the snake."

Morgan looked at the board doubtfully. "Uh—you know, Eddie feeds you shit sandwiches, but he'd skip the Wonderbread if he caught *me* working his gig."

"When did he put you on his list?"

"Since I told him a toot don't buy a touch. If anything goes blewie, he'll have my tits for tea."

"Listen. Nothing's going to go wrong. The truck's taking the stage feed. It's premixed and filtered. It goes straight out over the line from here. I'll just be a minute."

Morgan shook her head. "Where's your relief?"

"Supposed to be here half an hour ago. Damned if I know."

The headache was a dull, rusty ice pick sliding into his ear. "Listen, hon, I really need it." He turned up the wattage in his smile. "Give me a break."

Morgan rubbed her thumb along a straggly fringe of

pale red hair, and sighed. "All right, but I have to be back to the Metro trailer in fifteen minutes. Don't bitch me up."

Adam patted Morgan on the back and swung out of the trailer. It felt like nitroglycerin was sliding back and forth inside his brainpan.

Slosh.

Boom.

Outside now, Adam carefully picked his way through the mass of coiled cables. In the heat, they shimmered like sleeping snakes. The music had stopped, and now the voice of Eddie Roach echoed over the speakers.

". . . it for Jo Mama. Hey, now, before we bring up Donnie Arthur and Roadkill, we're gonna do a little video for you on screens two and three. So hang in there. We're gonna jam *all night long!*"

Adam could see one of the huge video screens rigged at the corner of the stage. On it, Eddie was twenty feet tall, decked in his usual bone-tight sharkskin suit, even though the temperature was ninety-three and climbing. Eddie's face was covered with sweat, and Adam could see that his coordination was way off. His smiles looked grafted on. The long weeks of preparation, the last one with virtually no sleep at all, were beginning to take their toll. This was Eddie's big chance, the first time that the Bash was broadcast live, nationally. The exposure that he'd always wanted, right in front of him, and if that meant propping himself up with chemicals, so be it. For Eddie's sake, Adam hoped he was the only one who could see how close to total collapse the man was.

Grimacing, Adam found the honeywagon, hustled inside, and tried to urinate loudly enough to drown out the sound of Eddie's voice.

". . . Hey, one last thought for the people still coming in on the Ventura Freeway. A little warning not to get caught indulging in auto-eroticism. For those who don't know, that's doing sixty-nine in a fifty-five-mile zone."

Adam closed his eyes. It smelled *bad* in the toilet, as if someone preceding him had been sick. He wouldn't have been surprised. He smelled a lot of sickness now; rancid fats and colds, body odor and unwashed teeth, fear and fatigue and hunger on a whiff of acid breath.

It must be the diet, and the meditation. His system cleansing itself. Especially the meditation, but he didn't want to think about that. Just thinking about that seemed to slow his breathing, send a warm, dry wind whistling through his bones as if there were a hole torn in his reality.

He didn't want to think about that now.

Or about Micki, and the miracle that the last six months had become.

He zipped himself and left the honeywagon, looking around. Needed to stretch his legs before going back.

Before . . .

He didn't *want* to go back, he suddenly realized. He wanted to stay out here, and watch the people.

His eye continued to pick out one miniature tableau after another through the fences: a mother nursing her child, a brown, glistening nipple escaping its mouth for an instant, milk shining white on its rose-petal lips. A plump woman lolling on a sleeping bag, a yellow towel shielding her face. A couple cuddling together in the shadow of one of the water tanks: the boy's hand, black against her pale yellow shirt, slipping beneath her waistband. The long white expanse of her neck as she leaned back and opened her mouth for a kiss.

A group of kids passing around a bottle of Blue Nun, one of them coughing, and the others laughing.

The details piled up behind one another like the wind-whipped pages of a child's picture book, until he felt confused, lost, uncertain of the proper order of things. What was important? What trivial?

Then a voice sounded over the loudspeakers, and it came to Adam that it had been speaking for several minutes. "Adam Ludlum, please report to the main trailer. It is urgent that Adam—"

A bit sadly, Adam turned and headed back to the trailers.

He hadn't gotten more than halfway back when Eddie Roach came flying down the narrow corridor between the trailers and the generator cables, screaming, "You *idiot!* I had him." Eddie was almost apoplectic with rage, his pale little face drawn tightly, breathing shallowly, harshly, in short, gasping pants. His fingers were crooked into claws.

Adam shook his head vaguely. "What are you talking about?"

"Stukka was here, you asshole. Jo Mama never gives interviews. He was going to give me five minutes. A KCOC exclusive. No network interference." Eddie's eyes were glazed. "I get him back to the trailer and what do I find out, you *puke?* I find out that you've gone off for a piss. Who the hell gave you permission? Would you tell me?"

Fumbling, Eddie pulled an acrylic plastic inhaler from his pocket, diddled a switch on the side, and sniffed deeply. His eyes glittered.

Adam felt a stab of pity. For the first time he didn't hear the hundreds of people who had laughed at Eddie's pathetic jokes; he heard the thousands who didn't. He saw Eddie strutting for television cameras that would never care to close in on the ruined face, the superstud radio image that was blasted by every public appearance. The manipulative little turd who had forced Adam to shame a man who had harmed no one.

And here a chance to interview one of America's favorite sex symbols, shot to hell because of a demanding bladder.

"Eddie, I was supposed to get my break two hours ago. I kept working," Adam said calmly. "I have rights."

Eddie's eyes flamed. "Rights? I'll show you rights you goddamn *worm.* I'll have your *job* for this. You wait and see." Eddie was flushing, chest heaving, and covered a momentary weakness in the legs with a snarl of anger.

"*Don't look at me like that, you shitsucking weirdo*! I don't know what you're doing in the dumpster, what the hell you're putting in your veins or up your nose—"

"I don't do drugs anymore, Eddie."

Eddie sneered. "You're on that steroid shit, and you know it. Look at the way your goddamn arms pump up, you muscle-bound freak. Nobody builds up as fast as you have. You're just a junkie, Ludlum. I saw that freak performance with Oo-ey or whatever his name is. You been shootin' up homogenized Bruce Lee brains or somethin'. I don't care, but you're weird, man, and you're through around here.''

He was screaming now, as much from exhaustion as anything else. Roadies were stopping their various labors to watch and listen. With an audience behind him, Eddie was both trapped and encouraged into going on. Deeper, further.

*Like Oei.*

"You're a loser, Ludlum, and you're trying to take me down with you. You try to hurt me? To screw me? I'll destroy you, you bastard.''

"You're letting the coke talk for you, Eddie," Adam said quietly. "Why don't you go get some sleep?''

Eddie's eyes flamed, and he slammed his palm against Adam's chest. "What the hell was that?''

The strike of the hand was a distant sensation, no pain, no discomfort. And yet something deeply buried flashed red and began to boil within Adam, and he smiled nastily. "You're sick, Eddie. You're a very sick man. You need to go and lie down. Let one of the other VJ's handle things for a while. You're losing it, man.''

Eddie was shaking now, sweat sticking his hair to his forehead. His legs quavered when he took another step toward Adam. When he swung again, Adam leaned his head lazily out of the way.

"Eddie,'' Adam purred, "you don't have it. Give it up and go away.'' From his peripheral vision, Adam could see the dozen witnesses they had attracted, the ones who could attest to the fact that Eddie threw every punch. Adam tried to calm him down. Honestly, there was nothing he could do but defend himself.

Eddie was shrieking now, screaming, chasing after Adam as he glided back and back, smiling kindly. Eddie's arms windmilled, missing, Adam always just barely out of distance. Eddie wanted to connect just once, to wipe that smile from Adam's face, to land just a single punch, although the pain in his chest was growing more severe. Adam was smiling more now, as if he knew about the dizziness, could read the pain, sensed that the heat was frying Eddie's brains in his head.

Then Adam stood still for a moment, and Eddie's left fist shot out, and Adam *caught* it. Caught it in midair, and smiled benevolently. He squeezed slowly and certainly, and Eddie, gut-punched with the sudden horrific knowledge of his error, knew that with another pound of pressure every bone in his hand would splinter.

Feet pattered up from behind Roach, as several orange-shirted roadies rescued him. "You're on stage, Eddie." They formed a barrier between Roach and Ludlum. "Let's cut this. We've got work to do."

Roach rubbed his hand, glaring at Adam. "Fix you, man, fix you. . . ." He sniffed from the inhaler again, turned a switch, and sniffed deeply up the other nostril, tottering off toward the stage, helped now by the roadies.

Adam stood where he was, watching the small, unsteady figure vanish, to be replaced a moment later by the twenty-foot-high Eddie on the washed-out color screen. The sharkskin Eddie, cool and hip and untouchable.

But he was staggering now, the fatigue and the heat and the drugs catching up with him all at the same moment. "And naow . . ." His speech was slurred, and there was silence behind the stage, broken only by a low, alarmed murmur.

"Hey, people. What'chu waitin' for? It's time to PAR-tay! I know *I* am. And I know you'll all take my pleasure . . ." He paused, looking into the camera, confused. He clutched at his left hand. "The same pleasure I . . ." He shook his head, and turned his back for a moment, sniffing from the inhaler again. A chorus of jeers swelled from the crowd, and behind the stage, Adam heard screams to get Eddie *off*.

"Hey, up yours, man." Somebody started from the wings to help him, to get him off, but he waved them back. "Get away from me, asshole, I'm fine, man, I'm—" He staggered back against one of the drum stands with a crash, and Adam distinctly heard him say, "Oh, I can't see—" before the stage erupted and the video blanked out.

Adam stood quietly, watching the darkened screen. He watched, and listened to the chaos around him, and felt something in his head pulse weakly, like a starved kitten feeding at a saucer of warm milk.

Or like another, darker creature, feeding on something equally warm. But thicker.

# Chapter Fifteen

## Thanksgiving

### Sunday, November 21.

Several of the nurses turned to look at Adam as he strode the halls of Good Samaritan. They admired the breadth of his shoulders, the trimness of his waist. The angles of his cheekbones, showing through his face for the first time in two decades, creating a kind of rugged handsomeness that was beyond his fondest dreams. Together with the squarely cut shoulder-length black hair, the overall effect was somewhat barbaric. He didn't walk like other men. His legs swung fully and sensuously from the hip, the muscles of his pelvic girdle somehow leading the rest of his body.

He knew they were watching, and didn't care at all. None of it mattered. Nothing mattered at all, except the man who was dying down the hall, alone, in a small, cheerless room at Good Samaritan Hospital.

The door was open, and through it he could see the hospital bed, and a bony pair of feet projecting from the end of the sheet. The television in the right upper corner of the room was on. It was always on, and always seemed to be showing an old, dull movie, as if the intrusion of quality would be too jarring to the patient.

Gunther Ludlum's eyes were wild and frightened when Adam entered, and he licked cracked lips and stretched out an emaciated hand. Tubes hung with terrible limpness from his arms, and Adam's nose wrinkled at the omnipresent, vaguely mentholated stench of decay.

"My son!" Gunther cried. "Where have you been, boy? They won't let me out of here. You've got to help me, please. . . ."

Adam took Gunther's hand, alarmed at the cool, waxy feel of the skin.

Gunther held up his arm, and pointed to the tubes trailing from it, tubes through which colorless liquid slowly pumped. "See? See what they're doing to me? If you loved . . . respected your father, you'd help. You wouldn't let them do this. They're giving me things." His voice lowered to a whisper, and he glanced at the door, licking his parched lips. "They've made me weak, boy. I've never been this weak before. You know that. You be a good boy. You get me out of here."

"You'll be leaving here soon, Father." Adam winced at the unintentional double entendre. "I'm getting you out for Thanksgiving. I promise. Micki and I just need to get your house ready. I can take care of you. I'm not working for KCOC—"

Gunther's hand flailed wildly.

"No, no. Don't worry, Father. I was ready to leave anyway. There was just an incident . . . some problems. Nothing to worry about. I can do free-lance work from home. It's all right."

Gunther's hands clutched at his, his breathing a slow hiss. The little plastic oxygen feeder in his nose fell out as Gunther moved uncomfortably. Adam fastened the strap behind Gunther's ear again.

"You promised me, Adam. Promised you'd show me. I can't help you anymore." With sudden fierce, dark humor, he grinned up. "Not until I kick their butts to let me out of here!" As if that challenge had drained him en-

tirely, he slumped into the pillows again. "Oh, Adam.
Oh, Adam . . ."

"What about what I *have* done, sir? My weight. Micki
and I are back together—"

Gunther's head whipped around. "When were you apart?"

"Uh . . . right." *Wrong subject.* "Does it hurt, Father?"

"Nothing hurts," Gunther said dully. "Nothing hurts
. . ." He was quiet, then suddenly began to thrash with
such violence Adam feared he would rip the tubes from his
arms. "Oh, God, Adam. Please, please help me."

"I'll do anything I can."

"Hold my hand." Gunther clutched out, and his eyes
were desperate. "I can't help you anymore. You have to
be strong now, Adam. Be strong for me, boy. For us."
Adam gripped his hand, and Gunther sighed. "God, that
feels good."

*Good?* Adam relaxed deeply, until his sense of touch
grew more sensitive, and he could feel every gnarled vein,
every hair on the back of his father's hand. Gunther sank
back into the bed, and was very quiet. For a moment,
Adam thought that his father was dead, then the sunken
chest began to move.

Adam closed his eyes.

At home, when he meditated, he could visualize an
individual neuron triggering, could watch a synapse firing.

And more. His reflexes, according to Dr. Culpepper,
were just a few thousandths of a second slower than the
fastest ever recorded. *He had done it! He had done the
impossible, and was improving his body at prodigious
rate.*

But at the moment, there was no feeling of pride. There
was no sensation but grief at the awful reality before him.

Gunther's nurse wheeled in a chair and the portable
oxygen apparatus, a little rectangular tank with rate of
flow adjustments along the top.

"Do you know how to operate this?" Her smile was
painted on. There was feeling there, and real concern, but
it seemed that the certainty of his father's death made her
pull that genuine concern back in. Gunther Ludlum was

soon to be an ex-patient, the late Gunther Ludlum, and meaningful concern was preserved for the living. Adam couldn't even find it within himself to be angry. "Set the control at 2.5," she said. "This unit will have to be recharged every four days."

"He'll only be out a week. Just for Thanksgiving," Adam said. "I just want . . . want him to be with me. There isn't much family, so I think that it would be nice."

"Are you taking me home, Adam?" Gunther mumbled on the bed. "That's good. You're a good boy. Always been a good boy. . . ."

Adam smiled weakly.

The nurse offered to helped Gunther out of the bed and into the wheelchair, but there wasn't really any need. His weight had dropped below a hundred pounds. To Adam, he was barely a wisp of cool air.

Adam deposited him gently in the wheelchair, and tied a safety belt across his lap.

Gunther tried to speak, to be alert, to do anything other than just sit, inert as a sack of kitty litter in a shopping cart. Adam looked down into the glistening pinkness of his bare scalp and fought back a withering tide of sadness.

The halls of Good Samaritan were more medicinally clean, but somehow less impersonal than those at Saint Martin's. The nurses seemed to know and like Gunther. Adam could tell how they cared by the very artificiality of their smiles. He wasn't fooled. Behind those false smiles was real pity, concern, the same sense of failure that Adam felt.

*Here we are, surrounded by millions of dollars of medical apparatus, and thousands of years of trained experience. And we can't stop an old man's body from turning against him. And so we sit back and smile as his son takes him home to die. Happy Thanksgiving.*

Micki was waiting down in the car, and watched silently as Adam spooned his father into the front seat. When he was finished, she drew him aside. "Adam, you're really sure this is the right thing to do?"

"It's his home." Adam slid into the rear, touching his father on the shoulder as Micki pulled away from the green hospital zone, and around the drive into the thin traffic.

"Hello, Mr. Ludlum," Micki said shyly. Her hands were steady on the wheel, Adam noted approvingly.

"I know you," Gunther said, with a torpid, lizardlike stare. "I like you."

Her hands gripped the wheel, hard. "I'm glad."

Adam touched Gunther's shoulder gently, felt the ancient bones through the fabric. "Just a few minutes," he said quietly. "Then we'll be home."

They turned the corner from Crenshaw Boulevard to Washington, and as they did they passed a billboard Adam had grown to hate, one of those nauseating creations with the smiling, muscular mountain climber with the cigarette dangling from his lips. Every twenty seconds a cloud of oiled steam jetted from some hidden mechanism, wafting away on the breeze.

He looked from that image to the shriveled man in the front seat of the car, and fought back an urge to scream.

The house sat between Venice and Washington boulevards on Virginia Road, one of a row of stately houses that had been erected in the 1930s, a semiexclusive neighborhood that had become less exclusive as the years went by, but had never fallen into the disrepair of neighborhoods barely a quarter mile to the east or west.

It was a big old rambling two-story house, one that Adam remembered with varied responses. Driving up to the side driveway, he looked back over the fence to the backyard where he had played as a child. The rusted swing set still stood. His name, scrawled with a pencil tip in wet cement, still caught rainwater by the cellar door.

The house had been all but deserted for the two years since Gunther's stroke, and Adam had come by only to inspect for damages and to see that the gardener was managing things. For the eight years before that, there had been so little contact between Adam and his father that the old house had become a strange and terrible place, a place of remembered isolation, memories of endless walks though lonely hallways. Of sitting alone in empty rooms.

Adam lifted his father out of the car and Micki hurried on ahead, opening the door.

He and Micki had worked hard for the past week to get the house into some kind of shape, so that Gunther could come home. The house still smelled of disinfectant-masked mildew, and Adam swore to himself that he would get the rest of the smell out of the air before Thanksgiving.

There was a bizarre, inverted *déjà vu* in carrying his father up the stairs. Gunther was weightless in his arms, as light as a baby and infinitely more fragile. Adam could feel his father's bones sliding under the skin, the atrophied muscles and withered tendons barely keeping the skeleton strung together. They floated up the stairs as if gliding on a rail.

Micki stood holding the door at the top of the stairs, but Adam had paused there, gazing into a mirror at the end of the hall. At the image within the mirror: his father in his arms, still dressed in his hospital gown beneath his Christmas bathrobe, thin arms weakly, almost frantically wrapped around Adam's neck, eyes tightly closed.

Adam looked at himself, and at the man in his arms. At the swell of muscle in his arms, and the play of tendons in his forearms.

And he began to grow dizzy, as if Gunther, in his weakness, was finally, reluctantly, giving Adam full permission to be strong. Impulsively, Adam bent and kissed his father's forehead.

At least the bedroom at the top of the stairs was clean, no smell of mildew or rot. Just good clean soap and water, and clean bedding. It had been his parents' bedroom, and Adam remembered it only too well. . . .

He laid his father on the bed, moved the fleshy sticks of his legs under the covers. He pulled the blankets up, and sat gently at the edge of the bed. "One of us will be in the house at all times," he said, in what he hoped was a cheerful voice. "There's a buzzer at the bedside, so there's nothing to worry about."

Gunther was twitching under the covers as if trying to get his arms out. His skeletal fingers gripped at the covers, his mouth working as if chewing food that wasn't there. "Thank you . . . thank you . . . and Adam . . ."

"I think that I'll go downstairs and start fixing the food for dinner. We stocked the refrigerator yesterday."

Gunther nodded vigorously. "A growing boy should eat, Adam. Adam, one more thing."

Adam pointed to the buzzer. "Remember, if you want anything, it's right here." He closed the bedroom door behind him.

"Adam," his father coughed out. "Please, Adam, just one cigarette. Please, Adam . . ."

Micki kissed him lightly on the cheek. "I'll just be a minute. I need to wash my hands."

She heard him grunt an answer, then trudge off downstairs. At the other side of the upstairs hall was the mirror that had caught Adam's gaze, and she stood before it for a while, pressing her fingers against the glass. The mirror was gold-veined, and very old. The carpet beneath her feet was a fuzzy comfort.

The bathroom beyond was filled with dusty bottles and tubes. They simply hadn't had time to clean the entire house, and much of it was still the way it was on the day that Gunther had crawled to the phone and dialed "0."

Gunther Ludlum had never recovered, his once iron health finally collapsing like a line of dominoes. *Plink, plink, plink*; stroke, heart attack, carcinoma. The triple crown of geriatrics.

She washed her hands, the first gush of water a brownish surge against the white of her palms.

Adam sat at a frayed gray vinyl-topped table, his head folded in his arms. They were strong arms now, rounded and tanned, sinewy with new muscle. But he was crying, and right now he needed her. He turned, grasping her around the waist. "I'm not going to make it," he said miserably.

"What? Make what?" She stroked his hair. She loved its fineness, like baby hair.

"That's my *father* up there." When he turned to lay his cheek against her dress she realized, perhaps for the first time, how very much he had changed. His cheekbones were clearly defined, the cords of his neck standing out in bunches where once there had been puffy skin.

"This was the house I grew up in, that was always too big for me. I can still remember stubbing my toe right there, right over there against that counter. I fell and hit my head, and I can remember that my father was on the other side of the house and I had to run around and around to find him, my head bleeding into my hands, and he wasn't *anywhere*. . . ."

She started to make a comforting reply, but he shushed her. "No, listen to me. I may not be able to get this out more than once. I meditate almost two hours a day now, and study for another three. I've always had the ability to manipulate my visual field, but it's stronger now. Much stronger. Something is happening inside me, and sometimes it feels like it's growing out of control."

He picked up a blue porcelain salt shaker from the table. "Do you see this? What is it?"

"It's a salt shaker, Adam. It's . . . shaped like a little Dutch boy." Her mind stuttered as she fought to think. "Metal top . . ."

"I don't see a salt shaker," he said. "There is kind of a gray fog there. Amorphous. Colorless. It's like I'm holding a handful of mist." He squinted as if trying to focus on a page of damnably small type "I can bring some color into it. I can see what I want to see, Micki." He was crying again, and the shaker was trembling in his hand. "It's not a salt shaker now, it's red and green, and it has little pink petals around the center, and thorns."

He looked up, the wetness streaking his cheeks, and his hands trembling. "Here, Darling, a rose."

She took the salt shaker from his hand. In his eyes, so

moist and steady, she knew that it was a rose, and she was afraid to contradict him.

"See?" he said. "Do you see now? I can do this. And you've seen the things that I can do with my body. And sometimes when I sit quietly, and just look at the wall, it begins to *melt*." He looked up at her quickly. "I *know* that some of it is illusion, Micki. But it's still power. You'd think it would mean something. You'd think that someone who can do things like that would be able to do something to help his father. Could do something . . ."

"Adam, it's not your responsibility. You're doing everything you can. Don't torture yourself."

"I just feel," he whispered, "that life is playing an enormous joke on me. That I can have everything I want from my mind and my body . . . and from you. All I have to do is lose my father. I guess the deal always reads a little like that, huh?"

He said nothing more, just sat there at the table, looking terribly miserable. She kissed the back of his neck. *The walls melt, Adam?*

The first thing she thought of was that she had to talk to Culpepper, or Algernon, or someone. Quickly.

The second thought was a sad, small voice that said, *And if my father were falling apart in front of me, I'd want to melt the walls, too.*

# November 25. Thanksgiving.

Adam sat in a corner of the room, watching his father. Gunther was hooked up to the large oxygen tank now, the one that read "Not for Life Support" and "Do Not Smoke in This Room" around the edges. Its whisper should have been below the threshold of hearing, but was not. He heard, or imagined that he heard, every sibilant hiss, every gurgle as the oxygen ran through the humidifier.

His father was asleep, but in ten minutes would have to be awakened for his medicine. Thanksgiving dinner had been a cheerless affair, for all of Micki's efforts. His father had eaten a forkful or two of turkey, and a little cranberry sauce, which was better than Adam had managed. He looked at the steaming, sumptuous, artistically arranged plate that Micki served him, and realized he would as soon eat dog vomit.

Very little light filtered into the room, and what there was was warped by imperfections in the glass, or by the lightshade perhaps, or by the arc lights above the billboard on the corner that blew puff after puff of clean white steam into the street.

His father hacked painfully in his sleep, one frail hand clutching at a sunken chest. The light surrounded the bed, enveloped it, tinting it yellow and red with an odd outer fringe of black.

A trick of the light, no doubt. He had to doubt his perception, because Micki didn't see it. So it probably wasn't there. Except that he saw it.

He hadn't seen it in the hospital, where everything was sterile and full of anesthetic cheer, and *I Love Lucy* and the *Scooby-Doo Puppy Power Hour* walked hand in hand in the rerun hall of fame.

It was here, in the dark and quiet of his father's home, his home, that he could see that dark fringe. The tears that filmed his eyes acted as a prism, a diffraction lens that somehow twisted the colors of the rainbow away from the bed, leaving behind that billowing black fringe.

The old, old man on the bed shifted, calling out "Harriet . . ." Gunther moved a withered right hand down to his crotch, stroking himself clumsily, a single tear welling from a cloudy eye and rolling down his ruined cheek.

Feeling guiltily voyeuristic, Adam watched as Gunther sought any kind of emotional contact with his ruined body. He groaned, and his hips moved, and then he was quiet, and the room was quiet except for the distant rumble of cars rolling along Washington Boulevard.

"Father?" Adam said, touching his father's shoulder as gently as he could.

Gunther's eyes flew open as if a mortar shell had exploded next to his ear. "Wh-what do you want?"

*He doesn't know who I am.* Adam subdued the flash of pain. That was pure ego hurt, and had no place in this room.

"It's me, Father. Adam."

"Adam. Yes, yes . . ." He scrambled to move the covers into place, and he was petulant, and almost childishly defiant. So many things, from so many different times and moods, were mixed into Gunther's eyes, but paramount among them was fear.

Adam switched on the lamp. "It's time for your medicine, Father." He poured a glass of water from the pitcher on the nightstand, took a pill from each of two bottles, and put them rattling in a plastic cup. "Here."

Gunther knocked the cup away. "No," he said. "No. Adam, you're my son. Why are you trying to hurt me?"

Adam steadied himself. "I'm not trying to hurt you. This is your medicine, and you have to take it, Father. It will help you get well."

Gunther pulled the sheets up around his neck, under his chin, and squashed himself into the wall, more than ever the image of a petulant child. He blinked hard at the pills, trying to remember who he was, where he was, why he felt so alien in his own bed.

"You're just sleepy, Father. You're still half asleep. It's all right. Just take the medicine, and then you can go back to sleep."

Gunther recoiled as if Adam were offering a handful of spiders. "You're trying to kill me," he whispered. "Why? Why, Adam? I love you. I've always loved you. . . ."

Afraid to take his eyes from Adam's hand, Gunther groped out desperately, finally finding his wallet on the nightstand next to the bed. He thumbed it open, fumbling out two ancient American Express traveler's checks. "Here," he said. "You want money? I'll give you a hundred . . . no, two hundred dollars. Just please, please let me live. . . ."

The room spun for Adam, and he staggered back against

the dresser, trying to breath, fighting just to stay on his feet.

He swallowed hard, and came a little closer to the bed. His father recoiled, and Adam stopped.

"Father, I don't want to hurt you. Not for any amount of money. I don't want money. I want *you*. Alive. Well. Please. There's nothing wrong with it."

"Then you take it," Gunther said harshly. "Let me see *you* take it."

"Father, this is *your* medicine. I can't take it. It could make me sick."

Gunther's gaze was pitiless.

"Father," Adam said desperately, "when I was a child you took care of me. You always took care of me. That's all that I want to do now, for you. Please. Help me. Help me help you. I don't want the doctors to have to come and stick you with needles. I want to know that you trust me not to hurt you. That everything is right between us. Please, Father. Help me."

Adam held out the cup. Timidly, Gunther's hand reached from under the covers, took the cup and the glass of water. He cocked his head sideways, until he seemed almost birdlike. He examined the two pills as if they were the last things that he would ever see in this world.

"You really want me to take these?"

Adam nodded slowly. "Yes, I really do."

Gunther took one of them, and put it between his lips, looking at Adam as if his son had just asked him to sign on the dotted line and then, *Hey, Dad. Eat this gun for me, would you? But let me spread the tarp out first. We don't wanna mess the rug, do we?*

"You're sure?"

Adam nodded.

Gunther swallowed the pills and water. His eyes, bright and accusing, closed slowly, and he sank back against his pillows. "There, Adam," he said. "I did what you asked. It's on you now. I hope that you can live with yourself."

Adam stared as his father sank into motionless sleep, then turned and walked from the room.

*      *      *

Adam looked in on Micki, who was still sleeping soundly. She hadn't heard any of the ruckus, and had felt none of the pain.

There was little urge to climb into the bed with her, to wake her up, to frighten her with the intensity of his need. And right then, he needed her so badly that his crotch flamed, cramped, and he wept with frustration.

Tomorrow. Tomorrow he would talk her into giving up her apartment and moving in with him. Tomorrow.

For now, he had to be alone.

He left the house, walking south toward the corner of Washington Boulevard and Crenshaw. His father's image hovered like a mirage: the sheets pulled up to his chin, frightened out of his mind by his own son, the hollow face and dark, lusterless eyes, the frizzy wiry fringe, withered hands that once had been firm and strong moving clumsily beneath the sheets. Adam could see it all too clearly, and the images swam in his head until he thought he would go mad.

There was no traffic on Washington as he walked along dazedly, and he ended up beneath the billboard at the corner of Crenshaw. He looked up at the thing, an inspiration to be like the healthy, young, athletic stud with the cigarette dangling from his lips.

There was no particular reason for him to move around to the back of the service station or find the service route up to the roof, but he did it.

The first rung of the ladder was at least four feet over his head, but he couldn't clearly remember the leap that hooked his fingers around it. His shoulders and arms bunched as he pulled himself up, but all that he could remember was his father's voice, and face, that terrible, sickly face. The utter fear and the way a trembling hand held out a handful of dollars and begged for life.

He was behind the billboard now, behind the mechanism that squirted thin tendrils of oiled steam. The amorphous clouds that drifted out over the boulevard, calling, *Here! Here! Here is sexuality. Here is health. Ignore the*

*fine print warning from the Surgeon General that we are
required to publish. It is black and white, and you are
passing too quickly to read it anyway. Notice the color and
the muscles and the beautiful woman in the background,
the things that you would notice if the poster was printed
in Urdu. Watch. Learn. Act.*

Adam put his hands on the mechanism, and it was hot to
the touch. A little sign atop it warned; "Do Not Open the
Housing Without Switching the Apparatus Off or to *Neutral.*" It thrummed, hummed, in his hands, and he felt
deeply into it, listening to it sigh and grunt as it expelled
puff after puff. He heard it, but didn't see it. All that he
could see was his father, pleading.

(please)

He set his weight and dug his heels into the roof.

(don't)

Adam's fingers dug into the apparatus until his fingers
pressed into the metal, and he was crying, not hearing the
cars beneath him or the steady, venomous hiss of the
machine, but only the sound of his father

(kill)

and a slight sensation of tension in his legs, and then
there was a sharp cracking sound, and the air whirled with
live steam.

It hissed, swirled around him, and he was sobbing now,
and screamed as he ripped it free and smashed it against
one of the angle irons keeping the billboard erect. Scream
and

(me. Why do you want to)

scream, and take the angle irons in hand. Hands suddenly not flesh, but part of the metal, directed by mind
that was not ordinary mind at all. Automatically finding
some balance between metal and board and the heels
digging into the roof, as he screamed and

(kill me? I'll pay you a hundred)

never noticed the lights coming on in the apartment
across the back fence, the face that appeared in the window, the sleepy voice that yelled, "What in the hell is
going on out—"

Adam turned to face the voice, and the man blanched, whispered, ''Sweet Jesus,'' and disappeared back into the apartment.

Adam uncoiled from his crouch, feeling the angle irons cut into his hand, hearing the roof shudder as the bracing struts popped free, feeling muscles in his back stretch to their limits as with a hideous groan the support brace warped and the sign lurched forward, sagging under its own weight, lurching drunkenly now.

(no, two hundred—)

The top of the sign tipped over, the electrical connections on the back of the sign snapped loose, and an entire row of bulbs along the top of the sign exploded into sparks and glass and melting plastic. Wooden beams beneath the supports gave way, and it screamed like a dinosaur tumbling over a cliff, and the billboard fell, shattering, grinding against the pavement below.

Adam stood atop the service station garage, crying, laughing, staring at the blood, black against his hands in the terrible light. Listening to the short circuits jump along the back of the billboard.

In the distance sirens whined, growing louder every moment, until finally it penetrated his consciousness that he was their quarry.

Lights flickered on all over the apartment building behind him, but no one would look out of their windows.

Adam climbed down from the roof, only now feeling pain in his torn hands, his strained shoulder, his elbow joints. His back felt as if a truck had run over it, and even his thigh muscles felt ripped and sore.

He dropped the last few feet, landing off balance, and stumbled against the trash cans with a rattle. The whining sirens and swiveling lights were no more than a block away, and Adam vaulted the fence that separated the service station from the residential side of the block.

He landed on the grass behind the house, and pivoted as a black shadow leapt from the bushes at him. Faster than thought, Adam sidestepped, and his foot whipped out in a hook kick, his foreleg accelerating so quickly that it was an invisible blur in the dark. There was a muffled sound of splintering bone, and a yelp cut suddenly, brutally short. The Doberman dropped like a sack of wet meal.

A second dog was coming, but stopped to sniff at the first, which lay, unmoving, whimpering as it died, shattered ribs piercing its lungs and kidneys.

The second dog snarled. Adam met its eyes, and in that moment he didn't exist, nothing existed but a dark and deadly void that boiled just below the most basic level of consciousness.

The dog growled. Then whined. Backed away, its bobbed tail quivering. Ran.

Adam vaulted the next fence and took an indirect route back to his house.

Micki heard Adam coming in the back door and met him there. His hands were covered with blood, he limped, and there was something in his face . . . something. Some arrangement of sinews beneath the skin, like the strained mask of a world-class sprinter crossing the finish line. Police sirens were howling out on Washington Boulevard, and Adam was still breathing hard. His feet were cut and bloody, spotched with mud up to the ankles.

His clothes were drenched with sweat.

"Adam?"

She might have been a glass transparency, a phantom, a wisp of vapor. He plodded past her to the bathroom, moving like an automaton.

He was still breathing hard as he ran water into the bathtub. He ripped his clothes off as if they were contaminated: not unbuttoning them, or unzipping, but shredding them. She had never seen human fingers rip corduroy like that.

He slipped into the water, mud and bits of plant matter floating to the surface like mosquito larvae in a pond. He lay back in the tub, staring into the ceiling. Blood fluxed away from his hands in little scarlet rivulets.

He stared up into the ceiling, stretching his fingers out

and tensing them. Stretching and tensing, and every time he did, the little ribbons of blood flowed away.

"I remember this tub," he said at last. "I got my first bath in this tub. I can still remember my mother's hands. They were so smooth." He looked up at her, his face a calm oval. "Warm. They were warm."

Adam reached out a hand to her. "Micki?" he said. "Stay with me. Please."

She smiled weakly. "I promised that I'd be here until after Thanksgiving. After that your father goes back to the hospital."

"And then?"

"And then I go back to my apartment."

He ran one warm, damp finger along her arm, leaving a silver streak edged with soap bubbles. "Please, just stay with me. I need you. I can't take care of this house by myself. I can't be here by myself. There are too many memories."

She pulled her robe tightly across her shoulders. "I can't stay here, Adam. I need someplace to go home to."

"This could be your home."

"No, Adam, not yet. Please. Everything is changing too fast. Give me time."

He looked up at her. It had to be the indirectness of the light, but his pupils seemed wider, darker, awesomely deeper.

"I'm running out of time," he whispered.

He took her hand.

"Adam, please . . ."

"You're mine, now, Micki. We both know that. It doesn't make sense to lie any longer."

His hand was terribly hot, and the distant wail of sirens burned in her ears, the sound of voices, of a fire engine trundling down Washington toward an imaginary blaze.

"What happened out there?"

"I need you."

"Adam, no . . . talk to me, please . . ."

His hands pulled her toward him. The tub radiated heat,

and she was no longer sure if it was from the water or his skin.

"Adam, don't do this. Something is happening to you. I know . . . I can feel—" Beads of perspiration sprang up on her forehead, and she was lost.

Adam's slippery wet arms wound around her, pulling her across the porcelain. The terrycloth fabric of her robe rubbed painfully against her swollen nipples, and she was trying to get the robe off, and couldn't quite.

"I need you," Adam repeated, kissing her neck, her shoulders. The water was burning hot. His skin scorched her, the slippery fire of the soapsuds flowed everywhere, caressing, lubricating, stealing the coolness she had fought so carefully to maintain. The heat was penetrating, warming, and once again she wasn't sure, couldn't tell whether the water warmed his skin, or vice versa. All she knew was that he radiated heat, fed the fever raging in her blood. A small, still voice cried for sanity, wailed that there was something wrong with the intensity, with the feel and smell of him, with the muscles that writhed beneath the oily patina of his skin.

With the pain of his fingers gripping her back. With the depth of her response, the way her body opened to receive him, the wet heaviness of her robe weighing her down, holding her down, melding them together like a cocoon.

But as he held her, and at last she gripped at him, at the taut muscle of his buttocks as they flexed and drove into her, the corded wedge of his back, the salt slipperiness of his tongue, all fear, all reservation, everything except touch and smell and taste, and raw animal consciousness were like hot soap bubbles cascading down the drain in a steaming spiral.

# Chapter Sixteen
## Thanksgiving II

"What a mess." Winston Gates kicked a shard of broken glass into the hole in the middle of the roof, listening to it tinkle down into the body shop below.

The fire department had already left, but the gawkers were there, everywhere, on the far side of Washington, and on Crenshaw. Local residents, passersby, a few drunks, siren chasers, and at least a half-dozen officers controlling the scene. In fact, there seemed to be everything except a sober witness.

He bit the top off a strand of King-B beef jerky. It looked to be a long time until breakfast, and his stomach was beating him to death.

Feeling gingerly for his handholds, he climbed down from the roof.

Doug Patterson met him as his booted feet touched down. He grinned at the fractured brown strand of twisted beef in Winston's hand. "Hey, Win. Don't tell me the turkey's already going light on you?"

"An Arby's deluxe don't cut it at three in the morning." He ground his hands into his pockets, looking again at the two "witnesses" who had come forward.

"Haven't you found anyone who wasn't stoned last night?"

Shelly Leibowitz, the cop who had answered the squawk, shrugged. "I tell you true. That guy didn't look drunk to me. He even volunteered to take a breath test."

"Crazy, then. Did you take a look at the damage up there? They're saying that someone did it with his bare hands. I hope it's not inappropriate, in this liberated age, to assume we're talking about a man."

Shelly grimaced. "This is all we've got, Win. You wouldn't have been called if it didn't tie in with your other beef."

"Thank God for small favors." The night felt warm, and entirely too quiet for a place that looked like the middle of a war zone. Something extraordinary had happened here. For long months the city, at least his peculiar little corner of it, had been quiet. No more weird murders, no need for another visit to the Temple of the Earth Heart. Just the usual generous helping of shootings and stabbings. But this . . .

There was something coming, and it was coming soon. And hard. He could feel it in his back teeth.

Doug, uncomfortable in Winston's silence, laughed loudly. "I think someone doesn't like cigarettes, and took it out on the Marlboro Man."

Win buried his hands in his pockets, stalking back to his car. Months of peace. And now this. It was coming. It was almost here.

"Hey, Win . . ."

"Yeah, Leibowitz?"

"Happy Thanksgiving."

He snorted. "See you in the movies." Winston took a last look at the ruined roof, the toppled billboard ripped from its foundations by a stress that he had trouble imagining. And he thought of the two witnesses who claimed that it was the work of a lone, bare-handed miscreant.

"Shit, Doug," he muttered, sliding in behind the steering wheel. "I don't want this case anymore. I want it closed. I want it dead."

"You're getting old, Cowboy. This one is starting to look damned interesting."

Winston stared at his hands. They weren't shaking, but somehow he felt as if they should be. "Interesting. Yeah. I'll remember you said that."

And he would.

# Chapter Seventeen
## Projections

*I speak tonight of energy. According to one of my students, who is an engineer, "energy" is the capacity to do work. Energy due to motion is kinetic energy. Kinetic energy is expressible as one-half the product of the mass and the second power of the velocity. If a boulder is perched atop a cliff it is said to have* potential *energy in regard to the lower level. It becomes capable of doing work as it crashes down.*

*I ask you to open your minds to another dimension. One in which correct perspective reveals the true energy all things have in relation to one another. One must see the truth of the thing. The mere act of seeing a fundamental reality involves one inexorably with the process itself. In truth, all life, all existence, is motion. Thought itself is motion, and the inertia of a powerful mind can cloud the reason and perception of those caught in its web. Reality is an interconnected web of forces more delicate than the gears of the finest clock made by the hand of man. The slightest introduction of disharmony into this infinitely subtle balance of forces can disrupt the entire . . .*

—Savagi, *Conversations with the Master*,
Metromedia recording. 1959

# Thursday, March 8. Fifteen months later.

Adam sat, motionless, in the Cage.

Just outside the 12 × 12 white-walled room called the Cage, in the basement of the UCLA physical sciences facility, were Dr. Culpepper, and Algernon Swain, and Micki Cappelotti. And the head of the physics department, a black woman named Deckart, who would have been attractive but for the disdainful expression on her face.

A twelve-lead electrocardiograph was attached to Adam's chest and back, and additional leads from a portable electroencephalograph were attached to his forehead. The darkened isolation chamber was wired for sound.

"In a minute," Culpepper said, "we're going to seal off the observation window. Adam wants no light, no interference. Luckily, the Faraday cage was available to us."

Algy cleared his throat. "Uh, Micki, a cage is a room with metal mesh woven into the walls. Used to create a decrease in electromagnetic static, or to reduce the possibility of eavesdropping. Adam wants the greatest isolation possible, not even that background sixty-hertz hum everybody in the civilized world has to put up with."

"He said that he's going to try something different, and wants witnesses," Culpepper said. He seemed relaxed, confident, and excited.

Deckart laughed harshly. "Culpepper, what is he going to do? Stop his heart? Come on."

Algernon glanced at her with the barest flicker of irritation crossing his round face. "I'm not sure what you find so absurd, Tanya," he said carefully. "I've looked into this since Adam first told me about it. There've been several documented cases of cardiac control, by reputable Yogis, confirmed by scientific observers."

She smiled tolerantly. "You aren't the first people who've used the cage. Thelma Moss and her psychic researchers did a decade ago. I'm very familiar with the literature. One of the most publicized cases was back in the fifties, when a guy who called himself Ramananda Yogi claimed to be able to stop his heart. Under a fluoroscope there was still a flicker around the left apex. In 1961 the All-India Institute of Medical Sciences in New Delhi studied four Yogis. One slowed his heart a little, and another produced a weaker beat, at least it sounded weaker through the stethoscope."

Culpepper pulled a metal panel down on the test room, fastening it securely at the bottom.

"There was a third gentleman named Shri Krishnamacharia who did a demonstration for a Dr. Brosse in 1935. The first electrocardiogram was made with a single electrode attached to the body. When they used multiple leads, they were able to pick up a heartbeat. I'm sorry if I'm raining on your parade, but none of that stuff has been proved."

Algernon had set up his two cases of portable diagnostic equipment on a cleared desk. A gooseneck microphone snaked out of the wall above the top edge of the desk. Micki sat next to Algernon, who was totally absorbed with the diagnostic output.

He glanced up at her. At first Algy tensed a little, then smiled with resignation. "Hi, Michelle. Haven't seen you for a while."

"Sometimes I think Adam hides us on opposite ends of his universe." Algy wouldn't meet her eyes squarely. "I know how you feel, and I'm sorry that it hurts you. I know Adam cares about you very much."

"Let's just leave it, Micki. Unrequited love makes for bad poetry and worse conversation."

"Maybe after this is all over, we can go for coffee."

"Plasma may end up being more appropriate."

Culpepper browsed the liquid crystal display of the respiratory monitor, hawing to himself. "He's taking this pretty far down. This is running thirteen: fifty-two: twenty-six: thirteen." He turned to Deckart. "That means that he's inhaling for thirteen seconds, holding the breath for fifty-two seconds, exhaling for twenty-six seconds, and leaving his lungs empty for thirteen. Then he starts the cycle over again. Pretty far out.''

''But his heartbeat has only slowed slightly. It's still well above sixty.'' Dr. Deckart frowned as she examined the readout.

''A breathing cycle of less than one per hundred seconds. Twenty-six seconds for the *exhalation*, for Christ's sake.''

''Sixty-eight,'' Deckart said. ''His heart rate is going *up*. And it is irregular.''

Culpepper shrugged. ''Well, maybe he can't maintain it. I don't understand this. He said that he had something to show us. Micki?''

She looked small and particularly helpless. ''I don't know. He spends hours down in the basement every day. He's turned it into a gym or something, and he won't let me down there. Sometimes I can hear him working out, but a lot of the time he's just down there, meditating.''

''Seventy-four . . .'' Deckart seemed perplexed. ''I'm a little surprised that it's climbing so fast. He seemed to be—eighty. Eighty-four.''

Culpepper politely moved Deckart to the side. ''He said that he was going to show us what we wanted to see. And that we weren't supposed to stop the experiment. I assumed that he was talking about stopping the heart, but I guess I was wrong. Eighty-eight, ninety-two . . .''

In the Cage there was darkness and silence such as Adam had never known. With nothing outside of him to distract, he was, quite naturally, pulled within.

The anatomical map of his brain exploded into focus.

Without any effort, the vista expanded, his mind going from the bundles and fibers of brain and spinal-chord macroanatomy to microanatomy, the level of individual brain circuits. He saw the sparks sizzle, the individual electrical messages speeding on their way, and he sped them or slowed them upon command.

He was falling, plunging into the fibrous branches of a

nerve cell. Shrinking, shrinking, swimming among the organelles, finally sliding along the twisting helix of his own DNA.

And then there was nothing but light, tiny balls of blistering light.

*I'm seeing . . .*

*This is . . .*

But the attempt at words failed, and Adam was suddenly rushing into the light, swept up in a surge of power where all human limits vanished, and he was everything he saw, everything an overloaded mind reconstructed in the only ways it knew how—with lights, and pressure, and a roar of sound that was a physical pressure.

Then the lights began to flow and link together like a connect-the-dots coloring-book picture, and suddenly there was a face in the light.

A face furred with golden hair, its lips curled back from a mouth full of razor teeth. As he watched, the hair began to disappear, and what remained was lizardlike, hungry, its eyes running with blood, its breath thick and corrupt, and it hissed at him, saying, "Now. Mine. Come to me, Adam—"

And it opened its reptilian arms to him, darkly crusted talons spread wide.

The mood in the room abruptly altered, and Algernon laughed uneasily. "Well, he sure put one over on us. He's worked out a way to *increase* heartbeat."

"Not so difficult." Deckart sniffed, and rubbed her temples as if they were tender. "Visualizing an intense athletic event or romantic encounter, or even an increase in temperature can do that. The average person—"

"We're up over a hundred now." Culpepper was grinning broadly. "And you can't tell me that he's doing push-ups in there. Respiration is still down. We'd be able to see if he was disturbing the leads."

"A hundred and twenty and climbing."

"Temperature?" Culpepper's smile was broken momentarily by a wince. He looked up at the lights. "Need to replace the bulbs in here, I think."

"Ninety-nine and stable. Pulse is up to a hundred and thirty-two."

Micki shifted uncomfortably in her seat. "I don't know about this. Is that healthy?"

"Oh, hell, yes. For an athlete in Adam's condition, a hundred and eighty wouldn't be dangerous."

"It had better not be." Algernon bit his lip, and a tiny, worried furrow had appeared between his eyes. "Because that's exactly where he's headed. Christ, it just took another jump, and he's over a hundred and fifty. Climbing."

Micki lowered her head. Algernon touched her gently on the shoulder. "What exactly has Adam been doing?" he asked. His voice wasn't as calm as it had been even a moment before, and when Micki looked in his eyes, there was a troubled vagueness there. "He used to tell me everything, but now . . ." He shook his head. "He's grown a lot more secretive, and I don't know what he's into—"

"One hundred and eighty. Climbing." Algernon was perspiring now, and the expression on his face was worried and growing more so by the moment. He looked like a man who had just run a race. "A hundred and ninety." He looked up, openly worried now. "Dr. Culpepper, I'd say he's proven his point, wouldn't you?"

"Let's wait." Culpepper fidgeted, stood, paced. He was still squinting. He shook his head and took off his glasses, peering through them at the light above his head. "Let's see what happens, shall we?"

"There is one difference," Micki said. She got up from the chair, and paced over to the metal sheet blocking light from the isolation room. "He's started talking about the *kundalini* more."

"*Kundalini?* What's that?"

"Indian mysticism," Micki said. "Self-directed human evolution. Adam's been talking about it for months. There are traces of the concept in just about every culture on the planet. The serpent myth in Genesis. Quetzalcoatl. The staff pictured in the Hippocratic oath. He thinks that Savagi has something to do with it."

"Savagi again?"

Micki gave a tinny, disgusted laugh. "Savagi. He's everywhere. Magazine articles, film clips. Everything Adam can get his hands on. Savagi believed that there was a perfect proportion of breathing patterns that would wake up what he called the reptile mind, a primitive sector of the human hindbrain. Adam thinks he's found it."

"Jesus," Algernon whispered. "He's up to two hundred and thirty."

Culpepper's head whipped around. "What?"

"Two hundred and forty. Two hundred and fifty."

Deckart had gone pale. "Stop the experiment. He's going too far."

"Oh, nonsense," Culpepper said, but his voice didn't agree with his words.

"Go ahead and stop it, Giles," she said. "I'm really not feeling well anyway."

He clucked, shaking his head, and put a hand almost humorously to his chest. "I'm pretty excited myself. Palpitations." He laughed. "Don't worry. He can't go too much higher."

Algernon turned at his console to look at Micki. Her blue eye was in shadow, and the green was staring at him, the questions in it alive and frightened.

Deckart sat down heavily on the corner of a desk. Her face was pinched, drawn, and beginning to lose color. Perspiration shone in silvery beads. "Giles . . ."

"Two hundred and eighty-five. Two hundred and ninety-five. Three hundred—"

Deckart was hyperventilating. "Just by sitting still, Giles? I don't believe it. He's . . . he's done something to the leads. You and I both know it, and—"

"Jesus Christ." Algernon gulped. "Three hundred and twenty. Dr. Culpepper, I'm going to stop him."

Culpepper lifted a restraining hand, then fatigue overwhelmed him. "I'm not feeling well myself. . . ."

Algernon flicked the switch on the goosenecked micro-

phone in front of him. "Adam," he said softly, "Adam
. . . please come out of it now. The experiment is over."

There was no reply. Behind him, Deckart fell off the
desk.

She hit the floor heavily, her hand clutching her chest.
Micki tore off her sweater, bundling it to pillow Deckart's
head.

"Call the medical center," she said frantically. "Dr.
Deckart is in trouble."

Algernon looked at Deckart writhing on the floor, eyes
rolling white in her head and foam coming to her lips. She
had bitten through her lip now, and blood frothed from the
wound.

Culpepper was on the phone, and managed to gasp out,
"Sports medicine building . . . please hurry . . ." before
dropping the receiver and sitting heavily, gasping for air
like a man who has just run a marathon. "Stop him,
Swain. For God's sake, stop him."

Algernon looked at the register. "Three hundred and
fifty. Climbing. *Adam*, you've got to stop. Deckart is
having some kind of seizure. Culpepper—"

For once, Culpepper was looking his age. All of the
athletically maintained youth seemed to drain out of him in
a single terrible instant, leaving him a hollow, withered
shell. He was barely able to sit upright, staring balefully at
the metal plate in the wall, beyond the plate, as if it
concealed something that he no longer wanted to see.

"Three hundred and eighty. Three hundred and ninety."
Algernon bolted from his seat. "Holy shit. Four hundred
and we've lost him."

Micki got up shakily from the floor. Deckart was barely
breathing, her eyes fixed and staring. She shook Algernon's
shoulder. "What do you mean 'we've lost him'?"

There was a straight line on the ECG now, just a
straight line, no sign of cardiac activity at all. The air in
the room seemed to shimmer.

"I'm going in."

Algernon reached out, put a restraining hand on her

arm. "Wait. Take care of Deckart. I think . . . I think that Adam is all right." Under his breath, he added, "I hope."

The outer door opened, and one of the guards entered the room, wild-eyed. He staggered back as if he'd run into a wall. "What in the hell is going on in here?"

"Take care of Deckart," Micki said. "We have an emergency here."

The guard, a healthy barrel-chested teenager, was suddenly red in the face, and sweating. "What . . . what the devil is going *on* here? Jesus . . . I feel *awful*."

Micki, cradling Deckart in her arms, screamed at them, "Help this woman!"

She staggered toward the door, tugged at the handle, sobbed in frustration. "Algernon, the damned door is stuck."

Swain was still gazing at his ECG readout in stunned disbelief, and looked up at her as if his chin were strapped to his shoes with heavy rubber thongs. "Micki, I don't feel very well. . . ."

Culpepper toppled from the table, tried to roll when he hit the ground, but just lay there like a lump of dough dropped from a pantry shelf.

His body arced as if he had grabbed hold of a live wire and he screamed, an endless, quavering sound.

The shimmering grew more distinct, and Micki blinked hard. *My contact lenses. They must be dirty. I can't see straight.* Everything was wobbling in her sight, and Deckart's hands, clutching at the air, seemed inhuman, skeletal, with only a vestige of black rubber stretched over the bones, eyes rolling white in her face as the skin stretched and stretched and finally split, shriveled like fruit rotting on the vine, and a smell like a belly-burst corpse writhing with maggots filled the room.

"Micki"—Algernon was heaving for breath, bright droplets of perspiration shining over his dark face—"you can stop him. You've got to. He's killing us."

Micki swallowed hard, and tugged at the door handle again, set herself, set her feet, against the door frame and pulled with all of her strength. "Adam! What are you doing? These people are your goddamn friends!"

There was another sound in the hallway, and two men bearing stretchers appeared there. Blood slimed the room. The air was dark with flies, flies swarming everywhere, blotting out the light, crawling into their mouths and noses and ears.

Micki lurched against the door, her eyes closed. "It's not real!" she screamed. "None of it's real. For God's sake, help me open this damned door!"

One orderly seemed frozen to the floor, but the other responded instantly, ramming his shoulder into the door to loosen the jamb, then setting his feet to pull. "It's so *hot* in here," he panted, wiping his brow. "Bobby, get over here. We need your help." To Micki: "Are you sure this thing isn't bolted?"

"Look for yourself," she snapped. "The door doesn't have a lock."

The two men put their backs to it, and the door creaked and strained in the jamb, and began to move. Both men were sweating profusely, their feet slipping on the slimy floor as they fought for traction.

But the door was moving, was open an inch now. Micki fought to jam her foot into the widening opening. Her toes burned with sudden pain. The door opened another inch, and another, and she slid sideways, through what felt like a wall of fire.

The door slammed shut behind her, and she was in the darkened chamber. There was a greater mass of darkness in the center. She stumbled toward it with her heart thundering in her throat.

The lights in the room flickered on, and for a second she was taken aback.

The muscles in Adam's face and neck were so distorted that it was as if there were air or fluid bladders under the skin, swelling until he was a beet-faced grotesquery, almost unidentifiable as the man she loved. Her world whirled.

"Adam . . . ." Every fiber of her being screamed for her to back away. He was shaking, his breathing a tortured,

hyperextended wheeze, spittle flying from his mouth, lips
stretched in an insane grimace with the strain of the effort.
It was Adam and something more, something that terrified
her, but she kissed him, pressed her lips against his even
as her heart felt ready to burst in her chest.

His mouth was cold and unyielding, hard and dry, but
she forced her tongue between his teeth and kissed him
more deeply, crying now, and squeezing his shoulder,
digging her fingernails in, and his pupils slid back down
and wobbled like those of a drunken fish.

"Micki," he said in a thick, syrupy voice, "what . . . ?"

She pillowed her head against his chest, and cried in
relief.

He was shaking, and she could see the fear and confusion in his eyes, the disorientation as he took in his
surroundings and realized where he was. His breathing
broke rhythm, grew wilder, louder, as he fought to nor-
malize it. She heard the jackhammer explosion of his
heartbeat slow, slow, the muscles in his chest relax, and as
the tension left him, he released a great sigh.

"Adam . . . Adam . . . Where were you?"

"I . . . don't know. Not sure. But I want to go back,
Micki. I want to go back."

"Back? Why?"

"The power. The hunger. It's real, Micki." He laughed
hysterically. "It's realer than any of this. Savagi knew
about it."

"Savagi," she sobbed. "Damn Savagi. He's all you
ever talk about anymore. I hate him."

He put a warm, damp hand over her mouth. "Shhh.
Don't say that. Don't even tease," he said, and she could
feel him pull back from her a little. "Don't say that." The
warning in his voice was as cold and hard and immovable
as a granite monolith. "Don't ever say that."

"Or what, Adam?"

He stared at her, through her. Little muscles in his
cheek spasmed.

He paused, the wildness finally draining from his eyes.
His breathing normalized. Behind her, the control room

door opened. There was no blood on the floor, not a single fly in the air. Deckart was being helped to a stretcher. Culpepper was staggering to his feet.

"Just don't," he said flatly. "It might not be safe."

# Chapter Eighteen

# Death Dream

> *Kundalini can be understood on both a physical and a metaphysical level. The root word* kunda *means "pool," and the kundalini of the world is the molten pool of primordial elements at the core of the Earth. . . .*
>
> *The kundalini of mankind is centered in the sexual region of each individual and is an "inner fire" with tremendous potential. . . .*
>
> *Sexual contact is particularly liable to stimulate and awaken the kundalini within. Lovers sometimes experience kundalini spontaneously, through the natural convergence of life energies during love-making.*
>
> —Nik Douglas and Penny Slinger, *Sexual Secrets*

*As individual branches originate from a common root, so do individual human beings share a common root of consciousness. We are apparently separated by time or distance, culture or sex, but all power is determined by our acceptance or rejection of these illusions. Intense experience of many kinds clears the mind of such notions, returning us to the root of all knowledge: unprejudiced, original perception. We are left naked and trembling before the ultimate reality:*

*that together we created this world and that together, we may change or destroy it utterly.*
— Savagi, *Death of the Soul*

# Tuesday, March 13. Day 112.

Micki walked back from the bus stop, a cold March wind whipping her skirt up around her calves. Fruitlessly, she strove to concentrate on the day's business at Good Life. Regardless of her attempted focus, her mind continued to slide back to the previous week's unresolved events.

The two alternate tracks of thought chased each other in diminishing circles, like rabid dogs biting at each other's tails and legs. All other thought, all other feeling, had fled howling from her mind.

And as she turned the corner onto Virginia Road, it was no longer possible to pretend that there was a sane resolution to the dilemma she faced.

Adam's house was foreboding to her now, full of dim spaces and dull night sounds.

*I'll stop, Micki. Really, I will. I'm not doing the meditations anymore. I don't need it.*

But when she woke in the middle of the night, the rhythmic sigh of his breathing filled the room, as if Savagi's spirit had hooked into Adam as tenaciously as a tapeworm.

But where a tapeworm drained strength, Adam seemed to generate more and more energy. Endless, almost obscene potency, his metamorphosis leaving no aspect of his body or mind intact. His sex drive had increased in the same geometrical progression as his strength and mental powers.

Although at times she tried to be nothing but a vessel for his release, he inevitably pulled her with him, tirelessly, with aching intensity, until her screams shook the house, and there was nothing in her world but the driving, hypnotic rhythm of his body, and the unwavering brightness of his eyes.

Her key slid stiffly in the lock, and as she nudged the door open with the tip of her shoe, she knew that something was wrong. "Adam?" She heeled the door shut behind her. "Adam?"

BeDoss greeted her at the door. (When had the orange and black fur ball grown up? It seemed only yesterday that he was about a measuring cup of hair and claws. And now he was grown, with an entire house to run around in. Still affectionate but somehow not quite so adorable. Dogs and cats, she reflected, are the price we pay for puppies and kittens.) The cat rubbed against her ankles and she took a moment to return the affection.

"Adam?" There was no answer, and no sound, but she knew beyond any doubt that he was in the house.

She walked back around to the kitchen, and found the cellar door standing open.

"Adam?" she called into the cellar's dark, rectangular mouth.

There was still no answer, but she walked carefully down the stairs, groping along with one hand, the other searching for the light switch.

She hesitated. He was probably meditating again, and might be upset if he was interrupted by a painfully bright burst of light. On the other hand, if she didn't turn it on, she could easily take a nasty spill.

She flicked the light on.

There were twenty steps down to the floor of the cellar. Four months earlier, there hadn't been anything down there but old books and magazines. Adam had seized the opportunity to build his gym. As she came down into the basement, she saw the heavy blue punching bag hanging from a rafter, it's sides scuffed and tarnished. Adam had broken three chains already.

And all around the walls, covering every square foot of pale yellow plaster, were clippings, Xeroxes, and reproductions of a withered, bearded man who peered at her from beneath wiry eyebrows. No camera had ever caught him smiling. Not for an instant was there any projection of normal human emotion. She tried not to meet that leathery face, but wherever her eyes went, there he was.

Adam sat in lotus position, spine straight, on the corner of his tatami mat.

His shoulder-length, square-cut hair was splayed around his shoulders, dark strands plastered to his face with sweat. Except for the thick muscles in his shoulders and upper arms, he was built more like a runner than a fighter, and becoming thinner by the month.

Without warning, without initiation of any kind, he *uncoiled* from that seated position and sprang twisting into the air, launching simultaneous kicks in opposite directions, his magnificent body stretched bowstring taut for a moment that seemed without time. Then he landed and folded back into the lotus.

And uncoiled again, both feet lashing to the front, striking the heavy bag with an impact that slammed it into the ceiling. He bounced off the ground, torqued, and kicked with the back of his foot as the bag came down. It bent double in the middle: there was a popping sound from the ceiling, and the metal brace, fastened into the ceiling's main crossbeam with four eight-inch screws, ripped free. The bag crashed into the wall. Plaster, chickenwire, plasterboard, and plywood surrendered with a roar and a shower of dust.

Adam stood, his back muscles swollen until he looked like a posing bodybuilder, then he relaxed and turned to face her. She froze. His eyes were dark, dead pits, the eyes of a man who had never smiled.

"Adam?"

"They forced Culpepper to kick me out of the program," he snarled. "I can kiss my work-study goodbye."

"Why?" Even more uneasy now, she came a little closer. "Did they say why?"

"Deckart claims that I falsified my instrumentation, slipped some kind of psychedelic gas into the ventilation system."

Micki came closer now, and said the words that she had

been afraid to ask for an entire week. "Adam . . . what *did* happen?"

"I touched the Oneness," he said reverently. "Can you understand? Even you? The place in which there is only one being, one isness."

"I still don't understand."

He stared down at his hands, tensing and relaxing them. "What I saw. You wouldn't believe what I saw. No one could."

"Try me. Please. Give me a chance."

"You'll laugh. No? All right. I'll try. There was a man named Feynman, who won the Nobel prize for his work in quantum electrodynamics." He frowned. "It was either Feynman, or another man, named Wheeler. Anyway, one of them suggested that a positron could be seen as an electron going backward in time. Do you see the implication? From that point of view there is really only one electron in the entire universe. It goes forward, and it's an electron. And then it goes backward, and it's a positron, and then it goes forward, and we think it's *another* electron, and then it goes backward, and forward, and backward . . .

"And there's only this one electron in the entire world, and its time path is knotted . . . knitted, creating all matter in the universe. Do you see?"

Micki shook her head slowly, but she had taken an almost imperceptible step backward. Her skin itched, as if she were standing beneath a power line.

Adam's voice had become shriller, more irritated. "If it is possible to stand aside from time, then all electrons are the same electron. If I can control a single electron in a single neuron in my brain, I can control all electrons. And I can run it forward and backward, forward and backward."

It was clear that he could read the growing confusion in her face, and his body was growing tense. Micki's skin crawled. She looked at the backs of her hands, her throat tightening as she watched the individual hairs on the back of her hand lift away from one another and stand up like fine brush bristles. "I still don't understand. It's only a theory . . . but if it were true, how could you control an electron?''

''There's a principle proposed by a man named Heisenberg dealing with that level of reality. It implies that the observation of a phenomenon involves the observer in the process. To observe is to control—''

''Yes, but—''

''*I saw, damn you! I saw!* All I've been doing is learning to feel inside myself, sharpening my perception, and there's *no end to it!*''

The last was a scream, a challenge, a plea for understanding hidden beneath a mask of rage. Micki took another step backward, casting about her for a stick of incense, of charred paper. *Something is burning, I can smell it.*

''You don't believe, and you were there. No wonder that bitch Deckart thinks Culpepper set it up.''

''She *believes* that? After what happened?''

His voice shook with rage. ''Of *course* not. She said that from her goddamn hospital bed, with her arm paralyzed and a needle up her nose. I hope she dies.''

''Adam!''

He was breathing hard, but still, even in the height of his exertion, she recognized the slow whistle of the pattern, that prolonged exhalation, the moment when his breathing seemed to stop altogether, like a beach awaiting the next kiss of the tide.

The blood roared in her ears, and the fillings in her back teeth were aching now. ''Adam, you can't stop, can you?''

''Culpepper will help me. He has to. He knows what I've found.''

''Adam, you need help.''

''I'M GETTING HELP!''

It *hurt*. The sound, the anger, and something more that she couldn't understand at all, but the air was burning, shimmering around Adam, and his hair was fluttering as if stirred by a tame whirlwind.

''I don't need this. You know what I'm going through. I lost my job, and I lost my work-study, and I'm losing my father. The only thing I have right now is this!'' He slapped his glistening pectorals with his palms. "This, dammit, and I'm going to make it the best in the world. I can do things that no one else can do, and you damn well know it. I've lost too much already, but if I have to lose you, I will, because I'm going all the way.''

"All the way . . . to what?''

His oiled, muscular body gleamed in the light. His face was cold. "I don't need anybody. I don't need anyone who doesn't understand.''

"Adam, this has gotten out of hand. You need an expert—''

"There are no experts. I am the expert. I've never been anybody, Micki. And now I can be somebody. If only you knew what it felt like. If only you knew the power.''

"What I know, Adam, is that I don't feel like watching you destroy yourself. I can't do that.''

"Then *get out*.''

A trick of the light. It had to be that, because suddenly a nimbus played about Adam's head, and within it, for just an instant, tiny, delicate lightnings crackled and died almost before they registered in the eye or mind. The buzzing in her ears grew painful, and the throb of her heartbeat was like the slow roll of a kettledrum. She staggered back. "Adam . . .''

He shut his eyes and turned his head, hissing. Suddenly the sensation of pressure, the itching, crawling feeling, and the pain faded. The smell of burning air dissipated like candle smoke in a breeze.

"I won't hurt you, Micki. Ever. But it's not safe for you here anymore. You have to go.''

His head was still turned. His fingers slowly bent into hooks, cables crawling in his arms. He was fighting some terrible inner battle. Fighting, and just barely winning a stalemate.

"All right,'' she said. "All right, Adam. I'll leave. But this isn't over. This isn't over by a long shot.''

She composed herself, smoothing her hair down, and backed out of the basement. "I love you.''

He swallowed hard, face still averted. "I . . ."

"I know," she said. "I think I know."

"You don't know anything. You couldn't know. No one knows." He sank down onto his side, curling up into a ball. Sweat glistened on his skin like amniotic fluid. "No one could ever know. . . ."

Micki climbed the stairs from the basement, up the living-room stairs to the bedroom that they shared.

Into a single large suitcase went as many of her belongings as she could pack. At first she folded garments with forced calm, but as images of the open cellar door and the darkness within, the sound of phantom footsteps on the stairs, up the stairs, came to her again and again, she began to pack more quickly. Then suddenly she was shoveling her clothes in breakneck, stuffing them, finding an old paper bag to jam more into, every instant hearing a heavy tread on the wooden slats outside the door.

She slammed the suitcase lid down, her blue frilled slip catching in the lock. She gripped her purse under her arm, the suitcase in one hand, and the shopping bag in the other, and fled down the stairs, and out of the front door, the aluminum screen slamming behind her with a hollow bang.

# Friday, March 30. Day 95.

Adam emptied the last of the brewer's yeast into the dark, purplish half quart of beef blood in the clear plastic receptacle of his Osterizer Pulse-Matic blender, threw in a short handful of vitamin capsules, and pushed the button marked "puree."

*Micki.*

He had to throw the bolt on that thought, or he wouldn't be able to help himself. Would have to call her, to touch her.

Micki. In the three weeks since their breakup, the thought

of her had colored everything in his life, and only the deepest meditations offered relief.

Adam turned off the blender, and poured the dark, pungent stew into a glass.

She'd see. She'd see when he started competing, started breaking world records.

The beef-blood mixture had a taste that went beyond taste. He *felt* it flowing down his throat, as if it were still alive. Fresh from the slaughterhouse in Compton, still warm, still—

*Can't breathe.*

Adam was dragged from a maze of daydreams choking, gagging for air. His eyes flew wide.

Blood clot!

No! How could—

And there, sitting on the sink, was the capful of anticoagulant that he had forgotten to blend in. His throat spasmed, and he clawed at it desperately. He could feel the knot of jellied blood sitting there, jamming his esophagus. His lungs strained to move it, and failed.

*Calm. Remain calm.* He could hold his breath for well over three minutes. There had to be a way.

He sat cross-legged on the floor, pressing his fingers against his diaphragm, and pushed, and pushed . . .

Nothing, and the room was starting to spin.

He clawed frantically at his throat now.

This wasn't right! It wasn't fair! To come so close, and now . . . And now . . .

He closed his eyes and quieted his hammering heart. The darkness grew almost total.

*I am here. If this is the moment, take me. I am ready.*

Waves of red light washed through the blackness, his body's final warning. He itched, he burned, he was racked by chills, and the sticky, gummy clotted mass in his throat seemed to swell with his panic.

*Quiet. If this is the moment of death, so be it.* But there was light within the darkness, and as he quieted, it pushed toward him.

He surrendered, and dove to the heart of his fear.

Down through the darkling corridors of his brain into their innermost chambers, the vista swelling exponentially with each passing moment.

*The light! The light!* Impossibly bright pinpoints of colorless brilliance, pulsing, swelling . . .

Closer. The energy was so intense that he felt flayed, but with death so close, he had no option but to move closer, and closer still. And the individual point fragmented into a nest of flaming bees, the bees moving around and around the surface in a sort of Brownian movement.

Closer. Into the heart of the darkness, until one of the "bees" swelled to fill his vision, revealed itself as a luminous cloud concealing a point of unimaginable brightness. Searing, burning, the entire universe coming together, roiling, flaming, and Adam screamed, *My mind my mind*

*OH GOD MY MIND*

Adam's head slammed into the floor, and he gagged, coughing, something slippery-thick between his teeth. The clot spewed up and out, and finally lay there on the kitchen floor, quivering like a blood-brown amoeba.

He gasped for breath, steadied himself, and then staggered to the telephone, dialing Culpepper's number. It rang almost a dozen times before the familiar twanging voice answered, "Hello?"

"Dr. Culpepper. It's Adam."

A moment's pause, and the harshness went out of the voice, replaced by something else. Fear. "Adam, it's almost midnight."

"I almost killed myself."

"What? What in the world are you talking about."

"I . . . I forgot to put the anticoagulant in the beef blood."

"Jesus, boy. You shouldn't be drinking that stuff in the first place. And now *this*."

Adam wiped the back of his hand across a sticky forehead. "I know. I know . . . but it tastes right. It's what my body wants right now. It's the right fuel."

"Not if you make another mistake like that. Adam, you're pushing yourself too hard. Just too hard. Stop drinking the beef blood."

"You don't understand. I'm not drinking it because it tastes good." He fought for the right word. "I feel . . . *compelled*. It doesn't taste good, it tastes *right*."

For the first time, Culpepper sounded like an old man to Adam. One who just wanted to get off the phone and get back to sleep. Dreamless sleep, if possible.

"You're not average, Adam. You're not . . . I tell you what. I don't care if they cut off my funding. You come into the lab next week. I want to run a series of tests. I'm . . . worried. Maybe I should have been worried months ago, but it's not too late."

Something within Adam growled. *He doesn't understand, either. No one understands. He doesn't understand, but he knows too much.*

Adam shook that thought out of his mind. "We'll see."

"I think you should stop, Adam. I can help you."

"We'll . . . see. Give me some time."

Adam said something else into the receiver, but he didn't hear himself say it, couldn't recall what it was. Then the line went dead, and he sat there.

If he couldn't trust Culpepper, whom could he trust? Algernon?

No. Algernon would just tell him to see another doctor besides Culpepper. But how could Algernon know? How could *anyone* know who hadn't experienced the Power?

If they knew how little food he ate, they would think it impossible. Or if they believed it, he would be locked up, locked up and treated like a freak.

Well, they would *never* . . .

The light from the window streamed in currents, and his eyes could detect individual motes of dust, follow them.

And the light itself was more than light. In the dimness, he could see a shell of colors around his own body. The warm air he exhaled glowed in the darkness. He couldn't actually *see* heat could he? And yet, how else could his brain make sense of it?

How else could he explain the fact that he could look at the wall and visualize a hole there. A hole peeling away like a rent in living flesh.

Just an illusion, but when he walked over to the wall and touched it . . .

It was *hot*.

Suddenly very conscious of his breathing, Adam threw on his clothes. He had to get *out* of there. To somewhere. Anywhere.

The building housing Bob's Cowboy stood at the corner of Santa Monica Boulevard and Highland Avenue, and had once been the largest roller skating rink in Southern California. But a decrease in the popularity of roller skating lead the owners to the decision that Country Western was a more direct path to a higher tax bracket. The entire building had been remodeled from top to bottom, and outfitted with a new sound system, a new look. The bucking bronco on the roof, for instance, had certainly not been there in the days of Roller Boogie.

An entrance ticket cost seven dollars at a front, barred window. A rather surly guard glanced at his driver's license and stamped the back of his hand as he entered.

The lobby of the Cowboy was carpeted with wood shavings and hung with neon blown to resemble the intertwined loops of a lariat. The people who passed him were dressed in fake buckskins and fifty-dollar jeans. Many of the women were startlingly bright redheads whose hair was braided tightly. The men were tall, or walked as if they were, and on the whole there was a healthy, hearty aura that made the animal in his mind retreat into its cave for a while. He breathed easier. Cowboy Western memorabilia covered the walls. Plaques, photos of rodeos, the result sheet for a mechanical bull-riding contest, a Miss Sundance beauty

contest announcement, rows of medals and ribbons won by
customers or employees, a notice organizing a bowling
team, and an entire bulletin board announcing horse shows.

The neon ceiling kept flashing, and at one branching
hall it split into two directions, the green twisting away
from the red. A sign said that following the red would take
him to the pool hall. He followed the green.

There was raucous sound ahead, and the smell of alcohol. Dry sawdust tickled his nose, and the floor vibrated
with stamping feet.

Bob's Cowboy was still hopping at almost one-thirty,
filled with men in flannel shirts who were still hoping to
find someone to soothe their emptiness, women in leather
tie-up boots looking for a quick intimacy fix.

The dance, the formalized sexual ritual, the men and
women moving through the room as in choreographed
arabesques, truncated *pas de deux*, bobbing and weaving
on the horseshoe dance floor, drawing close, flashes of
intimate conversation, drinks bought and shared, moments
of testing the electricity, generating the spark. It was
impossible not to see the patterns behind the patterns, and
Adam's mind was overwhelmed with music, and sound,
and thoughts that had never entered his mind before.

It was funny that he had never noticed the *smell* before,
the intertwining scent of dozens of human beings in heat,
only partially masked by perfume and cologne, melding
into a synergistically intoxicating web.

As he watched the dancing, an incredible sexual ache
began to boil in his crotch.

He would leave, that was what he would do. He would—

There was a soft touch on his shoulder, and he turned to
look into the eyes of a woman whose hair was incredibly
white, somewhere beyond ash blond, with brilliant blue
eyes. "Mind if I sit down?"

*Hell, yes, I mind. Get away from me.*

A flipbook of images flashed before his eyes. Where
had he seen her? Oh, yes, on the floor, dancing with a tall
thin man in denim overalls who seemed to have vanished.
Her body, in a red sequined dress that fit tighter than a

condom, was perfect. In five, maybe ten years it would be overripe, but tonight Adam couldn't turn away from it.

He touched the seat lightly. "I was saving it for you."

She laughed, flashing a small fortune in orthodontics. "Thank you." She brushed her fingers through her hair in a practiced movement, her hair spraying around her shoulders like a shawl.

She waited, and he could almost hear the gears turning in her mind. *I've gone as far as my courage will let me. It's up to you now*.

Adam turned, staring into the mirror, and waited. He already knew that he wasn't going to say a damned thing. Her tone, her posture, said that she was intrigued. Dimly, he remembered a time when he would have died if a woman as beautiful as this had sat next to him, let alone tried so hard to strike up a conversation.

*If she wants me, she can work for it*.

The utter, blatant cruelty of that jolted him from complacency, silenced the small voice.

She fidgeted, running her finger around the rim of a glass of light brown fluid she had ordered while his back was turned.

"What have you got there?" he asked, curious.

"A Washington Redskin," she said, her expression suddenly alight. "Scotch and cider. Try some?"

He nodded. She ordered him one and he took a sip. The apple juice smoothed out the scotch, but the alcohol hit his empty stomach like a bomb.

The room spun as his body fought to compensate. His heart trip-hammered, his blood raced as the alcohol was oxidized.

The yammering in his mind quieted, and the exploding lights behind his forehead darkened. He downed it as if it were beer, holding up two fingers to the bartender.

The girl, who had chattered on obliviously, was suddenly silent. She was staring at his hand.

A yellowish line of callus framed the edge, and the palm was taut with muscle. The fingertips looked squarish, almost deformed, and when he relaxed them there was something about the way they curled together that suggested a claw. She pressed his hand. It was as soft as a cat's paw.

"Who *are* you?" she asked, finally.

"Adam. Name's Adam. I'm just someone who didn't want to be lonely tonight. And you?"

"Monica Pember," she said, and they shook hands. "I just wanted to get the kinks out. I love to dance." She finished her first drink and started into the second one.

His head was swirling, buzzing, as his body fought to metabolize the alcohol.

"I don't dance," he said quietly. "I hope that doesn't rule out all possibilities." He drew a slow line along the back of her hand.

Monica stared at his hand, taking it in both of hers. "Your hand is *hot*. Have you got a fever?"

He smiled without humor. "We don't know each other, and maybe we never really could. But I'd really like you to come home with me."

She released his hand and leaned away from him, staring.

"I'm sorry." He pulled out his wallet and laid a couple of bills on the bar. "I shouldn't have—"

"No, wait." She pulled him around until she could look directly in his eyes, questioning at first, then taking his hand again. "You're kind of weird, but I like you. Why don't you let me get my coat?"

He watched her sway off to the coatroom, mind swirling. *You mean it's as easy as that? All I had to do was ask?*

Adam drove Monica to his house. She tried to catch her breath and think about what it was that put her on edge about him.

Twice during the ride she almost asked him to pull over to the side of the road and let her out. There was something about the way he wove effortlessly through the traffic that made her more than uncomfortable.

It seemed that the traffic opened up for him, that he simply turned the wheel and spaces appeared, or that he somehow knew where the holes would be before they came into existence.

His hands, strong and supple, played on the wheel, spinning the car like a boy, weaving it from lane to lane sinuously.

Yes, that was it. *Ease.* His total control of the situation was unbearably exciting, almost frightening.

He pulled into the driveway and killed the lights, then turned and looked at her.

He didn't move closer to her in the car. His face was thin but perfectly clear, except for a very slight scarring, perhaps a memorial to long-ago acne, and the dermoplasty that had removed all traces. His eyes were huge and dark and somehow sad when framed by the mane of black hair.

"We're here," he said. "You don't have to come in, Monica."

For an instant she doubted his words, then realized that he was sincerely offering her a way out. She leaned over in the car and kissed him. His mouth tasted like spice.

He swung out from his side of the Cortina and opened her door. "Please."

She gathered her handbag and followed him timidly up the stairs. Adam opened the front door and went in without waiting for her.

When she entered the house, he was standing at the bottom of the stairs, his hands folded like a little boy's.

Much of the house was filmed with dust, had not been picked up or cleaned. Books were stacked in tumbled profusion, and much of the furniture had been hastily slip-covered and never used.

"Is this your house?"

"It's my father's. He's in the hospital, and I'm kind of taking care of it for him."

"I hope he's going to be . . ."

Something in his expression made her stop. She closed the door behind her. "Are you sure that you want me to be here. I'll go . . ."

He held his hands out to her and pulled her closer. He didn't kiss her, didn't try to grind his body against her or grope her. Just held her, and again, she heard a silent voice cry out, and this time it screamed for help.

As if she weighed nothing at all, he picked Monica up and carried her upstairs.

He lay on his side next to her in the darkness, his breathing slow and steady. No, not steady. There was a rhythm there, something that Monica couldn't quite fathom, but that was like the tidal ebb and flow of an eternal ocean.

Physically, she was satisfied. If she had wanted to pick up a lover who would fill her sexual needs, she had found him. Control was no problem, no issue for this man. Neither was sensitivity to her most complex and spontaneous movements, or anticipation of her deepest needs.

Except one. Adam had never reached orgasm. Almost as if something were holding him back. She could see it in his eyes, a look that reminded her of her last boyfriend, a postal clerk named Roman. She had said "I love you" in the night, in the darkness, and Roman's breathing had almost stopped as he wondered what to say, what to do, how to deal with the awesome awkwardness of the moment.

So when this man, with his magnificent body and the soft, frightening hands, his gentle kisses and eyes that seemed lost in a world of pain, when he turned away from her at last, she could not sleep.

"Please," she said finally, touching his shoulder. "Let me help you. You've given me so much. . . ."

He seemed scared of her, unwilling to let go, but for the first time in months she found herself *wanting* to give something to someone, and she clung to him until he turned back to her, and she held him, rubbed him, kissed and whispered small encouragements, and finally rolled him onto his back and mounted him, moving in the special way she had, the one that usually made men scream with pleasure.

He looked at her with huge, dark eyes, questioning eyes, eyes that saw things that weren't in the room, weren't in her world, and he began to move stiffly, jerkily under her.

She felt as if she were one of those electric globes in a Frankenstein movie, sparks flying up and away, tearing her body into fragments, dissolving into fire. As she peaked again his back knotted under her fingers. His gasp was the first warning hiss of an exploding boiler.

There was a rippling sound, and she turned her head in time to be shocked by her reflection in the dresser mirror, her hair literally standing away from her head like pine needles, a glowing plasma surrounding both of their bodies just before the mirror *flexed* in its oval casing, distorting their reflections like fun house oddities. "Wait, stop!"

But he was thrusting powerfully now, panting, gasping for breath, and she screamed as the room turned inside out, and the lamp next to the bed burst into light and slivered crystal.

She screamed as the water glass at the side of the bed exploded. As cracks ran the length of the mirror, and it burst as if a pile driver had slammed it from the rear, spinning glass shards over the entire room.

As he thrust one last time his cry shivered the room. He felt *hot*, her skin flamed and prickled, reminding her of the time she had used an electric hot comb with wet hands and feet and her entire body had convulsed with the shock.

*I'm dead!* she howled silently, but as the mattress burst into flames she was still alive enough to throw herself free and dive clumsily to the floor.

Adam rolled from the mattress, beating at it with the blanket, with his hands, until the fire died down, and slow smoke filled the air.

She looked around the room, now strewn with glass and splinters, thickly misted. And she began to tremble. "Who are you?" she said. "*What* are you?"

His hands were smudged with soot and burned, his naked, perfectly formed body glazed with sweat. He said nothing.

Shaking, she pulled her underwear on, was still pulling her dress on as she stumbled from the room, watching him. "You're not human. I don't know what it is with you, mister, but I don't want anything to do with it."

He heard her hurry down the stairs. Heard the front door open, and shut, imagined her making her cab call from the telephone at the corner.

Adam glanced down at his hands. The singed flesh was shiny and melted, until he concentrated, and the skin grew darker, and then swelled with blisters.

The pain faded.

It was under control.

Everything was under control.

# Chapter Nineteen

## Goodbye

## Tuesday, April 24. Day 70.

The nurse, a short plump woman in crisp, spotless white, tiptoed silently through the room, tucking in this, straightening that, adjusting the curtains, the flowers, then circling out of the room as if she had never passed through at all.

She barely even looked at the bed, and at the thin, wild-maned figure sitting on its edge, holding the withered hand of Gunther Ludlum.

Whatever spark of life had remained in Gunther's face was almost extinguished now. His complexion resembled nothing so much as a pale piece of plastic fruit. His eyelids trembled, three-quarters closed. His mouth moved almost constantly, but no words came forth. His eyes moved jerkily, but saw nothing. Death, long making its slow approach, was coming in a rush now.

"Father," Adam whispered, "I don't know what to say, and I don't know if you can even hear me. I just wanted to say that I've always loved you, and always will."

Gunther's exhalation was a thin wheeze.

"I'm sorry for all of the things that I wasn't. I tried, God, I tried so hard. All I wanted, I think, was for you to approve of me. Silly, isn't it. So silly. Stupid. But there it is."

Adam held his father's gnarled hand to his cheek. It was shriveled and clawlike, and as cold as the hand of a corpse.

"I don't want to lose you."

Adam fought, searched for words to say, anything, and was lost. Finally, and because there was nothing else to do, he warmed his hands, visualized them in clouds of sparkling white mist, and soothed the lines in Gunther's face.

Slowly, some of the stress lines began to drop out, and Gunther relaxed, stopped moaning. One of his arms trembled slightly, disturbing the trailing tubes that lead to the upright rectangle of the chrome chemotherapy machine. Medical science's last attempt to arrest the deterioration was flowing into Gunther Ludlum's veins a sluggish drop at a time. There was a bubble in the tubing, but it remained in a bend of the tube, bobbing back and forth with each pulse of fluid.

"Rest, Father. It's all done now. Nothing left to do. You're going home. I'm fine. I'll be fine. You've done everything you could for me. I'll miss you. I'll miss you so much, but . . ." He bit his lip. "It's not bad, not so bad, I think. No more pain, no more."

Adam had to stop, his voice finally giving out. He lowered his face to Gunther's sunken chest, wanting to cry, ashamed that the tears wouldn't come.

"*Adam.*"

The word had to be in his own mind, couldn't have been Gunther's, but Adam looked up. The eyes were still closed, but were more relaxed now.

"Adam, stop."

"I can't help it, Father. I love you so much, and I've never been able to just tell you."

"Ad . . . am." The ancient lips barely moved. Gunther squeezed Adam's hand.

Adam sent more warmth into his father's body, and Gunther seemed to relax, the tension draining from him like water squeezed from a sponge. The dark fringe of Gunther's aura lightened, and his breathing grew calm. His eyes still closed, Gunther moved his lips silently.

Adam leaned close.

"Sorry," Gunther said. "Always . . ."

The voice weakened again, and Gunther was very quiet. Then he said, "I'm coming, I'm . . . Adam? I can't see."

"I'm here, Father."

"Adam? Don't leave me."

"I won't."

For a few minutes there was no sound in the room, just the hall sounds from outside, and the low hum of the air conditioner. Then: "Adam . . . I love you."

Adam prayed for tears, damned his dry eyes. He cradled his father in his arms, rocking gently until the light slanting in through the venetian blinds was a dim crosshatching on the damp bed covers.

There was nothing else said in the room, and two hours later, without any fuss or fanfare, Gunther Ludlum quietly stopped breathing.

# Chapter Twenty

## An Ending

*Friday, August 23, 1977, UPI. The body of the controversial health guru known as Savagi disappeared from the Colorado Springs Morgue this morning. Savagi, a Pakistani emigrant, had lived in this country from 1924 until death by apparent assassination two days ago. Police and the El Paso County Sheriff's department are investigating . . .*

## Thursday, April 26. Day 68.

\<Micki\>

The thought, the image flashed into Micki's mind suddenly, echoing in a spot in the back of her head, precisely one inch above the hairline. She forced it down, forced it back, and concentrated on the job at hand, inventorying pamphlets at the Good Life.

"Michelle. What are you trying to forget?"

She jerked as if someone had dropped an ice cube down the back of her neck. "Huh?" Donna Maria, her day manager, was standing over her, her cropped, punkishly pink-tinged hair and outrageously straight teeth barely showing above an armload of record albums. "What are you talking about?"

"If a demon prodded your behind with a pitchfork whenever you stopped to rest, you couldn't work more neurotically. Can a person work psychotically? I doubt it, but if they could, it would be you. So when are you going to take a break?"

"All right. In about five minutes." She shrugged. "It looks like nobody ever puts these back in order. Sometimes I think there's a sign around here that says, 'Please make a mess; Micki needs the work.' " She tried to sound breezy, but Donna's face didn't lose the thin, concerned smile. "You can't con me, Lady. It's that man of yours, I bet."

"He's not my man anymore."

Donna barked laughter and walked away.

Micki rubbed the spot at the back of her head, because the thought was there again, the one that said

<Micki>

So strongly that she wanted to shriek. Her recent life, the events of the past two years, had been neatly, desperately compartmentalized. Already, the incident at UCLA, the evening in Adam's basement had been tucked quietly away. Books in her own store spoke of the paradigmatic denial phenomenon, where an event that would threaten the participant or observer's structured world view is trivialized, rationalized, and explained away before the crack in the cosmic egg becomes fatally wide. Because without that structure, disorientation and, sometimes, insanity could result.

But the compartments were too full, and every time she turned her attention to one, the others began to spill open like overstuffed file drawers, their contents tumbling to the floor.

<MICKI>

She licked her lips nervously, pushing herself to a standing position, glancing around the store. He wasn't here, she hadn't heard his voice or name. But still, she knew beyond any doubt that she would see him, that he would come in today, because . . .

Because he had been in the previous Thursday, that's why. She heaved a sigh of relief. There was a *reason*, and that made things easier.

That lie dissolved before it could even completely solidify. He hadn't been in for weeks.

She was sweating now, and tucked the rest of the pamphlets back into their positions, dusted her hands on her dress, looking around the store. Things seemed very quiet. Altogether a good time to take a break.

She tucked the last of the pamphlets into a corner and sidled back to the break room, clicking the lock behind her. The teapot was steaming on its hotplate, and she sighed at the thought of a glass of Constant Comment tea. It would help to get a few kinks out first.

Micki plopped into an overstuffed wicker chair in the corner of the room. She could close her eyes for a moment. Not much more than that, or she might go to sleep.

She never even heard the door open. "Hello, Micki."

Adam's face was handsome and healthily gaunt, so thin that for a half second she doubted it was him. A distance runner's leanness. His eyes were very bright. He stood with his back to the door, hands behind him.

"How . . . did you get in? Did Donna give you the key?"

"No. No one saw me. That's the way I wanted it."

He smiled as he walked toward her, hips swinging freely, right hand outstretched. He seemed to be moving in slow motion, and his smile was just a mask. Trapped beneath the mask was a raw, animal scream.

He kissed her on the cheek.

"Adam, how are you?"

"Fine, just—" *I'm not fine*, his eyes said. *I'm not anything even distantly related to fine. Help me, Micki.* "Just fine." His eyes flickered from side to side. "Can we talk?"

"Of . . . of course. Tea?"

"I'd like that." Suddenly she was glad that he had

come, and was no longer confused about the precognitive flash. Why, he had probably been in the store all the time, and she had heard his voice.

Why, she had probably heard the familiar cough of his car as he parked it around to the side.

Why, . . .

They sat on opposite sides of the break room. The water heater, dry when she entered, was building up a new head of steam. She dropped her eyes to the floor, not wanting to meet his directly. If she did, she would melt, and she just couldn't let that happen.

"What's new, Adam?"

His face was blank for a moment, then he swallowed. "My father died Tuesday."

"Oh, Adam. I'm—"

"He started failing on Monday. I was with him for the last twenty hours."

The question she needed to ask almost caught in her throat. "Why didn't you call me?"

He couldn't have heard her, so lost was he in his own thoughts. "I was there. I was sitting next to him. He was barely breathing anymore. Just a wheeze. And it went on and on for hours. Got weaker and weaker, and then finally just . . ." He gestured with those absurdly delicate and expressive hands, and Micki's heart broke for him.

"Adam"—she grabbed his hands, held them tightly— "why couldn't you let me be there? For God's sake, I cared for him. I fed him. I've known Gunther almost as long as you have. I should have been there with you. *Why wouldn't you let me be with you?*"

"His breath, Micki," he said in a small voice. "It's all in the breath. It connects us, and binds us, and—" He shook with suppressed emotion, then was suddenly calm again. "There wasn't anything to be done, Micki. I just watched him die. That was all."

For a long time silence blanketed the room, and then he whispered, "Micki, I really need you to come back."

"You should have let me help, Adam." She pulled back away from him. "If only . . . But you don't understand, do you? You really don't. But this is the last straw. I can't take it. You've just shut me away and away, and I've tried to hold on and hope."

"I'm so close," he said, miserable. "I'm just so close."

"Adam," she said, "I want you to tell me the truth. Could you stop if you wanted to?"

A flash of fear in his eyes told her that she had struck bull's-eye. "I'm all right. Honestly."

"When was the last time you had a physical? Do you even know what's happening in your body anymore? Do you even *want* to know?"

Adam hung his head, wordless.

"When was the last time you talked to Culpepper? Or Algy? For God's sake, Algernon is your best friend, and you've shut him out of your life. Shut everyone out of your life."

"I don't want you out of my life, Micki. I can get it all back, Micki. It's not so bad. Just some side effects. I can deal with them. Please, come back to me."

"I love you, Adam. I won't watch you destroy yourself."

He stood, blinked a few times, and finally smiled. "Then I'm sorry, Micki. I guess that I won't see you again." He brushed a few strands of hair out of his eyes, and for a moment, he was the old Adam again. The urge to hold him was a physical craving.

They stood on opposite sides of the room, and Adam's fingers were twitching. Once again he seemed to be smaller than he was, and weaker, and younger, and far more frightened than this tanned, muscular man with the poise and balance of a professional dancer.

He pivoted, heel-toe, and left the room.

She stood with her fists balled up, leaning on the desk between piles of books and posters, vials of liquid incense and pressed, arranged flowers.

Coming out of the back room was like emerging from a dream, and she ran to the front window in time to see Adam walking down the main pavement, recently redone with little ceramic swirls set in the concrete.

A woman was talking to him out there, and she felt a

pang of jealousy, until she identified the thin, unattractive figure as a member of the Savagi sect. Micki had seen her there before, passing out her pitiful handful of tracts and speaking in that whining, nasal voice.

But now the woman approached Adam with something different in her manner. It was tentative, as if she was afraid of him. When they spoke, the woman lowered her head obsequiously.

Adam ignored her, and the woman dropped her hand away.

After he left she lifted her skirt at the sides and ran across the street to a car. She leaned in the window to speak to the driver, and pointed after Adam, who was disappearing around the corner.

The driver nodded, and started his car. He made a U-turn and headed after Adam. As the car passed the window she could see the driver: a cadaverously thin man with short graying hair and a somber smile that was somehow disturbing.

She wasn't really worried. Adam could more than protect himself. Still . . .

The woman with the tiny handful of tracts stood there, almost sadly, watching after them, then walked slowly back to her place beneath the fir tree in the Good Life's front yard.

There was something new in her face now. Hope. Light. Like a sun worshiper who has seen the first dawn.

# Tuesday, May 1. Day 63.

Adam drove aimlessly, trying to quiet the rush of blood in his ears, to make sense of the thousand jumbled thoughts vying for his attention.

His father. The burial arrangements. (Or cremation? Absurd, but an old Monty Python routine went through his mind: "*And he'll burn up, crackle crackle crackle, which of course could be a bit painful if he's not quite dead yet.''*)

There were things to be done, letters to write, attorneys to engage, all to do with his father's

(Death)

His head snapped around as if a quiet word had been spoken in the empty car, whispered lovingly in his ear. He whimpered, the sound breaking low in his throat.

He was salivating, swallowing heavily. His throat felt sore, and his head hurt almost constantly. His vision was a blurred nightmare.

He barely saw the other cars, yet avoided them effortlessly.

At another time, it might have been fun, weaving in between the worms. Worms? Strange how that image popped into his mind. The cars were like time-lapse photographs of automobiles, long, wavering vaguely metallic shapes thinning into insubstantiality at either end. There was a story about that, a science fiction story, but he couldn't remember it, and thinking about it made his head hurt.

He stopped at a traffic light, and a group of teenagers, laughing, talking, holding one another, moved across the pedestrian lane, not looking at him, but straggling, one stopping to kiss a tiny girl with short black hair and a gold ring in her nose.

The light turned red, and Adam honked. One of the boys turned defiantly and slammed his palm on the hood of the car.

Something red and wet leaped from Adam's mind, and his foot slammed down on the accelerator. The boy barely leaped to safety as the car roared past him.

He stood, screaming in the intersection, his girl friend holding onto his arm, flicking an angry, frightened finger after the disappearing Cortina.

Adam drove down Crenshaw Boulevard past 31st, and stopped the car before he even knew exactly where he was. He was parked in front of a pet shop, the fish tanks in the windows bubbling merrily away, tiny gold and silver creatures weaving through the water within a myriad of miniature castles and forests.

Suddenly it wasn't an aquarium anymore; it was the front window of a gymnasium, and white-suited figures were marching up and down across the floor, the sweat from their bodies steaming the mirrors lining the walls, and at the head of the class was a calm and beautiful man named Mitchell Shackley.

Entranced, Adam got out of the car and staggered toward the window.

Shackley? Here? But everyone said that he had gone far, far away. That he had finished his business here in America, had scaled every pinnacle and was ready for the next stage in his evolution. Was gone, had just disappeared, and would never be seen again.

But there he was, in that crackling white karate *gi*, as handsome, as dynamic and perfect of form, as blur-fast and awesomely powerful as he had ever been, and in Adam's vision Shackley's movement was even more beautiful than it had been in the past.

"*Sensei* . . ." Adam said, and tears started down his face at the sight. "Oh, God, *Sensei*. Help me." He pushed at the front door, pushed, and pushed, and it was locked.

It rattled in his hands. "Please, sir. I've done everything that I was supposed to do, and it's all coming apart."

He shook the door again, heard the chain jingle, the bolt shaking in the lock. "Please, *Sensei*." His hands gripped the sliding metal bars that protected the store from vandals, from thieves, that had been tested to a breaking strength of 1,200 psi.

"Can't you see me?"

He pulled at the bars, shook them frantically. Someone walking down the other side of the street pointed to him, and one of the passing cars slowed down to look more closely.

Adam screamed, "*Sensei!* Let me in, for God's sake." Something was ringing distantly, but he didn't really hear it or understand it until he looked down in his hand and saw the steel grating, twisted and broken, standing from the steel track as if ripped away by a machine. The lock on the door was buckled in, the links of the chain bent and distorted, and the door was hanging half open.

For a bare moment reality intruded, and once again he was standing in front of the aquarium, and there was nothing real but the gentle bubbles, and the silvery, swimming creatures, and the ring of the burglar alarm, and the twisted iron fence.

A chill rippled through him, and he ran back to his car, driving away as quickly as he could.

Everything had gone wrong, and was getting worse. There had to be an answer, and he had to find it.

What was happening? Who had caused it all? Why was it all so wrong, so

(Dead)

wrong?

Everything was swirling faster and faster now, as if all thought and all action were bringing him to a point that had been decided before he was born. There was something to do. There was something within him that was, that had been, burrowing its way to the surface for weeks, months, long years, and it was almost there. Almost.

He needed something to set it free. He needed someone to understand.

Monica. If only he'd had more time with her. Time to explain. She had been wonderful.

The pounding in his head was killing him, and he could barely think, but he knew what he had to do, and where he had to go.

Adam smiled, and guided his car off through the traffic.

# Chapter Twenty-one
## Bob's Cowboy

For some reason that he didn't completely understand, Adam parked a block southwest of Bob's Cowboy.

He sat in the car for a while, listening to the radio, listening to KCOC. There were no more admonitions to listen to Eddie Roach in the morning. Eddie Roach didn't work for KCOC. He didn't work in Los Angeles at all. As far as he knew, Eddie wasn't working in radio, anywhere, and after he left the hospital, he had disappeared.

But music was music, and the removal of a single purveyor of rock made as much real impact as the removal of a single cowflop from the Ponderosa's North Forty.

But the truth beyond that was that the radio was playing, and Adam couldn't hear it. The music reached his ears, but before it impacted on his mind it had been filtered, and the only sound that he heard from the 5¼-inch stereo speakers stapled into the corners of the floor was a sibilant hiss that would have greatly surprised KCOC's sound engineer.

Adam's eyes were open, but he wasn't totally awake.

Just as when he lay in his bed at night, eyes closed, and mind wandering in dream, he wasn't totally asleep. He could hear the sound of the house creaking, of BeDoss purring in the corner, could hear it when the cat would stop purring and watch him through slitted eyes.

BeDoss wouldn't sleep on the bed anymore, would barely allow Adam to pet him. Would sniff an extended hand and recoil.

Adam blinked hard. The colors seemed too bright, the sounds too sharp. He felt as if every body sensation had been amplified a hundred times. The beat of his heart was a roaring tide, the feeling of his body producing its dozens of metabolic waste products a constant tremor.

When he opened the car door and stepped out, the screech of the hinges bending and twisting was a blistering groan, and the whispering scrape of his tennis shoes on the cement like sandpaper against a live microphone.

The night was alive with noise, the stars so bright that he could almost feel their heat.

When he asked himself why he was there, where he was going, what he was doing, his mind answered not with words but with the image of a smile, a savage, feral gleam that whispered for him to be silent and simply follow his feet along.

He stopped at the corner, gazing down Santa Monica Boulevard at the neon glitter at the end of the block.

Chevy pickups and station wagons and four-wheelers and jeeps and Mustangs were pulling into the parking lot. There was laughter and good spirits in the air, and women with fully rounded bodies escorted by men who had that healthy, good-ol'-boy outdoorsy look, one gained by laboring in the sun for long hours, or by broiling in tanning parlors for short minutes.

He caught a glimpse of himself in a store window, and felt a fleeting moment of chagrin that his long hair was uncombed, slicking it back with his palm. A man said something about "hippie" as Adam brushed past, and a woman hugged her escort's arm more tightly, pulling close, as if there were a threat.

Tonight, a Loretta Lynn ballad about sexual reciprocity was blaring from the loudspeakers, and as he walked through the entranceway up to the front door, he suddenly became aware of the smell of perfume, beer, and human sweat, mingled together in a suffocating mass, and he had to concentrate on his balance, the seesaw of hips and spine, to keep from vomiting.

The security guard at the entrance was huge, and wore a dark brown vest with a tiny name embroidery that read "Ernie." Hard muscle bulged under the vest, and his hands were callused. His eyes were as cold as his smile was friendly, and he scanned the passing faces for potential troublemakers.

The man was palpably disturbed by something. Adam handed him his ticket and presented his wrist to be stamped.

Ernie was at least three inches taller than Adam, but Adam had the eerily distinct feeling that he was looking *down* on the security guard.

"Do I know you?" Ernie asked.

"I've come here before, if that's what you mean."

"Oh, yeah? Where'd you hear about us?" The man put on a smile that was supposed to be friendly, but betrayed the hint of a nervous tic. He was playing for time, running through a mental file of mug shots and doing his best to place Adam.

"A friend."

"Maybe I know your friend," Ernie said.

"Name's Algy." Adam felt his head pounding, fought to control his temper. "Listen, I came to find someone, not to play twenty questions. Do you mind?"

Ernie finally hunched his shoulders, giving up. "Yeah, sure. All right. Have a good time."

As he rounded another bend he caught a glimpse of the horseshoe-shaped dance floor. The couples gliding along it could have been riding a sliding mechanical belt, so elegant were their movements.

Some of them were beautiful, and some exceptionally plain. Some were whipcord slender or muscular specimens, others roughly sculpted blubber, but all of them radiated joy, and sharing, as if this were their way of ending the day together.

He walked up to the brass safety rail that separated the

drinkers from the dance floor. The neon above his head blinked insistently. He craned his neck back, and the flashing color washed over him, painting his face blue, then green, and then red. The music was slow and sweet, and with the smell of sawdust and alcohol and good healthy sweat he calmed the yammering thing in his mind, and almost had the strength to take control of himself and leave this place of happiness before something ruptured the bubble.

One of the brown-vested men brushed past him. There were eight of the security men in sight, and they scanned the room carefully. When their eyes met his, they stayed on him for a beat longer than casual interest, and sometimes one nudged another, as if recognizing trouble.

They were at the corners of the upper floor, and one walked the perimeter of the dance floor, and one by the men's room with the "Out of Order" sign across the doorknob. They carried themselves with the heartily aggressive nonchalance of former Marines, the physical posture that says "I can break your arm or your neck. I won't, because I'm such a great guy, but don't mess with me, pencilneck."

Very subtly, and at a distance, they were bracketing him. He hadn't done anything, *anything*, and already they had labeled him a troublemaker. Well, by God, if those monkeys were going to climb his tree before he even had a chance to . . .

He rubbed his temple, hard. There was a headache coming on, and it wasn't going to do anything or anyone any good if he lost control. Relax.

He wandered back until he found the back bar, and sat. Three bartenders worked it, and he didn't recognize two of them.

The third was the man from the previous night. Adam moved down to a stool at his end of the bar.

"Hey."

"Hey," the man answered, the corners of his mouth twitching in welcome. His oversized t-shirt was emblazoned "Bob's Cowboy. We cheat the other guy, and pass the savings on to you!"

He wiped the bar and slid in a napkin. "What'll it be?"

"How about your name?"

"Charlie'll do. What'll it be?"

"Heineken. And a little information. I met a girl in here the other night. Name of Monica. Remember her?"

"Oh, oh, yeah." He flashed a man-to-man smile. "Nice-looking action there. Didn't get the number?"

Adam laughed. "No, I didn't. Wondering if you'd seen her."

"No." The smile was gone as quickly as it had appeared, and a foaming glass of brew appeared on the bar. "Buck fifty."

Adam sat, drinking, listening to his breathing, to the sound of blood boiling in his ears, trying to calm himself.

He wanted to see her. To talk to her. It just wasn't fair.

There was so much happiness in the room. In every part of the room except his little corner of it. It just wasn't fair.

A couple stood in the corner of the dance floor, not really dancing at all. Their arms were locked around each other, their mouths glued together in totally unself-conscious intimacy.

Adam watched, watched as their bodies, locked together, swayed to the music ever so slightly, and was overwhelmed with a sudden wave of loneliness.

There, two booths down, a woman drank by herself. She even smiled at him briefly before turning back to her drink. Adam picked up his beer and walked over to her table. "Excuse me." She smiled up at him. Her face was a little thin, but the eyes were nice, and the hair. "I was wondering if you'd like some company?" He heard himself saying the words, but heard them as if from a distance.

The answer came from behind him, in the form of an enormous hand grasping at his shoulder. "No, she don't, Buddy." The room flashed red and Adam turned quickly, his spinning shoulder smacking the man's hand away.

The man was big, at least thirty pounds heavier than Adam, but carried much of it around the waist. He was more than slightly tipsy. "Sorry. I didn't mean anything."

"Yeah, well, get moving."

Adam nodded, stumbling back to the bar, the pounding in his ears rolling into thunder. All he wanted to do was disappear. "Again," he said to Charlie. The bartender looked at him doubtfully. A frosted glass was tilted under a tap, and a river of foam pissed into it. Charlie set the beer on the bar and spun it down to Adam, where it stopped gently, just inches from his nose.

Adam nodded, and took a sip. It tasted strange, unpleasant, but there was something in it that he needed. Yes, that was it. There was something in the beer that was going to make something else easier to do. Would make him feel freer.

Maybe Micki was right. Maybe he needed to go to see Culpepper. But he was healthy. More than perfectly healthy. Wasn't he?

*Your hand is hot. . . .*

Heat. He looked at the beer in his hand, concentrated on it, relaxing, visualizing the heat running to his hand, and his hand began to tingle. Yes, heat. If he concentrated . . .

He took another sip, and the beer was no longer cold. It was lukewarm at best, and he laughed out loud. If only they knew! If only their tiny minds could even *conceive*. He could see the heat surrounding the other patrons, the lights, layering the air currents. And by willing it, he could interact with that heat, and . . .

Suddenly the beer was steaming. Boiling. Foaming, and flowing over the edge and onto the bar, and Adam was laughing hysterically, laughing and crying because it was all so damned silly, and none of it made any difference.

The bartender was there almost instantly with a towel, frowning. "Hey, let's not make a mess here." He mopped and then touched the rag. "Hey, Buddy, this is *warm*. What the hell did you do? Barf on the bar?"

Adam wiped his hand across his face. "No, Charlie. I'm sorry. I just got a little carried away. Bring me another one, would you?"

"You've already had too much."

"Aw, come on."

"I can't. Now, don't cause any trouble."

"Trouble my ass. I just want another *beer*." Adam punctuated that with a slam of his fist on the bar that shivered the surface, knocking glasses sideways, making a hollow *boom* that thundered through the room.

The dancers stopped dancing, and the five-piece band stopped playing. All over Bob's Cowboy faces turned to watch him. Adam pushed at the cracked wood, smiling foolishly. "I'm sorry. Really. Don't know . . ."

Suddenly everything—his father, Micki, his job, his lost grant—all of it came boiling out like beer foam over the lip of the glass, and Adam was sobbing uncontrollably, unable to do anything but lay his face against the wet bar, choking on his own grief.

Charlie touched his arm. "Hey, Pal, are you all right?" Charlie jerked his hand back, looking at his fingers in confusion, rubbing them together.

The music and the lights were swarming in, and it was becoming more and more difficult to maintain. There was nothing threatening, only pain and sympathy in this man's face. But the thing inside Adam was growing, and it took more and more effort to keep it down.

"Why? I never hurt anyone. All I wanted was to grow. I just wanted to be someone—"

Charlie was out of his depth. "Listen, Pal . . . I'm sorry. I wish I could help." He backed off.

He walked away to wait on another customer. Adam, wrestling with his emotions, won. The anger was drowned in tears, and the tears became a torrent, and all of the regret and resentment boiled out of him and he was sobbing, and slammed his fist down on the bar, splinters and chips of shellac flying.

Adam smashed his hand down on the bar again. Mugs and glasses toppled off the counter, and customers were clearing away. He looked into the mirror and saw the face of a stranger, a haggard, fleshless human mannequin, so thin that the cords in his neck stood out like bundles of sisal as he shook with great whooping sobs.

He barely noticed the pain in his hand and then looked

at it, watching the blood run down, tiny slivers of glass like crystal boats gliding along a stream.

There was nothing here for him. Nothing anywhere, perhaps. He had passed some point that he hadn't even known was there, and the light within him had gone out.

Suddenly there was a gloved hand on his shoulder, and Adam turned to face one of the security guards.

The patch said that his name was Mars. "Come on, Bud, let's go." A second man stood behind him to the left, a third to the right.

So. That was the way it had to be. He stood up slowly, and turned from the bar, nodding his head, and walked toward the door, barely hearing their words, feeling only that something deep and irreparable had been broken inside him, died before it was born, a dead fetus rotting in its emotional womb.

Wallet. He had left his wallet at his seat, and Adam turned, grabbing it.

Mars said, "Hey, we told you—" and shoved his shoulder. The wallet whipped out of Adam's hand.

There is a very subtle difference between a push and a punch. A punch has the quality of brissance: it explodes through the target, accelerating as it goes. A push or a shove *decelerates* as it hits the target.

When physical emphasis is required, a push is the less hostile, more civilized thing to do. But Mars, bored, irritated that evening, and having received a final finger of farewell by the last ejected drunk, was in no mood to be as professional as he might have been, and that tiny difference in the focus of his energy was interpreted exactly as it was meant by the thing growing inside Adam. A direct message, animal to animal, smiles and politeness and civility notwithstanding. Adam turned, slid the wallet into his pocket, and snarled.

Mars grabbed his arm, jerking. In extremely precise coordination with that push Adam's right hand shot out in an open-palm blow to the guard's midsection that traveled twelve inches and struck like a hammer.

The security man gasped and staggered back, stumbling

against a table, and as he did, one of the men at Adam's side began an armlock, a standard maneuver that takes the subject's struggles and turns them into pain.

But he felt no resistance. That entire quadrant of Adam's body relaxed as if it had turned into overcooked spaghetti. Adam's right foot scythed along the floor, as if the lower body were unconnected to the upper. The guard's feet flew from underneath him. The lock and everything else were forgotten as he performed the arm-slapping-floor breakfall necessary to save himself from injury.

And the rest of it, almost all of the rest of it, right up until the end, happened in a kind of crazy slow motion that wasn't slow at all. That was hyperspeed, totally out of control yet so starkly crystalline that every facial expression, every movement, was more distinct than anything Adam had ever experienced.

The third guard punched, but punched directly into the point of Adam's elbow, shrieking as the finger bones shattered.

The second guard struggled to his knees, was smashed down again. Adam turned to meet the charge of the third guard, who moved in absurdly slow motion. Adam stepped in and kicked the guard in the stomach so hard the man dropped where he stood, purpling on the floor, diaphragm paralyzed.

A beefy customer tried to grab one of Adam's arms, and Adam felt the *thing* within him boil to the surface and *snarl*. He shrugged, and as he did, the man flew across the table and landed on another group of customers, who screamed, scrambling to get the hell out of the way.

Adam vaulted over the rail separating the upper from the lower floors. He landed lightly, spun and kneed over a table, spraying the entire contents into the guards that were running up.

*Stay away from me!* he tried to scream, but the words emerged from his throat as nothing more than a blood-maddened snarl.

One of the guards tried a flying tackle from the rear. Adam grabbed an arm and pivoted, heaving him into the rail headfirst with a horrific cracking sound. Adam, watching the carnage as if from a distant place, screamed *Stop it!* to a thing that was out of control and growing stronger by the moment.

Another guard squared off in a karate stance. Feinting with a kick, he moved straight in with a lunging boxer's punch. Adam leaned sideways, and the punch grazed his cheek. The bunched fingers of his own right hand speared deeply into the man's larynx. Something broke. Eyes bulged, and blood spurted darkly between clenched teeth.

Sticks and bottles and knives were kicked or wrenched from their owner's hands, counters flowing so smoothly from the initial movements that it seemed their owners voluntarily jammed their eyes and groins and joints into Adam's weapons. The crowd finally broke and ran, scrambling to get away from this capering, crimson-smeared *thing* that crushed armed men into bleeding bundles of rags.

And all Adam could hear was his own heartbeat. He stalked across the floor to the men's room. The door was locked, an "Out of Order" sign slung across the doorknob.

His palm slammed against the door three times: on the first, the hinges shrieked in protest, and on the second, they cracked and ripped from the jamb, the screws flying loose, and on the third the door lurched in the frame and burst away.

The room was empty save for urinals and a row of pay toilets. Adam ran to the window above the sink. It was grilled, but under the assault of his fingers the rusted wires crumpled like brittle vines. He got a foot up on the sink and was about to lever himself through when he heard the sound behind him, and turned.

Mars had followed him, face smeared with blood, scalp torn, one arm dangling useless. He clutched a folding knife in his good left hand.

"Come on, cocksucker," the security guard wheezed. "I got something for your ass." And he lunged.

Adam didn't see the bleeding, pitifully afraid man lunging with the palmed sliver of steel. He saw only the gem, a ruby gem rotating in the crown of Mars's head, a beckoning star, a glistening treasure so lovely that the hunger grew to monstrously strong proportions.

Adam ignored the knife, ignored it as it slashed once, twice, three times. He caught Mars by the hair. It should have been *impossible* for him to stand right in front of a man with a knife and remain untouchable. But he did so, and with that hair grip whipped Mars around, torquing his entire body to generate the power.

Mars howled in pain and fear, the scream chopped off in mid-note as Adam cracked the security man's body like a whip, a feat of such strength and speed and coordination that Mars didn't even realize that his neck was broken, just lay where he crashed onto the floor, his bowels and bladder releasing in a warm tide. He gazed up into the face above him, whispered "Mother" softly as the edge of Adam's hand smashed down onto and into his forehead.

The thing that had been Adam Ludlum cradled the security guard's ruptured head in its hands, seeing only the glistening red thing inside. The hunger grew, and he wedged his thumbs into the cracked skull and levered, the sound of splitting bones a primitive music to him.

But when he looked down into the pulpy mush of a shattered brain, he turned away with a start and was violently ill.

He heard the sound of sirens and returned to the thin grill protecting the window at the back of the lavatory. With crimson-slippery fingers, he wrenched the bars out, broke the glass, and was through the window and into the alley with the speed of a cat wiggling through a pet-door.

And as he ran to his car, he finally knew why he had parked where he had, and realized for the first time that part of him had known exactly what was going to happen that night, had relished the thought, and concealed it from his conscious mind.

And he knew for the first time just how badly he was losing the fight.

# Chapter Twenty-two

## Aftermath

*"Déjà vu,* Man. I told you it wasn't over."

Winston Gates poked at one of the broken tables with his toe. The metal rim was broken, the inch-thick glass shattered. What impact a human body had to have had to do damage like that, he could hardly imagine.

Three ambulances were still carting away the wounded. Fourteen men needed immediate attention. Three were badly injured, but all were expected to pull through.

Incredibly, there had only been one fatality, and Gates was saving that mess for last.

"One man. One man did all of this?"

Doug Patterson was coming back out of the lavatory, and his expression was sour. "Man, I have *never* seen anything like this before. Whoever this cat was, he came to play."

One of the security guards, a beefy specimen who had given his name as Redbone, was still sitting on the floor, nursing an arm that was twisted the wrong way. He had bitten almost completely through his lower lip, but was relaxed now that he had received a shot of painkiller. He waited for the stretcher.

Gates knelt down, searching Redbone's face for an answer. "Had you ever seen this man before?"

"No," he rasped, "and I hope to God I never see him again. You don't understand what it was like in here."

"I've got eyes."

"No," Redbone said vehemently. His rust-colored beard shook as he fought to keep his teeth from chattering. In better circumstances Redbone would have been a strong-featured, good-looking man, but now he looked frightened and lost. "You don't understand. *No* one human being should have been able to do that. I don't care who he was."

"Not even Bruce Lee?" Patterson tried to laugh.

"Screw Bruce Lee. The Incredible Hulk shouldn't have been able to do this. Not the way we're trained."

Gates looked at Redbone, at the USMC tattoo on his arm, the thick ridges of muscle flaring out from the neck to the shoulder, the thin razor scar on his cheek, and nodded his head. "Were all of them trained as well as you?"

"Some better. Mars Peach was Cal State Judo Champion *before* he went Ranger, for Chris'sakes. He and I handled six drunken sailors last Christmas. And this guy went through Mars like he wasn't nothing but a faggot."

Patterson glanced over at Gates, and Winston could tell he was on the edge of a smart-assed comment. Mercifully, it remained in the planning stages.

The paramedics arrived with a stretcher for Redbone. "One last thing. Have you ever, anywhere, seen anything that reminded you of this guy? I mean, a gorilla on angel dust? What? What was it like?"

The painkillers were making Redbone drowsy, but he blinked hard, trying to think. "He moved like the best frigging karate man who ever lived, gone apeshit. Crazy. He was all right one minute, just kind of crying in his beer. Then Mars pushed him, and kind of sent him over the line. I guess that comes the closest. Scared the hell out of me, even before the shit hit the fan. Made my hair crawl."

"Best karate man in the world. Is that some particular image for you? Somebody's name come to mind?"

"Sure. Mitch Shackley, man. Best *I* ever saw, at least in this country. Screw that. He was the best."

Gates flipped out his notebook and jotted the name down. "And where can I find this man?"

"It wasn't Shackley." He laughed. "I'd recognize him in a sec. But if you can find Mitch, you let me know. He disappeared about five years ago. Mitch closed his school, sold his house. Nobody knows."

The drug was stealing consciousness from Redbone rapidly. "One more thing," he said, his voice slurring. "The air. The air was burning. You could smell it, man. . . ."

He closed his eyes as they strapped him to the stretcher, and was gone.

"Come on, Doug," Winston sighed. "Let's check the nasty part."

There was a dark blue chalk outline on the tile where Marston Peach had died. There was still blood smeared on the floor and the wall of the toilet stall.

"It's the same," Gates sighed. "I can feel it. And it's going to get a lot worse before it gets better, unless we can find this bastard."

His eyes scanned from the outline on the floor to the ruined toilet stall, to the heavy, bloodstained metal grill that had been ripped away like cheesecloth. "What kind of man could do all of this?"

"I got no idea. But one thing is for sure."

"What's that?"

The sun blinders on Doug's glasses flipped up, and his bright green eyes were deadly cold. "Brother, if I run into the sucker that did this, I'm putting his brains on the wall before I even *think* about the Miranda."

"You're a class act, Doug."

They made one more sweep of the bar before leaving for the morgue. He played the tape of the witnesses over and over in his mind as he looked, and was almost sure that there was something that he was missing.

*"He reached for his wallet, and Mars shoved him. . . ."*

On his third look-through, he found what he was looking for. There were just two scraps of cardboard lying on the floor. He picked up the first, and it was a silvered card for a place called InfraSystems Computer Ware.

The other was for a store called Good Life.

"Ever heard of either of these?" Patterson took them both, shook his head, then squinted. "You know, maybe I've heard of Good Life. Metaphysics. Incense, that kind of stuff. Over in Venice somewhere, maybe."

Gates slipped both cards into an envelope and slid it into his pocket. "We'll check it. I think we should get to the morgue. I want to see if they've come up with anything."

The room was a shambles, the wreckage scattered from wall to wall. The stench of yeast and alcohol and blood mingled with the sawdust and sweat, forming a stiflingly thick stew of aromas. He tried to visualize what it must have been like to be in the room when it was happening, and his imagination quailed.

"Come on," he said in disgust. "Let's go do something useful."

# Wednesday, May 2. Day 62.

Patterson was quiet in the elevator down to the basement of the Wilshire Police Department, and that in itself Gates found interesting enough to pull him out of his mood. "What's on the mind, Doug?"

"Something on the squawk box. A store on Crenshaw Boulevard last night. Bare-handed damage to solid steel grating. I think we had better look into it."

"Might be a connection." Gates shrugged. "Worth checking. In fact, we had better check any instances of abnormal strength. We've probably got a juiced up weightlifter type. Kung fu nut. Something."

The elevator jostled to a stop, and the doors sighed open.

There was always something sad about the basement, and Gates had long since gone from dislike to a kind of accepting hollowness over it. He knew that every time he came down he was going to see something that he didn't want to see. And yet the job demanded that he do exactly that, time after hideous time. The little girls, the old men, the boys caught in gang violence, the drug overdoses . . . no, he didn't get many of those. Those wouldn't be the cases given Gates. It was always the bizarre ones, the jobs that were just a hair this side of a Glad Bag—the housewife who cured her headache with a shotgun, the bookie whose irate boss threw him off the San Diego Freeway overpass at rush hour . . .

That was what he got, and he already knew that this was going to be worse than anything he had seen in a long time.

Gates stood silently in the doorway as Inosanto, their balding morgue tech, examined the body of a young black girl with a strange gash between her breasts. The Filipino hummed as his slender fingers probed the wound.

Gates cleared his throat, and Inosanto whipped around. "Gates! I didn't know you were here!"

"Evidently not."

"Later, Darling," he said, pulling the rubber sheet up over her face. He turned to the adjacent slab. "We've got a doozy here. Bruises in the shape of handprints here on the wrist. Note the discoloration." He looked up at Gates questioningly. "Do you have any idea how much pressure it takes to interrupt scapular access like this? We're dealing with maniac strength here."

"Wonderful."

"Let's make this official." He snapped on a plastic-cased cassette recorder and raised his voice for its condenser mike. "The deceased is a thirty-year-old Caucasian male who demonstrates a dramatic and unusual penetrating injury of the brain. The seven-centimeter-diameter point of entry is located in the median frontal area. This superficial wound has been created by the avulsion of two flaps composed of skin, muscle, and bone which were then displaced laterally." He lightly traced the edges of the wound with a thick finger. Doug turned away. "The jagged medial edge of each flap, further, demonstrates crush injury and contusion. The paucity of bleeding noted from the edges is probably secondary to spasms of the frontalis muscles, compressing ripped blood vessels. The path of penetration through the brain tissue itself follows an inferoposterior course, extending through the frontal lobes and destroying most of the corpus callosum. . . .''

Gates felt a little dizzy. He shouldn't have been. Lord knew, he'd been to enough autopsies. But still, he balanced uneasily on the edge of overload, and he had a strong, sudden urge to crawl away somewhere and go to sleep. Or maybe just curl up with Arlene. God, that would be nice. . . .

Inosanto droned on. "While its etiology is not yet clear, this wound is unlikely to have been inflicted by a projectile for several reasons. First, the skin surrounding the avulsed area is devoid of powder burns or scatter, though such a large superficial wound would imply close-range firing or exploding shells. Second, gross examination has failed to reveal a projectile . . .''

The morgue tech spoke and moved like an automaton, and Gates's sense of unreality grew more acute. He began wondering about things that should have seemed superfluous: What was Marston Peach's last meal? When had he last made love? What were his last thoughts? Had it been the image of a parent or loved one, or a final, defiant curse? And what if his consciousness in some way was still connected with the body? Would Inosanto's probing hands and instruments or the impersonal, somnambulant monotone of the autopsy report be more offensive?

"In fact, evidence for a two-step injury is furnished by the superficial crushing previously noted, as a powerful *external* force is thus indicated. The nature of this force, however, is not readily apparent.

"Immediate cause of death appears to have been uncal herniation—''

"Uncle who?''

Inosanto looked pained. "Uncal herniation. Tentorial pressure cone.''

"Thanks,'' Winston said. "That clears it up perfectly.''

"Let's try again. That is the herniation of the uncus, midbrain, and adjacent structures into the incisure of the tentorium as a result of a sharp pressure gradient from above—"

"I'm sorry I asked. Please continue."

"—with associated compression of the brainstem and cessation of vegetative function. The herniation itself is indisputably secondary to the displacement of tissue produced by the creation of the penetration path. Rapid stoppage of circulation is further indicated by the minimal subarachnoid and intracranial hemorrhage despite the severity of the wound." Inosanto clicked off his microphone. "And that about concludes it. Off the record, I would suspect some kind of martial arts training. Pretty intense. I've heard stories about the Japanese emperor's bodyguards, or perhaps the Shaolin monks. There just isn't a whole lot of evidence for a human being who can inflict this kind of damage with his bare hands."

Patterson was perspiring lightly, and his face was pale. "Crying in his beer one minute, and the next a bare-handed maniac that can wipe out a dozen trained men? This is comic-book stuff."

"So send for Superman," Inosanto said. "You might need him."

Winston tried to laugh. "Inosanto, if you come across anything you think I need, you know where to find me."

"You know it. Mostly I think you're going to need a bazooka."

Doug patted his sidearm, a Styer GB 9-mm loaded with SuperVel hollowpoints. He caressed its wood-grain grip nervously, then tried to disguise his nervousness with a laugh. "Listen, Win. I'm going down to the range for an hour or so. You want to come?"

Gates looked at the corpse on the slab and winced. There was something, something that niggled at the back of his mind, but when he couldn't get at it, he let it go—there would be another time.

"Yeah, I guess so," Gates said, and swung his coat over his shoulder, following Patterson out.

"Well. What's first?"

"You wanted to hit the firing range. Then lunch."

"You can think of *food* after that?"

"Wishful thinking. I'm hoping my stomach will settle by then. Then I guess we check out that storefront on Crenshaw."

"And then?"

"The lab will have pulled any fingerprints from the cards by then. If there's a lead, we follow it. Otherwise, we pick up a sketch of the killer, and visit InfraSystems, and a place called the Good Life."

"I'm ready for the Good Life," Patterson said.

"Ain't we all."

The elevator door hissed shut.

# Chapter Twenty-three
## First Contact

## Thursday, May 3. Day 61.

Despite the earplugs and muffs worn on the firing range, Winston Gates's ears were still ringing, a kind of sharp vibration that bypassed his ears to hammer his brain directly.

Doug Patterson hunched over the steering wheel, his eyes almost as bright as they had appeared just a half an hour ago on the range. It was always an experience to watch Doug: his reflexes were staggering, and Winston's distinct impression was that he had joined the force eight years before to have an excuse to continue playing cowboy long past adolescence.

His Styer GB automatic was an awesome sidearm, carrying an incredible nineteen cartridges. Gas-operated, it utilized a delayed blowback to soften the recoil. In any hands, such a tool was deadly. In Doug Patterson's, the Styer became something on the edge of the fantastic. Doug could put five shots in a five-inch target in ten seconds at twenty-five yards. Winston had seen Doug draw and fire on an ex-Army drill sergeant who already had the drop on him, putting a 9-mm slug between the man's eyes before his brain could send the message to his hands to pull the trigger.

"Whattaya think, my man?" Patterson asked. An Armour Hams delivery truck blared its horn at them as Doug swerved within inches of its front bumper.

Gates sighed, glancing at his notebook. He started a new one for every case, but this one already had sixty pages of information in it—there was simply too much connection with the other fourteen, no, fifteen, killings that they had identified nationwide. Another Judd? "I don't think the computer place meant anything in particular. Christ, my nephew Carl has a computer, and he's retarded. It's just a mail-order house for disks and other items, and their cards pop up all over town. No help. I have a better feeling about Good Life."

"Why? It's just a bookstore. Their cards are going to pop up everywhere, too."

"Yeah, but I bet it carries books on karate, meditation, all of that Eastern stuff. Maybe he's linked to the Temple of the Earth Heart, and maybe not, but I'll bet our killer is knee-deep in mantras."

"I'll tell you"—Patterson patted his side arm—"Gun fu beats all of that chop-sockie stuff."

"I'd like to reel this one in alive, Doug," Gates said quietly.

"Be better if it worked that way, but if it don't, better he than me. Or thee, for that matter."

"Mighty white of you."

A young uniformed officer whose nameplate read "Regents" met Gates and Patterson in front of the pet store. The iron gates had been ripped away like coat-hanger wire, and a tumbler of acid splashed into Gates's stomach.

"Witnesses?"

"Several. Descriptions of a male Caucasian driving a Toyota or Datsun. Haven't been able to lift prints yet."

"All right, then. Keep us posted."

Regents nodded. "This never would have happened back in the old days."

"Why?"

"This was Shackley's school, man, that's why. He was a neighborhood institution."

"Mitchell Shackley? Karate instructor?"

"That's the man." Regents nodded.

"Well," Gates sighed, flipping out his notebook, "that settles that. Second time our man's name has come up. There's *something* there, that's for sure. Regents, tell me: Was he really as good as they say?"

"Better. He wasn't the kind of man who's easy to forget."

"Where's Shackley now?"

"Nobody knows. He closed up the school about five years ago. There was some trouble. I heard talk about a Dojo war—whatever it was, he left in a *hurry*. I heard rumors he went to Tibet or somewhere."

Already suspecting the answer, Gates took a sheet of folded paper out of his pocket and handed it to Regents. "Did he look anything like this? This is the official composite on the killer. Pretty wild, but if you'd listened to the descriptions that we got, you'd be surprised that the drawing didn't look like a combination of Lon Chaney and Rocky Balboa."

The Xerox was truly bizarre. It was a copy of a picture actually drawn by one of the women who had been in Bob's Cowboy the night before. The eyes dominated the picture, although they were mere slits in a black and white etching. They were brilliant, volcanic, and framed in hair that had grown long and wild and somehow gave the impression of greasiness.

But most explicitly, and disturbingly, there was the distinct impression of feral energy. Something, some arrangement of the muscles, made Gates feel that the artist had had an animal in mind rather than a human being.

Regents shook his head. "Nothing. This guy looks like a freak. Shackley was fairly short, real elegant. He'd be almost sixty years old by now. No connection there."

"All right. Thanks."

\* \* \*

Gates and Patterson pulled up outside the Good Life bookstore. Once again Winston had the distinct feeling that there was something alive here, that it wasn't another dead lead.

There were a few scruffy-looking types outside the front door, and they gave him the creeps. He nudged Doug. "Recognize her? Temple of the Earth Heart, buddy."

The anorexic Sylvia recognized them as well, and backed away as the two officers approached the front door.

Just before they reached the door she screamed out to them, "Gates! Soon, man. He's back. You'll see. He's returned. All praise to Savagi. The great one has returned."

"Great," Gates said, and kept walking. Behind him, Doug was frowning.

The younger man spun on his heel. "We had another murder last night, and now you're telling me that Savagi has returned. What's the connection, lady?"

Her mouth stopped as if it had run into a wall. "No. Blasphemer! We do not countenance murder. That is your word, your world. We are love, and life."

"Uh-huh. You people are going to talk to us today. Count on it."

"You'll see!" she shrieked at him. "He was betrayed, but he has come back! He is revealed to us, and this time, his seed will take root. Your world is *ending*, fool. And you don't see it, you don't even see it—"

When the door slammed shut behind him, Gates heaved a sigh of relief. "Jesus God. So this is where the lost and lonely go."

"Everyone needs somewhere, my man." Patterson scanned the racks. "Look at this stuff, will you? Some of these diets are enough to gag a maggot. Come on."

He had spotted a shelf labeled "Tai Chi, Martial Arts" and browsed through it. Most of the covers portrayed white- or black-suited figures engaged in explosive action. "So you were right. Our Karate Kid might have shopped here."

A tall olive-skinned girl with straight short dark hair was counting money at the cash register. She flashed them a brilliant smile. "We'll be closing in five minutes, gentlemen. Can I help you?"

"Police business." Winston flashed the badge, and the girl's eyebrows raised a fraction.

"We're looking for the owner," Patterson said, and Gates looked around, scanning psychedelic posters and the incense, and the workers behind the counter.

"Michelle is out right now. I'm Donna Maria. What's the problem? Parking again?"

"No. We had a little situation over in Hollywood last night. Several people injured, one dead. Ever seen this man before?"

Gates reached into his suit pocket and pulled out the folded Xerox.

Donna shook her head, but she was looking very closely at the picture, and her eyes were troubled.

"What's the matter?" Gates asked quietly.

"I . . . don't know. I'm one of those people who has trouble identifying someone from a photograph, and a drawing. *Madre Dios*, it looks like whoever drew this was watching *Movie Macabre*. Nobody really looks like that . . . but there's something about it. There are so many weird types that hang out in here. I'm sorry."

"Not half as sorry as I am. Can we ask the other employees?"

"Sure. Anyone who's still here. Go ahead. Good luck. Ugh. What a creep."

The Good Life was closing up, and Gates watched the cash register through the window.

He scanned the street. It was mostly deserted, except for a few last straggling customers making their way to various cars. There came a Barracuda, its sleek dark predatory shape gliding through darkened streets. Behind it rolled a dark-green compact car. It killed its lights quickly and turned its wheels to the curb. A dark thin shape climbed out with a disturbingly fluid flowing movement.

*"Like a Toyota or Datsun or something. . . ."*

Gates couldn't quite see the license plate from where he was, but . . .

"Come on, Doug. Let's take a look."

"Why not," Patterson grunted. "So far the Good Life has yielded diddly."

Dusk was falling quickly, and the street was mostly deserted. The figure was still walking through shadows as the two men approached, but then stopped still, hands hanging limply by his sides. Nothing threatening, nothing that should have been at all alarming, but Gates was profoundly grateful for the feel of the .38 against his side, and for the memory of Doug's skills.

When they were within twelve yards, the man turned and bolted, cutting across a weed-infested lawn to the alley beyond.

"Bingo," Doug snarled, and limped after him. Gates scanned the street behind them, then drew his revolver and followed.

Doug waited for him at the mouth of the alley, Styer drawn and leveled. They had a good view down to the far end. All of the lampposts were glaring brightly, throwing one another's shadows at odd angles all over the gravel-coated stretch of concrete.

There were a few trash cans, but nothing large enough for a man to hide in or behind. The branch of an avocado tree hung heavy over the fence.

"He might have vaulted the fence. Nothing to stop that. Hell," Doug said, and the first sign of nervousness crept into his voice. "*I* could do that. Easy. He could be anywhere by now."

Sudden alarms blared in the back of Gates's mind, and the hair at the back of his head itched fiercely. "Yeah, he could be anywhere, including right here. I think—" Gates had halted his forward motion, and begun to turn, and that very slight alteration of momentum was all that saved him as something skimmed out of the darkness and hit him low on the forehead instead of slamming into his temple. The world exploded into red and black, and he fell. His palms scraped on gravel and new pain ripped through him, but he fought to keep his balance and his mind. As he came rolling up, he saw something that he would never forget.

With hardly a sound, a thin, pale man with wild hair and eyes so bright they seemed to *glow* dropped from the branches of the avocado tree. It had to be a trick of the light, but the air *danced* around his body, wavered as if a heat mirage.

Doug saw the figure out of the corner of his eye, and turned, turned with that easy, swivel movement that was so incredibly fast, bringing the gun into line. But the wild-eyed man was moving directly into him, faster than anything human had any right to move. But even something moving as fast as the Wild Man couldn't stop him from getting off a shot.

One shot, which hit the man at a distance of six feet, directly in the abdomen. There wasn't even a moment of hesitation, and no time to pull the trigger a second time. The Wild Man spun like a top, and a scything motion of the legs ripped the gun from Doug's hand as if he'd thrust it into a garbage disposal.

The momentum of the first kick carried into the second one, a dancing, whirling motion that dropped a heel from overhead, smashing into Doug's collarbone with the distinct creak of splintering bone.

Doug fell limply, his scream a weak whistling sound.

Winston Gates struggled to pull his gun from the ground, but it was so heavy, too heavy, and everything was spinning. The gun was glued to the gravel. He looked up, directly into the eyes of the Wild Man, and all of the remaining strength drained from his mind and body.

The eyes were vast, ancient, infinitely compelling; there was something overwhelmingly sexual about them that hit him like a physical blow to the groin. In the diffuse light, the man seemed haloed with a reddish aura.

Gates groped for the gun with a final, desperate effort. The Wild Man's eyes widened, and the gun fell from nerveless fingers. Gates fell to his elbows, utterly drained.

Satisfied, the Wild Man turned back to Doug Patterson, his face fish-belly white, as pale as dead flesh.

He hauled Patterson up with one hand, and stared into his face, seemed to be looking deeply into Doug's wide, terrified eyes, perhaps at a spot behind them. Then, very deliberately, the right hand came up, and crashed down, and there was a hideously loud crunch. Patterson convulsed, and went totally limp. The Wild Man bent over his body and . . .

And . . .

And that was when consciousness mercifully released Gates from its grasp and he fell headlong into a tossing, inky sea.

# Chapter Twenty-four

## Healing

Adam couldn't remember driving home. He couldn't remember any of the events of the evening, just awoke unable to move his arms or legs, with his Cortina parked in his carport. The engine was still running, and he bobbled up from the sea of memory long enough to notice the carport door swinging shut. He noticed it, and it meant something, but he couldn't figure what. The remote-control box lay in his hand, and he giggled, and closed his hand on it. He tightened until the box splintered into a noncohesive collection of fragments. He looked at the splinters, not totally understanding what it was that he had done, but feeling content.

Blood drooled down the front of his shirt, and when he rolled the shirt up, the bullet hole was a second belly button, huge and now oozing only slightly. There didn't have to be much blood. Internal bleeding.

He could feel the damage, feel the wound, and knew that if he didn't get to a hospital, he was going to die. It was as simple as that.

But that wasn't the worst that could happen. Judging by his fragmented memories, the worst had already occurred.

When he concentrated, the events of the past few hours began to come back to him. When he concentrated, and examined himself in the rearview mirror, saw the stranger's eyes, the face that was still distorted with a hatred that he did not feel, he could remember driving to the Good Life to see Micki.

She was his. She was his mate, and she could not leave him. She had no right, and he would see her, talk to her, force her to understand.

And then the other men, the young white man and the older black walked toward him from across the street, and after that he couldn't remember anything at all.

(Micki)

Adam gasped with sudden pain. He could feel things moving in his stomach, as if organs were collapsing, their fluids draining into one another. The pain had a strangely cleansing effect, felt *right* somehow, and he rode it out, rode the crest of his body's agony.

He was losing. Losing. He knew that he had done something dreadful, but couldn't remember what.

His hands gripped the steering wheel, and his entire body convulsed. Dying. He was dying, and it was good, because . . .

Because he was losing control. And losing control was bad because . . .

Because he might kill.

But killing was not bad. It had never been bad. There was nothing more natural than killing. All things killed, just in the process of life itself.

"No," he whispered weakly, and as the exhaust fumes swirled around the garage, he began to grow drowsy. What was wrong? Why drowsy? It felt good to sleep, to go to sleep, and heal

(And die)

No, no, go to sleep.

Adam tried to lie back and sleep, but a force stronger than his conscious will lifted him from the driver's seat, banged his shoulder against the door until it opened, and the fumes ate at his lungs and tore at his eyes more strongly.

He groaned, the forces of Death and

(Life) warring as he fought to close his eyes and surrender to it, but he shook convulsively. He crawled across the floor, his stomach wound bleeding again, and reached up to the garage-door control box.

He couldn't reach it, and settled back down to the floor.

This is a good place. A perfect place to die, and a perfect time.

Time. Again he had the sinking feeling in the pit of his stomach, so strong that he felt it even through the pain, and he saw himself rising, stretching out, and flicking the door switch. Impossible. He was far too weak now. Impossible.

But he was moving again, rising to his knees, although there was no strength left in his body, and he touched the switch.

The door hummed up, and a wave of fresh air wafted in. Adam collapsed back to the ground, wondering at the feeling of utter defeat. Why defeat? He would live. He would live to kill . . .

No. There was still the bullet. His fingers tore away the shirt and he looked at the wound. It was still trickling blood, and he was rocked by another convulsion.

Another rivulet of blood, and there was a pinkish white edge of flesh amid the darker red.

He watched, fascinated, not understanding. Again he convulsed, and gasped with the pain. It felt . . . it felt as if he was giving birth, his body pushing in rhythmic time to the breathing that had slowed and stretched, as if he were doing one of the exercises he had abandoned months ago.

Another spasm, and something dark appeared, surrounded by glistening white. He touched it as another tremor hit, and the bullet popped out of the wound, glistening, wetly dark.

It rolled to the floor.

As he watched, the wound ceased bleeding, and the flesh began to close. The sides of his mouth curled up in a smile that was totally at odds with the terror he felt, the utter confusion and fear over the thing that his body and mind had become, and he lay there on the floor of the garage.

Frightened. Bleeding. Healing.

Planning.

# Chapter Twenty-five

# Culpepper

*Savagi, the controversial health guru, today entered a plea of "not guilty" in the mutilation death of Riley Winterson, known as the "Newark giant." Due to the sensational and grisly nature of the killing, both prosecution and defense counsel predict a lengthy trial.*
*—San Francisco Star, August 15, 1947*

*Why did I enter such a plea? Because I am an honest man, and I truly do not remember. He threatened me, and he is dead. I was there, and I awoke from a dream state with blood on my hands and mouth. It is possible that I was the instrument of his death, but that is all. One might see it as a suicide. I am not . . . always in control of the Beast.*
*—Savagi, quoted in the San Francisco Star.*
*August 17, 1947*

## Friday morning, May 4. Day 60.

Dr. Giles Culpepper lived in a green two-story house in Culver City, a pretty thing with white trim along the roof and a manicured lawn. When he bought it in 1956 on a VA loan, it had been a single-story dwelling. In 1972, after an eighteen-month fight with the zoning commission, he built a second story onto the first to house his expanding library and office. His first wife had divorced him in '73, his second in '82, and he had lived alone since then. And alone he now sat, silhouetted on his office window shade.

And never had he felt so alone as at this moment. He sipped from a mug of lukewarm coffee, fingers leaving damp ovals on the paper as he scanned the reports stacked on his desk, hundreds of pages, bound and loose, concerning the mental and physical development of a man named Adam Ludlum. So much information, each separate piece unremarkable in and of itself, but together painting a picture that became more disturbing by the page.

And most disturbing of all were the most recent news clippings that he had collected.

Neon Killer? A maniac who projected radiation in the visible bands of the electromagnetic spectrum? Reality? Illusion?

*What had happened that night in the basement of the physical sciences building?*

The slaughter at Bob's Cowboy. Jesus Christ. How many human beings were capable of something like that? The composite picture in the paper was a grotesquery, virtually useless for identification: the witness was clearly hysterical. And yet, it *could* have been Adam. God in heaven. Yes it could.

And now the police investigator, Patterson. His head torn open, brain destroyed.

Culpepper rubbed weary eyes and held up a scrap of Xeroxed paper to the light. The final straw.

It was a copy of a news item from the *San Francisco Star*, dated August 1947. It told of a long-standing rivalry between two strongmen, Savagi and a 300-pound behemoth called the Newark Giant. The rivalry had persisted for a decade, with threats documented on both sides. And then . . .

The Giant had been found in Savagi's palatial home, head torn open. Like the policeman's. Dear Lord.

How much damage had he done by remaining silent? By living in hope? Whether it was all Adam, or partially Adam, or not Adam at all . . . Even if all he could accomplish was the clearing of his own conscience, he had to talk to the police now, before it was too late.

There was a sound outside the door of the study, and Culpepper froze as his hand touched the phone.

No sound now, nothing at all. And yet . . . was that the hint of a draft? Just the faintest touch of cold air wafting in beneath the closed door?

Culpepper pushed himself out of the swivel chair, feeling the ache in his arms, the grind of joints in his elbows as he did. Just a year ago that movement would have been effortless, but now . . .

He shut his mind on that thought, and listened again for the door.

There was nothing. No one on the far side of the door. It was his imagination that made the room chilly.

And yet . . .

His hand shook as he reached out and quietly turned the bolt, hearing it snick into the lock.

He felt so damned stupid. There was nothing out there, nothing at—

The door exploded, a shower of wood and glass splinters blowing Culpepper back into his desk. There was a tall, shadowed figure in the hall as the ruined door creaked back on its shattered hinges. It stood there, somehow reminiscent of nothing so much as an animal balanced upon its hind legs. It was the slight tilt of the head, the cant of a shoulder, the low, hungry growl, a sound like a human being imitating the snarl of a rabid dog. For a long moment, there was no motion, and no sound.

Then Culpepper whispered, "Adam?" and the figure leaped out of the doorway and was upon him, fingers like iron rods tearing the breath from his throat.

\* \* \*

Adam sat hunched over the wheel, eyes open wide. When he closed them, there was a light, lovely at first and then grotesque, a light that raced around inside his body as if he were breathing fire. His tissues and organs were laid out in his sight like delicate fibrous things, swelling and collapsing, pulsing with life like anemones.

He shook his head violently. What . . . ? How had he . . . ? Where . . . ? He looked around him, scanning the street. He couldn't remember driving here, didn't know how long he'd been sitting, barely conscious.

The radio was on at low volume, and he barely responded when he heard the announcer say, "And as the Neon Killer claims his third victim, police files across the country are being opened and cross-referenced, hoping that this madman . . .''

Adam turned the radio off. *His* hands glowed. He could see it. Could anyone else? They must, or the eye-witness reports would have been meaningless. Someone had seen him kill, watched him run flaming from the scene of the crime. He couldn't remember the incidents, but that meant nothing.

Culpepper's house was quiet and dark. He had never been here before, had found the number in the telephone book, the white '78 Camaro with the "SPORTMED" license plate told Adam that he'd found the right address.

It made sense for him to come here. There had to be a way out of this horror, and Culpepper could show him.

The bullet hole still leaked a little, and the shirt was stained red, but his body was healing.

But there was something wrong, he could feel it. Tissue had been pushed up out of the bullet hole, creating a new, "outie" belly button. Things felt . . . *strange* in his gut, as if organs were rearranging themselves somehow. But that was impossible, wasn't it? Wasn't everything that had happened to him impossible?

He peered across the street at the house number. It barely registered on him that he shouldn't have been able to see the number so clearly. How long ago had he thrown his glasses away? Things were so confused now, so uncertain, and yet disorientingly melded with that disturbing clarity.

It was three in the morning, but the light was still on in Culpepper's study. It should be all right. If he could just make it across the street, everything would be all right.

But Culpepper. The doctor would figure everything out. He could trust Culpepper. And then . . .

He knocked on the door twice, and got no reply.

Strange. The car was in the driveway, but maybe Culpepper wasn't home. Maybe this wasn't the right house. He touched the door, ran his hands flat against it, sniffing. It *was* Culpepper. He could smell the man's sweat.

Adam looked around into the street, and when he was sure that there was no one watching, he placed his palms flat against the door and dug in his heels. When he found the balance, he slid his palm under the doorknob and slapped hard, once. The lock shattered, and the door swung open.

The house yawned its emptiness, and even before he walked in, he could smell the death.

He hadn't been in the house before

(Had he?)

but it seemed somehow familiar, its shadowed halls, the endless yards of books along the walls, and the soft clicks and pops and hisses from clocks and pilot lights, refrigerators and cooling walls, the hundred small sounds that ordinarily jostle for position just below the level of consciousness.

Familiar. And growing more familiar as the smell of blood grew thicker, warmer, and as he walked up the carpeted stairway to the second floor. The door to Culpepper's study was shattered

(Like the rest-room door at the Cowboy?)

and leaning inward on warped hinges. He edged in through the shattered wood and glass, already knowing what he would find.

Culpepper sat on the floor with his back against a cabinet, chin resting on his chest. His head was a red ruin, cracked open to the bridge of his nose, the top of the skull

such a mass of savaged tissue that Adam whipped his head
to the side.

The room swam, dipped, and wove.

(Why did you do it?)

Adam sank to his knees, trying to make sense of it,
trying to find a pattern where the man with the shattered
head fit.

The bar.

The cop. Suddenly he remembered. Remembered—

Kicking. Then smashing. Then prying with a sound like
a fox breaking a nest of brittle twigs. The sweet wet red
pulp, oh, yes. . . .

Adam vomited, his stomach spasming painfully, helplessly clawing at the rug.

No, no, no. Please, God, no.

And the worst of Culpepper's death was that, once
again, Adam couldn't even remember. Which meant that
he couldn't know how many times . . .

"If they catch you," a voice whispered, "they'll kill
you."

"But if they don't catch me, I'll keep killing."

Where could he go? He couldn't go to the police. They
wouldn't believe him. Would never believe him. And he
had killed a cop. That was virtually a death sentence.

Algernon?

Micki?

One swift, stomach-churning glimpse of the mutilated
thing slumped against the wall, and that idea was dead. He
couldn't take a chance of hurting anyone else.

No. There was no one in the world . . .

Correct that. There was one man. But that would take
money.

He had 28,000 dollars, all that was left of Gunther
Ludlum's estate after the bills were settled.

So he had money. What he was running out of was
time.

# Sunday, May 6. Day 58.

Algernon Swain was in the midst of a nightmare. In it, the sports medicine building at UCLA had been razed, destroyed, stripped up from the ground in a roar of tortured steel and crumbling concrete. And he watched, unable to run.

*It was dark in the dream. Driverless, the Caterpillar tractors prowled through the gloom. Their headlights searched tirelessly, peeling aside the darkness as the fan-mouthed diesels peeled away the earth.*

*"No. Please stop," that was what he wanted to say, but the words stuck sideways in his mouth. Chunks of wood and concrete tumbled out of the ground, a swelling wave of detritus ahead of the thrusting plow.*

*Then, something broken and rotten burst through the surface. An arm. Twisted, attached to a broken shoulder, and then a grinning shattered skull, its brains oozing out of a gaping wound.*

*It was Culpepper. The iron-gray hair was clotted with dirt and blood, but it was him, and as his body arced up and crumbled beneath the rushing wave of dirt, the wave growing larger and larger, another body appeared, and another, and another, until it was like one of the newsreels of the tractors at Belsen digging the hideous mass graves, hundreds of shattered, limp bodies tumbling over and over one another in a mash of human death, reaching for him, coming faster and faster now. . . .*

Algernon sat bolt upright in his bed, shivering as the sweat dried on his naked body. The sheet was sopping, and he came back to consciousness in a series of leaps, each of them taking him further away from the mountain of corpses and toward a waking reality no less horrifying.

*Culpepper is dead. And we know* how, *don't we?*

There was no proof. None. Except for a trail of blood that lead from Bob's Cowboy *and who introduced Adam to the Cowboy, Algy old man?* to the dead officer outside the

Good Life to a murdered exercise physiology professor. Oh, yes, and the hideous picture on the second section of the *Los Angeles Times*, the artist's composite. It looked like a face caught in mid-scream, or an astronaut under high g stress. He hadn't seen Adam in two months. He had not returned calls, had stopped coming to UCLA months earlier than that. He couldn't have lost so much weight so quickly, could he? And even if he had, could that face be Adam's?

Could it?

There were just no more options. He had to go to the police.

The front doorbell rang, and he jerked his head around so quickly that he heard the vertebrae crunch. Who . . . ?

It rang again. Now he remembered. It had been that sound that pulled him up out of the nightmare. He should be grateful to whoever it was . . .

. . . who would come to his front door at five in the morning?

"Oh, shit." He rolled out of bed and pulled a robe over his thin, damp body, peeked quickly into his dresser mirror and packed down his hair a little, and went to the front door.

He peered through the security eye.

Adam.

Taking a deep breath, he opened the door.

Adam. He held a large brown cardboard box in his arms. To Algy's shame the first thing he did was mentally compare Adam to the face in the police artist's sketch. Yes, it might be. It just might. Shit *fire*.

"Algy," Adam said, "I . . . shouldn't have come, I know."

"No . . . please. Come in." He held the screen open, and Adam entered. Something moved inside the box.

Algy backed away, and sat on the arm of the couch.

"I'm going away," Adam said softly. "I think I'm in control now, but I don't want to stay long."

The robe just wasn't enough protection from the chill,

and Algy fought to keep his teeth from chattering. "Then it was you?"

"Yes. No. Maybe. I think I killed the policeman."

"And Culpepper?"

"I was there, Algy, but I don't know. I'm not sure. God, I hope not. But I'm going to try to get help."

There was silence for an impossibly long moment. Then Algy said, "Why? Why would you do it?"

Adam stood there, the wet cardboard box in his hands, and Algy felt the depth of his friend's fatigue. It was like something beyond death, and that impression combined with the unmistakable aura of physical power was terrifying. "Why?" Adam swallowed heavily, and his eyes flickered around the room as if searching for concealed assassins. "I . . . only remember the bar. They started it, Algy. They started it, and something inside me just let go. Something came to life. I can't defend it. I don't expect you to condone it. But it was like all of the frustration and all of the *mad* just . . . just . . ." He hung his head. "I don't want to be more trouble than I've been. I'll be gone soon. Wait one day, and then tell the police anything that you like. I never meant for any of it to happen." Beneath the long, dark, frazzled hair his eyes burned.

"What . . . do you want from me?"

Adam grimaced, and Algy finally realized that he was trying to smile. "I wanted to leave you something." He opened the box, and an orange and black puffball stuck its head out and meowed shrilly, then forced its paws up and scrabbled out. BeDoss gave Adam a dirty look and then bolted, hiding behind the couch. "Take care of him, would you?"

Algy felt his eyes burning, and bit his lip hard. "Are you coming back, Adam? We can help you. Someone can . . ."

Adam shook his head. "There's only one man who might. I'll find him if I can. Algy"—he reached into his pants pocket and pulled out an envelope—"give this to Micki, would you? I . . . know how you've always felt about her. You two will always be at least friends. Anything else is gravy. Take care of her, would you?"

They just looked at each other, then Algy left the couch, and it was Adam that backed up now, frightened for his friend. "Algy—"

"Shut the hell up." Algernon buried his face against Adam's chest, unashamed of the tears that streamed hotly down his cheeks. "I love you, Man. I am so sorry about all of this."

Shaking his head, holding his only friend closely, there was a moment in which Adam almost told Algy to call the police, to help him stop himself while there was still time. Then the moment was past, and Adam turned to the door.

"Hey, Ludlum!" Algy called out.

"Yeah?"

"Your cat craps in my drain, he sleeps in the blender."

"Fair enough." He smiled a last time, his gaunt face almost peaceful. "You're the best friend anyone ever had, Algy. Don't ever forget it."

And then he was gone.

BeDoss sniffed out from behind the couch, and padded up next to Algy. Algy bent and picked the cat up. BeDoss protested for a few seconds, then curled up in Algy's arms and began to purr. Algernon kissed BeDoss on the tip of his furry nose, and said, "Let's see if we can't find you some tuna, Sweetheart." BeDoss growled approval.

And then, he thought bleakly, he had to call Micki. And together they would march, hand in hand, down to the police department to sign the death warrant of their dearest friend.

# Chapter Twenty-six

## Katmandu

## Wednesday, May 9. Day 55.

Noise.

The squalling of infants, low moans, the drone of engines. The sounds were a nest of pastel yarn woven around Adam's ears, and he shook his head listlessly, not certain whether he was awake or asleep.

If he was asleep, the dream was an insane one. The people in the plane huddled in their seats, holding their heads and cursing in Nepalese. Babies tossed restlessly, their brown bodies swathed in robes and bathed in sweat, mothers holding them, glancing back at Adam and mumbling frantic Hindu prayers under their breaths.

No one sat in the seat next to Adam. The row behind him was empty. The row in front of him was occupied by one dark, sunburnt Newar tribesman who hadn't been able to find a seat elsewhere. He turned around and looked back at Adam fearfully, a streak of dried blood on his upper lip. His eyes were horribly bloodshot.

Across the aisle and up the row, a round, light-skinned infant awoke screaming from its nightmare, and the droning in Adam's head grew louder.

The stewardess, a small woman in a dull blue uniform, smiled uncertainly as she exited the pilot's cabin. She spoke a few quick words in a language Adam didn't recognize, then came back closer to his seat and tried to appear genial. She spoke in broken English. "The . . . pilot would wants to know if . . . if any passengers are operating the, the computers. Small computer? Have you?"

Adam shook his head.

"No?" Her smile was more transparently plastic now. "The radio, perhaps?" Her round face was strained. "It is illegal to operate such on an airplane. The instruments—"

"I'm sorry. Is there something wrong with the instruments?"

She glanced nervously up and down the seats, and then scurried on down the aisle.

He closed his eyes, and his eyelids seemed translucent. In his imagination the people around him looked so fragile, so weak. Brittle bones suspended in bags of thin syrup.

There was an almost playful urge to reach out and grab one of them, shake one of them, just to feel the bones break. With his eyes closed, he felt the heat of their bodies, smelled their fear.

He shut the blinders down on his mind, and tried to lose himself. It was easy—too easy. In his mind, the darkness solidified and separated into walls that twisted away into a false horizon. And stalking him through the depths of the maze was the Golden Man. Very real now. Very close. Very hungry.

Why had he come halfway around the world? It was ridiculous, and yet there seemed no better option open to him. And really, it was simple, once he had the money. A seven-day visa would be obtained on arrival at Tribhuvan airport. He had the three required photographs, taken in a booth on Hollywood Boulevard: his old photographs barely resembled him at all. The required cholera, smallpox, and typhoid vaccinations were still small red scars on his arms.

Pan Am to New York, to Frankfurt, and then on to Katmandu. Twenty-four hours of cramped spaces and wait-

ing, and waiting. But at the far end of the wait was the one
human being who might be able to help him. Had to.
Because if there was no help here . . .

Adam closed his eyes, and thought of death.


Adam felt like a giant in Tribhuvan airport. It was more
Europeanized than he would have expected. There was an
ancient, red, silver-handled Coca-Cola machine, beneath
an American Express sign. But still, he was so much taller
than the Rajput hillmen, the Brahmans, and Chetris that he
felt far more of a freak than he had in Los Angeles.

He felt relief when a touring group of Austrian students
walked by, with olive-drab duffel bags slung across their
broad shoulders. They talked animatedly, not paying any
attention to the thin American in the red nylon windbreaker, sitting with his luggage between his legs and his
head in his hands near the desk marked "Nagarkot Charter."

Outside, there would be pagoda-style Hindu temples,
vendors and pilgrims, tourists and shopkeepers. At another
time, in another life, he might have taken some pleasure in
being so far from home. Before this week, England twice
and Manila once had been the extent of his travels. But
there was no pleasure. There was nothing but a growing
sense of dread, only slightly alleviated by the approach of
the man he sought.

"Mr. Ludlum?" The man was fat and somber of face
even though his voice was pleasant. He looked to be some
indecipherable blend of European and Mongoloid. "I am
Rapti. You are the American seeking the Gauri Shankar
retreat?" Adam nodded as they shook hands. "Unfortu-
nately, the weather is still rather harsh, unusually so for
May. You must make the trip now? In a few weeks . . ."

Adam dug into his jacket and pulled out a wad of traveler's checks. "It's worth it to me. I can make it worth it to
you."

Rapti pulled at his beard, sighing. "You understand that
the path will be difficult to find. You have been there
before?"

"Yes," he lied.

Rapti's expression said that he knew Adam was lying, and was balancing his relative merits of being responsible for this crazy American's death, or allowing the same crazy American to give his ample funds to some less deserving soul. "Very well. We expect a break in the weather tomorrow. It will not last, and I suggest we take advantage of it."

"Done."

Below his window, someone was laughing, ringing a bell as they ran through the streets. The laughter blended into song, a tingling, high-pitched sound that was joyful and somehow plaintive at the same time.

Adam looked out at the mountains, crested and slicked with snow. Late flurries danced outside the windows, painting the streets white. A group of children ran past, trailing strings clustered with brass chimes, running and running into the darkness, swallowed at last by the snow, the endless tiny flakes of frozen night tumbling down and down from a dark and silent sky.

He turned back to his bed and lay back, closing his eyes. If he was fortunate, he might be able to sleep. Briefly. If not, it would be another bout of tossing, of watching the light show. Praying for dawn. And just praying.

Please. *Sensei.* You are my last hope.

# Thursday, May 10. Day 54.

Rapti brought the plane around in a long, slow curve, approaching a narrow strip of frozen ground. As he did, Adam watched the peak of Gauri Shankar as the mountain slowly expanded to fill the windows of Rapti's twin-engine cargo plane. He felt utterly dwarfed, and in that sensation, there was strange peace.

"You come to study *tumo*?" Rapti's hands on the controls were sure, but his question was asked with a thread of genuine unease.

"I'm here to find . . . someone."

"Not to study *tumo*? Then why are you not cold? It not even thirty degrees, and you wear only the light jacket."

Adam stared straight ahead, wishing that the little man would simply do his job and be quiet. Rapti flicked a finger at the compass ball on the plane's instrument panel. "Strange," he said, "it doesn't seem to be working very well. Do you have a magnet with you? No, I didn't suppose you would."

Rapti sank back into his own thoughts, circling the plane for his final approach to the crudely hewn landing strip. Cold wind buffeted the plane, and Adam's stomach rolled as it shuddered.

"*Sensei*," he whispered, "I'm coming."

Rapti killed the engines as they touched down, and as they taxied to a halt Adam watched the blur above the engine housing solidify into propellers. When the plane finally came to a complete halt, the pilot locked the breaks and unbuckled his seat belt. "We camp here tonight. You must walk the rest of the way."

Adam smelled the air. It was so utterly crisp and cold that it was like a blowtorch applied to his lungs. For the first time in months he felt clean, and hopeful.

He and Rapti spoke little to each other as the man prepared a meal of chicken curry and rice atop a gas stove. Tiny blue flames peaked out from beneath the burner, warming the interior of the cargo plane and lifting the darkness, but again and again Adam found Rapti glancing at him.

Once, the pilot shook his wrist. He shook it again, glanced at his watch, and laughed uneasily. "It is strange," he said. "The watch is new. Digital, it is called. It seems to be broken. As was the compass. Do you perhaps . . . ?"

Adam sat, silently cross-legged.

"No," Rapti said at last. "Somehow I thought not."

They ate in silence, Adam barely noticing the taste of the food. He remembered to mumble a few words of appreciation, which Rapti acknowledged with rote modesty.

When the dishes were packed away, Rapti set up a small

heater, and then backed away, rolling himself in a blanket. Adam was sure that Rapti wasn't unusually tired. This was withdrawal from the strange American, and Adam was content for it to be so.

In the dark, the single heating coil was a red pulsing eye. Sitting cross-legged, Adam stared into it, seeking answers that weren't there, waiting for morning.

Not asleep, not awake, Adam began to dream.

He dreamed that he walked along a narrow pathway, between ridges of barren, unscalable rock. The only way through the path was forward, and up. His legs burned, his lungs ached as he walked. He was so tired, so very tired.

"Father . . ." he whispered. As if beckoned by the words, Gunther Ludlum appeared in the path before him, a different man than Adam remembered.

This Gunther was strong, and no older than Adam, and smiled to him. "Go back," Gunther said, his voice kind. "You may not pass me. May never pass."

Adam strode forward until they stood face to face. His breath puffed out in front of him like clouds. His father's arms stretched out to halt him.

Adam's arms twined with his father's, and Adam began to push. Before his eyes, his father withered, grew older, the black hair turning white, the teeth discoloring and working free, the flesh withering against the bone.

Adam gasped in shock, for even as his father aged, the ravaged body expanded in Adam's arms, before his eyes, growing and growing until Adam was struggling against a giant, a giant crowned with snow, gazing down at Adam from the frigid heights with a vast regret as Adam's efforts grew more and more frantic.

"Out . . . of . . . my . . ." the words desolved into the hiss of something that loved neither him nor his father, something that whispered filth into Adam's mind, made his struggles something both larger and smaller than it should have been.

And his father, incredibly ancient and huge now, filled

the sky, filled the earth, calling forth from Adam the greatest effort of his life, all emotion and energy finally focusing, exploding through the barrier. With a great sigh his father, arms outstretched, toppled to the icy ground, dying once again.

And when the snows ceased their flurries, and the distant roll of thunder became a memory, Adam looked up, utterly alone, on a frozen blue plain beneath a pitiless moon. The plain was grooved, carved into an infinitely complex labyrinth, one that twisted and contorted in endless complexity to the far horizon. And one path through the labyrinth was marked in blood.

And the voice whispered in his ear: "Do you see? Do you see now? All that you had to do . . ."

And Adam screamed.

# Chapter Twenty-seven
## Ice Giants

## Saturday, May 12. Day 52.

The roughly hewn pathway up Gauri Shankar was only wide enough to walk single file. It wove like a ribbon of granite along the side of a valley that stretched away into blue-white vastness and mist dotted with flecks of black. With each passing minute the air grew thinner. Rapti puffed as he sang in a cracked, graceless voice. With each breath, frigid clouds of condensation wafted from his mouth.

Adam felt as if he were floating above the path, his feet putting only enough pressure on the ground to crack the frost. The weight of his pack was nothing, and the cold was nothing, and the labyrinth in his mind yawned to receive him.

The snow was falling lightly, but the ice on the mountainside to his left might have been there for decades since last it melted. There would be no real thaw up here, only false springs followed by bitterly cold winter nights.

"Not long now," Rapti called over his shoulder.

Adam nodded without speaking.

The path suddenly became much steeper. Here, human hands had chipped away the rock to make footholds, and a

knotted, tethered rope guided the way. Rapti adjusted his
backpack and set his feet, beginning to climb up.

Adam watched him for a few feet before following. The
man was a monkey, just a little monkey. A flower of
irritation blossomed within Adam, annoyance that he had
to rely on such as Rapti to get things accomplished. It
wasn't fair; it made no sense. He resented it, and as soon
as Rapti was no longer useful, perhaps there could be an
accident. Just the tap of a rock on the head at the proper
moment, and Rapti would go spinning off into the valley,
screaming as he fell, a sweeter music than any of his
loathsome . . .

The Golden Man, more dragon than man now, lizard
grin full of gleaming teeth, prowled hungrily in the labyrinth, just behind him now. Adam ran, putting bloodstained walls between himself and its hissing, gibbering
laughter. It scratched at the walls in mock frustration,
enjoying the game of Hide and Seek.

"That way," Rapti pointed. "We are here, and I can go
no farther. I make camp here, and leave tomorrow, at
noon."

Adam wiped snow away from his hood and shook Rapti's
hand, every movement totally conscious. The lizard-thing
was very close now, but Adam repeated over and over
again that Rapti was *a good man, who has discharged his
duties with honor and competence. I need him alive. He
must fly me down* . . .

And the dragon hissed, coiling in dark corridors.

The path twisted now, and the sun, low on the horizon,
was giving little light. No matter . . . his eyes saw better
in the dark than he would ever have believed possible.

He rounded the curve of the mountain, and found himself facing a colossus.

The monstrosity stood at least sixty feet high and glistened in the waning light like a tower of opaque glass. It
might have waited there for a thousand years, its colossal
grin smiling down on him, dwarfing him as it would any
creature that had ever lived. Its waist, as thick and round
as a stone Buddha's, nestled flush against the ground.

Although covered in snow, its ice shone blue in some places. It was old, thick ice, as if created through decades of patient molding, countless seasonal layers of snow carved and packed, blocks of frozen slush chopped and hauled and stacked, lovingly and reverently compiled over years or generations.

Its face was twisted, an expression that was part frown and part smile, clotted with snow, the suggestion of vast stalactite teeth gleaming fifty feet above him.

Adam turned and turned on his heels, head spinning now. There was another sculpture, this one vaguely bat-shaped, crouching, and ready to spring. Within its light outer shell of ice hung suspended an opaque core as dark as the heart of a dead star.

And there: something like a sky spirit, a delicate, spidery shape that seemed impossibly fragile. A complex of arches and thin, flaring sheets that curved in upon each other to dazzle and confuse the eye.

And there . . . and over there . . .

Adam walked through a forest of demons, ice spirits, godlings frozen in a blast of gelid air. Among these blue-white immortals who guarded the pass, he felt as a speck of cosmic detritus floating in the void. Before their purity and grandeur the Golden Man-Dragon withered, howled as it retreated, and Adam came back into the light, breathing pure air.

He drew his jacket tighter around his collar. There was no trail now. There were only the statues, and the mountains, and a vast, aching loneliness that he had no words for, and no way to cleanse.

He began to cry, his eyes burning until it seemed that the sobs would drown out the whistle of the wind. He collapsed to his knees in the snow, suddenly utterly lost, all strength drained.

Micki. The love of his life. Gone, lost forever now. Everything in his past sacrificed in the search, offered up to the compulsion to find something he didn't understand anymore. The addiction to the unknown.

Gunther. There were no words for the grief that suddenly flooded him, as if he had had to travel halfway around the world to find his own feelings. No words, just images, endless images suddenly gushing from an open heart. Fragments of memories, thought forever lost.

His father: teaching him to read. Gunther's strong hands helping Adam from the branches of a tree. His warm arms enfolding Adam, holding him, loving him. Images, buried amid the pain, suddenly springing up as if all that had ever existed between them was love and trust.

And over it all, the very, very last words Gunther had spoken.

"Adam . . . I love you."

All of the tears that would not, could not come before flooded from Adam's eyes in a torrent, freezing on his face.

"You have come a long way to cry," a voice said, soft, but audible above the wind. Adam looked up, shocked at the sound.

There, some thirty yards distant, sitting cross-legged in the snow, was the figure of a naked man.

Adam ran now, and joy surged through him. Shackley. It had to be. Bearded now. Older, thinner, perhaps . . .

Adam stopped short ten yards from the man. Circled him cautiously.

The snow beneath the old man was melted into liquid. The man gleamed in the darkness like a beacon, but whether he truly glowed, or that luminescence existed only in Adam's tortured mind, he could not say.

Finally, the bearded man opened his eyes.

They were large, and soft and very brown, and gently inquisitive.

Ice-fingered, the wind plucked at Adam.

"Did you know I was coming?"

"Since before you were born."

The cold was suddenly numbing, through the thermal reflective clothing, the wool, cotton, and leather that bundled him, and Adam fought to center himself.

"Where are the rest of you?"

"I was sent to meet you."

Adam paused, afraid to ask the question that he had come halfway around the world to ask. "Where is Mitchell Shackley?"

The bearded man shook his head. "You did not come to find Shackley. You came to find your father. Why do you not see? Both are dead."

A sledgehammer slammed Adam over the heart and he staggered, sank to his knees next to the man with the moat of melted water around his body, his skin prickling with the heat. The wind was increasing, and from far away Adam could hear himself begin to cry, the sounds of a lost child.

"Death is life's winter. Without death, there is no re-birth, no renewal."

There was something, almost humor, in the man's voice, and Adam looked up. "Rebirth?"

"Yes. We come to winter in fear, carrying our burden of lies and regrets. You. Your father. Mitchell Shackley. He came to find his ending, and, as you must, discovered it to be a new beginning. As did his, your search must end where it began."

For a moment there was confusion, and then a bubble of laughter that forced its way up to the surface, and Adam was roaring, kneeling in the snow, laughing and tears mingling freely, emotion flowing unchecked for the first time in months.

When the gale had passed, the bearded man was still staring at him. "You have killed," the man said.

"Yes."

"You will kill again."

"I don't want to. I don't understand what's happening to me."

"Come here," the man said. He closed his eyes, and extended his hands.

They enfolded Adam's, and Adam wanted to weep with relief at the penetrating warmth in the touch. "Please," he said. "Help me."

"I cannot," the bearded man said regretfully. "The fruit you have borne is diseased. Rejoice that winter comes for you. Death is the gift.'' He withdrew his hands, and folded them, closing his eyes. "Go."

Adam shook his head disbelievingly. "That's it? That's all? Just like that? 'Death is the gift'?" Suddenly the Man-Dragon was alive within him, its voice hissing insistently. "You can't just tell me that. There has to be more than that."

The bearded man's eyes opened again. "A great power awakens in the world, one that has slumbered for ages. Your teacher thought it was over. He was wrong. Power does not corrupt. It attracts and nurtures both corruption and growth. The evil that was destroyed is less than the evil that lives. You are not the power. You are the prize. If not you, another, or another, until the seed that was planted millennia ago comes to fruition. Winter will come, and with it the death of all Man's dreams. It is your decision whether spring will follow. Yours alone."

"Me?"

"You must suffer, and you must die. And in the end, the future resides in your hands. Are you brave?"

Adam stared at him. "I don't understand."

"All things come to their ending. Soon. Two moons, no more. You will decide." The faintest of smiles played on the old man's face. "You are a good man," he said simply. "Do not forget this, whatever happens. There are impurities in the human spirit. Things of violence and death. They will, they must work their way to the surface, and burst into the open like pustules. But in the end, you will decide."

The old man said a few more things, including a name.

Then Adam stood, feeling utterly alone, and terrified, and went his way. Leaving the bearded man who sat cross-legged in the forest of giants, the starlight painting them silver and royal amethyst. He went back down the mountain, knowing that he was without a home, possibly without a future, but with something that he had not had for a terribly long time.

Hope.

# Chapter Twenty-eight
## Homecoming

## Thursday, May 31. Day 33.

The cab dropped Adam Ludlum off on the darkened street in front of the Temple of the Earth Heart. He had no luggage—that had been left in Mexico City after his return flight. Hitched rides brought him to Tijuana. There he had walked across the border to San Diego, and the Trailways bus depot.

There was no way to tell who knew of his existence, who he was, what he had done. Who might have his picture.

The temple was darkened, save for a few lights on the upper floor, and a very faint sound of clinking, as if someone were washing dishes.

Should he knock? Where else did he have to go? Here he might find rest, and comfort, and understanding. He even felt *drawn* to the temple, as if some deep part of him yearned for the fellowship.

He raised his hand to knock, but before his hand touched the wood, the door opened.

Sylvia was dressed simply, her body painfully thin
*as yours is thin*

but elegant and innocently sensuous in the flowing white of her robes. She smiled shyly.

*And welcome little fishes in with . . .*

"Hello, Mr. Ludlum," Sylvia said.

The door opened more widely, and Kevin Dearborne was beside her, quiet, certain, calm. An infinite reservoir of dark strength, and Adam felt the pull.

"Savagi is dead," Kevin Dearborne said. "Betrayed by his own Judas. But the spark lives on, doesn't it?"

Adam's head buzzed with confusion. "I need to rest." And an answering voice sang softly,

*Not here. Do not trust them.*

"You had to come to us. You need us. And we need you."

"Why?" His head was buzzing, as if the weight of two months without sleep had fallen on him all at once. Reality itself was rending, its fabric twisting and splitting under the strain.

"Why? Because we are the only ones who understand what is happening to you. The only ones who can help." Dearborne put out his hand, and for a moment, to Adam's tormented gaze, he seemed not a human being at all, but an animated shadow, a fragment of darkness torn from the heart of the earth. Cunning. Powerful. Hungry.

Adam took a step back. "No. I shouldn't."

"You must," Dearborne said quietly. "You killed many of them. Many of the slow and stupid creatures. They will find you, and try to kill you. The change is not yet complete in you. You have great potential." His voice and face were urgent, almost pleading, and Adam was swayed. "More than anyone I have known. More than me. More than Savagi. You are the one. You must let nothing hold you from your destiny."

His breathing ragged, Adam backed away from the door. "Go away," he mumbled, the words thick in his throat. "Just go away."

"You'll be back, Adam." Dearborne's voice was muffled through the door. "You know that, more than anyone."

Adam staggered out into the street, wandering out into the gloom.

He wandered out across the street, pausing to examine his reflection in a car window. He saw the face of a stranger. A powerful, oddly haggard face. The only thing that was truly familiar were the eyes. They were his old eyes. Hunted. Frightened.

But still waiting for something to happen.

*Not long now*, the Man-Dragon said.

*Ready or not, here I come.*

# Chapter Twenty-nine
## Second Contact

## Monday, June 25. Day 8.

Winston fumbled with the front-door latch, and rubbed at his eyes. "Hi."

Arlene Cheviot held out a stack of papers to him. "Welcome to the land of the living." She leaned forward and pecked his mouth.

"Hey. None of that. I haven't brushed my teeth yet."

"So brush 'em. I haven't got all day."

He grunted and groped toward the kitchen, pulling a tube of toothpaste from the refrigerator.

"Helluva place to keep it."

He grinned, scratching at two days' growth of beard. "Helps me wake up. Wait a sec." He clomped back to a half bathroom off his back porch. Arlene sat sedately, folding her legs as she listened to the gargling, scrubbing sounds from the rear of the house.

Winston emerged from the kitchen looking decidedly more awake. "Now then, where were we?"

She stood, and he folded her into his arms, kissing her heartily.

"Mmmm. Much better." She pushed him away, and

looked at him carefully. "How are you? You tried to come
in for a couple of days last week . . ."

"Oh, not too bad." He sat heavily on the couch, thumbing through the papers she had deposited on the coffee
table. "The whispers were the worst. Worse than the pity,
or those humiliating hospital interviews. Worse than that
damned forensics man explaining how an avocado pit
could fracture my skull." His mouth twisted wryly. "For
instance, if it was shot out of a *cannon*. Nearly killed by a
goddamn piece of fruit."

He reached across the table and took her hand.

"Oh, Winston," she said finally. "It *would* be funny if
Doug hadn't been killed."

Arlene came across to sit next to him, leaning her head
on his shoulder. She was wearing a touch of makeup
today. Even those few brushstrokes dissolved the hardness
in her face, and she was achingly lovely.

"I hope you know how sorry I am."

Gates nodded wordlessly. The face in the alley glowed
in his vision like a floating Halloween mask.

He flipped through the files, pulling out the one marked
"Brain-Eater" in red pen. A momentary whorl of dizziness surrounded him, and he fought for balance. His eyes
felt scratchy and tired. "Adam Ludlum. A man goes nuts,
just nuts, and does something like this. Who can figure it?
Somewhere in this mess is the answer, Chev, and I'm
going to find it."

"Cappelotti and Swain gave us their statements while
you were in the hospital."

"Damn, I'm sorry I missed that. What did you think
about them?"

"All the words are on the paper, but my gut says they
were on the level. Scared, not sure what the hell was
happening. We've got the UCLA material, and combed
Ludlum's house. He's disappeared."

"I still think the trail is going to lead right back to the
Temple of the Earth Heart, but I don't know when.

"Look at the coroner's report," he said softly. "Poor

Doug. Arm, leg, neck broken. Skull cracked open. Part of his freaking *brain* removed.''

"Some kind of devil-worship ceremony?"

"I don't know. No sign of anything like that in Ludlum's past. Just this Savagi stuff. Seems to have driven him crackers. Hell, I don't care what the reports say. The man must have been juiced up on angel dust . . . something.''

Arlene Cheviot looked at the photographs of the carnage at Bob's Cowboy. The picture of Doug Patterson's body in the alley. Dr. Culpepper, crumpled in his library. Carter Pelz. Mars Peach, the former California State Judo Champion. A dozen others. All very dead.

"One man did all of this."

Gates gave her a twisted little smile. "Let's hope to hell it was. I'd hate to think that there were two of these maniacs running around.''

"Have you seen this one?" She dropped a clipping from the *Times* on the coffee table.

There was a small article about the killing in the newspaper, another like the Pelz killing, just an anonymous nobody down in the Mission district. Nobody would have cared except for the bizarre underpinnings.

"Neon Killer." He shook his head in disgust. "Christ, they must be selling papers.''

Chev searched through the files until she found a fanfold sheet torn from a telex machine. "Well, we've got national press. The fifteen other murders, maybe another two or three that are being linked into the pattern. Twenty empty brainpans. No glowing man, however. Sometimes a tall figure was seen running cat-quick from the site.''

"No glow. Was anyone ever convicted?"

"Never."

She threw another sheet of paper on the desk. "You might find this interesting.''

Gates opened it, and read, "The UCLA Humanities department in conjunction with the New York Institute of Synergetics presents an evening with Patanjal. Come hear the words of this controversial, enlightened, and enlightening man.''

And it ran on, giving time and place specifications. At the bottom of the page was the request, "No photography, please."

Gates shrugged. "Some Yogi, right? Why is this interesting?"

"We weren't interested until we found out someone else was."

"Who?"

"The secretary of the humanities department reads the mail that is sent 'in care of.' Especially in this case, since there seems to be some controversy around this man. Anyway, she got this letter."

She opened her purse and extracted a neatly folded sheet of paper.

Winston raised an eyebrow, and then unfolded it.

In broad, rather childish handwriting, the letter read, "Please, *Sensei*, help me. I will come to talk to you on Monday. If you cannot help me, I may be lost. Please."

And it was signed, "Adam Ludlum."

Winston felt his heart thundering in his chest. "Is this for real?"

"We've compared it with writing samples at his house. Seems to be real. It was mailed from Santa Monica. We're taking it seriously. Tyler Hall is going to be covered. It's not our jurisdiction, but we've been invited."

"Patanjal." For the first time, a smile broke out on Gates's troubled face. "Well," he said, "let's go to a lecture."

The posters were up on Wilshire Boulevard and on Westwood on the outskirts of the Village.

MONDAY, JUNE TWENTY-FIFTH
LAHIRA PATANJAL
SPEAKS ON YOGA, MYSTICISM, AND CHRISTIANITY
SEVEN-THIRTY, TYLER HALL

Winston walked past one of the posters on the campus itself, and glared at it. "I don't have a clue how to feel about this. Whether or not to hope it's the real thing."

"Let's hope it is."

He sighed. "You haven't seen what this man can do, Arlene. Pictures just don't cut it." Once again, the request "No photography, please" was emblazoned across the bottom of the poster.

"I read about his book. The *Daily News* synopsis of the *Reader's Digest* condensation or some such."

"Yeah. Right. Well, the linkage is just too damn strong. I can smell it. The Wild Man is going to be here tonight."

They walked up the stairs to the auditorium. An officer of the LAPD met them there, and introduced himself as Sergeant Dysan. "Winston Gates?"

"That's me. Thanks for letting me in on this. I'm not officially back on duty for two more days."

"I knew Patterson when he worked out of West Hollywood," Dysan replied.

"Then let's nail this bastard today."

Dysan nodded soberly. "You know it. We figure that Ludlum is wearing Kevlar and probably dusted to the gills."

He smiled hastily. "Doesn't matter this time. We've got enough men and equipment to take him for sure. We've got the roofs covered, officers backstage, and plainclothesmen seeded in the audience. The university asked for that even before there was any flap about the Neon Killer."

The hall was empty now, its 2,400 seats stiffly at attention, awaiting 2,400 attentive occupants.

"What do you know about this guy Patanjal."

"Not a lot. Doing this one limited lecture tour. No television. No radio. No auditoriums over twenty-five hundred seats. No photography. There's been trouble about this book that he wrote, but only from loonytunes."

"What about?"

"Saying that Christ didn't die on the cross." Dysan took a dark, thin cigar out of his pocket and lit it, inhaling deeply. "What the hell. When my wife found out the duty I was pulling, she said that I should let them, and I'll quote her, 'Shoot the bastard.' End quote. Wonderful stuff, religion. Brings out the best in people."

"Well, when can I meet him?"

"Now, if you want to. He's up in the projection room checking his slides right now." Dysan pointed up to the top of the auditorium, and through the projection slots Gates could vaguely see a shadowy shape moving back and forth.

"Coming, Chev?"

"Wouldn't miss it."

They knocked on the projection-room door twice before there was any answer.

"Yes?" a softly modulated voice asked as the door swung open.

"Mr. Patanjal?" Gates asked. He showed his credentials. "I'm Inspector Gates, and this is Officer Arlene Cheviot. I'd like to speak with you."

There were two people in the room: a student and an older man that Gates assumed was a college professor.

Meeting Patanjal in person was another abrupt modification of the mental image Gates had built up. The man seemed in his early fifties, and wore a finely tailored blue business suit, and had the body of a champion swimmer beneath it. His hair was very black, receding at the sides, but somehow the high forehead softened his face. A warm smile curled a mouth that Gates found a little hard. His eyes were as black as onyx. They caught the light merrily, but Gates had the feeling that they had seen a lot. Too much, perhaps. But the overall impression was positive, that Patanjal would be a good man to spend an hour's easy conversation with. He was shorter than Gates would have expected, barely five foot seven, with gentle self-mockery in his expression.

"The quarters are a bit cramped, but I'm sure we can make do."

He held a final slide up to the light, then slid it into the projection carousel. "That will be all for now, Howard. Thank you."

His assistant nodded and left the room.

"Well, now. I suppose that you're going to tell me that you are here to protect me, and that I needn't worry."

"No, as a matter of fact not. I don't know anything about the threats against your life. I'm sure that the LAPD can handle anything along that line. I'm more concerned with this."

Gates pulled a sheaf of clippings from his pocket and handed them over. Patanjal read them quickly, efficiently, as if there were an optical scan instead of a brain behind the dark eyes.

He handed them back. "Yes?"

"We believe that the man who committed these crimes may come to your lecture tonight."

Patanjal sat lightly, and folded his fingers. His hands were strong but very fine, with the kind of aliveness Gates would have ordinarily associated with a concert pianist. "Well, what is it exactly that I can do for you?"

"I was wondering if you can remember anyone in your past who might have been capable of this kind of violence."

Patanjal templed his fingers ruminatively, and closed his eyes. "Perhaps. I have had . . . many associations in my life, and some of them have involved the potential for violence." He paused, as if he were about to say something, but then changed his mind. "Not now, not anymore. For many years. I hope that this person is captured soon." The skin at the corners of his black eyes crinkled. "But not at my talk, for goodness' sake."

Patanjal smiled again. "And now, if there is nothing more I can help you with at the moment, I must get back to my preparations."

"Of course."

Arlene stopped. "By the way. Why don't you like your picture taken?"

"That's a matter of personal conviction," he said, holding her gaze levelly. "Now, excuse me, please?"

Gates knew that Patanjal watched as they left the room, and wasn't sure what those black eyes held. Only that they held more than Gates knew. And that they were waiting for something.

*        *        *

The crowd had been trickling in for almost half an hour.
Gates stood in one of the balconies, the two-way LAPD
radio swinging from his belt, the flat-nosed bulk of a Taser
stun pistol snug in its black holster. He watched every
face, hoping that one of them would trigger a memory.

Glow. There had been no glow that night in the alley.
Why would a killer paint himself with phosphorus?

There was a tiny voice in the back of his mind that said,
"Maybe he didn't paint himself."

But Gates shut down that voice with brutal speed. That
way lay madness.

The auditorium was over half full, and the trickle of
people had turned into a torrent.

He lifted his radio and whispered into it, "Arlene,
anything interesting backstage?"

The radio crackled then spoke back to him. "No, Win.
All security is tight. If he's coming in, he's buying a ticket
like everyone else."

"All we can do is wait then." The house lights were
going down as the crowd filled the auditorium, dammit,
and it was getting harder and harder to make out the faces.
Never mind. Just a trace. Just the hint of an outline. There
was no way that the killer could blend into the crowd.
There was just something too alien about him. Something
would betray him.

The lights went all of the way down, and the rotund
chairman of the humanities department strode onto the
stage. "Good evening," he said. "Tonight it is my very
great pleasure . . ."

Gates tuned out the oleaginous pleasantries and scanned
the crowd. There. The aquiline silhouette, the long, ratty
hair.

No. That person shifted, and the full outline of a breast
presented itself.

There . . . No, not that one either.

There was a round of applause as Patanjal strode onto
the stage, and a few boos and catcalls. He paused before
speaking, and when he spoke, it was with an entirely

higher level of intensity that he had used in the projection room.

"I'm glad that a few of you feel strongly enough to express your feelings. Because just as I'm sure that most of you are genuinely glad to see me, there are others who are offended. Terribly, deeply offended, and yet in the name of courtesy will not express their anger.

"Tonight, I will attempt to answer any and all questions. I am not in any way antiempathetic to the Christian religion. I was raised in the Episcopalian faith, and it was my childhood observation that good and strong people consistently fell short of the goals that they set for themselves, that they routinely allowed others to make moral judgments that human beings can only make for themselves. This sent me in a lifelong search for, well, let's be extravagant and call it truth.

"For if Christ was God, then his sacrifice was a meaningless charade. If he was a man, an enlightened, fearfully advanced man, then his sacrifice and actions are more than meaningful. He is calling us to be not 'Christian' but 'Christlike,' an infinitely more difficult, noble, and rewarding pathway. . . ."

As Patanjal went on, Gates found himself relaxing. Whatever this man had written, it was easy to understand why he both challenged and attracted. And the Neon Killer, listening to the soft, comforting voice, would almost certainly be soothed.

". . . The techniques of suspended animation that would have been necessary are quite within the scope of known Yogic practices."

Patanjal began to show slides. Slides of the Mediterranean area. Of land and sea routes to Indian ports. Of ships and artists' conceptions of docks. Of Yogic homilies and Christian artifacts. And on, and on.

And when he was through, the lights in the room came up, and Patanjal asked for questions.

The first woman who stood up was stout, and in her mid-fifties by Gates's estimate, and her face was tightly drawn. "*Mr.* Patanjal, how does it feel to know that you are going to burn in hell?"

Lovely. Gates smiled to himself, waiting for an explosion.

"Madame," Patanjal said quietly, "the divine force which you believe in and the one in which I believe are obviously two different beings. If in a sincere quest for understanding and knowledge I have erred, I am deeply sorry, and await a sign from the Almighty that will teach me the error of my ways. I simply believe in the virtues of sincere intellectual curiosity. An eagerness to use the mind and feelings that God himself gave me to inquire into mysteries rather than merely accept the explanations that other *men* have passed down through the years. If for this I will be cast into fires everlasting, then God is indeed the malign thug of which Mark Twain wrote, and his hell could certainly be no more insufferable than his heaven."

Gates choked back a guffaw on that one, and hefted his walkie-talkie. "Chev, the old boy is pretty sharp."

The speaker crackled softly. "Wish I was out in front. How does it look out there?"

Patanjal called on another of the waving hands, and comments were exchanged. "So far, so good. Maybe our boy didn't come."

The second speaker sat down, and Patanjal called on another.

Gates held his breath.

An almost painfully thin arm was raised, and when Patanjal took it, the man stood up. Tall, thin, shabbily dressed in a naval jacket. Although he didn't say a word, suddenly every eye in the auditorium was drawn to him.

"Chev," Gates whispered, "I think we've got our man."

Patanjal gazed out into the audience for a long moment, and then spoke, "Yes? Your question?"

"Sir"—the voice was very quiet, and yet carried across the entire room—"I've read your book. Yours, and others. You have stated that the biblical miracles are the result of men learning to channel all the forces that act upon them. To utilize more of their minds in order to find a new balance. How can this process be approached?"

There was something in the voice that told Gates that the question hid something greater than itself. Without understanding why, while damning the emotion for its insufferable inappropriateness, Gates found himself feeling pity.

"Jesus," he whispered under his breath. "Chev, we've got him all right, and we have to figure out how to work this. Judging by the past, we can't just arrest him now. He'll resist, and people are going to be hurt. Badly. What suggestions?"

Patanjal seemed frozen to the podium for a moment, then cleared his throat. "It doesn't seem possible to predict a clear-cut path to such powers. The path is too fraught with illusion. One can only go so far, take the bearings, and reorient. Most are lost along the way. It takes a uniquely pure spirit totally given to self-sacrifice. Years of meditation . . ." He stopped in mid-phrase, and watched the man's face more carefully now. "Pardon me, sir, but . . . do I know you?"

The man lowered his head, fighting to gather himself, then went on. "The process. What if there is one door that is more easily opened? More direct, more powerful?"

"At what cost," Patanjal whispered. "Are you a follower of Savagi?"

The audience was confused, looked at the tall, dark figure who stood in their midst. The man didn't look at all like the pictures that had flooded the newspapers. The profile that Gates could see was thin, but almost nobly handsome. Childish in a strange way. And definitely Adam Ludlum.

Security was moving in to cover the doors. Adam didn't look around, but Gates had absolutely no doubt that he knew that they were there.

"How?" Adam said. "If the door can be opened, why can't I close it?"

"Our eyes and ears filter but a small part of the vibratory spectrum." Patanjal seemed unable to take his eyes from the tall, sad figure in front of him. "Similarly, our minds filter reality to a small fragment of what actually is.

Once the lie is seen as such, it is like cracking a dam. Difficult to stop the waters once the crack begins to spread.''

"I'm seeing things. Too much. I'd always heard that we are the world we see. That it is us. I've found the balance point. His teaching is the fulcrum. It's real, and realer all the time. Please . . . how do I close the door?'' The voice was pleading now, and Patanjal stepped out from behind the podium. The entire room was still, every eye focused on the man who stood in the middle of the auditorium, begging for understanding.

"Savagi didn't know either,'' Patanjal said sadly. "It . . . led to his destruction. Perhaps there is time, if one were to stop now. Put aside those teachings.''

"It's too late. I thought that it could be controlled, but that was an illusion. It feeds on death.''

"Perhaps together''—Patanjal moved to the edge of the stage, no longer using the microphone, but still his voice carried to every corner of the room—"perhaps together we can fight this thing.''

"*Sensei*,'' Adam Ludlum said, and his voice was breaking, "I don't want to hurt anyone.'' He looked around the room. "I think I should leave.''

Abruptly, he turned and began edging his way out of the auditorium. Before he got to the door two security guards closed in to meet him.

Adam looked at them both, and it seemed to Gates that there was a huge and awful struggle going on in that mind. He looked back at Patanjal, who looked after him with an expression that Gates couldn't even pretend to read. "Fight it,'' Patanjal called out. He put the microphone back into its holder. "I'll help you, I swear.''

The tall man was screaming now as the two security guards began to drag him toward the back of the auditorium, and Gates cursed and ran down the back stairs, the voice, the terrible, haunted voice ringing in the auditorium; "Help me. Help me please. . . .''

# Chapter Thirty

## Massacre

*Tellin' you all the Zomby Troof,*
*Here I'm is, the ZOMBY WOOF.*
　　　　—Frank Zappa, *The Zomby Woof*

"Help me . . ."

That pleading voice, and the roar of a confused and frightened crowd rang in Winston Gates's ears as he pushed through the fire doors. The walkie-talkie beeped and crackled at his belt, and as he ran he scooped it up in one hand and pressed it to receive.

A half-dozen voices exploded into speech at once:

"Got 'im! Got the sonuvabitch!"

"Need a squad car in front of Tyler Hall *now*."

"Watch his head, dammit."

And above them all was a steady, rhythmic crackle, like waves of static thrown out by an electric generator.

By the time Gates reached the lobby of Tyler Hall, the commotion was ear-splitting.

Four beefy security men, each of them larger than Ludlum, were lurching with him from couch to chair to desk. At first Gates thought that they were slamming him against the wall, but then it was clear that he was bouncing

281

*them* back and forth, all four of them, and that they were definitely getting the worst of it.

*Four men*. Incredible. But they had him now.

Adam Ludlum screamed and bucked.

One of the four security men whipped face first against a pillar, and blood gushed from his nose.

"Please, please," Ludlum yelled. "Leave me alone. I don't want to kill you—"

The man with the bleeding nose screamed something obscene and tripped their prisoner. Ludlum sprawled face-down on the ground, and lay there, trembling, long dark hair splayed like a shawl.

Not just trembling: he *convulsed*, as if electric currents were smashing through his body.

The walkie-talkie in Gates's hand suddenly drowned in static, and, as Gates watched in horror, the hairs on the back of his hand stood up away from the skin. The men holding Ludlum down were twitching as if attacked by a swarm of invisible ants. The hair splayed up away from their heads in spikes, like the quills of an angry porcupine.

Two uniformed LAPD officers joined the fray, and Gates heard the snap of cuffs as they clicked into place.

Ludlum arched his back, looked imploringly at Gates, and for a moment Winston felt himself losing balance, wavering on the edge of a pit. There was nothing danger-ous or fearful in that expression, just an engulfing, crippling despair. "Please . . . help me."

The injured security man hissed, "Son of a bitch," and kicked Ludlum in the back. One of the LAPD officers jumped the security man and wrestled his arms back, hauling him away.

Ludlum's face had darkened and twisted with rage as the blow landed. His mouth opened wider and wider, until Gates saw the back of Ludlum's throat, saw his white teeth stained red with fresh blood, and the prisoner screeched "*Senseiii!*"

The cords in the face stood out in ridges, more muscle and tendon than Gates had ever seen in a human face before, stretching it, contorting it into a mask that combined all of the anger and pain that could possibly exist in one man's universe. And more. Much more.

Gates *saw* Ludlum's arms swell, the skin beneath the handcuffs suddenly well blood. Heard the tortured creak of metal.

"Watch out!" he yelled as the cuffs burst, and Ludlum rose to one knee.

There were four men hanging onto him, one riding his back. *Four!* But there was a sudden blur of motion, and an elbow or a shoulder jolted back—Gates couldn't be sure which—and one of the security men flew away from Ludlum as if shot out of a cannon. Their suspect threw himself onto his back, and there was a cracking sound as a head met the marble floor. Ludlum was on his feet, and then down, then on his feet again. Someone tried a flying tackle, and Gates, running now in what seemed to be slow motion, running but making pitifully little forward progress, running and running, saw Ludlum twist aside. The officer's hand caught only a khaki pocket which ripped diagonally. Ludlum snarled, and his hand blurred as it speared a pale throat. The officer's body knotted with pain as blood gushed from his mouth, and he crumpled to the ground.

A uniformed officer fired his Taser pistol at point-blank range, and Ludlum spasmed and turned on him. Gates scrambled to pull his own Taser and fired, felt the tiny jolt as the steel needle and the wire flew from the flat nose and penetrated the suspect's flesh.

The Wild Man spasmed, thrashing, winding the wire around himself. The wire tautened, then, with a single violent convulsion, snapped. Gates scrambled for his gun, and barely saw the blur as a leg cocked and speared into his stomach.

Agony exploded, destroying logic and vision as the radio flew from his hands. Gates dropped, hands clutching cracked ribs. Through slitted eyes he watched the second officer die, the victim of an acrobatic, leaping, twisting motion that took the Wild Man clear off the ground, cartwheeling him into the officer with a sound like ice cubes under the mallet.

Then in a blur of motion, Ludlum was gone.

Ten seconds. The whole thing couldn't have taken more than ten seconds, and half a dozen men lay broken on the floor like so many road kills.

Chev and the other officers came running up from behind the aisle, and two of them helped Winston to his feet.

"What happened out here?" she asked, wide-eyed.

Pain shot through him, and he tasted bile, but nothing short of death was stopping him this time. "Damned if I know." His voice was a pain-filled rasp. "But whatever it is, it ends tonight." He scooped his walkie-talkie from the floor and shook it to life. "All units in the vicinity of Tyler Hall. Suspect is approximately six feet tall, wearing a navy jacket. Unarmed but extremely dangerous." He paused and surveyed the damage. One of the men was bleeding weakly from the ears. Another's head was turned at an impossible angle, and Gates felt sick. "Shoot on sight."

They hobbled to the front door as a chorus of shots broke out, and the sound of breaking glass, and more screams.

The distant form of the Wild Man galloped across the grass. A squad car was wheels up on the lawn, with one figure sprawled limply, and another down on one knee, firing as the suspect disappeared.

Students, dazed and frightened, watched the carnage with expressions that ranged from fascination to terror. A second squad car pulled up to the front steps, and a young officer rolled his window down to yell out. "Inspector Gates, sir. We've got the campus sealed off. Do you need a lift?"

Gates hobbled to the passenger seat, and waved Arlene around to the driver's position. "Let her drive, son. She puts both of us to shame."

He checked the rack beneath the dashboard and couldn't repress a grunt of satisfaction at what he found: a regulation Remington pump shotgun, loaded and ready.

They wheeled the car around on the drive and started after Ludlum. The radio was buzzing: "Nothing in sight and—*there he is!* God *damn* he is moving! Going to cut him off at—" A burst of static garbled the words, then there was nothing.

The whine of sirens filled the air.

Winston's ears were hammered by the sound of tires smoking against the pavement, of yowling, tortured brakes, and the staccato explosion of gunshots.

Arlene skimmed down the main path, and Gates caught sight of a second police car pulling out of a vicious skid, pursuing a running, ragged figure that galloped out onto Westwood Boulevard.

The sirens were blaring, but a car backing blindly out of a driveway took the front bumper of the police car in front of them. The vehicles linked and dragged each other into an inverted V, blocking Westwood.

Arlene swung her steering wheel hard to avoid a crack-up, jumping the black and white up onto the sidewalk. Two wire frame trash baskets erupted in a shower of paper and plastic, and pedestrians dove for the protection of a ginger-bread front Baskin-Robbins doorway as they roared by. Gates's heartbeat did a staccato jitterbug. In the next moment the tires bumped as they leaped down over the curb, and they were back on the boulevard.

The Wild Man was only half a block ahead, just reaching Weyburn Avenue. A police car slammed across the intersection, fishtailing to seal it, the doors swinging open. "Halt!"

Without breaking stride, the suspect *vaulted the car*, performed a leaping movement of some kind that sent his whole body whirling through the air. His heel smashed into the driver's door and slammed it shut, crushing the officer's jaw and legs. The second officer braced himself and got off a shot.

The Wild Man flinched and staggered, but kept running.

Arlene hit the brakes hard and the car slewed in a dizzying half circle before she regained control. The young officer in the backseat looked green as Arlene threw the car into reverse and skimmed it backward around the other vehicle.

When they cleared the far side, Gates looked back at the car: its door was smashed in as if by a wrecking ball, and the officer hung on the door, broken and hideously still. Blood slimed the glass under his face.

Ludlum was weaving through the traffic like a broken field runner, and Gates could hear a loudspeaker now: "Clear the streets! This is a police emergency. Clear the streets!"

A police car came skidding off Wilshire, siren blaring, immediately swerving to avoid a red and white Chevy van spinning out of control. The black and white jumped the curb, slamming into a hydrant, shattering its right headlight and sending a glittering, foaming stream of water arcing across the street.

And Gates saw it, saw what was going to happen. Because all of the pedestrians had *not* cleared out of the street and a blond woman dragging two children across the intersection of Kinross and Westwood put on a burst of speed to escape the slewing van.

The little girl on her left lost her grip, kept up with her mother for two strides and then stumbled, her tiny mitted hands stretching out to keep her face from the pavement.

The mother was almost to the sidewalk, and safety, before she turned, realizing what was happening. The chrome bumper of the van was only a few yards away from the little girl who cowered in the middle of the street, and there was nothing, nothing to be done.

Gates held his breath, because Ludlum had swerved, moving faster than any animal ever birthed by nature, darting like a hummingbird, changing directions with the impossible, inertia-defying angularity of a bumblebee. He scooped up the girl as he moved, picking her up in stick-thin, bloodstained arms, spinning, riding out the shock as the bumper of the Chevy smashed into him at full speed. He stumbled and fell, rolling like a gymnast, protecting her with his shoulders and back. And when he came up he wheeled like a human top under perfect control, and set the sobbing child on the pavement as lightly as a snowflake.

Gates still hadn't breathed. All motion in his universe froze as Ludlum seemed to be frozen, in stillness as volcanically dynamic as his movement. The Wild Man stood looking at the girl, at his hands, smeared with his own blood. At the street, and the incredible carnage of crushed automobiles and smashed hydrants vomiting fountains of foaming white, and something seemed to go out of him.

Then from the corner of his eye, Gates saw the officer climbing shakily out of the wet, crashed police car, pulling his service pistol and drawing a careful bead. A scream of "wait!" stuck in Gates's throat as the .38 revolver fired once and then again. Ludlum's head snapped back.

His hands slapped to his forehead, and Gates saw red oozing between pale thin fingers as Ludlum's knees buckled slightly. Howling like a wounded wolf, Ludlum fled into a sidewalk mall.

"Jesus Christ." They stopped the patrol car. Gates unclipped the Remington from beneath the dashboard. Arlene gripped his arm.

"Winston . . ."

"I don't know. I'll *try* to take him alive, but I don't know." Before there was time to change his mind, he swung out from the passenger side, ribs aching, shotgun at port arms. The young officer scrambled out of the other side, revolver leveled. "Cover the side," Winston barked.

A grinding, crashing sound beckoned him to the back of the complex, and he limped on, ignoring the pain of his broken ribs and the sudden taste of blood in his mouth. "Police, dammit!" The crowd was confused, as terrified as he, and a row of smashed merchandise led him to the back. There was another crashing sound in the back of the store, and Gates followed it. The pain in his side ripped at his lungs, and each breath was torture as he struggled up an unpainted flight of wooden stairs and into the storeroom.

Darkness, splintered shadows of cones and boxes and cylinders. The room's only window was set with iron burglar bars: there was no escape. In the back of the shop one shadow seemed more massively dark than any of the others. Gates paused, heart hammering in his chest.

Gates felt himself shaking, gritted his teeth together to keep them from chattering. It was insane: he held the shotgun. He had cornered a trapped, injured madman, and yet he felt naked and utterly vulnerable.

He forced courage into his voice. "Don't move. I don't want to have to kill you, but I will if you make just one wrong move."

The shadow whimpered, and Gates took another step into the room. Something glittered in the corner, reflecting a streetlamp, and Gates squinted against the light.

The Wild Man moved with baffling speed, and one of the wooden storage boxes sailed through the air directly at Gates.

Gates cursed, firing. There was a scream—perhaps his own, perhaps that of the Wild Man—as the raft of cartons clubbed him in face and chest.

Stars exploded behind his eyes, his gasp of pain lost in the metallic cacophony of concrete and steel bars being wrenched apart. Gates fired again in the direction of the noise, the shot deflected by the boxes. There was a moment of clarity, an image of a thin, bleeding figure wriggling through a window, half-inch iron bars twisted out of the way like sticks of taffy.

A clear moment, and Gates pumped the shotgun and fired again. In a burst of smoke and sparks and ear-numbing sound, the silhouette jolted out of the window and onto Kinross Avenue a story below.

"Bingo," Gates said disgustedly.

There on the sidewalk under the window was a splotch of blood. Limping away from it, holding his stomach and head, was Adam Ludlum.

Disbelieving, reeling from the emotional gut punch, Gates aimed the shotgun again, and then lowered it. He just couldn't—even if the range had been right. There was something terribly wrong here. He couldn't understand even a fingernail fragment of it, but there was something *wrong*.

He ran back out of the shop, holding his side as if he could squeeze the pain away.

As Gates hit the street and cleared the corner he saw Arlene's police car in pursuit, and there stood Adam Ludlum at the driveway of the Kinross parking lot.

Blood drenched his jacket; a flap of scalp was torn away from his forehead, hanging to mask one eye. One arm looked to have been almost completely torn away, and a fragment of bone protruded from his left shin.

Ludlum stood, and then he screamed, a sound that would haunt Winston Gates for the rest of his life.

The ground shook as the roar built. The windows of the oncoming patrol car slivered and spiderwebbed with cracks.

The car slid and spun, doing at least forty mph, and hit the restraint spikes in the parking lot driveway.

As it hit, the windows *exploded* out of the car. The front tires shredded like paper, and the car stumped onto its nose, hit a concrete stopper, and flipped over, smashing against a black Oldsmobile with a sound like metal dinosaurs colliding in mortal combat. Black smoke boiled from the undercarriage. Gates shook his head, dazed and startled to find himself on his knees.

He staggered to his feet and quickly scanned the lot for Adam Ludlum, but he was nowhere in sight.

Chev was pulling herself out of the car window. Ignoring the pain in his side, Gates helped her out. As her feet left the window, flames began to lick from the underside of the Oldsmobile.

He cradled her head in his arms, and she looked up at him. "He isn't human, Winston. He isn't."

"You're in shock," he whispered. Police and ambulance sirens mingled. They almost, but not quite drowned out the thunder of his own breathing.

With a soft *whumph* the fuel lines burst into flame.

Chev closed her eyes. "Yes. I'm in shock. And he's not human."

She went limp in his arms. Winston Gates leaned back against the car, watching the patrol car burn, afraid to label the emotion that was engulfing him now, larger and stronger than any emotion he had ever known.

# Chapter Thirty-one
## Shattered

Adam could no longer move. He lay in an alley some-where, covered with sheets of damp, moldy cardboard that smelled like rotten bologna. Sirens howled around him, but he heard them distantly, without concern.

Light. His world was filled with lights, dancing, fluxing. Pretty lights. Pretty, pretty . . . calling.

Broken ribs stood out from his chest, and his skin peeled away from his skull. He was blind in one eye, and one ear was gone. There was something wrong with his head. With his brain. He couldn't think clearly. It felt as if part of him had died.

The flow of blood from his wounds, which had drenched the ground around him had slowed to a trickle, seemingly because there was no blood left.

How that could be, he didn't know. There wasn't a lot that he could be sure of, nothing that existed beyond the sensation of hundreds of alien pieces of metal invading his body, of his shattered bones hanging in his body like splinters suspended in Jell-O. Flies buzzed over the wounds, and he was too weak to shoo them away. Ants swarmed at the blood, investigated the ruptures in his flesh with tiny, questing pincers.

How long he lay there, it was impossible to say. But the

night came, and somehow no one found him, and still he breathed.

He felt his body encapsulate the pellets of lead and steel, form cysts, and push them slowly to the surface.

Tiny, shiny red beads. Slimed with flesh and clotted blood, glistening, lying on the ground, covered with ants. Each of them a symbol, a mark of passage, another piece of himself left behind as he crossed some nameless threshold.

Sometimes he hallucinated that he was alone.

He wasn't alone, of course. The Golden Man stood over him, crouched over him, next to him, its reptilian visage alternating with the mammalian. Fading in and out. The golden one hissed softly of the wonders to come. Adam shuddered as his bones knit, as they found each other in the shattered matrix of his flesh and, in the best way they could, made him whole.

Sometimes the numbness went away, and he whimpered, curled onto his side. The reality around him wavered, rippled, the brick walls melting away until he was alone on a plain vaster than all of creation. The light finally becoming brighter and brighter until it overwhelmed everything.

And became night. Which became something from the heart of darkness, or the heart of the sun, light and dark dancing together until they were an indistinguishable fusion. And in that land of absolute light and shadow his skin and bone and blood melded to create a cocoon, within which something infinitely strange and terrible could grow.

Winston Gates sat at his desk at the Wilshire Police Department. There was noise all around him, endless beehive activity as the movement and progress of the sweeping police net was coordinated. Phones rang, and people ran past his desk: he had spent the last five hours in meetings and conferences, and still had a stack of papers on his desk to complete, but his heart just wasn't in it. He peered down at the newsstand below his window. It was deserted, and there were no newspapers on the rack. It seemed that half of the cars cruising under his window had blinking red lights atop them.

His head pounded unmercifully, and he fought to put the pieces together. How could such a thing happen? He *saw* Ludlum take a round to the head. At least one, and keep going. And a Remington round to the midsection. How much abuse could a human body take?

But he couldn't bring himself to hate the man. There was something in his face. When Ludlum put the little girl down on the sidewalk, just before the .38 slammed into his forehead. When he cowered in the darkened storage room, just before Gates blew him out the window with the shotgun.

The memory of the whimpering scream made Gates cringe.

There was someone standing next to the desk, and Gates pulled his attention back to the present.

"Mr. Gates," Patanjal said softly.

"Mr. Shackley," Gates answered. "I think I can safely call you that."

"I suppose so." Patanjal/Shackley sat lightly in a wooden chair by Gates's desk. His face was quietly expectant.

"Coffee?"

"Never. Have you any juice?"

"Never." They stared at each other for a long time, in silence. "Well, I'm glad that you don't deny that you're Mitchell Shackley."

"No. I tried that. Plastic surgery in Hong Kong. The new name. Disappearing for five years."

"Do you mind telling me about that?"

"It was . . . a religious matter." The unlined face was serene. "There are things a man must do in life that . . . cause changes. I lived through one of those things. I'm afraid that I don't care to comment more at this time."

Gates sighed. Rain was beginning to fall outside the window, and in the parking lot of the 7-Eleven, a bony dog padded forlornly through the wet. "You know Adam Ludlum?"

"He was a student. He left my school about eight years ago. I hadn't seen or heard of him since."

"Do you know why he might have wanted to talk to you?"

Shackley sighed. "I assume he needed a friend. Remembered and recognized me. I had no contact with him except what you saw."

Gates drummed his fingers on the table. "You've already given statements to the West LAPD."

"Twice." He smiled. "I'm not as young as I used to be. I'm really tired."

"Me, too. I appreciate your coming in. I guess . . . I just hoped you might want to say something to me."

Shackley paused, and again Gates had the feeling that he was about to speak. "No. Not at this time. But, Inspector, if you locate Adam, consider me a resource. I will do anything in my power to help."

"I appreciate that."

Shackley stood, and turned.

"Shackley," Gates said.

The man stopped, but didn't turn. "Yes, Inspector?"

"I know there's more. You're not exactly lying, but there's more. We'll talk again."

"I'm sure we will," he said. "I'll be at the Sheraton Wilshire for the next three days if you want me." And he left.

They came for Adam when he was in a state beyond time, beyond pain. When they strode down the alley he could not see them, he could only sense that they were there. He cried, *No! Leave me alone. I don't want . . .*

"You are Adam Ludlum," Kevin Dearborne said. "We have watched you, and found you, and now you are ours. You belong to us, and we to you."

Adam tried to make a sound. There was no sound that would emerge, but the plea *Help me* was the closest he could come. *Someone help me.*

"Yes," Kevin said. "We will help. We are the only ones who can. We're going to take you home."

And Adam's consciousness slipped away as they loaded him carefully onto a cot and carried him to the rickety yellow school bus waiting in the alley mouth.

# Chapter Thirty-two
## The Kundalini Equation

*Absence diminishes mediocre passions and increases
great ones, as the wind blows out candles and fans
fires.*

—La Rochefoucauld, Reflections; or,
Sentences and Moral Maxims

## Sunday, July 1. Day 2.

Algernon pulled his VW Rabbit into the parking lot
beside the Good Life bookstore, and turned off the motor.
Beside him, Micki was asleep, exhausted, the nutmeg
ringlets of her hair limp and flaccid, new stress lines eating
the glow from her complexion.

"Micki. Michelle. Wake up." He glanced at his watch.
It was almost four-thirty in the morning, and they had been
going at it all night. In the backseat of the car was a
collection of disks and files that he had copied out of the
computer at UCLA, protected in hidden files, and printed
out the first chance that they had. It was everything, and it
wasn't enough.

Michelle stirred groggily, and opened her eyes. They

wouldn't focus at first. Then slowly she assimilated her surroundings. "Algy?"

"You're home. Do you want to keep working, or . . . ?" He left the question open. He felt so tired, but knew that sleep would elude him until he had exhausted every erg of energy in his body. "We should have done something sooner, Micki. We should have spoken up. It was so damned stupid."

Micki took his hands in hers. "We didn't know. You saw the pictures: every muscle in his face was distorted. We couldn't be sure until Culpepper. And now they're looking for him. Going to kill him."

"I hate to say this, Michelle," Algy said quietly, "but I'm not sure Adam wouldn't want that."

"You read the reports, for God's sake. We can't even be sure they *can* kill him."

"Then just what the hell do we think we're doing?"

She released his hand, rubbed at her eyes with fingers that shook. "What he did, he did for himself, but because of us, don't you understand that? If anyone can get to him, it's us. He's still Adam. Somewhere out there, if he's alive at all, he's still Adam."

Together they carted the boxes into the bedroom at the rear of the bookstore, clumping them onto the floor.

Algy sighed. "All right. This should be the rest of the notes, but I can't be sure. A lot of it is Culpepper's transcription of Adam's verbal notes. A lot of it just doesn't make sense. Take this file: 'The Kundalini Equation.' "

"What about it?" Micki turned on the coffee maker in the kitchenette.

He traced his finger along a column of figures in a computer printout. "Look at this. What he has here is a listing of the specific effects of different cycles of inhalation-exhalation on the body and mind. Carbon dioxide. I think that he believed that there was a particular threshold with the breathing. Probably something in concert with visualization and physical exercise. Some combination. A balance, an 'equation' if you will, that takes you over the edge.''

"But who would ever develop something as hideous as this?''

"Jesus, who can say? You read the stuff on Savagi. What do you think? The man obviously didn't have all of the fudge in his filling.'' Algy sat on the edge of her bed, distantly aware of the intimacy of their situation, instantly rejecting the implications or possibilities. "Listen to me. I can't explain everything happening here, but a few things are of interest. Let's look at the range of effects: psychological, biological/physiological, psychic, and electrodynamic.''

"What?'' Micki thumped down on the bed next to him, and Algy closed his eyes. She smelled of fatigue and thirty-six hours without a shower, but his mind still battled to stay on the track.

"Look at the reports. At least a dozen people reported their skin crawling, their hair standing on end. In one sense that might have been merely emotional. But it could also be symptomatic of electrostatic repulsion.''

"I remember—'' Micki thought back, trying desperately to whip the fog from her mind. "I remember my digital watch stopping at his house.''

Algy kept his eyes closed, as his mind raced through possibilities. "I'm just guessing now, but listen to me anyway. Remember that the first distinct manifestations of Adam's power came when he was in the Faraday cage, cut off from the otherwise omnipresent electromagnetic static. The kind of quiet that Tibetan holy men get atop mountains.

"Listen. Most of the world's religions have a strong foundation in the belief in miracles. Jesus, Buddha, Mohammed, Moses—all of their legends, myths, heritages, whatever you want to call them, are built on miracles. They are an essential part of most religious philosophies. And yet there is so little evidence for miracles in today's world that many rational churchgoers have to keep their spiritual and secular lives totally separate.''

Algy took a deep breath, as if steeling himself for what he was about to say.

"But what if . . . what if some of those accounts are true? What if just once in human history someone made a seed sprout by looking at it, or turned a cloud against the wind, or made a single pebble leap into the air with the force of mind alone. If any of that is true, then literally anything is possible. It opens doors to things I'm not sure I want to think about. What if, just for instance, the manipulations and miracles mentioned in the Bible and other holy books are a result of the manipulation of various manifestations of electromagnetism? Psychic phenomena as electromagnetic communication between living antennas . . . I'm sorry. Am I getting punchy?"

Something kept Micki from automatically laughing out loud. "Adam mentioned something about electrons once. About sensing them, or seeing them." She gestured helplessly. "I don't really remember. What if it's true? What if somehow he's managed to do this? Why has there been so much violence?"

"Christ," he said in disgust. "I don't know. I suspect any strong emotion focuses the mind, shuts out distractions. Why violence? Bloodlust? Berserker rage?" He drummed his fingers on the file. "This is a stab in the dark. The forces of creation and destruction are balanced in a human being, or in the universe, for that matter. Call it the life/death complex. It drives us like the stroke of a piston. The drive to kill what we were yesterday by becoming something new today. Great athletes, artists, statesmen . . . consistently jump from one near-disaster to another, and the most skillful of them skirt the edge, never quite falling in. And they're celebrated for it. But let the life drive gain dominance and you can get fear of risk, leading to mediocrity. Let the death urge get out of control, and the career self-destructs.

"The explosion of emotions from an act of violence is more powerful than a similar brief act of love, and often has more lasting consequences. How long does it take to raise and nurture a human being, and how long to extinguish him? So from one twisted perspective, the path of destruction, the 'Dark Side of the Force,' as Darth Vader put it, is more immediately rewarding. And I think that that was the path that Savagi followed, the path that Adam tripped onto.''

"Where could it all lead? If you're right. God, I hope you're wrong.''

Algy ran a hand through his wiry hair. "I don't know. I don't have any idea. The heat of a nuclear fireball is produced by electrostatic repulsion. There's just no way to say what the limits are.'' He yawned, the weight of two sleepless days suddenly falling on his shoulders like a shelf of mud. "Besides, I'm babbling by now. I think I need to sleep. I need to get home.''

"Algy, there's a couch out in the reading room. Could I maybe make that up for you? I'd really rather not be here alone tonight.''

He opened his mouth, then shut it fast, before he said what was really on his mind. Instead, he gave her only the weariest of wan smiles. "Sure. I can make it up myself. You try to get some sleep.''

She looked at him with eyes that were haunted and darkly ringed. "Do you really think that I'm going to be able to sleep before I know what in the hell is going on?''

"I know that you've got to give it a shot,'' he said. "Now, listen. We can keep going in the morning. There has to be a clue in all of this. Something that will at least let us know what he's done to himself. If it's possible to help him. Hell,'' he added, "if it's even possible to *stop* him.''

As during the previous three nights, Micki couldn't sleep. She lay staring at the ceiling, tossing, feeling unendurably hot. The visions that came to her were cobwebby and sticky, filled with echoing voices and questioning eyes.

Finally, in desperation, she got up quietly and turned on the light again. There were boxes of fanfold paper, and stolen files and stacks of Adam's notes made in the same omnipresent scrawl.

Her eyes burned as she pored over them, searching, searching, but for what? She wasn't even sure. All she knew was that she had failed someone who loved and needed her desperately.

She turned on the radio, diddling the dial until she found station KCOC. At first she lost herself in the sway of the music. But her smile failed as she remembered Adam, remembered the station, remembered all of the things that had happened since he had been there. The song ended, and the announcer said, "And we'll be back after a word from our sponsor, and a quick weather report."

She was about to change the dial when something stayed her hand. She continued looking through the stack. The commercial, a face cream spiel aimed at every insecure teen who had ever compared her face to the Sea of Tranquillity, ended after a wretched but mercifully brief jingle. The weather was predicted to be mild and warm, and the weatherman stopped to laugh. "Hey, glad you're down here in Los Angeles, aren't you? Our cousins up in San Francisco haven't seen the sun for three days, and the weather bureau can't even tell them when they're going to get relief—"

San Francisco.

She browsed through the letters, through the stacks of clippings and notes, until she came to a brief article on a failed health farm called "Pah-Dishah." There was very little about it, just a picture of a forlorn row of bungalows and a stretch of grass that looked like it got burned back about twice a year. Its location was given as Porter Creek, not fifty miles north of San Francisco.

San Francisco. Now that the name of the town had come into her head, it didn't seem to want to leave.

She rubbed her eyes, and shook her head. Sleep. She needed sleep. When was the last time she had slept? Seventy-two hours before, at least. Why was this happening?

She turned off the light and went back to her couch, lying down. The image of San Francisco came to her, a town she knew in sunlight and sometimes in fog, but not in rain. She saw the umbrellas bending under the blast, and the wind whistling savagely from the bay. She shivered with the image.

Then she was wrenched out of that scene, shocked by the sudden inversion of colors, the pain that racked her body, that made her arch her back, gasping, thrashing, crying out. *She was Adam!* Her eyes were fixed open, and she was in a school bus, driving, driving, and the people who were around her were staring at her with something that might have been mistaken for sympathy were it not for the stark hunger in their gaze.

She whimpered.

The bus turned off a road, and there was a flare of fear. Her mind reached out and grazed the side of the bus. The paint bubbled, then smoked and burst into flame. The bus careened wildly, and slammed into a ditch. The side of the bus peeled back further, and she crawled toward the hole, through the hole, and away, trying to get away, but there was nowhere to go, and she couldn't run, could barely crawl.

Then they came, dozens of the Children of the Earth Heart. Cadaverously thin, radiating physical strength and power that was totally disorienting. Their saffron robes shimmered in the sunlight as they carried her to a row of vaguely military barracks.

They were singing, or humming, and something within her that was strong and hungry twitched in response, leaped, danced like a homicidal idiot child.

She screamed.

Algernon shook her shoulder, and when she pulled herself out of the vision, her hands formed into claws and raked at him. He backed away, aghast. "Micki? What is it?"

It took a few moments for her eyes to refocus, and then she dissolved into tears, clutching at him. "I know where he is," she said. "I've got to go to him."

"Where . . . do you think he is?"

"San Francisco. Somewhere north of San Francisco."

Her eyes were pleading, and Algernon sighed. "How far is it?"

"We can . . . drive there. One night."

"Drive there." *How far? How far do you go for a friend?*

Or for Micki. He turned from her, feeling the cold place in his chest. "Micki." He shook his head slowly. "I've gone as far as I think I can. I love Adam. You know that." He turned slowly. "The problem is, that I love you too."

"Algernon—"

"Be quiet, Micki. Just be quiet. I may not be able to get this out twice. I've always loved you, and I never had a chance because you and Adam were always breaking up and getting back together. There just wasn't ever a chance for me to even find out if you would have laughed in my face."

"Algy . . . I never laughed at you."

"You never looked at me, either. Not the way I wanted." He closed his eyes, sorry now that he had begun to speak. "It's too late now. Whatever is going to happen, I'm sure of that. I'll help you. I'll go with you. If Adam is still alive I'll do what I can. If he isn't, you can cry on my shoulder if you want, then go your way. I don't, I really don't want to lay anything on you when you don't need it. I just wanted to say it now, in case I never had another chance. I've seen your eyes in a hundred women's faces. I'd do anything for you."

She was silent, but reached out a hand for his, and he took it, and she came to him and hugged him, held him closely, so closely that for a moment their bodies seemed to melt together. Then he pushed her away, and held a quieting finger to her lips. "All right. BeDoss is on an automatic feeder. He'll hold for a couple of days . . ."

Micki smiled bleakly. "If his cat box gets too full, there's always the sink."

"Jesus, don't remind me." He wiped his eyes. "All right Miss Cappelotti. Let's get going before I come to my senses."

*     *     *

Outside the Good Life, Winston Gates sat in his car, Arlene by his side. They had been sleeping alternately for the past two days. Now he was awake and Arlene was asleep, and he took a pull of coffee from his thermos. There was an ending here, something that was more important than any considerations of time or discomfort. Something. And the fact that he couldn't understand it didn't change a thing.

A light flashed on on the porch. Swain and Cappelotti came out, carrying light suitcases. "Bingo," he said under his breath.

Without turning his lights on, Gates started his car and cruised after them.

Arlene, next to him, stirred groggily to wakefulness. "We're moving?" She sat up straight, and looked at Gates carefully. "You're sure this is what you want to do?"

"You don't have to come," he said. "I don't know where all of this is heading, only that I have to go."

She looked at the people in the car ahead of them. "I don't know what the hell we can do that the entire Los Angeles Police Department couldn't."

"Maybe nothing. But maybe it's just being crazy enough to care that makes the difference. Maybe."

"Yeah. Maybe."

They turned onto the Santa Monica Freeway, following the blinking red right turn indicator of the Rabbit in front of them.

# Chapter Thirty-three
## San Francisco

## Monday, July 2. Day 1.

Winston Gates didn't like the Bay City. He never had. He was that rarest of creatures, a born and raised Angeleno. Driving was his natural mode of transport. The trip up Highway 5 had been a pleasure, even when the skeletal shogun-warrior frames of the electrical transformers glowered sullenly along the side of the road. But as they neared the Bay area, the pleasant Los Angeles weather dissolved into a wet hell.

San Francisco is many wonderful things, but a driver's paradise is not among them. The city seemed a twisted warren of roads that began and ended at random. The street signs might as well have been printed in Arabic, and even the cab drivers couldn't seem to give concise directions.

Arlene Cheviot was back at the motor hotel where Micki Cappelotti and Swain had taken rooms. If necessary, she could continue to follow them. He doubted if that would be necessary: Adam Ludlum's two friends had literally driven all day, and had to be in desperate need of sleep.

Meanwhile, he needed to check on his own contacts.

The weather was horrendous, a continuous driving sheet

of rain that stole the oxygen from the air. His windshield wipers were going at full speed, and even so, between beats reality blurred to a distorted gel of melting ice.

He turned into the driveway of the Columbus Street police station, and waited for a minute, watching his breath fog the window.

Dragging Arlene along with him up to San Francisco was crazy, and could cost them both dearly if things went wrong. On the other hand, if even half of his instincts were correct, there was far, far more at stake than their careers.

Or lives.

Gates could still remember what Shackley told him: "*I will do anything in my power to help.*"

He would come. And there was an implication, an unspoken assertion that there were things Shackley knew, could accomplish, that the police department couldn't. What that might be, Gates didn't know. Even thinking about it too hard made his head hurt.

Growling, he turned up his collar and left the car. Rain pelted against his face in snail-sized drops. The parking lot was filled with comfortingly familiar blue and white police cars, and a few damp faces turned to watch him as he crossed the lot, as if wondering exactly what business he had there.

The front door swung heavily to his touch, and the officer of the day smiled at him as he wiped his feet on the welcome mat.

"Pretty wet." The desk man smiled bleakly. "What can I do for you?"

"Winston Gates, LAPD. I need to talk to someone in Homicide."

In five minutes a tall, pleasant-faced man appeared. He smoked a hand-carved pipe, and his discrete potbelly was well disguised with a carefully tailored waistcoat. He had clearly come in from out of the rain no more than thirty minutes before: his pants cuffs were still damp.

They shook hands, hard. "Bill Janus." His eyes were extremely deepset. "How can I help you?"

"Some coffee would help," Gates said, "and then a little talk."

"Yeah, LA ain't SF, and I wouldn't trade 'em." Janus looked at Winston over the cup of coffee. "Shouldn't drink this stuff. Plays hell with my stomach." He laughed at a private joke, then leaned back in his chair. "Anyway, heard about the Croissant Constituency? Damn Yuppies are moving into the low-rent districts, driving up the values. Working man can't get a decent roof in the city. Had to move over to Berkeley myself. Most of my men live farther out than that."

"Thing's have gotten weird down in LA, too." Gates chuckled. The coffee was hot, and bitter, and unsullied by cream or sugar. "Month ago I was making an investigation upstairs from a cheese wholesaler. A truck had dropped off half a ton of Brie in the alley next door. Company refused to take delivery, saying the cheese was rotten. Truck just dumped it there. People were sick for blocks. This work ain't what it used to be, Janus."

Janus chuckled, then turned serious. "Yeah. We know about the whole Westwood thing, and we read the other reports. And you think that this guy is up in this area?"

"It seems to be a pretty decent possibility."

" 'Decent' isn't the word I would have chosen. Why weren't we warned?"

"You just got the first word I've given. I followed his lady friend up here without departmental approval. I think that what we're into here is something very special. I'm not sure what to believe."

"You're telling me that you think that there's something to this Neon Killer bullshit?"

"I tell you what. Let's you and I just believe that this is a maniacal black belt strung out on angel dust, and that he's into devil worship and Kevlar underwear. Let's just say that I want him for my own private reasons. He killed my partner, and I want to pull the trigger on him. It doesn't make me look any better, but it might be easier to believe. God knows that I don't believe what I'm beginning to suspect is the truth.''

"And what is that?"

Gates took another pull of the coffee. "That there's something special about this guy Ludlum. I tell you that I saw this man eat a dozen bullets, including a shotgun blast, and walk away from it. And he was more powerful the second time I saw him than the first. There's no question about it.''

Janus looked at him with confusion in his hooded eyes. "If you're so afraid of this man, why are you tackling him by yourself?"

"I don't know. I only know that he's had two chances to kill me, and didn't take them. I think that there's a reason for it. I don't think he wanted to hurt *anybody*. There's something driving him, and I'm beginning to think it isn't drugs. I don't want any more dead officers. Nobody's going to believe what I think. If he's just a man, then he's dead somewhere. If there's something else going on, then maybe he would *want* to be helped out of his misery. Maybe we should be just a little bit frightened.''

Janus sighed, rubbing his stomach. "Well, Win, I can see that I'm not going to be able to talk you out of this one, so I guess I might as well tell you.''

"Tell me what?"

"We've had a copycat killing up here. Either that, or you're right. Your boy is in San Francisco.''

The cell block was cold, as they always seemed to be, except when they were too hot. Gates shuddered as they walked up the stairs, his damaged ribs nudging him painfully with every step. "That thing down in the morgue. Yeah, that's the same cranial mutilation all right. There can't be any doubt about it.''

"We have a suspect this time," Janus said. "Weirdo. Panhandles around the neighborhood for some fringie group. Christ, we've got so many of them around here that they trip over each other's robes. Anyway, somebody recognized him, and we picked him up on the other side of town the next day. And guess what? Traces of phosphorescent paint in his beard. Could be your Neon Killer.''

Gates snorted. "We'll see."

The cell door clanged open electronically. "Cell fourteen. We want to see the prisoner. Arlan Hubbock.''

"Right down here."

The jailer, a red-faced, porcine man who seemed ripe for retirement, levered himself from behind the desk and grabbed his clipboard, rattling it along the rows of bars. "All right, Hubbock, you've got company." His face went ashen. "Aw, *shit*." He fumbled for his keys.

Janus was the first into the cell, and the one to examine the body. "I don't get it," he whispered. "I really don't get it. How could a man do something like this to himself?"

Hubbock's hands still gripped the bars. His forehead was crushed in like an eggshell, as if he had rammed his head into the bars with the force of an express train.

The jailer ran back down the hall, rapping out numbers on the telephone. Janus sucked his cheeks as if trying to work up a spitball. "Well, for sure we're not going to learn anything from this guy.''

"Don't bet on it," Gates said, turning on his heel. "Where in the hell is the property room? I want to take a look at what was in this guy's pockets. And I want to look at it *now*."

# Chapter Thirty-four

## Interlude

Adam was in intolerable pain. His body was a trap, a suffocating web of misery intense enough to cloud any perception of the world beyond it. He did not know where or what he was anymore. There was no longer logic or thought, only the fight for survival.

And he sought escape in the only manner open to him. He pulled his consciousness into his mind, more deeply than he had ever done before.

And he fell, shrinking into his brain, down to the tissue level, to the synaptic level, to a place where there were shapes without form and color without light.

And there, he loosed his scream.

Adam saw. Adam *was*. Incapable of standing apart from that which he observed, now at a singularity more starkly terrible than any dreamed by technological man.

Primal mind, primal matter. One.

Innately there is a perfect balance between forces in the universe. The electric charges on an electron and a proton are identical, to the extent that instrumentation can measure.

The tiniest change in balance can make electrons slightly more negative than protons are positive. So small a change as one part in $10^{-30}$ could be enough to completely disintegrate matter.

Adam's pain became the pain of this primal matter, this basic isness at the core of our universe, creating a field of electrostatic disruption.

Each atom of oxygen in the air around him became slightly negatively charged. And those negative charges repelled one another. Every atom repelled every other atom in the field. The sphere swelled as his scream grew, disrupting the charges of oxygen atoms as it expanded. It grew until it was a mile across, and more.

The air molecules pushed against one another, warming one another, lowering the atmospheric density so that there was an enormous mass of electrically charged air, now expanding and floating upward like a giant balloon. Winds of staggering power ripped the California northwest. Rain followed swiftly, and as the atmosphere struggled to regain electrical balance, the sky danced with lightning. It coiled, flaming along the underside of the massed clouds, striking to the earth below, arcing across the darkness, the roll of thunder impossibly but unmistakably echoing in steady, ominous cadence.

By the time that Gates made it back to the Holiday Inn, the weather was stupefyingly bad. He could remember few California storms so intense. The raindrops struck his skin so hard that they felt like hail. The radio weather bulletins carried an unnerving edge of hysteria.

None of the weather patterns seemed to match what had been predicted for the month. None of the hot-air/cold-air masses that drifted off the coast of California, wafted in from Hawaii, down from Alaska, or up from the Gulf of Mexico seemed to explain it.

"*This is starting to look damned interesting.*" The irony of Doug's flippant sentiment was crushing.

The streets were almost empty when he reached the inn, but one car, his station wagon, was still there. Arlene Cheviot was still in the front seat, and nodded to him as he tapped on the glass. He slid in next to her, glad for her warmth.

"Any action?"

"Nothing. They never came out. Maybe they're playing footsie in there. Maybe they just drove up for a little action."

The door to the room opened, and Swain staggered into view, pantless, shirttails flapping in the wind, wildly searching the parking lot. He disappeared back inside and reappeared two minutes later fully dressed.

"This could be it."

"It's something, that's for sure."

But Swain didn't get into his Rabbit, he merely looked through the window. Then he staggered across the parking lot like a drunken man, and finally stood in the middle of the rain-swept concrete driveway, screaming something to the clouds.

"I think that maybe we should get over there."

"I think you're right."

Arlene gunned the engine, and she swung the station wagon in a huge arc, pulling into the parking lot. Winston Gates turned up his collar, and marched over to Swain, who looked utterly miserable.

"Is there a problem here?"

Algernon looked at him blankly for a minute, then with puzzlement, recognition, and suspicion.

"So you're here. Then you've got Micki. What is this all about? We haven't broken any law."

"I don't have her," Gates said, chewing on the inside of his cheek. "You're telling me she's disappeared?"

"Gone. Vanished. I just laid my head down for a second. It didn't feel like I was asleep at all. The next thing I knew, half an hour had passed, and she was gone."

Gates turned to Arlene. "Could you have nodded off?"

She hunched her eyebrows together, and tried so hard to think that Gates felt sorry for her. Finally, she shook her head. "No. I'm sure that I didn't. I couldn't have."

"Jesus Christ." Algernon sat in the middle of the parking lot, looking pitifully small and sad and wet. "This was the stupidest idea. If anything happens to her, I'll never forgive myself."

Lightning flashed, and the clouds above were flushed

with sudden luminescence that rolled and crackled until the clouds looked like illuminated tissues of a living thing. Gates swore that he could make out veins and arteries, the shadowy ribs and a phantasmal heart, beating, beating, growing stronger by the moment.

He rubbed his head. "All right, all right. I don't believe any of this. I'm just not built to believe it. But whatever is going on here is more important than what I believe. I think it's time that we got some help. I'm calling Shackley. If possible, he can land in San Jose and come in by bus. Lord knows, he'll never be able to land at SF Airport. Neither will anyone else." He pulled his collar up tight. "And in a little while, this whole damned city is going to be sealed off."

Outside their motel room, the wind howled. Gates felt more bone weary than at any moment of his life. The rain battered at the roof, the windows oozed water, and everything outside that hadn't been battened down came tumbling by. The sound of shattering glass jarred him, and somewhere nearby, a siren howled in the night.

Arlene cursed in the bathroom as the hot water went cold. She stalked out with her hair plastered down across her face, and a wet towel wrapped around her hips, barely covering the tips of her breasts.

Looking at her, seeing her like that, awakened in him a wave of longing so strong that it felt like fear.

She smiled sadly at him, turning off the light as she sat at the edge of the bed.

For a long time she just sat there, and he lay on his side of the bed, the sheet pulled up around his naked body, and watched her. Her shoulders were quite broad for a woman, and seen from the back it would have been easy to mistake her for a man, and a strong man at that.

"It sounds like the end of the world, doesn't it?" she said, softly. "It just doesn't sound like wind."

He traced the line of her shoulders. So warm, so soft. The cruel sharpness of the wind outside suddenly touched him deeply, and he saw Arlene sprawled dead on the ground, her head torn open, her lovely eyes staring sightlessly.

She turned to him. "We've never talked about things like love, Winston," she said. "I never let you close enough for that. But in case something happens tomorrow" —her voice caught raggedly—"I mean—"

He turned her, and pulled her down to him. In the room's dim light, she was wholly beautiful. To the lonely, frightened animal that cried within the man, she was everything he could have ever desired to hold, and the only pain was in coming to that realization too late.

Too late for anything but . . .

"Tomorrow," she said. "We don't know. No one could know. I just wanted to say that I care, Winston. I might seem like I avoid you sometimes. It took Doug's death to pull me out of my hole this time. But I care. I always have. And if we get out of this alive, I'll show you."

There were so many things to say, and no time in which to say them. He lifted the blanket for her, sighing as she dropped the towel and slid under, pressing her body warmly against him.

"To hell with tomorrow," Winston said, the words seemingly torn from the pit of his stomach. "Show me now."

Two men? Or was it a man and a woman? They called to Micki, whispering to her from outside the window of the motel. In a sudden wave of fear, she had tried to wake Algy. She shook and slapped him, but he was asleep as though drugged. Then she couldn't even remember why she wanted to wake him.

She had opened the door of the motel, opened it to the wind and the driving rain, and smiled timidly to the two people standing there. Yes, a man and a woman.

She had seen the woman before. Thin, pock-faced. A core of murderous jealousy neatly shrouded in external gestures of friendship and trust.

Micki stumbled forward like a drunk tottering down

stairs, needing just a touch on either arm to guide her into the waiting car.

Once, walking in a dream, Micki lost her footing, and the woman's grip on her arm tightened cruelly, until pain shot up Micki's side and into her ear as if a spike had been driven into the bone.

Everywhere around them was violent cold, but the windshield of their car was barely misted, as if the weather were parting for them as they drove. Water droplets jumped about on the wipers like imps, and the rubbery squeak of the blades was a high, giggling voice.

In an hour, perhaps more, the car reached its destination, pulling into a parking lot at the side of a complex of low buildings that looked like an abandoned summer camp. She was numb by then, the rush of noises and visions totally overwhelming her. Sanity had finally given way, and what rushed in to replace it was a feeling of emptiness beyond calm, something that leaked in from beyond a barrier normally inviolate, and she whimpered at its nearness.

Strong but gentle hands grasped her. But lost in the fluxing illusions, she couldn't be sure what was real and what wasn't, knowing only that their touch burned, pulled her into a flaming whirlpool whose center was Adam. And somehow she knew that in the center of that whirlpool there would be safety.

Much of the rest of it was a blur, a crazed nightmare in which sleep and wakefulness folded together, in which sound and smell were differing aspects of the same reality. Nothing of her experience seemed real until they took her to the long, low building that they called the Temple.

There were several concentric rings of worshipers, humming, softly chanting a harmonic phrase that was arousing and magnetic. It quickened her breathing and sped her heartbeat, and guided her into the center of the Temple.

And there in the center was a roughly man-sized basket. Its outlines were unclear, as if she were viewing the entire scene through a diffraction lens. Its precise shape and dimensions were indeterminable, as if it existed only partially in this time and space, and more wholly in another.

And then she saw Adam.

He wasn't a man anymore, not in the way that men conceive of men. He seemed to be enshrouded in a chrysalis of some kind, a membranous material that covered him, but his face, hollowed to the bone, was glistening and vaguely reptilian, like the face of an undeveloped embryo. His eyes, huge and dark, rolled to look up at her. His lips twitched, but the word that she heard didn't match them at all.

*Micki . . .*

The woman Sylvia hissed behind her.

"I found him. I charted his progress. But he will not accept me. Go to him, then, damn you."

The man who had come for Micki held her fast, gripping her arms as another came and levered up the basket, the basket where the Adam-thing waited, its face shrouded in webbing, eyes lizard-dull or bright as flaring stars as they passed between bars of shadow.

And the man behind her whispered in her ear, "We will have His children. You are His queen."

# Chapter Thirty-five

## Shackley

## Tuesday, July 3. Day 0.

A confused weather department could say only that the winds were approaching gale force, and that there was no practical end in sight. Businesses were closing under the onslaught; the bus depot closed twenty minutes after a nearly empty Greyhound coach delivered Shackley to them.

Few cars crept along the streets. Their headlights wavered in the midday darkness, their tires slewed through the pools of murky water that flooded the streets.

Shackley seemed tired, but behind and before the fatigue was a sense of anticipation that was impossible to disguise. Winston and Arlene were able to pick him out immediately from the lightness of his step.

Winston grabbed his bag and helped him to the car. "Thank you so much for coming."

Shackley's reply was cautious. "When you know the rest of the story, you might not be so glad."

He settled back into the seat and closed his eyes.

The car jerked, and started off. The sewers and storm-drains were overflowing. Water gushed up through the manhole covers, roiled brownly in the gutters, arced in unending sheets from the sky. Cars crept through the horrid weather with highbeams engaged, crawling in low gear. There was no traction: the slightest touch on the brakes and the car slid dizzyingly, threatening to spin.

They slid into the station parking lot, banging a patrol car as they slid into a space. Winston looked at the dent ruefully, and cleared his throat. "Just a little paint," he muttered. He prudently backed up and found a space farther down the lot.

The morgue was ready for them by the time they arrived. The station was almost empty, although the phones were ringing constantly, and Gates could hear the news over every radio, every one-sided conversation. Roads out, bridges washed away, telephone lines down: "We've lost Cook County!" The increasingly beleaguered expressions on the faces of the officers accentuated the armed camp feeling. The radios themselves were nearly drowned in a torrent of static, peaking and dying in short cycles.

Janus and Algernon Swain was already in the morgue, examining Hubbock's corpse.

The skull was driven in, and Gates couldn't help but feel that it had been with a single terrible thrust.

Swain shook his head as they approached, then extended his hand to Shackley. "My name's Algernon. Adam told me so much about you. It seems strange to be meeting you under these circumstances. This is all such a mess. I feel crazy just for starting to believe the things I'm believing."

Shackley laid a comforting hand on Algernon's shoulder. "We try to live our lives 'logically.' Logic is a representation of reality, not reality itself. If you confuse them, you can no longer perceive what is."

He peeled the sheet completely away from Hubbock's body, folding it, and handed it to Gates. "The cause of death is obvious."

Gates pushed the sheet onto a nearby table. "Any idea why he might have done it? I mean, why he did it this way?"

Shackley seemed to ignore the question. "Were there any traces of drugs in his system?"

Janus handed Shackley a clipboard holding the autopsy results. "Listen. I don't know what it is that you people are looking for, and ordinarily I'd be as pissed as hell for you coming in here without any prior communication, but . . . there's something wrong happening here. I can feel it. Everyone can, and maybe it's time for a little cooperation. No. No drugs in the system. The only really unusual thing is the phosphorescent paint under his nails."

"Paint?"

Shackley's black eyes glittered. "There is much that I do not understand here. Look here." He pointed out the swollen joints in the arms and wrists. "This is a condition that is similar to what doctors call acromegaly. I believe that it is symptomatic of a secondary anabolic state. Induced."

"Drugs?" Arlene asked. "Steroids of some kind?"

"No. The joints, the paint, and the head injury all point to Savagi. Savagi was known to use a phosphorescent effect to convince the gullible that they were seeing his aura."

Algy winced. "Savagi is wormfood."

"He didn't exist in a vacuum. Someone would have filled the void."

Gates hesitated a moment, then asked it. "Do you know a man named Dearborne? Kevin Dearborne?"

Shackley's black eyes seemed to grow darker still. "We . . . knew each other. He would be the perfect one. God yes."

Gates could feel that there was more, and that it was nearing the surface, but bided his time. "Dearborne was capable of killing someone to make a point? To the victim? Witnesses? The papers picked it up . . ."

"Adam would have been conscious of his own aura. If he were confused enough, he might think others could see it also. Maybe Dearborne was trying to convince Adam that he wasn't alone . . ." Shackley paused thoughtfully. "Or that he was experiencing memory lapses, during which he killed indiscriminately."

Gates glanced at Hubbock's ghastly head wound. "And the brain injury?"

"The sixth *chakra* is located near what you call the pineal gland. Savagists are taught to meditate upon it. To awaken it. To see"—he smiled self-consciously—"or imagine that they see it in other people. It is supposed to be the source of power, of paranormal phenomenon."

"And by destroying it . . ." Algernon said haltingly, "a compulsive killer might destroy the 'evil' within him?"

"Perhaps. It happened before."

Algernon made a spitting sound. "Savagi. Just who the hell was he? I mean, really?"

Shackley pushed himself away from the table and sat. He said nothing at first, and it was clear that he was at war with himself. Finally, when he spoke, it was in the tones of a man who had fought for years to come to terms with a basically untenable position.

"Savagi wasn't his real name. I never learned it. He was the youngest son of a Brahman family in Kashmir. That's Pakistan now, but in 1924 it was still part of the Indian Territory. When he wished to marry he found himself at a strange impasse. According to tradition, he was compelled to fight for his bride. An archaic tradition, and the battle would not normally be to the death, but still the contests were often brutal.

"His grandfather, who ruled the family with an iron hand, refused to allow his grandson to learn the techniques of the warrior which had been passed down in their family. I do not know what techniques these might have been. I am aware that they are the root of what is today called kung fu and karate.

"Savagi knew that his family owned a unique collection of ancient books. Disobeying his grandfather, he slipped into the study late one night and spent the entire night searching among the scrolls for something that might help him win the woman he loved."

"Oh, Jesus," Algy whispered. "No wonder Adam understood Savagi's mind."

"And he found something. A translation of an ancient

scroll. He shouldn't have even been able to read it, but some incautious soul had made a partial translation perhaps a generation before, and Savagi was entranced. The scroll stated that physical techniques of war and hunting are literally a blind, a smoke screen. That the reality of combat is something quite different. That within every man is a pure Essence. But as white light striking a prism produces the rainbow, it is possible to separate out of this essence a priest, a leader, a hunter—or a beast. A warrior-demon, as it were. Not something supernatural, but the essence of the killing rage, manifested not only in actions but in the structure of the body itself.

"And then the scroll went on to give what instructions it could. Savagi began to practice the rites. When it was time to take his bride, he defeated his opponent easily, and brutally. His grandfather guessed what had happened, and burned the scroll, demanding that Savagi turn over any and all notes that he may have made. Savagi denied any involvement with the scroll, and was banished from his family dwelling. There was no wedding, nothing but a young man with an ancient secret who left India for America."

He sighed heavily. "The rest, I'm afraid, is history. The phenomenal strongman demonstrations, the assault charges—he had part of this secret, enough to make him unusual, and enough to drive him mad. His followers received a diluted version of the secret from him. He wrote tracts that were even more watered down. Virtually worthless."

"Worthless? What in the hell happened to Adam then?"

"Obviously there were clues that Adam was intelligent enough to find. He was motivated enough to fill in the blanks, to correct Savagi's errors. How long ago did he begin studying Savagi?"

"Two years ago. Maybe three."

"Incredible." Shackley shook his head in reluctant admiration. "I remember Adam. He had real potential, and was afraid to reach it. It almost seemed he didn't have *permission* to succeed."

Algy raised his hand uncomfortably. "May I try a piece of coffee-table psychoanalysis?"

"Please, do."

"Adam never got over his need for parenting. Hell, he chased after Micki as if she was his mother. He damn near worshiped you, Shackley, and it tore his guts out to 'fail' at karate. That's how he saw his whole life, as a series of failures. It wasn't until his father, his real father, began to die, slowly and painfully, that Adam began to take responsibility for his life."

"Role reversal," Arlene murmured. "The elderly parent becoming child."

"Exactly. Taking responsibility for his father meant taking it for himself. Adam tried to make up for lost time. But that damned dependent pattern was still wired into his head—he looked for another male figure to identify with—even if it was a dead man, Savagi." He shrugged. "I don't know if any of this makes sense. Maybe I shouldn't have even said it."

Shackley hugged Algy warmly. "I think you knew your friend exceptionally well. And I need all of the information I can get. I don't know how this is going to end." His voice flattened. "Probably in death. It ended in death before. As you may know, Savagi was assassinated."

Shackley scanned each of them in turn.

Arlene's tentative voice broke the silence. "How do you know so much?"

"That's easy," he said. "I was one of Savagi's followers. I killed him."

"What . . ." Gates felt shock and relief mingling in the same dizzying instant. Game time was over. The truth was about to emerge at last, and with it, invaluable answers.

"I was a fool," Shackley continued, now that he had their complete attention. "I was a karate instructor, and had been contacted by the Temple of Inner Light. That's what they called it then, and it was located in Colorado Springs. As time went on, I saw where Savagi was going with his studies. He scared the hell out of me. I knew that there had been killings that could be traced back to his students. Not to him. To my knowledge, Savagi only directly killed one man. There were others. He didn't *order* them, but he *caused* them, don't you see . . ."

The prayer circle had continued for three days now, and Shackley was almost unconscious with fatigue and the constant, ceaseless humming and chanting. His head was dizzy and light, and although he had been allowed to stretch his legs only three hours before, his knees ached abominably. His thighs were badly chafed from the small package taped snugly between his legs.

Without breaking rhythm with the chant, he looked at the man next to him. Anderson, a club-fisted young bull of a man, shuddered. Anderson would break soon. He was strong, but didn't have the mastery of physical self that came only with time.

But even Shackley was trembling, losing it. There was no turning back now. He was becoming disoriented. It would have to be soon.

There were sixty of them in the room, a low bungalow that had once been a mess hall for an Air Force cook's training facility. Now the entire camp, with all of its twelve cabins and recreational facilities, belonged to the Temple of Inner Light. And the people in the room, kneeling in their cotton drawstring pants, meditating without ceasing for fifty-six hours, would soon be allowed into the presence of Savagi.

And then . . .

The door opened and Shackley watched out of the corner of his eye as Kevin Dearborne entered the room, crossed to where Shackley sat, edging between rows of the Faithful.

Acceptance into the very exclusive group was by invitation only, but there was no apparent pattern for most of them: housewives, cab drivers, an accountant, the editor of a Detroit newspaper. The other half was more interesting, and included several former Special Forces personnel; two mercenaries; a powerlifter; Anderson, a ranked middleweight boxer; and Shackley.

Whenever Shackley came up to the camp some ten miles north of the U.S. Air Force Academy, many faces and life positions had changed, but a few remained constant. Practitioners of violent or explosive sports were always represented. Trained killers, like the military men. And Dearborne.

Most especially, Dearborne frightened him. The one time he had been to the camp and Dearborne had been absent, another of those damned murders had taken place, this one in Missouri. Frightened. Because Savagi's mixture of methods worked better than it should have. With them, Shackley's already acute skills skyrocketed, until competition was meaningless. Anderson was clearing his division with extraordinary brutality. But there was something different about Dearborne.

After years in the martial arts, twenty months of Savagic meditation had turned Shackley's world around. He had gained speed, power, control of pain, and a kind of killer fighting instinct that took instinctive reflex to a new, wondrous, and frightening level. One other thing it had done: opened the door to the reading of auras, the mental trick that takes perception of heat and odor and body language and through a kind of synesthesia creates the impression of color. A field of fluxing hue that tells of mood and health and mental balance.

And what Shackley's newly opened senses told him was that Kevin Dearborne was a killer.

Dearborne tapped Shackley on the shoulder. "Come." Behind the angelic face, the high cheekbones, and the fair curly hair was a psychopath, an untapped reservoir of animal rage that Savagi's art was fine-tuning.

Shackley stood, ignoring the pain in his knees, and waited as Dearborne tapped Anderson. Then the two of them followed the taller man from the bungalow.

Their path wove through a stand of yellow pines to a bungalow that stood apart from the others. Two men guarded the door, as they did twenty-four hours a day. It swung open, then closed behind them.

At first he was sealed in darkness, then the strange synesthesia took place again, and Shackley saw the light. It leapt like a solar flare, blinding his mind's eye with its extreme radiance.

"Greetings," a voice whispered. Shackley's eyes were adjusting a little better. He could see now, enough to make out a figure in flowing robes, seated upon a cushion. Thin, skeleton thin, thinner than any of the pictures taken of him. The aura was purple around the outer edge, and a kind of glowing black inside.

Shackley felt sick, and fought to find his center. He could feel Savagi's eyes upon him, Savagi's mind probing him, and knew that a moment's error, a single instant in which the mental shields slipped, would be his undoing.

"Come," Savagi said. The voice was rasping, and heavily accented. "Closer. You have been chosen. You are strong. You may have the qualities I am looking for." Savagi turned from one of them to the other, and Shackley could hear the man's neck creak. He stifled a scream, controlled the urge to wheel and flee while there was still time.

Savagi's gaze was merciless, and Shackley strove to harness all of the strength and balance he had ever known. If it cost him his life later, this was one time that he must not fail. There was too much at stake.

He pressed the fear down, back into the core of his heart, and at last Savagi's gaze slipped past him, and the ancient voice rasped again. "Each of you knows the killing energy. If you would be one of mine, you must take the final step. If you are not committed, speak now. This is your last chance to withdraw."

He didn't know, couldn't really know, but still suspected what was about to happen. Shackley whispered his affirmative, and heard Anderson grunt the same.

Dearborne knelt beside the shadowed figure of Savagi for a few moments, whispering. Shackley strained to pierce the darkness, but could make out no more than the silhouette of a man with barely enough life force to sit upright, a shell of the vigorous Yogi promoted in the books and pamphlets. It must have been years since the last photograph had been taken.

Dearborne went to the back of the building, and emerged with a shallow bowl in each hand, extending one to Anderson, and the other to Shackley.

Anderson grunted with satisfaction as he ate something from the bowl.

Shackley felt around the lip of the bowl, finding a rough wooden spoon there. Something in the bowl, something as thin as mush, moved sluggishly. He hefted the spoon, brought a portion of the contents closer to his face, until the warm, syrupy salt stench of clotting blood gagged him.

"Whose head did you break, Kevin?" he asked softly.

"That is not a question you want answered. Either eat, or—"

Shackley threw the bowl at Dearborne's voice, and stomped Anderson's leg with the fastest, hardest kick he had ever thrown in his life. The bone splintered, and Anderson went down and sideways, into Dearborne, screeching in pain and confusion. Then Shackley tore his pants away and went for the gun. It was a small weapon, a .22 tiny enough to hide taped between his legs for three days. But the hollowpoint bullets each contained a drop of liquid mercury beneath their soldered tips. It was the most lethal small weapon that Shackley knew of.

Savagi screamed "*hold*" in a voice that was like a physical restraint, and Shackley froze, time slowing to a crawl.

He was a dead man, and more would die unless he could force himself to move. His heart slowed, his lungs stopped pumping as if filling with phlegm. His nerves burned with dark fire. He fought to regain his balance, ignoring all pain, all sensation, tunneling his perception down to a pinpoint. Funneled all strength and consciousness into his wrist, just his wrist, bending it toward Savagi.

Hardly three seconds could have passed since Shackley's first movement: Dearborne was still struggling to his feet. But to Shackley it felt like hours, days, and his mind swam in agony as he fought the force of Savagi's will. All strength focused down to his finger now, just his finger, curling around the trigger. Oh, God. To sleep. To lay down and rest. Sleep.

*Just another ounce of pressure—*

The gun bucked in his hand, and a bullet slammed into Savagi's head. The Yogi shrieked, and Shackley stumbled back, released from the paralysis by what seemed to be a solid wall of fire. He fired again and again, and both bullets hit, he *saw* them hit, and Savagi slammed over backward into the floor, his head a misshapen ruin.

But he wasn't dead yet. Half of his head blown away and the man called Savagi was crawling toward him, hissing his hatred, trailing blood and viscera across the mat, reaching for Shackley with hands like claws, eyes glowing in the darkness.

Shackley staggered back, coming to his senses as Anderson thrashed and screamed, holding his leg. Dearborne was cursing, feet tangling around Anderson. Shackley panicked, firing his last two rounds into Savagi's body. The door of the cabin whirred open, and one of the guards entered—

And from there it was a blur. Screaming, and weeping, and the memory of a brief, frantic struggle, and then breaking away. Hiding among the trees, and working his way deeper into the forest, his heart pounding with fear, the chorus of sudden, wrathful screams splitting the night behind him . . .

Shackley's face was taut, lined. "I'll never forget that night. Savagi should have been dead. Anything human would have been dead. His body was shattered. His head pulped. *But he was still moving.* There was still something alive in him. I won't call it life, but it was animation and it was malevolent. And hungry. God, it was so hungry." He wiped his hand across his brow, looked at the slick of moisture glistening on his palm. Shackley sighed massively, and his shoulders relaxed as if he had unloaded a burden that had bent him beneath its weight for years.

"I couldn't go back to my school, ever. I left the country. It took Savagi a month to die. Five shots, three of them to the head. Heavy-metal poisoning. He still lasted a month." Shackley shook his head wonderingly. "I thought that after the years, with a new name and a new face, I could come back. Live some kind of life here. Then I heard about the killings, and knew that the cult was still alive. Still growing.'' He looked up at them, no challenge or plea for understanding in his face. "That's the story."

"So you killed him," Gates said. "And that didn't stop it. I seem to remember his corpse being stolen from the morgue . . ."

"I don't know anything about that, but I can guess."

"I don't see how this helps," Arlene said.

Janus stared. "You've got to be kidding. You've just heard a confession of murder and you don't even comment on it."

"Bill," Gates replied grimly, "we've got much bigger fish to fry, all right? And we're at a dead end."

"I'm not sure," Algy added, almost reluctantly. "Micki found a clipping file that belonged to Adam. There was mention of a health farm up here, a place called Pah-Dishah. Does that sound familiar to anyone?"

Shackley templed his hands ruminatively. "Pah-Dishah. Savagi spoke of it. An ancient city."

"The article said it was in Porter Creek. Where in the hell is that?"

"About fifty miles north," Janus said. "Do you think that's where your friends are?"

"Friends?" Gates said in disgust. "Let's not take this too far. My 'friend' killed at least five policemen."

"You know damn well we're up against something we don't understand." Algy pulled the sheet from its shelf, and began spreading it over Hubbock's body. "So was Adam. I swear that if Adam was in his right mind, he could never hurt anyone. If he has any idea what he's doing, he probably just wants to die."

"We might have to do him that favor. I hope you understand that."

Algy gripped Gates's shoulders. "All right. Maybe we'll have to kill him. But for God's sake, realize that he was once a good and decent . . ." His voice wavered, and he sat heavily, tears starting from his eyes. "I just . . . he was my friend, that's all. I . . ." He swallowed hard, and looked up defiantly. "He was my *friend*. I should have stopped him, should have helped him. Instead, I helped him do it to himself, and we were all so excited with the results that even when things started looking funny to us, we were too damned blind to stop.''

Arlene sat next to him, held his head in her arms. "Well, then. What do we do? The roads are being washed out.''

Gates scratched his head. "Listen. Can we get any serious information on the location of the old health farm? Somebody must have it.''

"And how do we get there?'' Algy said glumly.

Janus gritted his teeth. "I shouldn't tell you this, but there's a truck dealership right down the street. They've closed down. Everything's closed down. Most people are scared as hell. If you're not one of them, you'll probably find the keys to one of their big four-wheel drive offroad vehicles in the office.''

He paced back to the door. "I don't know what the hell is going on, but I read the report about your partner, and about the goddamn Marlboro sign, and the massacre out at UCLA, and the Neon Killer. And now I hear the weather people sounding more frightened than I've ever heard them, and air traffic being rerouted around San Francisco, and people being swept off the goddamn streets, and I don't even know what else . . .'' He stopped, and you could almost see the steam releasing itself from some pressurized place behind his ears. "All right, all right. Just . . . just find this girl. And if your Neon Killer is up there''—he glanced at Algernon, who wilted under the gaze—"don't take any chances.''

He looked at Shackley. "And for all of our sakes I hope to God that you are just a crazy, lying old man.''

Shackley smiled faintly.

"One more thing.'' He paused, as if unsure he wanted the answer to the next question. "You said you could guess. Why did they steal Savagi's body?''

"I thought I made that clear,'' Shackley said flatly. "They're cannibals.''

# Chapter Thirty-six
## The Eye of the Storm

"—and the present downpour continues. Just one more inch of rain, and San Francisco's all-time twenty-four-hour record will be broken. Winds have exceeded gale force; civil authorities urge that all noncritical traffic remain off the streets. We—"

Gates reached out and turned the radio off.

The Grevstad Motors parking lot *was* deserted, and in the rain, steadily cooling, sleeting the windshield into a glazed nightmare, it was easy to see why.

The rain filled every hollow on the ground and overflowed the sewers. It slammed down onto his head like hail as he fought his way out of the car to the office.

Winston turned his back to the door and slammed his elbow through the glass. The howling wind made it easy to ignore the klaxon of the alarm. A moment's probing found the inside latch and unlocked the door. His flashlight beam splashed around the room until it fastened on the rack of keys behind the desk, and he searched them until he found a tag labeled "Scout 4 × 4."

He considered leaving a note of apology, then decided against it. If things went well, no apology would be needed. And if things went badly . . .

\* \* \*

The cab was just large enough for the four of them: Arlene, Algernon, Winston, and Shackley.

The Scout swayed and fishtailed through the puddles. The Golden Gate Bridge was deserted, all of the booths closed in the middle of the week.

Cars were cracked up all along the road, and the sky overhead was the ugliest gray-brown that Winston could ever remember, veined with lightning, shaking with a continuous roll of thunder. The Scout shuddered on its suspension as Arlene piloted it skillfully across the bridge. The wind hit them, and slammed again, and then again. The heater, pumping at full bore, barely compensated for the numbing cold.

It was becoming impossible to pull anything in on the radio. Its last faint cracklings were about storm damage; then with a final burst of static, the speakers died.

The road was littered with the wreckage of small cars, swept to the sides and broken like soft-shelled beetles. The wounded and dead were tangled in metal or lay tumbled on the road. A few people peeped out from under the crumpled roofs of their cars, waving handkerchiefs at the Scout as it rumbled past. Bodies lay face down in pools of violently choppy water. An ambulance was spilled onto its side, and ahead of them, the only other car on the road, a Mercury Montego, slewed into a tailspin. If there had been any other vehicles near, the Montego's occupants would have been dead. As it was, the Mercury slid to a stop, and the wheels spun helplessly, churning water into the air.

Gates leaned over and kissed Arlene's hairline. "I think that there are a couple of emergency blankets in the back. Now might be a good time. We can't turn around now."

"I don't want to. I've got to see this through, Win." She smiled at him, and the numbness eased. Algernon looked sick to his stomach. In the backseat Shackley sat cross-legged, eyes closed, expression totally neutral. Without opening his eyes, he reached into the back, found the emergency blankets, and passed them forward.

The windshield wipers were groaning, slapping back

and forth ineffectually. Arlene seemed to be driving less by sight than instinct.

They hit the freeway, and traveled up through Mill Valley. Fifteen minutes in, the crumpled body of an over-turned semi loomed out of the driving rain with shocking suddenness. Arlene spun the wheel frantically, and the car hydroplaned dizzily, and Winston grabbed at the dash-board, whipping forward, seatbelt cutting painfully into his chest.

They slammed against the center divider, and lights and smells exploded as his head rebounded off the window.

"Jesus . . ." His fingers probed his head, found noth-ing broken or cut, just a large sore spot. "Is everyone all right?"

Arlene sucked air and gasped "Fine."

Algernon was crawling up from behind the seat, Shackley helping him gently.

*Turn back.* There was an uncomfortably strong urge to retreat, a veritable wave of resistance, of warning, of antagonism. But within it was a second message, one that beckoned him, beckoned them all, and welcomed them, urged them. Begged them, and it was a small, urgent voice that Gates couldn't deny.

For a moment he couldn't see anything through the windshields, only impressions of light and darkness. Ar-lene downshifted to first, bumping into stalled and smashed vehicles. The road was a graveyard of wind and rain-swept cars, freezing now, covered with sleet, hail tumbling down on them in a solid curtain.

Then, almost imperceptibly, it lightened, just enough for Gates to make out the turnoff sign for Porter Creek.

The lights up ahead were off, power lines down or owners fled to huddle in their beds, aware that something was terribly wrong.

Abruptly, the storm abated, just stopped as if they had stepped through a shower curtain. It was so impossibly sudden that Arlene put the engine into neutral, and rolled the window down.

The air was briskly cool, but not cold. A light curtain of

mist hung in the air, but when Gates looked behind them he saw only an opaque wall of rain and sleet and killing wind.

There was almost no sound in the calm, and Algy twisted uncomfortably in his seat. "It's like the eye of a hurricane, isn't it?"

"Check the numbers. The camp should be around the next corner," Gates said, surprised to hear himself whisper. Arlene killed the motor.

For a long time they sat there, looking out. The hills around them were almost violently green, and the fog drifted around them, rolled up over them with the caressing touch of a lover.

There was no sound, and there were no birds overhead, and nothing moving.

"This is it," Arlene said calmly. Far behind them, the storm clouds roiled and billowed. They shone pinkish.

"I can't help but feel that this is a womb. It's warm in here. Moist. Humid. Safe. And alien. Stupid isn't it?"

Shackley rolled down his window, and smelled the air. "Insane, perhaps. But there's nothing stupid about any of it."

Gates checked his revolver, examined each bullet individually, then slid them back in. He clucked to himself. "If he's here, this popgun won't kill him. I don't know what I'm doing. It would be crazy to try to *help* Ludlum . . ."

"Yes," Shackley said, smiling. "Let's indulge our insanity, shall we?"

Algy nodded. Arlene checked her .38. Shackley watched the clouds, boiling in slow motion, patches of dark cotton jaggedly etched with lightning.

They crept around the periphery of the camp, looking down on the emerald expanse of the lawns, snarled now with weeds and unmanaged bushes. Winston Gates sat back on his heels and spread the brush, looking, evaluating, trying to quell the queasy feeling in the pit of his stomach.

It was too warm, especially with the wall of clouds that

boiled on the horizon like a living thing, behind every stand of trees, every rise of hill: an enveloping pinkish-gray dome of crawling, angry clouds aflame with lightning.

No birds. No sound.

Algy pointed to a long, low, red-tile roofed building in the center of the mall. "That's the place, Gates." Algernon pointed at the hall. "Note the concentric rings of discoloration starting out from the hall." The rings were brown toward the center, but increasingly pale toward the outer edge. "Whatever is in there is putting out a lot of . . . well, let's call it heat. In pulses. And has been for a while. You can almost see the air shimmer."

There was a commotion at the edge of the camp, and two acolytes dragged Micki from one of the peripheral cabins. Her head hung weakly, the ringlets of her curls dangling like limp wires.

Algernon growled, and his face tightened as he half rose from his crouch. Gates put his hand on Algy's shoulder. "Now listen, Swain. We can't move until we know what the score is."

"They have *Micki*."

"And if we want her back alive, you'd better start using your head."

Arlene checked the action on her revolver. "I don't think that woman knows where in the hell she is, and I think it's time we ask some questions."

Gates looked at Shackley. "Are you coming?"

"I'm going to circle around to the other side. By myself. It may take a few minutes. Do any of you wish to follow me? No? All right. I hope I'll see you down there in a few minutes."

"Be careful. And Shackley? Thanks for being here."

Without a sound, Shackley spun around and was gone.

The three of them crept down to the bushes. When the two men passed, Gates leaped out, jamming the pistol up under the first one's jaw. "Not a move or a word." The man released Micki and she crumpled to the ground.

One second the acolyte was standing there, and in the next he had moved—not so quickly as Adam Ludlum, but faster than Gates could react. The man's hand slapped out in a flat arc, impacting against Winston's chest, smashing him back as if a tree branch had whipped into him.

Arlene hopped a step back and fired twice. The acolyte flopped backward, scratched at the chest wound with fingers that were cadaver-thin. He glared at them balefully, and clambered to his feet.

"Gates!" Algy yelled, and Winston spun as quickly as he could, running into what felt like the bumper of a truck. Something struck him two thunderous blows, on the jaw and the left arm. He hit the ground, rolling, trying to find the pistol that had spilled from a numb hand.

Dearborne. Arlene was down. The big man grinned at him, holding Gates's pistol in one hand and Algernon Swain in the other. Suspended by the throat, Algernon's feet dangled a full foot above the ground.

Algy's already dark face purpled.

Gates tried to move, but all of the strength had drained from his arms and legs. From the corner of his eye, he saw Arlene, frozen in the hands of two Children in red-splotched, saffron robes.

Algernon managed to force out a scream, a hissing squeal of pain and terror.

Dearborne cooed and stroked Algernon's hair with the barrel of the gun. He rubbed it slowly around Algy's eyes, his mouth, daubing at the wetness bleeding from his flat nose. "Shh. Shh. I'm happy for you, little one. You're about to see the *light*."

Algernon's right foot lashed out, catching Dearborne solidly in the groin. The big man grunted, and Algernon almost twisted free. Then Dearborne grinned savagely, straightened, and closed his hand. Algy thrashed, hands raking out, fingernails clawing at the cherubic face, ripping away flesh from the corner of Dearborne's smile. Blood ran over his nails as his hands spasmed, and there was a flat, ugly crunch. Algernon's arms and legs thrashed in one violent spasm, then he went limp.

Gates squeezed his eyes shut, attempted futilely to block out the wet sounds that followed. Impossibly strong hands lifted him from the ground. Dearborne grinned through red-stained teeth. His breath reeked of blood; it coated his tongue and ran in glistening rivulets from the torn corner of his mouth.

Algy sprawled bonelessly on the grass, his head mercifully concealed in shadow.

With great effort, Gates managed to control his bladder. He met Dearborne's gaze as squarely as he could. "No fluorescent paint this time?"

"You're rather clever, Inspector. No. Deception is no longer necessary. I honored Culpepper and the others with a meaningful death. But a police bullet in the brain has diminished Adam's rational faculties perfectly, and it is no longer necessary to provide illusions for his guidance.

"This is a glorious day. Our master has returned again. And this time, we win. Do you know of the Earth Heart, Inspector? I think not. All of the times that you intruded into our temple, and you never once thought to ask."

*He could kill me now, or I can keep him amused for another few minutes. And maybe . . .*

"All right. What is it?"

"Soon, Inspector. Listen to the thunder. Don't you hear its rhythm?"

Gates hated to admit it, but it was true. The flash of the lightning and the roll of the thunder seemed somehow in time with the steady, monotonous chanting from the low building.

"This time we are in control. This time there will be no mistake. Come. It is time for you to meet Adam. And then"—he wiped his grin with the back of a crimsoned hand—"then, Inspector, you are invited for dinner."

# Chapter Thirty-seven
## The Earth Heart

The bungalow was filled with the Children. They knelt, sat cross-legged, prayed with eyes shut tightly, humming or chanting in an endlessly intertwined harmonic round.

And outside, impossibly, the thunder rolled on, in time with the chant, the throb of a colossal drum.

Men, black and white, young and old, naked from the waist up, formed the outer ranks of the Children. The women were in the inner circle, their voices lighter and higher. Their bodies glistened with oil and sweat.

The sound was hypnotic. No one was touching Gates, but he had no strength to move. His jaw and arm and side hurt so damned much that he was surprised that he could think at all. The music, fiercely compelling, urged him to forget the pain. All he wanted to do was move to the center of the room, luxuriate in the rhythm.

Beside him, Arlene wavered, almost fell to her knees, eyelashes fluttering as if she had been drugged. Micki lay in a motionless heap by the doorway.

*Stay alert! For God's sake keep your head.*

*Where was Shackley?*

Dearborne ushered them through the rings of worshipers. He stepped on a woman's leg, and her eyes flickered

335

open. Dearborne hissed at her: "Back *down*, you fool." The acolyte bowed her head and continued to mumble.

Within the center ring was a basket, the contents almost lost in darkness, except for a hint of an outline, a tortured face, eyes stretched wide in perpetual agony, cloudy with some kind of slimy, fibrous membrane.

"This is where it happens, Inspector. Here you die. Your flesh, and your woman's flesh, will feed a god."

"What?" His own voice sounded distant, like something coming from the depths of a cave. "What is it all about?"

Dearborne spoke flatly, without undue emphasis, but the flame of fanaticism burned behind his words. "Men no longer hear the voice of God, Inspector. He speaks in a whisper, and we have deafened ourselves with the roar of our televisions and radios, the thousand electromagnetic pollutions that have destroyed our subtle senses. We will give them back to Man."

"What in the hell are you talking about?"

"The Earth Heart, you fool. The core of the Earth, the billion billion tons of molten metal that create the Earth's magnetic field. Don't you realize that Adam is tampering with the basic stuff of our universe? We cannot oppose him—but we can channel him, subtly, carefully, because he has lost so many of his faculties.

"Listen to the storm, Inspector. It is Adam's living rage." In mindless agreement, the hall trembled on its foundations, rocked by the thunder. The chanting was no longer some manner of martial dirge. Suddenly it was a staggeringly blasphemous psalmody, offered in dark homage to the forces of chaos. "As the balance of charges continues to shift, ultimately the Earth's magnetic field will flip. It has happened before, and what might it do this time? Change our planet from a dipole to a quadripole or a multipole? No one knows. But when it happens, it will not take a year or a month as when it occurs naturally. It will happen within seconds." Dearborne paused, relishing the moment. "Have you heard of an electromagnetic pulse?"

Gates wavered, trying to stay awake. The music was intense, its pull so strong. When he closed his eyes, he saw blood. "Doesn't . . . that have something to do with the effects of a nuclear war?"

"Yes. But Adam can cause an energy pulse stronger than anything dreamed of. Melting circuits. All magnetic storage media instantly erased. Communications disrupted all over the planet. And in the silence that follows, men will once again hear the true voice of God. The serpent within our own mind, a God of death and fire. A thousand minds like Adam's awakening. And that is just the beginning, Gates. Adam is taking the first true steps on his journey. You, on the other hand, are ending yours."

"You're out of your fucking mind."

"What happens here, today, will redefine reality and fantasy."

"ADAM!"

Shackley's voice rang from the doorway like a clap of thunder. *The command tone.* How many times had Gates heard references to it in police work, used it himself in the field. Paralyzing. Controlling. With it, and the accompanying body postures, a handful of men could control a crowd. But Shackley's projection was so powerful that it was as if Gates were hearing it for the first time.

Kevin Dearborne turned to the door to face the newcomer. His face, at first haughty, became questioning. "So. There is another of you."

Dearborne motioned to two of his people, and they flew at Shackley.

The old man was standing in the doorway, hands peacefully at his sides, eyes locked upon Dearborne. There might have been movement at the moment the two Savagists should have touched him. There *had* to have been movement, because the two men collided with each other as if Shackley had simply dissolved.

Both of the men slid to the ground and lay still. Gates had no doubt that they were dead. The old man had advanced a single step closer.

Dearborne exhaled harshly. "*Shackley.*"

Mitchell Shackley took another step forward. "I swore

never to use the filth I learned from Savagi. I traveled halfway around the world to cleanse myself.''

"Cleanse yourself." The acid rage in those two words was shocking. "You ran like a traitorous, murdering coward. How *dare* you set foot in this sacred place?"

Behind Shackley, two of the meditating acolytes silently rose. One was the stick figure of Sylvia, eyes aflame. She bared her teeth as she drew a thin, gleaming knife, and lunged.

*Shackley didn't move.* He couldn't have: there wasn't time, and Gates's eyes could distinguish nothing. Yet both Children were tangled together now. The knife protruded from Sylvia's neck. The other's head lolled limply. Sylvia's eyes stretched wide, her cry of anger and pain impaled in her throat; she sank to the floor, hands outstretched, trying to reach Shackley with her dying breath. Then she was still.

The meditative hums rose and crashed in a violent wave, and Dearborne forced himself to be calm.

"Judas," he hissed. "I can kill you. You know that."

"Maybe," Shackley said calmly, and proceeded another step. "But not easily, and you can't afford a brawl. And it's going to be a brawl, I guarantee you. You need everyone here to concentrate in order to control Adam, don't you? We'll see how well you've taught them, how strong their concentration is."

Dearborne's eyes flew wide, and anger burst from him as a tangible essence. Gates remembered too vividly the sudden, convulsive physical scream that Adam had loosed at UCLA, so in a way he was prepared. Dearborne's civilized veneer fell from him like a skin of ice, and with an impossibly swift lunge forward he became a torrent of teeth and nails and murderous insanity.

Shackley was *gone* and then *gone* and then *gone*, twisting and spinning out of the way of Dearborne's attack. Every time Dearborne grazed Shackley, skin and clothes were ripped brutally away.

Mitchell Shackley ran, jumped, heaved the furnishings,

the incense pots, the meditating acolytes at Dearborne—
anything to keep the man at a distance.

It had to be an illusion, but Dearborne seemed to *swell*
as he pursued Shackley, and in the light his face no longer
seemed wholly human. He moved more like some kind of
reptilian goblin or capering demon than an angry human
being. Once, finally, he caught Shackley in a corner pocket
formed by a stove and a support post. Only then, without
option, did Shackley stand his ground and fight.

If Adam Ludlum had been something beyond human,
now Gates had an opportunity to see just exactly what it
was to be a human being at its highest level of efficiency.
In a sustained, eye-baffling phrase of movement Shackley's
legs and arms, knees and elbows and shoulders cannoned
out and snapped back as if his spine were elastic, attaining
the percussive speed of the most explosive drum solo in
history. Dearborne's skin and bone split; teeth, shattered
and wrenched bloody from their sockets, flew to the floor.
Nothing human could have stood up to that assault, that
magnificent moment, that culmination of a lifetime of
sacrifice and pain and dedication.

But that which animated Dearborne, which kept him on
his feet and forced his faltering body through the windmill
of death, grasped Shackley in its arms and slowly began to
tear him apart.

Gates *heard* the bones and muscles give in Shackley's
shoulder, and despair rose like a gray tide.

Then Shackley's head rammed forward, crushing Dearborne's nose and slamming his head back. Dearborne
howled, forcing his way back in and Shackley *bit*. Dearborne
tossed Shackley aside like a bundle of rags, clasping a
crimsoned hand to a streaming, empty eye socket.

"ADAM!!!"

The meditating acolytes were awakening now. They had
lost the pulse-maddening flow of the chant. It was dissolving into disharmony, and as it did—

Adam was free. The sounds which had formed a cage, a
shielded channel for his thoughts and emotions, were dis-

rupted at last, and he roamed free in the labyrinth of his mind.

Free. But not alone. *It* was there with him, the killer in his own mind. Survival instinct, death drive, reptilian hindbrain. Whatever name he or others had given to it, it lived now, stalked him, fighting for mastery of his soul.

He saw without seeing, knew without thinking. Without the limitation of identity he was anchored to nothing in our world, had been reduced by force of mind to a focus more intense than the fabric of time or space or matter could bear.

And in that timeless space, he turned to face his darker self.

The Golden Man. Fluxing between mammal and reptile, golden fur and fangs and scales mingling and flowing together, now humping toward him in the dark corridors of his mind.

Every instinct told him to run, to flee, or to surrender.

But there was nowhere to run. This was the moment that the battle would be lost or won, and retreat was unimaginable.

He was no longer Adam Ludlum. He was, in that instant, the essence of himself, that thing that he had sought all of his life. And when the sum total of all the hatred, all the anger, all of the festering unfulfilled hungers within the human spirit, that dark dragon of his isness rose up and came for him, he was ready.

He joined with it, shrieking his joy as it shrieked its hatred, embraced it as its talons tore at him.

He was not conscious of evasions or blocks, or any attempt to preserve himself, just purely and absolutely committed to the death of the evil within him, to the final purging of all in his spirit which craved destruction and chaos, which embraced the death of the universe.

And the two forces within what had been Adam Ludlum joined in battle, life against death. Locked together as the nails and teeth of the lizard-thing fastened in his spiritual flesh, seeking fear.

But there was no fear in Adam, not of death, or of life. The dragon found no purchase for its claws: Adam's flesh parted like butter, refused to resist. The lizard-thing found its claws tearing its own skin, its jaws fastened in its own vitals, and Death was consumed by its fear of Life, consumed until there was nothing, nothing at all, but Adam's pure essence.

Alive. Standing naked among the beckoning stars.

He could live. Could return to his flesh. Could heal, could have all worldly things.

But at what cost? Abandoning the infinite?

*Join us*, whispered the stars. *Join those who have gone beyond. Guide, and protect, and learn. Open yourself to new mysteries, to wonders beyond the veil of flesh. Return to the ocean of your birth, and in surrendering, conquer all—*

*But, to die? To voluntarily deny life? To abandon the sweetness of rainswept air, the intoxicating glow of physical exertion, the touch of a warm hand . . .*

*Micki.*

*He would give anything to hold her again. To share her night, Adam would sacrifice eternity itself.*

*His vision swelled to encompass San Francisco, California, the Americas, the Earth itself. This was his world, and it awaited him . . .*

*Then, almost incidentally, his gaze rested upon a crumpled body, a corpse sprawled in the bushes of Pah-Dishah. Its blood congealed in the dust. Its head was shattered, its eyes were open and staring and still.*

*Algernon Swain. His friend. His best and only friend, who had given all that a man could. Who had sacrificed everything in the name of love.*

*Adam, who had no eyes, wept in shame. How could he have forgotten Algernon, even for a moment? There was, after all, one price too high to pay.*

*There is a balance in the universe, a law of conservation which governs both matter and energy. Adam could not create life from ashes. But he could offer his own life force, and welcome death as the gift it truly was.*

*He merged with Algy, sank to the very core of his friend's body, where the million physical processes of life were slowing, stopping, leaving only a cooling husk.*

*And there, Adam expended his spark of living fire.*

*He watched as that fire swept hungrily through Algy, as it warmed his bones and sent blood surging through flaccid veins. As tissues healed at impossible speed. As a still, cooling heart trembled, then began to beat . . .*

*Adam withdrew from Algernon Swain. Exhausted, exalted, but for the first time in his existence, totally prepared.*

*There was only one thing left to do . . .*


Gates felt it before he heard it. Felt the hum that penetrated his skin. He imagined that sailors in a submarine struck by a depth charge must have felt something similar to what followed. The space in the room *bent*, and the pressure in his ears was painfully fierce.

The walls wavered—or it seemed they did. The entire room distorted like something seen in a fun house mirror, or a fever dream. Something like a bubble of cold fire burst from the basket, burning harsh shadows into the walls.

Limping, blood streaming from a hundred wounds, Mitchell Shackley grinned through torn lips. "I've won, Kevin. *We've* won. He's awake."

Dearborne crouched. Fear and indecision clouded his rage. His good eye shifted from Gates to the basket and back. "I—"

The pitiful figure in the basket was suddenly pitiful no longer, a figure no longer, nothing but a burst of radiance that hurt the eyes. With shocking clarity, Gates felt his mind *probed*, like fingers reaching up through the roof of his mouth and searching, searching for lies or deceit.

And retreat, satisfied.

Arlene's body stiffened, and she moaned in pain.

"Relax, Arlene," he whispered. "Let him do it. We don't have anything to fear—"

*I hope.*

Then Dearborne screamed, a sound that began as a word, but ended as something inarticulate and animal.

Because it was too late for words or thoughts, and the ball of light was expanding. When it touched one of the Children he screamed and burst into flames, and the stench of flesh filled the air.

Gates was blinded, and when the wall of light touched

him, he felt himself open, felt himself touched by a soundless voice saying, Thank you. Thank you so very much—

The light rolled across the cabin and touched the walls, and as it did, the walls and roof exploded, flew away into fragments carrying flame and fury out into the camp—

The withering grass, and the brush, and the wood crackled and burst into flame. Stone walls melted, and the rock puddled. The clouds boiled with flame and lightning, and from somewhere far away there came a scream of elemental fury and triumph. . . .

# Chapter Thirty-eight

## Epilogue

## Wednesday, July 11.

The Los Angeles Airport, surrounded by the concrete ramps of its new two-level delivery system, was jammed by an endless stream of travelers and cars. Flights from the San Francisco Bay area had doubled in the past week. Although the nightmare was over, many just wanted to leave.

Micki shivered, watching as Shackley checked in at the Eastern Airlines counter. He shouldered his bag and came to her, bending to kiss her cheek. He smelled very clean and very tired, as if the weight of years had fallen upon him with drastic suddenness. Half his face was covered in bandages, and he favored his left leg. His right arm hung in a sling. But the strength that had saved them all a few days before still shimmered beneath the surface like a shoal of fish flashing over a reef.

He shook Winston's good hand. Gates gazed at him, eyes filled with wonder. "What now for you, Shackley? Mitch? Can I call you that?"

"I'd prefer it, Winston."

Then Shackley bent to the wheelchair at her side, grasping the hands of the thin, ashen-faced man who sat, terribly frail but, incredibly, alive.

Algernon. Algy gripped at Shackley's hand like a drowning man clutching a plank.

For an instant Shackley's weariness seemed to vanish, and Micki saw again the man who emerged from the rubble of the Earth Heart encampment: looking to the sky, eyes alight with wonder as a crackling aurora of flame ate away the storm clouds. The teacher become student. The Master revealed, inevitably, as a child, a child striving with all that is alive and good within him to lift a veil of ultimate mystery. A blind man given one glorious moment of perfect sight.

He helped them one at a time from the wreckage, and together they searched the rubble, stepping around the charred and blasted corpses of the Children. Some were mere smudges of wet carbon, like twisted, blackened logs after a forest fire. They searched, following a thin wailing sound. Walking and then running, all of them running until they found the impossible.

Algernon lay curled on his side, the gaping wound in his head healed with pinkish scar tissue. He looked up at them with the eyes of a child, remembering nothing, mercifully unaware of what had happened.

In the two days that had followed, some of that memory had returned. Not all, but some.

Algernon gazed into Shackley's eyes, unwilling to release his hand. "It's going to take time," Shackley said gently. "His mind will return. He won't remember everything . . . but he'll be whole again."

Micki wrapped her arms around Algernon tightly, helped Shackley pull gently free. She still shook, hadn't been able to stop shaking since they had all crawled out of the ruins of the lodge. "We have time. I'll take care of him. We'll take care of each other."

"I'm sure that's what Adam wanted." He laughed, a clear, mellow sound. "I can't finish the lecture tour. I can't tell what I've seen, and anything less would be a deceit."

Arlene hugged him, then kissed him, tears sparkling in her eyes. "I hope . . . you're right about Adam."

"The body in the wreckage. The thing that didn't seem to be human. What did the coroner say, Winston?"

Gates sighed, wishing he didn't have to remember. "She said it was like the body was structured like an amphibian, but the bones and tendons so strong that the surgical drills and band saws wouldn't take them apart."

Shackley shook his head. "They'll never learn anything looking at the physical manifestation of Adam's spirit. What Adam is now has nothing to do with the corruption that molded and twisted his body. He's beyond that now."

Algy's thin, trembling arms stretched out. "I . . . know you, all of you. I . . ." He began to cry uncontrollably. "I don't understand. I don't understand anything."

Shackley kissed Algy's forehead.

"Shackley. Mitch. Patanjal." Gates smiled. "It's pretty obvious why everyone feels about you the way they do. Thanks for everything."

"In months, or years, you'll start wondering if all of this ever happened," Shackley said soberly. "Don't forget. Don't ever forget. Help each other remember. Love each other. That's really all there is to do in this life." He smiled at Micki, and kissed her cheek.

Then, with a final regretful smile, Shackley turned and left them.

"His name . . ." Algy said haltingly. "Shackley? Shack . . ." his face tautened. "Adam's teacher. Adam. Where's . . ." He licked his lips briefly, sudden alarm touching his face.

"It's all right," Micki said, and gave him her hand. He gripped it with sudden, fierce strength. "We'll talk about it later. We'll talk about everything." She pushed his chair toward the front door.

Gates put his arm around Micki. Together he and Arlene walked her to the front of the airport. "You know, I don't have the foggiest notion how to feel about all of this."

At the front door, a neatly dressed young man approached Gates and said, "Would you care to make a donation to the Unification Church, sir?"

Winston dug into his pocket, wincing as he did. "That

shoulder *hurts*—'' but he managed to fumble out his wallet, extracting a five. He received three flowers in return.

"God loves you," the kid said dewily.

"Yeah, but He doesn't get sloppy about it."

The kid looked confused, but managed to maintain his smile as he wandered off.

"What a cynic." Arlene elbowed him in his good side.

"Purely a protective mechanism." He fixed one of the flowers in her hair. "It's that, or straight into a monastery, I promise you." He inserted the second stalk over Micki's ear, and tousled her hair lightly. The third flower went into Algernon's hair.

Arlene waved a cab over to the curb as Micki took a deep breath. The air was rain-swept, and crisply cool, as clean as the sunlight burning away the morning clouds.

"Air smells good, Micki," Algernon said.

She held his hand desperately tight. Her eyes burned again, and she almost stumbled, but caught herself. This was a time for strength. She had to be strong, if not for herself, for Algy.

*Damn you, Adam Ludlum*, she said to herself, suddenly laughing through the pain. *You knew just what it would take, didn't you?*

"Better than good," she said. For a moment the pain faded, and she felt whole, and calm. "It smells better than good, Algy."

It smelled like life.

The End

# Acknowledgments

A very special thanks to Dr. Jonathan Post, for introductions to both a delightful Franco-Nipponese restaurant and the mysteries of the electroweak force.

To Otis Allred, Toni Young, Pam Davis, Meghan Lancaster, Jayne Miyori Dunagin, Anita Anderson, Tom McDunnough, Dawn Atkins, Mary Mason, Ray "Bruce" Doss, Bobbi Laurens, Rick Foss, Charles Fuller, Daniel Pinal, Karen Malcor, Larry Niven, Marty Corbett, the staff of radio station KFAC, the staff of the West Coast 6-Day Training, Dr. Charles Garfield of the Peak Performance Center, Dr. Richard Landers for a delightfully gruesome autopsy report, Frank Robinson, the Staff of Body Dynamics/Nautilus Plus in Santa Monica, and Barry Workman of Workman and Associates.

To my instructor and friend, Rex Kimball: peace to you, wherever life may lead.

To my editor, Beth Meacham, who once again extended her trust, and my agent Eleanor Wood, for endlessly cheerful encouragement.

To my darling sister Joyce, endless thanks for a lifetime of support.

And, finally, to my mother—all that I am, or might ever aspire to, is but the flowering of the seed you nurtured so well, and at such cost. Rest in peace.

—Steven Barnes